I'll Always Have *Paris*

Kevin Russell

Copyright © 2022 Kevin Russell
All rights reserved
First Edition

Fulton Books
Meadville, PA

Published by Fulton Books 2022

ISBN 978-1-63985-476-9 (paperback)
ISBN 979-8-88505-862-9 (hardcover)
ISBN 978-1-63985-477-6 (digital)

Printed in the United States of America

Acknowledgments

I want to thank all of those who supported me throughout writing this book.

To my best friend, Armine, you have been invaluable to me for the past many years.

My kids, Eric and Sofia; family; and friends were the inspiration of the characters in this book. Some others have come and gone throughout the process, but played a vital role in helping me stay focused on completing this book. Many thanks to Vanessa for encouraging me endlessly to have this published. So I thank everyone that has been in my life. I love you all.

Chapter 1

Standing in a room that seemed all too familiar to her now, Marcela looked at her suitcase that was almost full with clothes for her trip. The sun was filling her room with natural light, and she could feel the warmth of the sun reflecting off the window. She wasn't quite sure what she should even be taking. Taking this trip was absurd! She was a planner, not the spontaneous person she had always wished she could be. Never in her lifetime could she remember doing something like this! This wasn't going to a city right next to her that she had been a thousand times. This is even a different county! Could she really go through with this? It was a scary thought, but she had every intention of doing it.

Her flight for Paris was leaving very early the next morning. Marcela had yet to look for a hotel and had no intention of doing so until she was there. It was Paris after all! There had to be thousands of hotels in the city. The question was, would there be one that she could actually afford? That thought scared her, and she thought again how irresponsible this trip was. Who books a flight to another country without having at least the hotel arranged? She couldn't think of a single friend of hers that would do that.

She put those thoughts out of her head for the moment and continued to find things she thought she'd need for the trip. This posed a bit of a challenge considering she had no idea what things she would be doing. Luckily, she had found a great last-minute deal on a flight from Barcelona to Paris that allowed for an open-ended return. She just had to give forty-eight hours' notice. She was told that spring was a good time to find deals on flights, and luckily, it was. Given that her financial situation wasn't all she had hoped for, she would be extremely limited on what she could afford for hotel, eating, and seeing as many usual tourist attractions that most visitors go to Paris for.

Suddenly, her thoughts turned to her mother. She could see her mom standing in front of her bed and looking down at Marcela's suitcase. Her mom's look was somber but content at the same time. "Don't forget to bring a few nice dresses and such, dear. Who knows what trouble you will find when you're there!" She could hear her mother telling her as she winked at her. She always winked when she said things that would make Marcela uncomfortable. She wondered if over time those little details would drop away or if she would always remember her mom the same way.

Marcela's mother was the optimistic one of the family. Her mom always would mention casually how everything worked out for a reason. One of her mom's favorite songs was "All You Need Is Love" sung by The Beatles. She said that's how life was supposed to be lived. All you needed was love. She needed love from family, friends, and most of all, from a partner that would show her love each and every day for the rest of her life. Her mother somehow believed in true love even though her husband had left her for another woman years before and cut off all contact with them. Even after he left her with Marcela and without any financial support, she still believed in true love. She would preach about finding love but would never act on it herself. She was still an attractive woman, and when approached by someone with romantic interests, she would tell them that she had everything in life that she needed but thanked them for the compliment. Marcela wished she could make the same excuses, but she knew her mother would frown upon that. Not that she was being approached by any men for romantic interests anyways.

She pushed the visions and thoughts of her mom standing there out of her mind. It couldn't be healthy to have those kinds of thoughts too often. But they comforted her, so she let them run their course. Even though it had been a few weeks since the sudden death of her mother, she could still feel her right there with her. She would dream of her almost every night. Even when she was awake, her mom would randomly appear in her thoughts in times like cooking dinner, sitting, and watching TV or doing simple, everyday tasks. Sometimes she'd found herself answering questions out loud that her mother would ask her. She was hoping that this was a normal thing to do. But in all honesty, she was too afraid to ask or tell anyone about it.

It wasn't even like she had many people to even talk to these days. After she ended things with her longtime boyfriend, Lee, just about a year ago, all she really had left was her best friend, Antonio, and her mother until now. Now her mother was gone, and she wasn't sure what her best friend would say about her seeing and talking to her mom who wasn't really there. She didn't want to chance that he might react in a way that would make her sound mentally unhealthy. He was never the one to be quick to judge or criticize anyone that she was aware of. But she didn't think she could handle him thinking she was not dealing with her mother's death well, which she really wasn't! Or worse yet, going crazy. He was the one of the few friends she had left.

She was now going through her closet, looking for any dresses that she thought would be appropriate for a place like Paris. Looking through her clothes, she didn't even realize until that moment that she had very little to choose from what she thought she'd want to wear there. She grabbed the few dresses she had and threw them in her bag. She went over her list she had in her head and couldn't think of anything she needed to pack until she was finished getting ready in the morning.

She looked sadly down on her bag and had to deal with the reality of what she had to work with and needed to focus on things that would make her happier on her trip. She closed her bag and put it in the corner of her room. It was getting close to time to meet Antonio out for dinner and a drink. She always looked forward to seeing him and the easy, effortless way their banter fell into place. They were alike in so many ways that sometimes it scared her. It was like they could read each other's thoughts. If he had interest in the opposite sex, she was sure they would have dated sometime in their life. But she was happy that it was what it was. Friendship kept things simple. And simple was just what she thought she needed!

When Marcela arrived, Antonio was already sitting in a booth they always sat in. This was their go-to place to eat, talk, and enjoy a bit of time together. It wasn't anything fancy, like most things in her life, but to her, it was perfect! The food was amazing, the prices fair, and a great place to have a conversation with someone without having to yell across the table. They had found this place many years ago, and it was a place everyone there knew everyone. It was a nice feeling.

Antonio had been her friend for about six years now. They had met through her previous boyfriend and had instantly connected. She would never forget how they met. There was at a firework show that evening, and she had always really enjoyed watching fireworks. Her boyfriend didn't really care for them but wanted to appease her, so he agreed to go, and they both had invited some friends.

She met Antonio just before the show began, and most of their other friends were talking among one another. They began talking, and both really enjoyed the fireworks while everyone else was mainly enjoying their drinks. After the show was done, they exchanged numbers and promised to talk very soon. They followed through with their promises, and those talks turned into an everyday event, and they had been friends ever since.

Like herself, Antonio was in his late twenties. He was not from Barcelona originally but took up residence there during school. He was an extremely attractive guy, intelligent, witty, and driven. Basically, everything she could think someone would want in a man. He worked in the medical profession at a local hospital.

She walked over, and they exchanged the customary hellos with a hug and kisses on each cheek. She sat across from him and noticed that he had already ordered a glass of house cabernet for her. He had ordered his usual favorite beer, Mikkeller, for himself. He lifted his glass as she did the same, and they made a toast and had a drink. It was apparent that the taste was refreshing to both of them. Neither of them drank often, but they enjoyed a drink here and there when they got together.

Even though they had been friends for several years now and had always been able to talk to each other about anything, she was nervous about talking about the trip with him. She also knew he was going to ask how she was dealing with her mother's passing. She really wasn't ready to talk about any of it, but he always had a way of making her open up. She wondered how he'd react to the fact that she was going on a trip with everything up in the air. She hoped he'd understand!

The conversation started out light. It was now the middle of April, and the temperature was finally warming up a bit. He caught her up on the events, or lack thereof, in his life for the past few weeks and then turned his attention to her. He asked how she was doing, how work was going, if she had she been sleeping, and so on. She was mostly honest about everything and brushed over the things that she didn't want to discuss. When it came to questions about her trip, she couldn't hold back the truth. She could see the concern in his eyes, but he chose to keep whatever thoughts he had about it to himself. She was thankful he didn't express his concern! His eyes could never hide anything.

One of the other great things about Antonio was that he was well traveled. He was able to offer advice on where to go and things he thought she'd enjoy doing, especially on a budget. But one big difference between the two of them, he was the adventurous one! They sat and enjoyed their dinner and a few drinks talking about the upcoming trip and normal life stuff. She wasn't ready for the night to end, but she knew it would by the time she got to sleep, if she even could. It would be time to get up before she knew it. She had to be up incredibly early to finish up packing the odds and ends and get to the airport.

They finished up their drinks, paid the tab, and said their goodbyes. He gave her a big hug, and she suddenly felt a bit more reassured. She wished he could come with her to help her make sure she got out and enjoyed the things you were supposed to do on vacation instead of staying in the hotel room and letting the sadness she felt sink in even deeper. But she knew she needed to do this on her own! She had always relied on her mom or lately Antonio to help her get through the negative things that came up in her life. It was time to be the independent woman she was intended to be.

It didn't seem like minutes before she closed her eyes, and when her alarm was waking her up, she jumped up and looked around to make sure there was nothing she was forgetting. It had been a long time since she had gone anywhere. Even when she was dating, her boyfriend would ask her to go away for weekend trips and such, but she would never allow herself to take the time to do those things. She had opened her own jewelry shop a few years back, and soon after that, the economy had bottomed out, and she couldn't afford to have employees. So that meant she had to be there from open to close every day.

She felt like she had packed way more than she needed, but in her mind, she knew the minute she got on the plane, she'd remember something else she needed. She was absolutely exhausted! She tried to sleep soon after arriving home, but sleep never came. Her mind was preoccupied by nervousness and still thinking about her mom and going over her list of things she needed to take.

She made it to the airport with plenty of time to spare. All she kept thinking was that she should turn right back around, go home, and go back to her normal routine. Home was safe. She knew what to expect, where do go, and what she'd do every day. Even though her mind was pulling her back to home, her feet kept moving toward her gate, and ultimately her feet won, and she found herself standing at her gate.

She couldn't even sit as she waited for her flight. She walked through the different shops that offered everything from books to snacks to restaurants and bars. She bought a few snacks and a book she doubted she would read, but she wanted something to distract her thoughts from what the very near future held. It was finally time to head back to her gate, and she should be boarding the flight any time now.

Marcela made her way to her seat. She had been lucky enough to get a seat by the window. The flight was pretty full, but each row only had three seats for each side of the plane. A man took the seat on the aisle, but they were fortunate enough not to have someone take the middle seat. She didn't take that much room, being only five seven, and she was of average body size. But the way airlines have streamlined their planes, it didn't leave much room even for smaller people. The man in the other seat smiled and said hello, and she said hello back but quickly turned her head to look out the window. Even though he seemed nice enough, conversation was not what she wanted right now. There would be questions to answer, possibly some explanations, and the look that people gave you when they knew you had lost someone close to you.

As the plane started to leave the terminal, it began to rain. She had noticed the clouds rolling in before but thought nothing of it until now. Although she had flown a few times in her life, the thought of flying through a storm scared her. This was not the start to the getaway that she wanted! This was supposed to be relaxing, not stressful. Now she understood why she'd hear parents dreading going on family vacations. The wants and needs of everyone involved would be anything but relaxing.

They made their way to the runway and took off shortly after. The first few minutes was quite bumpy and had lots of turbulence, but once they got above the storm, everything calmed down, and she could breathe again. She continued to blankly look out the window. Even though they were above the clouds, it wasn't as bright out as she was expecting. The hum from the engines put her into a daze, and without realizing it, she started to doze off.

⁓

Marcela was sitting with her mother in the living room talking and watching TV. They were both sitting on the couch. Her mom was making comments about the show that made them both laugh a lot. Her mom always had a great sense of humor and could make anyone laugh. There were very few times that Marcela saw her upset or not smiling. It was her nature to be happy in life!

Her mom made another comment that made them laugh. Suddenly, the laughter turned to coughing and then choking. Marcela quickly got up and stood in front of her mom. She could see the fear in her mother's eyes. She had no clue what to do. She grabbed her phone and called for an ambulance as she helped her mom lay down on the floor. They hadn't been eating or drinking, so she knew that she couldn't be choking on something. All she could do was look into her mother's eyes, hold her hand, and let her know she wasn't alone. Her breathing stopped, and her eyes were wide open, still staring into Marcela's eyes.

~

Marcela was jolted awake by the plane landing. She was in such a deep sleep that she didn't hear any announcements from the flight crew. Her heart was racing, and she was breathing much too fast. She could feel sweat running down from her forehead. She could still see the visions of her dream even though she was awake now. Luckily, her head was still turned toward the window, so she didn't think anyone could see the panic she was in.

The plane made its way to the gate as she collected herself and steadied her breathing. Her heart was still racing, but after taking some deep breaths, it slowed some. She looked out the window more and tried to push her thoughts to other things. It was sunny out, and from what the weather report had said and claimed before she left, it was supposed to be very pleasant. She started to think about and unfortunately worry about the next step of her trip. She had to find a hotel that she could afford and hopefully wasn't going to be too far from several attractions she wanted to see.

Chapter 2

It didn't take as long as she thought to make it off the plane, get through customs, and retrieve her luggage. Now it was time to deal with reality. She had no idea where she was going or what she was going to do. But once again, one foot kept going in front of the other, like they knew where they were going. Her feet must have known what they were doing as she made it out of the airport and found her way to the line of taxis waiting.

There was a short wait as there were several people waiting for a ride to whisk them away to destinations that they already had planned. She wanted to distract herself, so she played a game with herself. She tried to guess who were tourists and who were residents. When it was her turn, the driver came and took her luggage, and she got into the car. The driver made his way back to the driver seat, and he asked, "Où aller?"

Marcela didn't know any French, and it hadn't occurred to her until now that she should have at least attempted to learn some of the basics. She stared at him blankly for a moment and asked in one word, "Inglés?" She only spoke Spanish and a decent amount of English. She was hoping that being such a tourist city that he would speak English as well as French.

He sighed and seemed instantly irritated but answered, "Yes, where do you want to go?"

This was the part she feared the most! She had no idea where she was going. Her English was far from perfect, but she knew enough to get by. She sat there still staring blankly, but after a few seconds of silence and an impatient look on his face, she said, "Please take me to a hotel that is very inexpensive but in an area that is easy to get to see the sites of the city."

Now he was not only impatient but annoyed too! "What are you talking about, lady? I need to know where you want to go. I can't just drive around aimlessly unless you have lots of money to drive around all day!" he said in a curt way.

Feeling completely embarrassed, she said, "I've never been here before, and I can't afford an expensive place to stay. You should know the city well enough to…," she started with tears welling up in her eyes. She looked away, trying not to let him see her cry.

But he had seen the look in her eyes change and felt bad that he had been so rude. He wanted to say something, anything really, but he had no words. He turned his attention to the road in front of him, put the car into drive, and started their way out of the airport. He looked in his rearview mirror and could see she was still looking away. He stayed silent but now knew exactly where he was taking her.

She sat there looking out the window because she was too scared to face forward and catch him looking at her through the mirror. She wondered where he was taking her but just couldn't bear the thought of asking after the exchange they already had. So she just kept her gaze on the scenery they were passing and praying for a miracle. Why would he care what hotel he was taking her to? As long as she paid him for the trip, he had no reason at all to help her.

The driver, still feeling bad about how he had spoken to her, started some light conversation. Just the basics to start. Where was she from? Was she here for business or pleasure? The usual questions you'd expect from someone that didn't really know what to say but wanted to break the ice and make both feel more comfortable. She was happy that he had started some kind of dialogue as she felt uncomfortable with the awkward silence.

It wasn't a short drive. They were driving for over an hour now. She was getting worried about how much it was going to cost and looked at the meter. It didn't show anything. How could she have not looked before? Was this guy going to rip her off? She didn't have any money to waste! As if she didn't have enough to worry about, now she was genuinely worried about this. She finally got the courage to ask, "Where are we going? I'm limited on what I can spend and can't afford to drive around the city as I thought you were joking about!" she said, half joking, but worried at the same time.

He looked in the mirror and caught her eye. "You have nothing to worry about. You know, it's a custom for drivers to not charge visitors for trips when they don't know where they're going!" he said with a wink.

She didn't even know how to respond. Was he serious? They had been driving for over an hour now. She really wished things were different, and she didn't have to watch every penny she spent, but it was the reality she was dealing with. "What do you mean? I can't afford to play games! Where are we going?" she said with a little fire in her voice. She couldn't afford to be taken advantage of monetarily or emotionally right now.

He thought carefully about what to say next. She was clearly upset, and he didn't want to make it worse. "I'm taking you to hotel in the Moulin Rouge district. It's a smaller hotel, and it will be a good spot to be able to see many of our sites easily. I think you'll find the hotel pleasant. And there is no need to worry about the cost of the ride. The stupid meter must have shut off, and I didn't notice. So I can't charge you for the ride!"

She knew that he was lying to make her feel better, but she was also grateful for his generosity. She wasn't sure what to say. She had assumed this guy was still annoyed with her and was going to spin her around in circles and waste her money and time. But he wasn't! He was being very kind. Still unsure what to say, she softly said, "Thank you, sir." She didn't know what else to say, so she looked back out the window at all the buildings, and for the first time on this trip, she felt herself relax just the tiniest bit.

After close to an hour and a half, they made their way through some smaller streets. It looked very cozy but definitely not what she expected. She envisioned it like she had seen it on TV. Big streets, lots of fancy shops and restaurants, and swanky hotels. This was going to be less money for sure, but now she wondered how safe this area was. She was, after all, a female traveling alone and would be an easy target for anyone looking for trouble.

He slowed the car and came to a stop in from of a smaller building. It looked incredibly old, and now some of the tension that had disappeared were coming back. She wanted inexpensive, but she wasn't looking for something that likely had more insects and rodents than guests. "Please don't tell me this is the place you are thinking of me staying!" she said worriedly.

"I know it doesn't look like much, but I assure you that you will be very happy here. I have known the owner for more years than I can count. The building is old, but he keeps it well kept inside."

"Well, what about the area? Is it safe?"

"I can't think of a safer neighborhood than here. Most of the people here are locals, and they take pride in their home here. Many years ago, there were smaller hotels here, but now just a few. So unless a traveler was told about this place, you wouldn't know it existed."

She was still very unsure and had yet to move to get out of the car. He sensed her hesitation and then offered, "I know you don't have any reason to trust me, but I'm asking you to give it a chance." He took a moment to collect his thoughts, and continued, "I'll make a deal with you, try it out, and I'll give you my cell phone number. If you don't like it here, I will come pick you up free of charge and take you somewhere else." He was now turned in his seat looking at her.

Marcela was in shock! Why was he being so nice to her now? She thought about it for a second. It wasn't a bad offer. And if he was so confident that she'd like it, maybe it would be okay. Some of the best places she had been to eat were places that looked less than desirable from the outside. With that in mind, she made up her mind. She would try it out. "You've got a deal!" she said and opened her door. He got out on his side of the car and retrieved her luggage and led the way to the entrance of the hotel.

The driver held the door for her, and she entered what appeared to be a small lobby area with the front desk off to the right. There was a large area rug on the middle of the floor that looked like it must have been the original rug put there when this place opened. There was a crystal chandelier centered in the middle of the room. The walls needed painted and the furniture updated. But she could see past all that. She had an image in her head of how this place must have looked many years ago. It might have been called elegant then, but now she'd call it charming, oddly enough.

"Bonjour, Rocco," the driver said to the person behind the counter. Marcela was a few steps behind her driver, and she couldn't yet see who he was speaking with. But at least it was a word she understood!

"Bonjour, Matisse," came a man's voice from behind the counter. She made her away around the driver and could now see the man standing there. He caught her gaze and smiled at her. She guessed he must have been well over eighty. His face was wrinkled by what appeared to be too much sun over the years, and it seemed he must have lost weight at some point with how his skin hung a bit. His body was tall and frail. His smile was big and genuine even though he didn't have many teeth that she could see. Between his eyes and smile, she knew she could talk to him for days and not even get close to all the stories this man could tell about life!

The driver, whom now she knew was named Matisse, and the old man, Rocco, were conversing in French, and she couldn't understand a word of what was being said. So instead of pretending to know what was going on, she walked around the small room and looked at the art on the walls and little things like the molding around the walls and the details that she could see. Her friend Antonio had taught her to take in everything up to the smallest detail. With just a little money and lots of motivation, this place could be spectacular!

The men were finished talking, and Matisse came to her and told her everything was all set. He held a piece of paper in his hand and started to hand it to her. She reached for it and saw that it had his name and number written on it. "I hope you didn't think I forgot! I hope you don't need it, but if you don't mind, let me know how you like staying here and how your trip is going. It has been a true pleasure!" he said and turned to leave.

"Matisse, wait! I know you said there was no charge for the ride, but I don't feel right about it. Please let me pay you for trip and your time. You have been so very kind!"

He stepped closer to her as she was reaching into her purse. He put his hand gently on her arm, and she looked back up at him. He was looking into her eyes, smiling warmly. He took another half a step forward and put both hands just below her shoulders and quickly kissed both her cheeks. "Welcome to Paris, madam!" And without another word, he turned and walked out the door.

While Matisse had embraced Marcela, Rocco had made his way around the counter and walked toward her. She could see he was holding a key in his hand and nothing else. Her emotions seemed to be on a roller-coaster ride that she wasn't used to. Just as soon as she had relaxed and forgot about the rest of the world, the world came crashing back down in reality. Where was the paperwork they always filled out when checking into a hotel? What was this going to be costing her?

She looked at his smiling eyes and asked in English, "What is your rate per night?"

He kept looking at her with the same expression, and she knew then that he didn't have any idea what she was saying. She wanted to protest and demand he tell her what it was going to cost her. But she knew it was just going to be a waste of energy. She would take whatever her gave her at this point and figure out the rest later this afternoon. It was getting close to lunchtime, and she had missed breakfast on the flight because she had fallen asleep.

She put on her best fake smile and gave him a look that said, "Let's go!" He adverted his eyes toward the stairway that was at the far end of the room. For the size of the room, the stairway seemed wider than she would have thought should have been. He stopped her and put his hand out to take her luggage. She shook her head no and kept holding onto the suitcase. He was smaller than she was, and she thought his arm might break off if he tried to carry it. But he didn't move a muscle but just kept looking at her with his hand out.

She relented and let him take the suitcase. She was surprised that when he took it, it seemed effortless for him to carry. It was packed full of everything except the kitchen sink! This man had her very curious what his life had been and what it was now. Holding her suitcase now, he started up the stairs. Now she realized why they were so wide. There was no elevator! It had to be wide to be able to get everything to and from the rooms.

They made their way up two flights of stairs. There was old art on each wall that she would have to check out later. Even though he was much older, he was quick and moved with a purpose. When they made it to the third floor, they went to the right and to the end of the hallway, which was only lined with two rooms on each side. He went to the door on the far left and put the key in and opened the door for her and stood off to the side.

She stepped inside. The room was quite small but looked that it had everything she needed. There was a full-sized bed with outdated linens, a dresser that she was sure would be considered an antique, a doorway that led to one of the smallest bathrooms she had ever seen, and another door that opened up to be a very small closet. There was hardly any room to get around in the room given its size. But it wasn't like she was going to be throwing a party in here. It was plenty big enough for her, and she started to realize that Matisse was probably right after all. She walked back over toward Rocco. He put her luggage next to the bed and handed her the key and left the room, closing the door behind him.

She wanted to stop him to say and ask so many things but knew it was pointless. He wouldn't understand her. She couldn't imagine that this place would cost a lot per night, but the fact that she didn't know weighed in her mind. She would have to find an app on the phone that she could either learn how to say the things she needed to say or, in a desperate situation, translate them on her phone and just show it to whoever she was trying to communicate with. And then they could enter in what they needed to say and translate back and forth. She was hoping that for most of her trip, she could get away without having to talk to many people, and if she did, it would be minimal. She pushed the thought out of her head and looked over the room once more.

There was a window that overlooked the street she had come in on. The window was open, and she peered outside. There were some beautiful flowers planted in pots along the railing out of each window in the building. With the window being open, she could smell the sweet scent they were giving off. She loved the springtime! The vibrant colors, the crispness of the air in the mornings, even the brightness of the sky seemed clearer this time of year. And her favorite part was the smell of everything. She loved the scent of fresh cut grass, flowers blooming, and most of all, the smell that a rainstorm would produce. Everything in the spring was fresh and new, just like how she wanted this vacation to take an effect on her life. She wanted to feel fresh and new.

Again, catching all the details, she noticed lights strung across the buildings. She looked from left to right and saw the lights for blocks on either side. Some were solid color strands, and others were multicolored lights, much like you'd see at Christmas time. It was a beautiful mess during the day, but she imagined that at night it would be beautiful and bring life to this same street and make it feel cozy. She looked forward to seeing what it would look like this evening!

As she was still taking in the scents from outside, she could smell what she guessed to be fresh bread or something like that of a bakery. Now it was what she thought of when she would think of Paris—the food and the fresh bakeries. At that moment, it reminded her that she was famished. She only had a banana on her way out of the house this morning and missed breakfast on the plane. It was time to go and find something delicious to start her trip with.

Marcela picked up her suitcase and laid it out on the bed. She wasn't ready to fully unpack yet but wanted to change out of the clothes she had worn for her flight. She unzipped her bag and sorted out some of her clothes and put them on the bed. It seemed warm enough already outside to wear a pair of shorts and a top to match. She looked through what she had. She was still disappointed in the selection she had to choose from but finally picked out a pair of black shorts and a creamed-colored sleeveless blouse. It was simple, but she liked the way it shaped her body. She was slightly taller than average at five seven. Her build was also very average, and she knew that if she just put a little effort in, it would tone up very nicely. Not that she looked bad now by any means, she thought.

She quickly changed and stood in front of a full-length mirror that was in between the closet and the bathroom doors. Her outfit looked fine, but she wished she had made the time to get at least a little sun before taking this trip. But her work schedule didn't allow time for things like that. She looked again in the mirror and decided to keep her hair in a ponytail. It just needed a little work. She freed her hair from the band, and it cascaded over her shoulders. She had been letting her hair grow over the last year, and it was now down about three inches below her shoulders. Her hair was a lighter shade of brown, and it would lighten some more during the summer months if she got any time to spend out in the sun, that was.

Happy with her clothes and hair, now she just needed a touch up of makeup. She had never been one to use much makeup, if any at all. But she decided to apply some around her eyes to hide the shade of blue that came from not sleeping much the night before. She got her makeup bag out of the suitcase and headed into the bathroom. Her eyes were deep green in color. She used the smallest amount possible of concealer around her eyes and a light mascara that made her eyes seem to sparkle.

She closed her eyes for a moment and took a deep breath. When she opened her eyes, her mom was standing almost beside her looking into the mirror with her. "You have always been so beautiful my baby! Go out there and enjoy yourself!" her mom said to her while smiling at their reflection.

Marcela almost spoke back out loud, but instead closed her eyes again and saw an image of when she was young, maybe ten or eleven, and her mom was brushing her hair and had said those exact words to her. She was all dressed up for her first church dance, and she was so nervous. She had begged her mom to let her stay home, but her mother was insistent. She did go, and much to her surprise, she really did enjoy herself very much. It was the first time boys actually paid attention to her. She usually didn't get dressed up for anything, and she wasn't noticed by anyone.

She let the memory consume her for just a moment longer, and a single tear had formed in her eye. She took another deep breath and opened her eyes again. Her mother was no longer there, and she was back to the woman she had become over the years. She could still see that little girl in herself, but that little girl that was carefree was long gone now! There was some sadness in her again, but she was determined to push on today and get out there and enjoy!

She went back to the bedroom and found her purse and made sure she had everything she needed to head out. Her plan was to find something to eat for lunch first. She was hoping she'd find a small café of some sort. After that, she would explore the area and see if there was anything close by that would interest her. She would also download the translation app on her phone at lunch so she could hopefully get by when she went places that only spoke French. From what she could see from her hotel, it looked like this area she was in was more for people that lived there rather than visitors, so she had to be prepared. Not to mention trying to figure out what the hotel was going to cost her. That had a huge determination on how long she could stay at that hotel and what she could afford to do once that was settled.

Marcela grabbed her purse and headed out the door. She made note of what room number she was in because it wasn't printed on the key. She walked down the short hallway and started down the stairway. As she made her way down, she could hear voices coming from the lobby area. When she got close to the bottom of the stairs, she could see several men sitting around a foldable table. As small as the lobby was, it took most of the area up. Rocco was among the men sitting there.

As the one facing her saw her making her way down the stairs, he stopped what he was saying to another and smiled at her. This prompted the others to turn and look in her direction. All the men sitting there looked to be about the same age as Rocco. Rocco, as well as all the others, smiled at her. "Bonjour!" one of the men said, and the others followed.

She looked at the men for a moment as she kept walking toward them and, with all the confidence she had, said, "Bonjour!" She gave a nervous smile to Rocco, and he quickly said something to the other men at the table. She wished she knew what he was saying. By the smiles that stayed on the men's faces and that not one of them even seemed to hear that Rocco was even speaking, it was apparent she had become the center of attention. She tried to play it cool and kept the smile on her face as she walked by them. She tried her best to avoid eye contact with anyone as she didn't want to get stuck in a conversation that she would not understand. She walked quickly past the men. She made it to the entrance and opened the door. As the door opened, the sun beamed right into her eyes. It caught her off guard, and suddenly she was off balance. She had run into something and found herself falling backward. By instinct, she braced for impact, but something caught her before she was flat on her back.

A shadow appeared in front of her and blocked the sun from her eyes. Her sight started to come back, and she saw that it wasn't something that she ran into. It was someone! She looked at him for a few seconds, but it felt like an eternity! Now she also realized that she was still bent backward, and his face was awfully close to hers. Her mind seemed slow to function, but things started to make sense. She had run straight into him, and he was also the one who kept her from splitting her head open on the ground.

She couldn't move. She felt paralyzed. All she could do was lay there stiff in his arms and stare at his face. The first thing she noticed was his hazel eyes. They were mesmerizing! Not that unusual in color but the way they penetrated her, she felt that he really could see her soul. She also noticed his smile. It was a gentle and kind smile. His face was tanned, and his facial features were strong. It looked like it had been a few days since he had shaved, but it was still short enough to look attractive.

"Bonjour!" he said. His smile did not change nor did the intensity of the look in his eyes.

There seemed to be a billion words in her mind, but nothing made it to her mouth. She was still laying there motionless. *Say something, anything*, she kept telling herself. Still nothing came out. She now felt her body moving toward his and closer to his face. She was in such a daze. She couldn't comprehend what was happening right then. His scent was now filling her senses. She didn't know what the fragrance was, but it had her head spinning.

She was now back on her feet, but she felt unsteady. His right arm was still around her waist and his hand pressed into her lower back. His body and face moved back slightly, but his eyes never left hers. "Est-ce que ça va?" he said.

Marcela wasn't sure if it was shock or if something was really wrong with her. Her mouth betrayed her and sat motionless. She closed her eyes for a moment. She had to! She had to collect herself before she got more embarrassed than she knew she was going to be if she didn't pull herself together. She opened her eyes, and as soon as she looked back into his eyes, his smile returned. In that instance, the world felt right, wonderful, like nothing she had ever felt in her life. Now she could feel a smile forming on her face. "Hello!" she said instinctively.

As soon as the words left her mouth, she could see a puzzled look on his face. What had she done wrong? He studied her face a moment longer and asked, "Are you American?"

Now she understood his puzzled look. She had said hello in English. He had a slight accent, and she wasn't sure exactly what it was right away, but it wasn't French. Her mouth had now decided to take over, and she was speaking before she even realized what she was thinking. "No, I am Spanish. I am here on vacation. Where is your accent from?"

"I am from the Tuscany region of Italy. What part of Spain are you from?" he asked. He realized that his arm was still around her waist. He gently pulled his arm back to his side and took a half step back as not to invade her personal space.

"I'm from Barcelona." She was now smiling back at him and felt like a girl in high school being talked to by the guy she had a crush on. Her stomach had the little butterflies, her heart racing a bit too fast and too hard. She had to concentrate not to put her hand in her hair and twirl it around. The way this made her feel almost made her laugh because she was so happy.

"Oh, I love Barcelona. I haven't been there in several months now, but I always enjoy being there when I get to go. What brought you here to Paris?"

She was still studying him. He looked like he was normally a clean-cut guy. His dark-brown hair was a bit windblown and his face unshaven. She would guess he was in his mid to late thirties. He was what she thought to be the perfect height, tall but not to the point that he stood out. He was wearing jeans and a simple royal-blue polo shirt. Without noticing she did, she looked at his ring finger and didn't see a ring. She quickly looked back up at him, hoping he didn't notice. He raised his eyebrows, and she realized that she wasn't speaking again. "I'm sorry, I'm here on vacation," she said much too quickly. Her English not being as good as she would have liked, it sounded a little rushed.

"Oh, very nice! Are you visiting friends or relatives?"

Her senses were back with her again, and she was determined to stay focused on the conversation and not on the beating of her heart. "No. I'm here just seeing the sights the city has to offer. I have never been here, and I thought I should finally check out what it's all about."

He tilted his head slightly and again had that little confused look on his face. "How in the world did you find this hotel? It isn't listed on any travel site or web search!"

Now she had to let out a nervous laugh and sigh. "Let's not talk about that! You will either have to stand here all day listening to me ramble on or you'll take off running!"

His smiled got even bigger, and he let out a little laugh and rubbed the back of his neck. "Well, I guess you're right! I don't have time to stand here all day. So would you allow me to take you to dinner and you can tell me then?"

She was almost speechless again. She didn't think her heart could be beating any harder or faster. "I'd love to! But maybe we can pursue a better topic. Speaking of which, do you happen to know this hotel at all?"

"I'm actually staying here. I have for many years now. I know it doesn't look like much, but you can't get much better than what you will get here. Is everything okay?"

"Oh, the hotel seems fine. It's just that, well…" She felt stupid for even continuing this thought, but she needed to get this figured out, and this was probably her best opportunity. "I came in this morning, and long story short, I was basically shown a room and given a key. That's about all I know!"

He let out another laugh. "I take it you met Rocco. And seeing that you don't seem to speak French, I'm glad you came here. Rocco is the owner of the hotel. He has owned it since the day it opened. He doesn't believe in the modern ways of running a business, but he has quite a remarkable reputation. I can talk to him for you. What exactly would you like me to find out?"

"Well, the most important thing I can think of is how much I am paying for each night. I'm on a budget and need to make sure of everything I spend so I know what all I can do!"

"Let me make sure I understand this correctly. Do you not know how long you are staying?" he asked in all seriousness.

This is exactly the conversation she was trying to avoid. She didn't want him to think she was the irresponsible person she was being. However, it was a logical question that she would ask if the roles were reversed. "If you can just find out what it is per night, I'll try to explain it better tonight. That is, if you would still like to have dinner with me!" She did her best imitation of a child batting their eyes to get the answer they wanted.

"I think I can handle that. And yes, I would be honored if you accompanied me to dinner." He looked at his watch and back to her. "I hate to admit it, but I have to get to a meeting soon. Would you like to meet in the lobby around 6:30 p.m.?"

"That works fine for me. May I inquire about a dress code?"

"It should be a beautiful evening and a bit warmer than usual for this time of year. So perhaps you can keep that in mind, and if you like my company at dinner, we could take a walk, and I can show you around a little bit."

"I will try to keep that in mind! There's just one thing you missed!" as she raised one brow.

"And what is that?" he asked.

"You didn't tell me your name!" she said, trying to give a somber look.

"Oh my! I sincerely apologize. Everything happened so fast, and that's not an excuse… I'm sorry! My name is Anastasio. And what would your name be?"

"I'm Marcela," she said, putting the smile back on her face. "I look forward to seeing you this evening! Now you better run along so you can get to your meeting!"

"Thank you, Marcela! I am looking forward to this evening as well! I hope you enjoy the rest of your afternoon. Oh, and you may want to find some sunglasses. You don't need to be bumping into strangers all day! I'll see you at 6:30 p.m."

And with that, he moved past her, still keeping her gaze until he was inside the hotel. She turned and started walking down the street to an unknown destination. But now she didn't feel one bit lost. Her mom entered her mind, "Enjoy your trip, my baby girl."

Marcela didn't have to walk too far until she was in an area bustling with people, shops, cafés, basically all the things she could think that she would like to visit today. The weather was absolutely perfect. After walking past several places, she decided to sit at a small café that had tables out on the sidewalk. She took a seat at one of the tables, and she sat facing the street so she could see the people walking by. Her whole life she had always enjoyed watching people, no matter where it might be.

There were menus already sitting on the table along with a small vase with a single red tulip. It looked like each table had the same setup. There were a few people sitting at other tables, but the café was pretty quiet. She picked up her menu and opened it up. Upon first glance, she saw something written and again shook her head. Why didn't her mind comprehend that this was a different country? But looking at it further, she saw that after each item listed, there was the same thing listed in English.

She was looking through the menu but didn't really see anything other than Anastasio's face when it was inches away from hers. The intensity in his eyes was still penetrating her soul. She was in disbelief over what had transpired just thirty minutes ago. One second, she couldn't wait to get out of the space she was in, and the next, she just had a moment she would spend the rest of her life thinking about. Something she thought impossible for so many years, in an instant, became a dream that she wondered if she'd wake from or hoped she wouldn't anyways.

A waitress appeared out of what seemed like thin air, pulling her back into reality. "Bonjour! Bonne après-midi. Savez-vous ce que vous voudriez?" the waitress asked as Marcela stared blankly into the menu. The waitress paused and waited patiently for a response. Feeling a bit awkward, she asked, "Madam?"

"Do you speak Spanish or English?" she asked in English.

"English, I speak English!" she exclaimed. "This is the famous Moulin Rouge district. If you don't speak English here, you better not need your job!"

"Wait, are you telling me this is the Moulin Rouge district?" Marcela asked.

"I sure hope so, or otherwise, I'm going to have a lot of angry customers coming back there and yelling at me!"

"I had no idea. What a fantastic surprise!" Marcela was truly shocked that she was in such a historic place. So many things had happened here. She quickly looked over the menu and decided on a meat-and-cheese platter with fresh fruit and an expresso. The waitress wrote down her order and disappeared. Another man appeared and poured her fresh water.

As she awaited her lunch, she sat and enjoyed the warmth of the sun and watching the different people walking by. She liked playing a game when she was with her best friend, Antonio. One would have to pick out a person and describe who that person was based on what they were wearing, how they walked, and whatever other information their appearance offered. Of course, they would never know if they were right or not, but it was a fun game nonetheless. Now she was playing the game by herself, and it was still fun. She often wondered if they got it right.

It didn't take long at all for her food to arrive. Everything looked so fresh and appetizing. She had already finished her expresso and ordered another. She sat in silence as she ate and watched the people walking by. Even though she liked playing the guessing game, her mind was somewhere else or, better said, on someone else. Anastasio consumed her thoughts. Who was he? What did he do for a living? What was he doing here in Paris? Was he interested in taking her to dinner just to be nice, or could he be interested in her? She was hoping she'd get the answers she wanted tonight but was also afraid the answers wouldn't be what she hoped them to be. And what did she expect anyways? She was on vacation in another country. She lived in Spain, and he lived in Italy. The thought made her feel a little sad again, so she did her best to push it out of her thoughts.

She finished her lunch and was very satisfied. So far, Paris lived up to its reputation for its food. She had halfway managed to keep Anastasio out of her mind, but the thought of him did come more often than she'd liked to admit. His look when he was holding her in his arms. The way he took interest in her right away. The flirtation she felt between them. There was an instant connection between them, for her at least. Marcela hoped the feeling was mutual.

As the waitress came back around to take her plates away and leave the bill, Marcela couldn't help but wonder what her evening was going to be like. Was it going to be an actual date? What was she going to wear? Where were they going? Did she even remember how to be with someone she didn't know? These thoughts started to make her nervous. She closed her eyes for a moment trying to clear her head and just enjoy the day and how amazing it was turning out in spite of so much uncertainty she had just hours before. The day seemed to be falling into place.

Marcela paid the bill and had a goal in mind. She needed to find something new to wear for tonight. She had brought some things that would have worked. But she wanted something new for the first date she had in a long time even if it wasn't really a date. She was attracted to Anastasio. It wasn't only his looks. There was something about him. Without any words, she had suddenly felt desired as he looked into her eyes. And without even knowing it, she needed to be desired. So now her quest was to find something to wear that would make her feel desirable.

She walked down the street, and it was filled with all kinds of shops. She would pick an occasional one and unfortunately wasn't finding anything that stood out to her. About an hour after her search began, she found the perfect boutique type of shop she was looking for. They offered trendy but classics options that were at affordable prices. The shop owner was very friendly and helpful. "My name is

Jacqueline. I run this little place I call home." She wasn't the usual salesperson that said the usual "Oh, that looks amazing on you" just to get the sale. She gave her honest opinion on each outfit that Marcela tried on.

Marcela certainly felt what she meant as she owned her own same place that she definitely called home. She felt like she had tried on everything that Jacqueline had to offer, but the last dress that she tried on seemed to be meant for her! It seemed to fit her every curve like it was designed specifically for her. It was black, sleeveless, and just the perfect length, she thought. To her, her breast size wasn't exactly what she would call big, but with this dress, her cleavage looked amazing. She could see that her hips and waistline looked nice in it as well. When she looked at the price tag, she was even more pleased.

This was the dress she would wear for the evening. That was no longer even a question. She had never thought herself as a beautiful woman. She felt beautiful now. The dress was absolutely perfect. "I'll take it, Jacqueline!" she exclaimed with excitement.

"Do you need anything else to accompany your dress? Shoes or accessories perhaps?"

Even though she was feeling a little bit embarrassed about answering the question, she answered with confidence. "I have the shoes covered, but I need some things to wear underneath, if you know what I mean."

"You mean, the unmentionables?" It was more of a statement than a question.

"Um, yes, I guess you could say that. Not that I'm—" Marcela started.

Jacqueline cut her off purposely. "I know, dear. Most of us aren't. But it is nice to feel sexy every now and then. Let me show you what we have to offer. I think you will like some things I have here!" Jacqueline said as she led her toward the back of the shop.

Marcela found herself looking at some of the most beautiful lingerie she had ever seen. For being a small boutique, she had quite the selection. She had everything from plain old stockings to elaborate outfits. She looked over all the selections, and most of the things she couldn't see herself wearing, but others were very sexy. She wanted to make herself look and feel sexy for her date. She tried on several selections and decided upon a simple thong-and-bra combination with thigh-high stockings that she thought looked and felt amazing. And luckily for her, the price was in her budget.

She wanted to shop more, but after taking her time at lunch and then looking through several shops before finding this new outfit, she was feeling pressed for time. Jacqueline rang up the items, and Marcela paid for the things. She thanked Jacqueline for her assistance and promised that she'd be back soon to find some more things. She really looked forward to getting ready for the evening. From what she could remember, she never dressed up like this before for a date.

"Good luck tonight!" Jacqueline said. Through the course of shopping, Marcela had told her about the date and how it all came about. Jacqueline agreed that it sounded as this man, Anastasio, was interested in Marcela. Jacqueline already liked Marcela and really hoped the evening was going to go even better than Marcela expected.

"Thank you so much, Jacqueline. I promise I will let you know how it goes when I come back!" Marcela took the bags and left the shop. She had been fortunate enough to be one of those people that had a great sense of direction. As she made her way back to her hotel, she kept an eye out for shops she might have not seen the first time around. Each shop she did go into, she quickly glanced over the clothes and found that most of the pricing were in her range. She was hoping she had a reason to buy a few new things after this date to go on more with this new man that she had just met.

She made it back to the hotel, and the same men were still sitting around the table playing cards. The only difference this time was she took her time to get through the lobby as she had found a new sense of confidence, and she felt great. The men all stopped and turned toward her and said their hellos, and she repeated it back and then headed up the stairs to her room.

It was now about 3:30 p.m., and so that meant she had about three hours to get herself prepared for the evening. She was still tired from not sleeping the night before and now the excitement and nervousness of the day. She decided she had about an hour or so to nap to try to get a little rest. She put her suitcase on the rack next to the bed that was perfect size for her bag. She took off her shorts and top and climbed into the bed. It was quite warm out, and since there was no air conditioner, she left the window open, which let in a slight breeze. Luckily, there was also a ceiling fan that was on that cooled the room down some. She set the alarm on her phone and closed her eyes.

She must have been even more tired than she had thought. All she remembered was closing her eyes and then the alarm seemed to be going off right away. She didn't know if she had dreamed or not, but now that she was waking back up, she was already daydreaming. She was dreaming about seeing Anastasio! After about fifteen minutes of lying there thinking about what she needed to do, she felt reenergized and went and turned on the shower.

As she let the shower warm up, she went out and got the things she needed for the shower and laid out her clothes on the bed. Once she had everything in place, she took off the rest of her clothes and got into the shower. Even though the room was already warm, the hot water felt good on her body. She put her head under the shower and let the water cascade down her down her shoulders. Then she turned around and let the water hit her directly on the middle of her neck and shoulders. She wished she had the money and the time for a massage. But this was definitely relaxing her as she grabbed the soap and loofah and lathered up her body. She loved the smell of the lavender that the soap had. She took her time, making sure to get every part of her body. She wanted to feel clean, sexy, and radiant, like she had never known.

About halfway through cleaning her body, she shut her eyes. Without even realizing it, she started imagining that Anastasio was cleaning her body. He was taking his time, and she really felt as if he was really there. He took his time, starting with each leg, then making his way upward. She found herself getting aroused, and this wasn't something normal for her. But she felt like it was completely natural right now. She dropped the loofah, and her hands roamed her body, like she imagined he would be doing. She even felt him washing and shampooing her hair.

After her body was completely clean, she stayed there with her eyes closed, feeling his hands roaming her body. Not once did he ever touch her in the places guys always go right for. All the touches were light and teasing. His hands were getting ever so close but then would move in another direction. Before she knew it, she found herself in a very intense orgasm. She had never experienced anything like it before and definitely not when she was alone.

She opened her eyes again, and she almost lost her balance because her legs had become weak, and they were shaking. If just thoughts of him could do this to her, what would real life be like with him? She wasn't the type to normally think about things like this, but this time, she really hoped she'd find out! She regained her balance and got out of the shower and started to dry off.

Marcela took her time getting ready. First, she put lotion on each leg, feeling the smoothness of her skin. She then applied it over her stomach and on her breasts. Immediately she felt that same feeling she had in the shower but had to focus on something else. She didn't have time for things like that right now. She had a real date soon. So she continued to put lotion on her arms, shoulders, and the places she could reach on her back.

She put her hair up in a towel and went out to the bedroom, where she had laid out the new clothes she was going to wear. She found a small pair of scissors to cut the tags off each piece of clothing. She slipped on the black lace thong first. The material felt good against her silky smooth skin. She then put on the matching bra and stood in front of the mirror. She turned this way and that and was pleased with the way her body looked. She wasn't one to visit gyms or go for runs, but she did her best to stay in shape by eating the right things, going for walks with her mom or best friend, and things like that. Satisfied with how she looked, she went back into the bathroom.

She had never cared for wearing much makeup, and she didn't feel like she really needed it. She had gotten the genes from her mother. Rarely did she have blemishes or things that needed to be covered up. She applied just enough to make her eyes really stand out. She wasn't one for lipstick either but put a little gloss on her lips to make them look fuller.

Now for the hardest part, getting her hair to do exactly what she wanted. She had naturally wavy hair, and on some days, it seemed to have a mind of its own, and she felt like all she could do was put it in a ponytail and call it a day. That couldn't happen tonight! She removed the towel and dried it some with the towel before starting to brush it and blow dry it. There really must have been an angel with her today because everything kept turning out better than she had expected. Even though it was warm out, there was no humidity, and her hair fell in such a way that even she didn't know if she could recreate it.

Marcela still had a little time to spare, so she straightened up the bed and put away some things in the closet and dresser. She stopped in front of the full-length mirror several times to make sure she wasn't missing something that could possibly make her more desirable. But each time she looked, she was pleased with what she saw. She was her mother's beautiful baby! That made her wonder if her own mother had ever felt this way. She guessed she probably did when she was younger.

She finally was ready to put on her stockings and dress. She put on each stocking very slowly to not rip them. She had never really worn thigh-high stockings. With her legs fresh from the lotion, the material of the stockings felt amazing. She watched herself in the mirror as she did, and she felt she was the lead character in a movie. She then put on her new dress. She couldn't believe how she felt and how amazing the clothes that Jacqueline had helped her pick out looked on her. And after she zipped up the dress, she looked and made sure that she hadn't missed a tag or if something didn't look right.

The last thing she did before she left the room was put on her favorite perfume. She sprayed it on her wrist and some on her neck. She loved the way it smelled and hoped Anastasio would think the same thing. It was that time now! She took one last look in the mirror and took a deep breath. She felt like this was one of the fairy-tale evenings she had read about when she was a child. She grabbed her purse and the room key and proceeded out of the room to go meet Anastasio. Could he make the night continue to be a fairy tale?

Chapter 3

When Marcela came downstairs, she immediately saw Anastasio standing there waiting for her. She had thought before that he was very attractive, but now seeing him dressed up, he looked even more handsome. She was relieved to see the way he dressed matched up with what she was wearing. He was wearing a pair of nice black slacks and a classic white button-down shirt. The contrast made his tanned face look even darker. Even though he was older than her, the years had been kind to him.

Anastasio had also taken his time to get ready for the date he had planned. His slacks were already pressed and ready to go. He had several shirts to choose from but decided on a white one that he really liked. The fit was perfect on him. He wanted tonight to go very well, and he had decided to treat himself to a manicure and pedicure after he was done with his meetings. He was supposed to have had meetings in the late afternoon but changed them to a few days later so he had time to plan out the evening and to get ready. He wanted it all to be a surprise to her what his plans were.

She noticed that he had shaved since they met, and now his dark hair was redone and not windblown as it was earlier. He stood there with a smile on his face and delight in his eyes. His eyes met hers, and she swore she felt her heart start to beat a little faster and harder. Marcela continued her pace down the stairs, feeling like she was a princess entering the ball. She felt better about herself than she ever felt before.

When she got most of the way to him, he started to approach her. Their eyes never left each other. Before she even realized she had taken another step, she was within reaching distance of him. He leaned in and put one arm around her back and pulled her into him. He gave her a small, delicate kiss on the cheek and whispered, "You look absolutely stunning, Marcela!"

He didn't back away right away but just held her there for a few more seconds. She had to admit that it felt great having him hold her close. And also, there was the fact that she needed that time to compose herself from the compliment he had just given her. Her expression had to be a cross between a sheepish grin and shock. He finally released her and again looked straight into her eyes. It took him a few seconds to say anything, and she could see he was also visibly shaken by this encounter. "Shall we?" he asked as he held his arm out to have her put hers inside of his.

"I didn't ask, but I hope you like French and Italian food," he said as he opened the front door of the lobby leading to the street.

"I do. I think I have to being here in Paris," she said as she pushed her elbow into his rib playfully if only to relax herself a bit and the intense moment she just felt.

He laughed casually and walked her to a taxi that was already waiting for them. She wondered if he had already arranged this or if it was just a coincidence. Anastasio opened the door for her, and she got in. He closed the door and went around to the other side and sat beside her. Without a word, the driver pulled away and started down the street. He knew she was curious by the way she looked over at him.

"I hired him for the evening. His name is Bernard. He speaks very little English, so don't think it rude of him if he doesn't speak with you too much. I didn't think I should keep you waiting around on the streets dressed so nice," he said without moving his eyes from her. The relaxation she felt now disappeared again with him gazing into her eyes.

Sensing the change in her look, he broke their eye contact and looked out the window. He pointed out a few buildings on the way that he knew a little bit about, and she took interest in learning and felt at ease again. As they were looking out the windows, she realized that they were now sitting only inches from each other. He leaned toward her to show her a building, or he'd point at one she'd have to lean toward him. Each time she got closer to him, she could smell the scent of his cologne. She loved the way it filled her senses with the pleasant scent.

The drive wasn't too long, and it seemed even shorter as she was studying the different sights as they drove. The taxi stopped in front of a restaurant called La Cremaillere. From the outside, it looked very nice. As she was still looking out the window at the restaurant, Bernard had already made it to her door to open it for her. She could get used to being treated like this, she thought.

Bernard held out his hand to help her out of the back seat. He had a broad smile on his face, and it was endearing to see. He said something to her in French, but she had no idea what and was too embarrassed to ask. But she had a feeling he was complimenting her. She was now standing, and he released her hand and turned to leave. Anastasio was now beside her and taking her arm again.

He held the door for her as they entered the restaurant. He approached the host, and they were immediately taken to a table. Their table was in the back of the restaurant in a little courtyard they had set up with tables. In the middle of the courtyard, there was a small man-made fountain. The sound the cascading water created was relaxing. The table was set for two and was small but cozy and intimate.

They sat and were greeted quickly by their waiter. He spoke in French, and she had no idea what he was saying, but just the sound of language and being there with Anastasio made it sound so pleasant to her ears. Anastasio replied in French, which she could easily tell that he was fluent in the language. He stopped speaking, and the waiter smiled and left. Anastasio turned his attention back to her and smiled. "I hope you don't mind, I took the liberty of ordering us a bottle of Sancerre. It's a Sauvignon blanc made here in France."

"That sounds absolutely perfect! I have to say, I'm very impressed with your skills. You speak Italian, English, and French? You seem to be very talented!" she said with admiration. She really meant what she said. He seemed well-spoken in several languages, was well-dressed, had manners that she forgot men could have, and carried himself very well. And she guessed this was the man he was, not just a facade put on to impress her.

They picked up their menus and browsed the selection. There was a mix of French and Italian foods listed. Some of the names she didn't know and had to ask Anastasio what they were. She loved hearing him tell her anything. He had passion in his voice. Even just describing the food, his descriptions made her feel that she could taste the food without even trying it. After asking him about several dishes, she decided on the salmon. It sounded perfect the way he described it.

They sat down their menus, and the waiter returned with the bottle of wine and two wineglasses. He presented the wine to Anastasio, and with a nod, the waiter uncorked the wine and poured a taste into his glass. With precision, Anastasio evaluated the wine and tasted it. He seemed pleased with the taste, and the waiter poured Marcela her glass and then back to Anastasio.

Anastasio then spoke to the waiter to order. It sounded so pleasant to hear him speak. "Nous commencerons avec l'Assiette Crémaillère. La belle dame prendra un Dos de Saumon à la plancha et son beurre Nantais, avec un gratin dauphinois. Quant à moi, je prendrais les pates aux deux saumons. Merci." The waiter turned and left again, and Anastasio brought his attention back to her.

"May I ask what any of that meant?" she asked, truly interested.

He smiled. "Of course. I ordered us appetizer of country ham and cheese. For you I ordered the salmon you requested, and for me, I ordered pasta with smoked salmon."

"That sounds lovely. Thank you. So where did learn French and English?" she asked.

"Well, I started learning French at an early age. My father owns a vineyard, and his dreams are for one day for me to take over the business. So he made me learn French starting at five and English when I was nine. I didn't mind though. It's great to be able to communicate with so many people. And you know, if I didn't learn other languages, all I'd be able to do is stare into your beautiful eyes and pray that you know what I'm thinking about. I can understand Spanish but haven't mastered it yet!"

Marcela was amazed by the way all his comments made her heart skip a beat. It took her several moments to speak again. She studied his eyes for a moment to see if she could in fact know what he was thinking. He had a playful expression on his face, and his eyes were lit up with happiness. She felt she did know what he was thinking but was too embarrassed now to say that.

She leaned in as if to really scan his eyes with a serious expression on her face. She moved side to side as if she could see more this way. His smile got bigger as he watched her look at him. Back and forth she went. She stopped finally and pursed her lips as if to say something and looked again. She finally drew a little closer and said, "Yes, I do know what you are thinking!"

She didn't offer any more information, and he laughed a bit. "And what is it that I'm thinking about?"

"Well, it's simple really. You were just thinking if you ordered the right meal for yourself or if I did a better job of choosing!" she said with a smile.

He let out a bigger laugh now that was genuine. He had to shake his head a little at her as he continued to laugh. She joined in the laughter as well as they looked at each other. After a few moments, he finally said, "How did you know? But I figured if yours was better, I'd just steal some of it anyways."

They both smiled, and he brought his wineglass up to toast. She lifted her glass as well and placed it in front of his. He looked into her eyes and said, "To a beautiful evening together, to getting to know each other a little, and to looking at the most stunning woman I have met in a long time!"

He pushed his glass forward, and she did as well. There was a clink of the glasses, and they both drank their first sip of wine together. As they did, he made sure to keep eye contact, as was customary for good luck in a toast. Her mind was still on the words he had said, and the thoughts warmed her whole body. She believed the words this man said without a doubt. She was in trouble for sure with this man!

The wine was refreshing and sweet. She loved the taste and the lightness of the sweet nectar that connected with her taste buds. She generally enjoyed wine, but now it was just refreshing and different sitting here with Anastasio. They took a few more sips as they smiled and looked at each other. All her senses were heightened, and it made everything seem to come to life instantly!

"So, Marcela, what brought you on this trip to France?" he asked as he sat down his wine and rested his chin on his hands.

"Well, I needed a getaway, wanted to meet an interesting Italian man, and haven't been to Paris before, so I thought, I should just go and see what it is like. So here I am!" she said as she lifted one brow and smiled.

"I know there is much more to this story, but I won't press for it now. But I do hope you meet that man you are looking for. You said you are staying for a week?"

"I am hoping for a week, but not knowing what I am paying for the hotel doesn't help me to figure that out." She again thought about the trip and how irresponsible she was being, not having much to fund this trip and planning it better or doing any planning instead of just getting on a plane for that matter.

"About that, I did have a chance to meet with Rocco. He really took a liking to you apparently! He told me that it is his pleasure to have you staying there and to just give him what fits into your budget. He doesn't run his place like the normal hotel. That's why I choose to stay with him anytime I come here. He is one of the friendliest people I have had the pleasure to meet."

"That seems so strange to me. I'm not used to people wanting to do something nice for someone and not wanting something in return. I don't really know what to think about it. It wouldn't seem fair to him I mean."

"Trust me, when I tell you that Rocco is a different breed and if he likes you, there is a something very good inside of you. He cares more about people than he ever has about money from what I've gathered. He is honored to have you in his place. I really wouldn't worry about it," he said with a serious expression. He then smiled and looked into her beautiful brown eyes.

Marcela looked back at him again, and all her concern about money and the hotel washed away as she looked at him. Something about the way he looked at her made her feel that all was right in the world and that everything would be okay. It was a strange but invigorating feeling! She had never felt something like this just by looking at someone, especially someone she didn't really know.

Their appetizer of ham and cheese arrived, and the waiter set it on in the middle of the table. Each of them was given a small plate. The waiter asked Anastasio a question, and he answered with a smile, and the waiter nodded and left the table. Anastasio turned his attention to the food in front of them and seemed to be pleased with it. He asked for her plate. She handed him her plate, and he put a few pieces of ham and cheese on it and handed it back to her. He then did the same for his plate and looked back at her.

"Bon appetite!" he said and cut a small piece of ham and cheese and put it in his mouth. His eyes lit up upon the taste and nodded in approval of the taste. She cut hers and tasted it as well. She was surprised how good the food tasted. It seemed so simple, but the flavor was quite pleasurable. They continued to eat and were quiet for a few minutes as they enjoyed the appetizer in front of them.

"That was quite delicious. I had no idea that ham and cheese could be so good. Thank you for ordering that for us. Such a treat. I can't wait to taste the main course now. I'm sure it will be amazing!" she said, clearly happy.

"Yes, that was very tasty. I have only been here a few times, and this is the first time I have tried that. I shouldn't be surprised by anything we get here as everything I have tried has been better than any other place I have found here in Paris. I'm sure you will enjoy your salmon just as much, if not more than the appetizer."

"If the appetizer and the company is any indication of what the rest of the dinner will be like, I'm sure I will never experience anything else like it." She was surprised once again by the candidness of thoughts that she voiced.

Anastasio opened his mouth to say something, but no words came out. He was not a shy person, but her statement shook his thoughts, and he had no words. All he could do was just stare at her and smile. He had hoped she would enjoy his company as much as he enjoyed hers, and now he knew that she was.

As if the waiter knew that this was an awkward moment, he came with their entrées, and he placed it in front of them. The presentation was perfect! Its aroma filled the air. Marcela wasn't starving but felt that she could eat every last bit of this meal. Anastasio looked at her and smiled. He mixed his pasta and put a small amount on his fork. He took a bite and made a face of sheer pleasure and then smiled again. She tried her salmon first and was sure she made the same face without even trying. It was the best she had ever had.

"I cannot believe how good this is. I think I could eat this every day. Is all their food this good?" she asked.

"I haven't had everything here, but everything I have had has been terrific!"

They both continued to slowly eat with casual banter in between bites. Even when they weren't talking, the air was filled with sounds of laughter and talking from other tables that seemed like all the people that were here were happy. The sounds of the fountain they sat next to also filled her ears with the smoothing sound that made this place seem even cozier than it really was. All that combined made any silence between them extremely comfortable. Their looks were saying more than words ever could.

As they finished their meal and the waiter kept their wineglasses full, Marcela leaned back in her chair and gazed at Anastasio in the waning light of the end of the day. "So tell me a little more about you now. All I really know is that you are handsome, charming, have great taste in cuisine, and speak various languages without flaw!"

"What is it that you would like to know? I'm an open book, but I'd rather you ask specific questions rather than me rambling on about myself," he said, leaning forward a bit to lessen the space between them.

"Let's start with why you are here. You said you were on business. What is it that you do?"

"I work with my father. Our family has a small vineyard in Italy that has been in the family for a long time. Right now, I am trying to get us more customers here in France to help our sales. Since the economy has weakened all across Europe and all the competition there is out there now, things aren't what they used to be!" he said, ending with a sigh. "I am just trying to do whatever I can to help save the vineyard for my family. It is killing my father that he may lose what our family has had for many generations. He takes it as a personal loss, not that the world is changing, and with it, the smaller people lose. Sorry, that may have been way too much information, but as I said, I'm incredibly open!" he said with a grim face.

"I'm so sorry. Do you think things will get better? With your charm, I would guess you can find people that would love to have your wine!"

He let out a small laugh. "I wish that's all it took, but most places either have the wines they want to carry and don't want to even listen or the wine they buy is much cheaper because these big vineyards produce much more wine and they can charge less. I just have to hope that we find a few new restaurants and bars to buy, and we'll make it through until we figure out what to do next," he said with a little less of a serious expression.

"You sound like you know what you need to do. I'm sure it will all work out in the end!" she said as she reached out for his hand without even knowing she was.

He grabbed her hand lightly, and as soon as their hands touched, her heartbeat sped up just enough for her to notice. They looked at each other and smiled. He knew her words were right, and her touch made him relax. She could see the light coming back in his eyes. They sat in silence for a few minutes hand in hand and listened to the sounds of the waterfall beside them. Each lost in their own thoughts about each other.

They left the restaurant, and she saw the driver standing next to his taxi. She started toward the car, and Anastasio lightly touched her arm and stopped her. His touch on her bare arm felt warm and electrifying. He released her arm and bent his arm for her to put her arm inside his. She did just that, and she heard his voice say, "Let's take a walk before we leave if you don't mind."

"That would be nice," she replied. She hugged his arm a little tighter, and they began walking down the street. The sun was still out but fading now. The air was still hot, but she couldn't have felt better than she did right now. Their pace was slow and easy, and there were several couples out walking around as well. She looked at them and wondered if any of them could be as happy as she was right now. She doubted it was possible. Most weren't even walking hand in hand or touching. She wondered if they were together many years if he would still walk the same way with her. She was pretty sure she already knew that answer!

As they walked down the street, he would comment on different buildings and tell her a little of the history about them. There were lots of boutiques on this street, and they browsed the windows, and he would ask what types of things she liked, and she would point out things that interested her. She liked the fact that he seemed to take real interest in what she was interested in. Most men she had met would not stop and ask what she thought of something in a window, especially clothes for a woman! Most men she had first dates with tried to impress her with things about themselves that really didn't mean much to her. He was so different, and that impressed her more than anything.

They walked about fifteen blocks, and they decided to turn around and walk the other side of the street. The sun now was too low to see, but there was still some light showing between the buildings. This side of the street was much the same as the other. It was lined with many shops, bakeries, and lots of visitors strolling the streets and enjoying the scenery of the Moulin Rouge area they were in. Her arm was still in his arm, and she felt like she never wanted that to change. They weren't talking too much now, but it was a comfortable silence. They both were taking in the sights and enjoying the company of each other and people watching as they walked.

She saw the restaurant where they started on the other side of the street and spotted Bernard still waiting patiently for them. He didn't seem to be annoyed with waiting for them, and it looked like he was enjoying watching the people walk by as well. She wondered how much Anastasio had to pay him to keep him solely for them for the night. Anastasio had planned this evening out well for such short notice, she thought, and for someone he really didn't know for that matter.

They made it back to the car, and Bernard opened the door for them. She climbed back inside, and Anastasio sat next to her. He immediately took her hand in his as Bernard got into the car. He started the car, and they were off without any instructions from Anastasio. He had another plan apparently made in advance for them, and she was happy to see that he didn't just stop at dinner. She didn't want this night to end yet. She wasn't sure that she ever would want any night to end with him.

It was getting dark now, so she couldn't see as much about the buildings as she did when they came to the restaurant. There were interesting things to see still. Many of the shops had different color lights up to attract people of every nature. The sex shops had the red lights, just as she would have imagined, being the red-light district. There were still lots of people milling about, going in and out of the shops, or just walking enjoying the sights and the company they were in.

She leaned on his shoulder, and he let go of her hand and put his arm around her to bring her closer to him. She loved the smell of his skin but didn't get too close as she didn't want to make him feel uncomfortable. It felt great to have his arm around her as Bernard sped through the streets to the next unknown destination. Neither of them felt the need to say anything. The driver had the music playing softly, and his window was down giving her the smells of night. She noticed a few buildings now that she passed on the way to where she shopped and ate earlier during the day. She then realized that maybe dinner was the only plan, and that they were now heading back to the hotel. She took a deep breath and prayed that this wasn't going to be the end of the evening or more so, the end of seeing Anastasio!

As they neared where they were staying, a crowd of people were walking in the same direction. She saw lights strung across the buildings in multiple colors that you think of when you think of outdoor Christmas decorations. The lights seemed bright against the black sky. She could hear music coming from somewhere ahead very faintly. The crowd looked to be all local families. She saw every age, from babies to much older people, walking. She wondered if there was some kind of festival going on.

Within seconds, the car came to a stop near their hotel, and Anastasio said something to the driver, and he looked to her and smiled. "Are you ready for the next part of the evening plans?"

Before she could answer, Bernard was already out of the car and opening her door. He smiled at her as he again offered his hand to help her out of the car. She gladly accepted and as she stood. Anastasio was already coming around the back of the car and to her side. They were at the edge of what looked like a huge street festival. She could hear the music much louder now but still couldn't see where it was coming from with the throng of people coming and going. Everyone looked so happy! The children were playing and running around, while the parents talked to one another, and some had drinks in their hands. Anastasio thanked Bernard, and he smiled, nodded at them, and drove off.

Anastasio took her hand as he did in the car and smiled at her. He kept the attention of her eyes for a few moments and then said, "I thought you might like to see what the locals do for entertainment here!"

"Looks like a lot of fun! Is this only for anybody, or are the locals going to tie us up and beat us for joining in, or are they going to beat me with a stick since I don't belong here?" she asked in a playful manner.

He turned and looked at her and began to laugh. He liked that she had a sense of humor. "I think we will be safe. The locals get together once a month like this and have a street party. They welcome anyone with open arms that want to join in the fun. They are very friendly! Come on, let's walk around and see what they put together this month. I have been a few times, and it's always so much fun."

"They do this once a month? Wow, they really do it up well!" she said, looking around.

They walked through the thick crowd and saw everyone enjoying themselves. The music continued to get louder, and she saw more and more people dancing to the music. It was a mixture of instruments that she couldn't quite figure out. There was no one currently signing, just a fast-paced beat that sounded from that of a band that had played together for many years. She couldn't wait to get close enough to see what was being played and how many there were playing. This whole thing was very intriguing. She felt energized from the people around her, and she felt truly alive.

"Yes, they do this once a month. They take pride in getting together, mingling, and enjoying the company of each other. Most of the families have lived here all their lives, and their parents lived here before them. It's quite a tight group of people here. They are so nice and welcomed me with open arms just as they will you!" he said, still guiding her through the crowd.

Finally, they stopped at a spot where they could see the band playing. It was in the middle of a street, and most had to be at least in their sixties. Only one was young and distinctly young at that. Marcela guessed he was still in his teens. She saw two men playing guitar, one playing the saxophone, an old man playing the accordion like he was the youngest man there, one playing drums, one playing the fiddle, and the youngest playing a clarinet. They were all full of energy and zest. She wondered how long they had been playing tonight and if most of them had been playing together most of their lives.

Around the band many were dancing. It was hard to tell who the couples were, just friends, family, and so on. The people dancing would dance with one, then another, then another. The ages here were very mixed. She loved that everyone was smiling and laughing like they didn't have a care in the world. "Would you like a drink? They generally have wine and beer here," he asked as she watched the dancing.

She turned toward him. "I'd love one! If they have red wine, I'd prefer that but will take whatever they have." He released her hand and leaned in closer to her. "I'll be right back. Enjoy watching them because soon, I'm taking you out there, and others will be watching us," he said and winked at her.

Before she could say anything, he turned and walked away. Dancing? She didn't know how to dance. She kept watching the people dance as she thought of every excuse in the world that she could to tell him that she couldn't dance tonight. She couldn't come out and just say she couldn't dance. The thought terrified her. She didn't want to disappoint him with being the worst dancer on the planet. Maybe she could get him to drink enough to forget about dancing with her. Yes, that was going to be her plan!

Anastasio came back carrying two glasses of red wine. He handed her a glass and toasted once again, and they both took a drink. It was red wine, but she didn't know anything more than that. She did enjoy the taste, and it looked like he did as well. It was a nice distraction of her previous thoughts, but she still couldn't get the fear of trying to dance out of her head. "I hope you like the wine. It's just a table wine that the locals love to have here. I figured you might want this more than a beer." He paused and looked at her a little more deeply. He could see that something was on her mind now. "I can get you something else. You don't look like you like it!"

It took her a moment to figure out why he would say that. It hit her that her face must have shown her concern, not for the drink but worrying about dancing. She relaxed her face a bit. "No, the wine is great! I'm sorry, I just was thinking about something." She wanted to change the subject quickly so he couldn't ask her what she was thinking about. "How many times have you come to one of these?"

He didn't seem to notice the deflection and smiled at her again. "I don't know really. I'd guess around ten times or so. I have been coming here to Paris for a long time. I remember coming out of the hotel one night and heard the music and decided to investigate. I walked through the crowd and was afraid that everyone was looking at me, wondering what I am doing at their party. Within minutes of walking, an elder couple stopped me and introduced themselves. Before I knew it, they introduced me to so many people I couldn't remember anyone's name. They kept handing me drinks and made me feel more at home than I did at my own home. And if you knew my mother, that is hard to do!"

"Wow, that's really nice! I don't know very many places you can go and find people like that!"

"And now here you are. They will embrace you just as they have me!" he said and lifted his glass and put it to her glass. He started yet another toast. "To new people in our lives, new experiences, and enjoying every minute of it!"

They both lifted their glasses and drank the last of the glass. Within seconds, some people that were dancing close to them noticed Anastasio. They hugged him with excitement, and he introduced them to Marcela. She stuck out her hand to shake, but before she could even lift it halfway up, she was being hugged by the couple and kissed on the cheek. They said something in French, and she looked at Anastasio.

"They said it is a pleasure to meet you!"

They started to speak again, and Anastasio quickly nodded to them, and they smiled back at them. The couple turned and left as quickly as they came, and she turned to Anastasio. Before she could ask what they said, he said, "They want to have a drink with us. I told them it would be an honor! I hope it is okay that I answered for you as well without asking."

"I think that will be okay just this one time!" He smiled at her and put his right arm around her and pulled her close to him. She didn't resist and felt relaxed with the closeness they now had. His lips found her forehead, and he gave her a gentle kiss. She couldn't help but smile where he couldn't see as his chin rested right where he kissed. She saw the couple coming back and thought she wasn't ready to leave his embrace yet but knew she had to.

The couple lifted their glasses in a toast that she didn't understand, and they drank more wine. She would try to remember to ask Anastasio what they had said. They talked with Anastasio some more but kept their smiling faces pointed at Marcela, giving her the notion that they were speaking of her. He spoke back to them slower than they had but in a voice that sounded very sincere and confident. Even though she didn't know what he was saying, she could listen to his voice like this all night. It was dreamlike!

They kept drinking, and as their glasses got closer to empty, wine seemed to come from nowhere. Every time their glasses got close to empty, someone would come by with a jug of wine, and without asking, they would fill their glasses once again. They were now on their fourth glass, and Marcela was starting to feel the effects of it. The music was still going strong, and more people were dancing and laughing around them. She even found herself swaying her head to the music.

At several different times, people came up to say give their regards to Anastasio, and she could tell by the looks and smiles she received that she was the topic they were most intrigued with. She didn't ask him what they discussed, but she could tell that they were pleased with the answer he gave them. They seemed to approve of her being here with him. Each time he was speaking with someone, he managed to stay close to her and, most of the time, kept some kind of physical contact with her. She loved the way he made her feel that even though he was talking with others, she knew that his attention was still on her.

The drinks continued, and she found herself relaxing even more. She was now holding hands with Anastasio, and most of the other people had said their hellos, but all his attention was back on her. They talked mostly of the surrounding events but stayed quiet many times as well as they took in the atmosphere around them. The night air was still warm and humid, but the way she felt now, the weather was absolutely perfect to her.

Without any warning of the music slowing down, the band changed the beat to a much slower song. Before she even realized what he was doing, he was taking her hand and taking her to the spot where everyone was dancing. Her mind hesitated some, but her body betrayed her and followed him willingly to the dance area. Once they were there, he turned and faced her. He held her left hand still and pulled her closer with his right arm as he put it around the small of her back.

Their eyes were locked upon each other. As he looked at her, he felt as if he had been looking at her for years. He already knew her face well! Her eyes, her lips, and her hair were all familiar to him. He thought she might shy away from how he was staring at her, but her eyes never left his. Her body was tight against his as they swayed to the music. They didn't even attempt to say anything. The music went right along with the looks they gave each other. Her face seemed so familiar, and he wondered if his face felt familiar to her as well.

Marcela was surprised by how relaxed she was dancing with him. She always had two left feet and was lucky if she could walk without tripping over absolutely nothing. But here she was slow dancing and didn't miss a beat. Of course, it was slow music, and if something fast came on, she might cause damage to herself, him, or both of them. Even other people around might be in danger. That didn't matter at the moment though because she was happy being right where she was, dancing with him!

The wine had taken full effect now, and she relaxed even more. She moved her arms up and around his neck, and her fingers lightly traced the edges of his collar and his hair. Her chin rested on his upper chest, and his right hand was now wrapped around her lower back. His lips were on the side of her forehead, and occasionally he would give it a small kiss. Every time he did, she could feel her heartbeat speed up just a little. She wanted to make a move to kiss him, but as relaxed as she was, she was still too nervous to do something like that! She wasn't the type to ever take the first step. And often, when someone else tried, she would do what she could to avoid it. But she knew that if he tried, she would not resist him in the least.

They continued to dance just the way they had been. The band must have sensed the closeness they had because they kept the music slower than they had all night. One of the older men was singing now, and although his voice was kind of rough, she could tell that in his younger years he must have sounded like an angel. She couldn't understand the words but knew it sounded awfully familiar, and it was a beautiful love song. Anastasio hugged her even tighter as the songs continued.

Without any warning or even light rain that slowly turned into heavy rain, thunder struck, and a shower of rain poured on the crowd. The raindrops were warm but very large and heavy, soaking anything it dropped upon. The crowd and the band scurried under any cover they could find as quickly as their feet would take them there. Anastasio took her hand to lead her to cover as well, but after a few steps, Marcela stopped him by pulling back on his hand and stopping her feet. He turned and looked at her confused, thinking she might have tripped or something but realizing by her look that wasn't it at all. She wanted to be there!

He continued to look at her for a few seconds, trying to figure out her actions, and her eyes said everything that words couldn't. In one fluid motion, he moved closer to her, put his right hand behind her neck, and pulled her face to his and kissed her deep and passionately. He wasn't rough, but it was a wanting kiss. She kissed him back with the same rigorous passion and put her arms around his neck. His arms were wrapped around her with one hand in her hair pulling her head into his and the other pulling her body closer to his.

The rain was relentless, and the crowd that had taken cover turned and saw them in the middle of the rain, like they were in the middle of their own living room. Someone caught one of the band members attention, and he saw them as well. He quickly motioned to the others of what he was seeing, and they all smiled in unison and picked up their instruments. They huddled for a few seconds and then started a slow waltz. The rest of the crowd was now settling undercover and still watching the two in the rain. Most of them whispered to their own spouses and smiled at the couple as they took part in their own little kisses and hugs.

After a few minutes of kissing, Anastasio pulled back and cupped her chin with both his hands. He looked at her and, for the first time, heard the music playing. He could tell that she had just heard it too as her head turned toward the band. His head followed hers, and they turned to see the band smiling at them and nodding in approval. She knew the song sounded awfully familiar. She asked Anastasio what is was, and he replied that it was "Smoke Gets in Your Eyes." They scanned the crowd standing near the band, and they were all smiling at them and clapping along with the music. It was a surreal scene. They looked back at each other, and as soon as their eyes met, her lips turned into a big smile. His followed in return. She started laughing, and he did as well. She buried her head in his chest as she laughed, and he put his arms back around her. Her hands were on his chest, a sort of protection. She could still smell his cologne, and she also wanted to feel the closeness of him.

The clapping got a little louder, and Marcela leaned back in his arms and smiled at him. "Well, I think they want us to dance," she said with another small laugh.

"I think you are right!"

Still leaning back, she started to sway in his arms. She looked down at his shirt, and it was completely soaked through. She could see his dark skin through the material. He looked down to look at what she was looking at. He laughed and pulled away from her a little. He reached up and started to unbutton his shirt. She just stood there and watched with a smile as he did so. She could see his tanned chest now through the rain that was pounding onto it. Her own hair was matted, and many strands of hair were plastered to her forehead. She pushed her hair back off her face as he undid the last button of his shirt and removed it.

She couldn't help but to look at his body. His shoulders were broad and strong. He wasn't too big but very fit. His arms were muscular, and she loved the curves of them. His chest and stomach were in proportion to the rest of his upper body. It was firm and muscular, and although his abs weren't that of a twenty-year-old athlete, it was still very flat and firm. Without taking her eyes from his body, she moved closer and kissed the top of his chest lightly in various places. Being this close to his skin brought out his scent. That along with the smell of the rain and his cologne filled her senses with a sweet smell that invigorated her.

He pulled her head back and cupped her face in his hands again. He leaned in and kissed her again. This time much softer and slower but still with the passion of the kiss before. Her lips tingled, and her tongued probed his mouth. She could taste the rain entering into their mouths mixed with their own saliva. His hands moved and brushed her hair off her face and then moved through her hair and pulled her closer to him. She loved the way his touch felt anywhere he touched her.

She broke the kiss off and looked at him. They had a serious expression on their faces and were breathing heavy. Marcela dropped her hands from his neck and grabbed his left hand. Her eyes found his, and she gave him a half smile. Without a word, she started walking, pulling Anastasio in tow. Their pace was slow but sure. After a few minutes of walking, there they were, in front of their hotel. He held the door open for her, and she kept hold of his hand. They stopped for a moment to shake off some of the rain that was in their hair and dripping down their bodies. She once again led the way, and he followed as she took his hand in hers again. He didn't question or say anything. He just followed her to her room.

They walked into her room, and he shut the door behind them. She turned and faced him. There wasn't much room, so when she turned around, she was awfully close to him. He put his arms around her waist and pulled her to him. Their mouths found each other, and they embraced in another passionate kiss. Her hands made their way around to the front of his shirtless chest, and she ran her fingers over his smooth skin. She saw now that he had no hair on his chest or stomach. Sweat started to form on their foreheads as the air was stagnate and humid from the rain that was now slowing outside her window. The only light emitted was from the lights strung across the buildings and any lights coming from the other buildings.

She broke their intimate kiss off and moved to open the window and turned on the ceiling fan that hung above the bed. As she was opening the window, she stopped as she could hear talking through the wall next to her room. The walls must have been very thin as she could hear every word spoken. As usual, the man was speaking in French, and she couldn't understand what was being said. She could tell by the tone of his voice he was saying something romantic to whoever he was with. It sounded very sensual the way he was speaking. It was soft, slow, and articulate.

Marcela came back over to him, and she could tell he could hear the man next door as well. She put her arms around his waist this time, and he pulled her head into his chest. His body was warm and wet, but it felt good to feel his skin on hers. She felt very safe and comfortable wrapped up in his arms. They were both listening to the sounds of the man's voice next door.

The man next door was silent for a short time, and then she heard a woman's voice spoke like his, soft and sensual. Marcela could hear the man start speaking again and heard his words clearly, although she didn't know what was said. She heard, "Maîtresse, embrasse-moi, baise-moi, serre-moi, haleine contre haleine, échauffe-moi la vie, mille et mille baisers donne-moi je te prie. Amour veut tout sans nombre. Amour n'a point de loi."

As soon as her voice stopped, Anastasio started speaking softly into her ear, "Mistress, embrace me, kiss me, hold me tight, breath against breath, breathe me life, thousands and thousands of kisses give me I bet you. Love wants everything without condition. Love has no law."

She looked at him and smiled. "Thank you for the translation. It is very sweet!" As soon as she finished her words, he lowered his lips to hers and parted her lips with his. While they were kissing, he moved his hands down to the bottom of her dress and started to lift it slowly. His hands were gentle as he kept lifting upward as she raised her arms to let him take the dress completely off her.

He looked at her standing there in her new lacy black bra and panties. Her body was tight and incredibly beautiful. He touched each curve of her body, starting with her calves all the way up to her face. To him, her body was perfect! Her skin was smooth, yet hard from what he imagined, her working hard on it every day. Her legs were muscular, but still feminine. Although her breasts were covered by her bra, he could tell they were firm and, well, perfect for her body type.

He put one of his hands on her hip right above the top of her panties and moved his hand softly across her belly. It was moist from the rain and humidity in the air. He could feel her shutter a little as his hand made its way across her body. Her breathing got deeper, and he could feel her stomach tense and relax with each breath. He kept his eyes focused on where his hand was. He not only wanted to feel her body but also to see it and each reaction to his touch.

She took his hand, and she backed up to the bed as she looked intensely in his eyes. He didn't need any further instructions as he took control and laid her down softly. He stayed standing for a few seconds as he moved her legs onto the bed and got her comfortably in the middle of the bed. He kneeled on the bed next to her and leaned down to kiss her softly. As his lips found hers, his hand found where it had left off and started to roam her stomach and sides.

He pulled back from their kiss, and her arms went to pull his neck back to her. He gently pushed her arms back down to over her head and smiled at her. His eyes searched hers for a moment and then bent back toward her lips and came very close to kissing her, but his lips stayed just out of her reach. Each time she lifted her head to try to reach him, he moved just far enough back to stay out of reach. All she could feel was his warm breath upon her lips. She desired to feel his lips on hers again!

Marcela's body was on fire with desire as he straddled her and sat all the way up. He moved both his hands to her face and lightly traced the lines of her face, jaw, and chin. His fingers traced over her lips, and each time her lips parted, he let her tongue moisten the tips of his fingers as they continued to move around her mouth. She was torn between shutting her eyes and just feeling what he was doing or keeping them open and looking at his intense eyes as she felt his hands work their magic on her.

He sensed her hesitation and whispered for her to close her eyes. She did without question. She felt his body move off hers, and his hands lightly and slowly traced their way down to her feet. She didn't open her eyes but was curious what he was going to do. She felt a fire burning inside of her now that she had never felt before. Once his hands were on the bottom of her feet, she felt his weight shift on the bed and felt his hands taking off her high heels. Then he took her stockings off slowly one leg at a time. He took his time with everything he was doing, making her desire him even more. He then touched the bottom of her foot. She could feel light kisses follow everywhere his hands went.

Starting with the right foot, he caressed and kissed it slowly. He moved his way up to her ankle on top and both sides of it, his lips following everywhere his hands were, onto her shin and what he could touch and kiss of her lower leg with her lying on her back. Her skin was still smooth and silky from the lotion she had applied before the evening began. He could see her breathing was deep and steady. Little bits of perspiration dotting all over her body. He looked over her whole body and knew he would never forget this sight as long as he lived.

Anastasio moved up to her knees and thighs. She could feel tingling in her stomach and her body temperature rising with each new touch and kiss. His touch was very slow and his kisses tender and soft. Never in her life did she want someone as bad as she wanted him right now. She wanted to grab him and pull him on top of her, but her body couldn't get enough of this feeling she had right now. His hands and mouth were now at the top of her right leg close to her hip, and his hands wandered very close to between her legs. Carefully and deliberately, he came as close as he could to touching her most sensitive spot but didn't actually touch or kiss it. He teased her like that for a few seconds before sliding his hands back down her right leg and back to her foot.

He moved his hand to the left foot and started the whole process all over again. She started to wonder if it was possible to have an orgasm without actually being touched on her most sensitive areas. She could feel her juices flowing, and the heat between her legs was still growing as his hands and mouth repeated the same thing on the left as he did on the right. She didn't only want to be touched and kissed on her most sensitive spots now; she needed to be touched and kissed there!

She didn't get her wish as he moved up and over the top of her panties below her stomach. His breath was hot as he exhaled his breath through the material of her panties. His hands moved upward and traced the lines of her panties, and his mouth followed. She could no longer stay still and squirmed under him, and her body was yearning for more and more of his touch and kisses. His hands were now halfway up her stomach, and his lips and tongue found their way around her belly button. The feeling it gave her almost put her over the edge. She could feel her juices coming out of her and running down between up legs onto the bed.

Anastasio continued up to her chest and moved her bra down just a bit so he could caress and kiss around her breasts. The whole time, he was very gentle and in no rush. He moved in circles around her breasts, making the circles smaller and smaller until he was almost touching her nipples. Then he moved one hand and kissed in the same circular motion. When he made his way to her nipple, he would lift his head back and exhale deeply, and her nipple would harden each time.

He started his way up to her shoulders and neck. Each kiss felt like his tongue caused an electric reaction wherever his mouth touched. She tried again to reach up to pull him to her, but he resisted. He put her arms back to above her head and continued teasing her body. His hands traced her shoulder and down the right arm, down to her hand, and back up the back side of her arm, then across her neck to the other shoulder and down the other arm and back up.

The only sounds were her heavy breathing, and she could still hear the couple in the next room. Now it wasn't only the man speaking but now also a woman with the same tone that the man had. Feeling Anastasio touching and kissing her body and the couple speaking in that tone was driving her crazy. She wished she knew what they were saying, but she knew that even if she did understand, she wasn't capable of paying attention to anything outside of what she was feeling.

Her eyes were still closed, but she felt like she could see everything he was doing. The beads of perspiration had now turned to sweat, which didn't bother her. She felt him nudging her left shoulder, and he whispered, "I want you to turn over!"

She did just as he asked without any hesitation and felt his weight shift again, and he was back at her feet. He repeated the same process on the back of her legs, butt, and back as he did in the front. He didn't seem to miss a spot on her body. It made her think of the many times someone heard, "I want to kiss you all over." Well, this was certainly the way it should be. She felt incredible and cared for by Anastasio, a man she had only met for less than a day. While he had his hands on her back, he undid the clasp of her bra and moved the straps to the side.

When he reached her head this time, he laid his body completely on top of hers and kissed the side of her face. His arms were above her head, and he found her hands, and they interlocked fingers. She turned her head a little more toward his face and found his lips waiting for hers. His body was as hot as hers, and she could feel his sweat dripping down to her face. Instead of a feeling of irritation that generally came with sweating like this, it made her skin burn with desire with each droplet of sweat.

He lifted his body a bit so she could turn back over on her back. During the turn, their lips never separated. When she was completely turned, he didn't lie all the way back down on her. He let go of her hands and removed her bra from her arms. She didn't need him to say anything. She moved her hands quickly down to his pants. She found the buckle on his belt and undid it. She slid the belt off and found the button to his pants. She had no problem unbuttoning it and sliding down his zipper. He rose up a bit more, and she slid his pants down as far as she could reach.

Anastasio sat straight up and looked over her body for a moment. She could see he was pleased with what he saw. He stood up at the end of the bed and removed his shoes, socks, and then pants. He reached for his black boxer briefs, but she sat up quickly and reached for his hands. He was caught off guard and thought for a moment that she decided she wasn't ready. But as soon as the thought came, she put her hands on both sides of his waist and pulled down the boxers, leaving him completely naked.

She looked over his body, just as he had hers, and she was also very pleased with what she was seeing. He started toward her again and kneeled on the bed in front of her. He reached down and pulled at the thin straps of her panties. She arched her lower half of her body off the bed so he could take them off easier. He tossed them on the floor with the rest of his clothes and turned back to look at her body once more. They were both taking in the sight of each other. Both were incredibly pleased with what they saw.

He leaned down and kissed her lips and then moved down to her neck and kept going down until he reached her breasts. This time, he didn't tease her. He gently cupped it and sucked her nipple into his mouth. Her back arched, and her breathing became more rapid immediately. He flicked his tongue back and forth on her hardening nipple, and with his other hand, he cupped her other breast the same way. He moved his mouth over to the other breast and did the same thing. With each lick, she could feel a pulse inside of her that pushed more fluid out of her. She couldn't take any more. She needed him inside of her and now.

Marcela put her hands on his head and pulled him back up to her lips. Once he was kissing her again, her hand found his hardness and guided him into her. She could feel how wet she had become and couldn't believe what he had done to her. She didn't know it was possible to feel like this before anything had really happened. She put him in place, and he pushed slowly inside of her. Her body ached for him, and her hips pushed toward him as well inside. He was completely inside of her. She felt like she could explode in an orgasm at any second but tried to focus not to. She wanted to feel like this as long as she possibly could.

He kept the pace slow and steady. Pushing deeper and deeper inside of her. They continued to kiss, and when they weren't kissing, they kept their eyes on each other. When she looked at him, he felt as if she was going to push him over the edge, so he would start to kiss her again. Their hands both roamed each other wherever they could reach. She would grab his butt and pull him deeper into her. He would put his hand on her breasts and squeeze and pull lightly on them. Every touch made her tingle with pleasure that she didn't know existed inside of her. She knew she couldn't hold out much longer.

The way he was moving and breathing, she could tell he was close to orgasm. Sweat was dripping off both of them. His speed and intensity increased little by little. She was encouraging him by increasing her own tempo of moving her hips and pulling him in harder and faster with her hands. The passion in their kisses changed as well as their tongues darted in and out of each other's mouth.

He couldn't hold it any longer. She felt him try to pull back to ensure he didn't cum inside of her, but she held on to him even tighter. "It's okay, please cum inside of me. I want to feel all of you!"

With hearing her tell him that, Anastasio exploded inside of her. She could feel him pulsing inside of her for what seemed like forever. As he was filling her with his fluid, they locked eyes and felt the emotions each other had at that moment. Within seconds of his orgasm inside of her, she started her own orgasm that was more intense than anything she ever felt. She wasn't sure if it was going to stop.

They kept eye contact still and said no words. He leaned back in and kissed her slowly while he was still inside of her. He wasn't moving, but her hips were still moving slightly as she was still very aroused feeling him inside of her. While kissing, she could feel him getting extremely hard inside of her, and he started to thrust slowly back in and out of her. She was surprised but incredibly happy to feel him again.

He made love to her again with the same ending results. They finally collapsed beside each other. Their bodies were covered in sweat, and they were both trying to even out their breathing. He looked at her and smiled. His hand was on her belly, and he was moving it back and forth on the slippery skin. "I think it got a little hot in here!" he said with a laugh.

She laughed and looked over her body. She could see a layer of sweat covering every inch of her body. She placed her hand on his. "Would you join me for a quick shower?"

"I'd like that!" He got up and took her hand to help her up as well. She started the shower as he found two fresh towels and placed them close by. They got in the warm shower and hugged under the falling water. Although they were hot, the warm water cascading down their bodies felt amazing. They continued to hug and kiss each other as he got the soap and proceeded to lather her body all over. He took his time and covered her whole body. When he was done, she took the soap and did the same to him. He then shampooed and conditioned her hair. She loved the feel of his fingers massaging her head as he rubbed in the shampoo. It reminded her of any time she went for a haircut and got shampooed. But of course, his touch felt like something she never felt before.

They stayed a little longer in the shower, touching and kissing each other. When they got out, he held out her towel for her and helped dry her off. He made sure to slowly dry each inch of her body, from her head to the bottoms of her feet. She dried him the same way. This was almost as erotic as the feeling she felt in the shower. She couldn't believe how in one night she had more first-time feelings than she ever had in her life.

They left the bathroom, and he looked at his clothes on the floor. She saw his glance and knew what he was thinking. "You don't have to go. In fact, if you wouldn't mind, I'd love if you stay with me tonight."

He looked back at her, surprised she knew what he was thinking. "Nothing would make me happier. I just didn't want to assume anything!"

They went to the bed, and Marcela started to laugh as she looked at the sheets. She didn't see one dry spot for them to lie on. He followed her eyes and again knew what she was thinking. He grabbed the blanket off the floor and put it over the bed. "I don't think we will be needing to have this over us anyways."

She lay down on the bed, and he lay next to her. He laid on his back and put his arm under her neck and pulled her to him. She put her head on his chest, and her hand was on the other side of his chest, caressing his smooth chest and stomach. He had his hand on her back and rubbed and massaged lightly where his hand could reach. The rain outside had stopped, and a slight breeze blew in through the open window, making it not too hot to cuddle up with each other.

Marcela felt her eyes getting heavy. It really had been a long day with the flight, stress of the day, the excitement of the day, wine, and the physical effort just put out. She wasn't ready for the night to end but knew she couldn't fight the impeding sleep that was coming. "I hate for this night to end, but I'm starting to fall asleep. Thank you for such a wonderful evening, Anastasio. I couldn't imagine it being any better. I loved every minute of it!"

He leaned down and kissed her forehead, and she moved and kissed his lips one last time. She rested her head back on his chest and closed her eyes. Immediately her eyes closed, and she felt the weight of the world start lifting away as he started to speak. She could hear him, but it felt like a part of a dream. "Sleep well, Marcela. I couldn't imagine a better evening either. You are truly a dream come true. I loved every moment of today, from meeting you to thinking of you during the day to the whole evening together. Thank you!"

She drifted further into sleep. She wasn't sure if it was a dream or not, but she swore she heard him say, "I can't explain why, but I want you to know. I love you, Marcela. I loved you before I even met you!"

Chapter 4

The sun was shining, and the weather was absolutely perfect. There were few clouds in the sky cooling his skin as he lay on his towel. There was a slight breeze that kept him from getting too hot. As he scanned the beach, it looked pretty empty for a day like this. The sand was white and pure. In the background, he could see the rolling hills and small cliffs that ended at the sea. The seawater was a bluish green with white foam from the breaking waves. He could smell the salt in the air from the sea. People were sparsely spread out, making it easy to see everything and relax.

He took off his sunglasses and wiped his brow. The sun was bright as he looked out at the sea. He could see only one person swimming now, but he couldn't see them clearly even though he was only about five meters from the water's edge. He took a drink of water that he had brought with him and examined the area again. He didn't see any empty towels or belongings nearby and wondered where this person had come from. He didn't remember anyone walking to the sea.

He watched the person, more of just a figure right now, swim and plunge in and out of the waves. He didn't know why, but he was drawn to just watching this person and waiting to catch a glimpse of who it was. Even when he tried to turn his head and look at something else, he found that he was always looking at this person in the sea.

Suddenly the person started swimming toward the beach. The breeze picked up a bit more, and a cloud covered the brightness of the sun. This made it easier to see who was there. It was a woman. He couldn't tell more than that yet. She was in a one-piece silver bathing suit. She was getting much closer now, and it seemed she was swimming right toward him. He looked around to see if he had somehow missed an empty towel near him and saw that there was not any around. In fact, now he didn't see anyone on the beach anymore. Where did everyone go? He turned his attention back to the woman and continued to look at her swimming toward him.

She emerged from the sea and was awfully close to him now. He couldn't take his eyes off her even though he tried as hard as he could. She seemed to be looking straight into his eyes. Her walk was slow but had a purpose. It seemed the purpose was to walk straight to him. Her body was lean and firm. She had tanned skin, and her hair was wet and went straight down her shoulders. She didn't appear to be too young or old either. Her eyes sparkled even from this distance. Her lips were parted slightly and looked very inviting. He couldn't take his eyes off her even if he had the will to do so.

Without any thought process or effort, he found himself standing up to face her. He hadn't even realized that he had gotten up. It didn't matter now. She was almost right in front of him. She was coming to him. She walked to him, and as she drew near, his hand reached out for hers. She put out hers and, when she was close enough, took his hand in hers. He looked down at her hand on his, and it felt so right and natural to hold it. He looked back up into her green eyes. They were still sparkling. The breeze died down, and the sun started to reappear.

She leaned toward him, and his body did the same without any instruction from his brain. Her lips parted, and her lips touched his. He felt electric pulses shoot through his lips that shot all the way to his feet. It was a short but powerful kiss! He didn't know that just the lips touching each other could do that. She pulled back and looked into his eyes again. A smile appeared on her face, and she put her hand on the side of his face. He couldn't place it, but he felt like he had seen her before. Maybe he even knew her.

~

"Anastasio." Marcela put her hand on Anastasio's face and gave him a kiss. He stirred a little but didn't wake. His lips did respond to hers and kissed her. She pulled back, and he looked like he was trying to say something, but nothing was coming out. She got close to his ear and whispered, "Good morning, Anastasio!"

His eyes opened slowly, and he smiled at her. It took him a moment to realize that Marcela was above him, and it was her eyes he was seeing. His dream had been so real. He felt confused for a moment but started to come to. He tried to clear his thoughts and said, "Good morning!"

He kissed her lips again and pulled her on top of him. They kissed and held each other and enjoyed being lazy and in each other's company. There was no rush to get up. They lay there and took turns kissing and looking into each other's eyes. Their bodies were pressed together, and her skin felt soft and smooth against his. He wasn't sure if he would ever get used to the way she made him feel when she was near him.

As they were kissing, she started to pull him on top of her. It didn't take much prodding to get him to lie on top of her. As like the night before, their lips never left each other. The only difference this time was that he took control and entered her slowly. The passion between them was ridiculous! In one fluid motion, he turned onto his back, and she was now on top of him. She pulled back so she could watch his face as she was on top of him as she controlled the speed and intensity. There was something about her eyes that made him go crazy. It was the same eyes as the dream he was having about the beach.

They made love another two times before they finally collapsed. He rolled off her but stayed by her side. They exchanged little kisses and smiles. His hand caressed the side of her face. He heard his stomach growl and realized that he was famished. He figured she must be as well. He heard her start laughing at him as she must have heard his stomach growl as well. She smiled and said, "Would you like to go find something to eat?"

"I think that would be a great idea! May I take you to breakfast?"

"I would love to! Think we can make it out of this bed and actually make it to breakfast?" she asked as they kept stopping to kiss each other.

"Okay, okay. Let's get up! We can come back to this later!" he said with a smile. "How long do you need to get ready? I will have to go to my room as I don't think I should be wearing what I was wearing last night when we leave the hotel. We don't want to start any rumors," he said with a wink.

"I can hurry. Just a quick shower, and I can throw on some clothes. With the sounds coming out of you, I think we should hurry before you eat me." She laughed at her own joke.

He laughed as well. "I think I will be okay. Why don't you come to my room when you are ready? I will shower quickly and get ready."

"Sounds good. What room are you in?"

"Room 304. It's at the end of the hall. Or maybe I should just shower with you here!" he said with a laugh. She giggled and gave him a playful push toward his clothes that were on the floor. With that, he threw on his pants and picked up the rest of his clothes. He gave her a kiss and headed to the door. Just before he shut it, he peaked back in. "I look forward to spending the morning with you. Clothed and unclothed! See you in a few minutes." He shut the door and headed to his room to get ready, and she headed to the shower herself.

She picked out a simple sundress and sandals that matched. It took about twenty minutes for her to get ready. She got her purse and left and to make her way to his room. He opened the door and looked as he had just finished getting ready too. He was wearing a pair of khaki shorts and a light-blue polo shirt. He grabbed his wallet and room key, and they made their way out of the hotel.

When they made it down the stairs, the same group of men were sitting around the table playing cards. They must have gone home at some point because they were wearing different clothes, but they were all sitting in the exact same spots as the last time she saw them. They all looked up at Anastasio and Marcela as they came into view from the stairs. The men were all smiling a knowing smile. No words were exchanged. Just glances around the table and back to the couple.

They left the hotel, and Anastasio indicated that there was café in the same direction the street party that they had just attended was at. They walked hand in hand, enjoying the sun shining down on them. It wasn't long before they arrived at the café. They decided to sit outside and enjoy the sun and people watching. She planned to tell him about the game that she liked to play while people watching.

Anastasio helped translate the menu, and they both ordered breakfast and fruit. As soon as the waitress left, they started to play the game she just told him about. It proved to be interesting and fun, and they laughed continuously as they made up stories for the people passing by. He liked to come up with the most random jobs and lifestyles he could think of. At times, she almost spit out her water as he made a comment that caught her off guard.

Their food came, and they ate and picked at the fruit, feeding each other occasionally as they talked and laughed. She thought things like this only happened in movies. No one had ever fed her before. It was such a sweet gesture. The food was now gone, and they just sat making small talk and holding hands. It was beautiful out. The rain and humidity were now gone and a slight breeze that made it very pleasant.

He looked at her and gave her a serious look that almost made her think something was wrong. Then he smiled at her and said, "I was thinking, you just got here and haven't been here before, so how would you like to spend the day seeing some sights with me as your tour guide?"

"I think that sounds like a wonderful plan. But…," she replied.

"Oh, I'm sorry, you probably already have your day planned. I was just…"

She stopped him midway through his sentence. "But you have to allow me to take you to dinner for your services."

"You drive a hard bargain, but I think that's doable. Do you need to go back to the hotel for anything, or do you want to leave from here?"

"We can go from here as long as we aren't going anywhere that I need to be dressed differently."

"You look absolute perfect. Shall we start our adventure?" he asked, and she nodded in response.

He paid the bill, and they found a taxi.

"Please take us to Le Sacré Coeur," he told the driver, and they sped off.

"Where are we going?"

"Le Sacré Coeur is an old Catholic church built on the highest point of the city. From there you can see the whole city surrounding it. I figured it was a good place to start, and we'll go from there."

"That sounds like it will be a lovely sight!"

He moved closer to her and whispered, "Not as lovely as the sight of you!"

She blushed and leaned over and kissed his cheek. "That's very sweet of you to say!"

The taxi made its way to the church, and they got out of the car. Marcela couldn't believe the view from here. She could literally see the whole city up there. The church itself was a magnificent view. It was a beautiful structure in all white. Before they went inside, they made sure to walk around the outside of the church to see all of it and the different views of the city. They made their way inside and took a tour of the church.

She learned that they started building it in 1875, and with many different complications, it wasn't completed until 1914. Then it was consecrated in 1919 after the end of World War I. There were so many interesting facts that she couldn't keep up. But more than the history of the church, she was amazed by its beauty. No matter how many old buildings and landmarks she had seen in her lifetime, it was still hard for her to believe that things like this were built so long ago.

They spent a few hours inside and outside the church. They decided to move on and go to see something completely different but incredibly famous in this district. They went to the Erotic Museum, also known as the Romantic Life Museum. They were going to see something that this church was built to fight against in this neighborhood. It was kind of ironic that these two clashing things were the biggest attractions and in the same area.

The museum was only opened in the late nineties and held erotic art from all over the world. She had grown up in a pretty conservative family, so seeing most of this was very new to her. The biggest surprise to her was how large the exhibit was. It consisted of five floors. Although it was new and unfamiliar to her, it was quite intriguing. She couldn't think of any other place that she could visit that was even remotely like this place.

They spent a few hours there, looking at all the art and artifacts that the museum had to offer. She couldn't believe how fast time was going. She really did find all the sights fascinating. The day was going by too fast, but she knew there was nothing she could do about that. She started to wonder if they were going to spend the evening together again or if they would part ways at the end of this journey. She did her best to push it from her mind. All she cared about right now, was being with Anastasio!

After they decided they saw all they wanted to see at the museum, they moved on to visiting some local art galleries that featured not only local artists but also artists from all over the world. Most of the galleries were small, but there were several of them within walking distance from one another. They visited several, and each one had its own style. She found it interesting that even being an artist in her own way with designing her own jewelry, the creativity that these people had was amazing.

He could tell she was getting tired. "Would you like to see more or call it a day? You are probably getting pretty tired now."

Again, she didn't want to think about the day ending, but she was tired. She hadn't done this much walking and other activities in so long that she was exhausted. But she did have a card to play to make sure to keep him around a bit longer. "I think we should go back and get ready for dinner. Remember, we had a deal! Just because we are leaving here doesn't mean you can get rid of me yet!"

"I wouldn't dream of wanting to get rid of you! Come on, let's get a taxi and go get ready. It seems I have a hot date tonight!"

"Oh yeah? Well, what about me?" she asked, nudging him.

Being witty himself, he didn't miss a beat. "Don't worry, we'll bring you!" And nudged her back.

They left and headed back to the hotel. They were quiet on the way back. It was a long but fun day visiting the museums and art galleries. They were still holding hands, and he pulled her closer to him. She put her head on his shoulder and closed her eyes. He put his arm around her and stroked her hair as they made their way back to the hotel. She loved that she felt she could never get tired of being next to him.

The driver dropped them off at the hotel, and Anastasio walked her to her room. She took his hand and gently pulled him inside. He didn't resist at all and followed her in. She turned around and look at him in the eyes. "Do we have a little time before we have to get ready?"

"Sure, dinner can wait. We can go anytime you like. I'm in no rush."

"Would you mind lying down with me for a short nap? I'd love to cuddle with you if you don't mind."

"I would love to!"

She got a little closer to him and started to lift his shirt over his head. As soon as it was off, she undid the button on his shorts and let them drop to the floor. "There, that's better!"

She walked to the other side of the bed and removed her dress. All she had left on was a white thong. He looked at her and was just as amazed as the first time he saw her with how she looked. He was sort of surprised that she already felt comfortable enough to get undressed in front of him. There was no question she was absolutely stunning in his eyes. She pulled back the covers and lay down. He lay next to her, and she put her head back on his chest. She kissed the side of his neck and then his lips quickly before resting her head. He stroked her hair and back again. Her skin felt warm and smooth. They both closed their eyes.

About an hour past before she woke to him kissing her forehead. "Well, hello, sleepyhead! How did you sleep?" he asked. He kissed her forehead one more time.

"I slept like a baby. What time is it? Did you sleep?" she said as she nuzzled her face into his chest.

"It's seven thirty. No, I didn't sleep. I was just enjoying holding you in my arms and listening to you breathe. Do you need to sleep more?"

"No, that was perfect. I just want to lay here for a moment. It is way too comfortable laying here with you to just jump out of bed."

All it took was one kiss, and before they knew it, they were making love again. Finally, after about thirty minutes, they decided to get up and get ready. They took a quick shower together. Even though it was quick, they still took time to kiss and hug under the cascading water. He helped dry her off again and left to get ready in his room as she started to get ready herself.

He met her back at her room shortly after, and now she was wearing jeans and a nice blouse. As instructed, he was dressed casually in jeans as well and, this time, a black shirt with white stripes. She could smell the same cologne on him as yesterday. She loved the way it smelled on him.

When they left the hotel, they passed the same men as usual. The men looked up but didn't seem the least bit surprised this time. They smiled and went back to playing cards. Marcela wondered if they talked about them after they left this morning. She was sure they did. She envisioned them gossiping like old women at a beauty parlor.

They had decided to keep it simple and to have a small dinner and a few drinks at a local pub. She wanted to see if the pubs here were any different than the ones back home. She had already painted a picture in her head of what it would be like. It would be smoke-filled and mostly men in the late thirties to upper forties. Most of them would not be in good shape. Of course, the place would smell of smoke and fried food. But she wanted to visit one despite all this.

It was only a few blocks away. They entered the pub, and it was nothing like she had thought. The air was clean and cool. It was well lit, and the crowd was very mixed but mostly younger, yuppie type of people. There was a bar in the middle and booths and tables surrounded it. The walls had all kinds of different types of sports pictures. Even though it was a different ambience than the tapas place that she liked to have dinner with Antonio and Lee, she got the same vibe from this place.

They chose a booth and looked over the menus. The waiter came, and they ordered beers while they decided what they were going to eat. Again, Anastasio helped her with the menu, and she decided on a sandwich, and he decided on a burger. The waiter came back with their drinks, and Anastasio placed their order.

While they waited for their food, they made small talk, and Marcela told him a little more about where she grew up and lived now. He was hoping she would bring up why she was on this trip, but it seemed she was still avoiding it. He asked other questions that he thought would get her to bring it up, but still she didn't remotely come close to telling him the reason she was there. He didn't want to push her too hard but was very curious. He just couldn't seem to come around to flat-out asking her.

"So I don't really know anything about you other than that you're in your family business and that you live in Italy, and there are some other things I know about you!" she said in a knowing way. "I guess I should have asked this before, but are you single, divorced, have kids, have a dog?" she said as she laughed a bit.

He laughed right along with her. "I am divorced. I got married right out of the university to a girl I had met in school. We had been dating a few years, and it just seemed like the step we were supposed to take. So we got engaged and then married a year later. We weren't an unhappy couple, but we weren't a happy couple either. At that time, business was great for the vineyard, and it kept me extremely busy and traveling a lot. Each time I went on a trip, the less we seemed to miss each other, and our love became kind of stagnant. She didn't do anything wrong, and we still talk here and there, but we didn't have the love for each other to carry us through life.

"We had talked about having kids, but I think we sensed that having a child wasn't the right move for us. Now I'm certainly glad we didn't as I don't think children shouldn't have to grow up in environments like that. I have always wanted kids though. And no dog either. I do have an impressive umbrella though! We divorced about five years after we married. Ever since then, I just haven't felt that spark, those butterflies you're supposed to get when you meet someone. Instant attraction and connection I think are important. Until last night, I wasn't sure I was going to feel that! But then here you come along!"

Their food arrived just as he finished talking about that. The food smelled delicious. They took their time eating and ordered another round of beer. The food was as good as it smelled. She thought that if she stayed here too long, she would gain a lot of weight. But for now, she was just going to enjoy it. As they finished their food, they made small talk about random things they each liked, where they have traveled, and so on. Their beer was getting low again. "What do you say to one more drink?" he asked.

"Sounds good to me!"

They ordered another round as the waiter cleared their food out of the way. He finally decided it wasn't ever going to get easier to ask her about it, and he didn't think she was just going to offer the information anytime soon. So he went for it. "Marcela, can I ask you something? It seems you don't want to talk about it, but what brought you on a spontaneous trip to Paris? If it's too personal of a question, you don't have to answer!"

She drank the last of her beer, and the new ones came. She took another very long drink and looked down at the table. She looked at him for a moment with tears in her eyes, and then back down at the table. "How about we finish our beer, we go back to the hotel, and I tell you there?"

"Sure. Hey, if you don't want to talk about it, you don't have to. I'm sorry to pry!" He now felt bad for bringing it up. He barely knew her but didn't like to see her upset or sad. And she was definitely sad now.

"No, it's fine. In fact, maybe it would be good to talk to you about it. Just not here."

"Okay." He reached out and put his hand on top of hers. "Marcela, I'm here for you. I know we just met, but I already care for you! I want to get to know everything about you!"

They finished their beer, and even though she argued that she was supposed to take him to dinner for being her tour guide, he grabbed the check before she could get to it and paid the waitress. She gave him a look, but she knew it was a battle she wasn't going to win. "Thank you, Anastasio. You didn't have to do that. I asked you to dinner."

"It was truly my pleasure!" He then put his hand out and helped her up, and she put her arm in his as they walked back to the hotel. They didn't talk on the way back to the hotel, but she felt extremely comfortable just being on his arm. This was something she could get very used to.

As if the men sitting at the table were a fixture, like a painting or a lamp, there the men were sitting at the table just talking. Anastasio exchanged greetings with them, and he and Marcela made their way upstairs. They went to the third floor to his room first to gather some clothes for him to wear for bed and the next morning. She just stood in the doorway but could tell that he was an exceptionally clean person just by how everything was perfectly arranged in his room. He quickly got some clothes and his toothbrush, and they headed down to Marcela's room.

When they got in her room, they took their time changing, brushing their teeth, and getting ready for bed. It seemed like they had been doing this for years together. They weren't running into each other or trying to do the same things at the same time. They were very limited on space that it would have made things near impossible. It's like they fit perfectly together without having to really try. She didn't know how they seemed to complement each other in everything they had done up to this point.

He brought his computer so they could have music to listen to if they wanted as they talked and lay in bed. He changed into a pair of silk boxers and no shirt. She put on a pair of cotton shorts and a loose-fitting tank top. Even when she wasn't trying, he thought she looked perfect. He was a lucky man to have met her just one day ago!

He pulled the covers back and got into bed as she washed her face. She finished up and climbed into bed, but instead of lying next to him, she sat in front of him, and he sat up with his back against the headboard. They were both sitting up, facing each other. She took his hand, kissed it, and interlocked her fingers into his. She drew her knees up to her chest with her chin resting on them. She held his hand to her face for a bit and then moved it down to her knee. Her knees were drawn up to her chest. He remained quiet and patient as she sorted through her thoughts. He could tell she didn't know where to begin, but he knew once she got started, her thoughts would flow out of her without any effort.

"I came because my life is a mess…" She paused to keep herself from crying uncontrollably. She got her composure and started to speak again. "I am almost thirty, and I have let my life and everything in it pass me by! I started college, like all my friends did, and followed what I thought I was supposed to do. I did well enough in school, but I just didn't feel like the things I was studying interested me as I thought they would. I found that I didn't want to do the normal jobs that people have. I have always loved designing, creating, and making many different things. After lots of thought, I decided to use my savings to design jewelry and open my own little shop. My mom and my friends helped me find a storefront and supported me as I frantically made jewelry. My best friend, Antonio, did most of the marketing for me, and I think he was responsible for getting me my first many customers. Anyways, my business did a little better than I expected. I was busy designing my stuff and hired someone to help me run the store. I didn't have much time to myself, but I thought if I just worked extremely hard for a few years, I would be able to slow down and take some time for myself.

"Well, it didn't. Even when I could slow down, I didn't know how slow down. All I knew was work. My friends and mom tried so many times to get me to do other things and wanted me to do things with other people. I was generally somewhat social before I started my jewelry shop, but then I let it take over my life. During that time, I met a man named Lee. We hit it off and started dating. We went to a firework show, and that's where I met my best friend, Antonio. So then our economy started to decline. When people must decide to either buy groceries and pay bills or buy jewelry, jewelry usually loses that battle. Things got slow, and I had to let my one employee go. So between trying to design new things and run the store, I went back to working nonstop."

She took a deep breath and wiped a tear away from her eye. She didn't look at Anastasio, and he didn't push for her to. He let her do this how she needed to. It was very apparent this wasn't easy for her. He thought she had a lot of courage to be telling him personal things like this when they had just met. He already had tremendous respect for her.

"Lee was very understanding…at first. He really did try to help me get my time under control, but I shut him out. I ended up letting him slip away. I blamed him for trying to spend time with him I didn't have. But really, I left him out of stupidity. It's only logical to want to spend time with the person you're dating. It wasn't his fault at all. He was, he is, a good man. He still keeps in contact with me and would be there for me anytime I need. So when I stopped seeing him, I cut everyone out of my life. Antonio and my mom were my best friends, and I wouldn't even let them do anything for me anymore. I didn't make any time to spend with them either. It was just me and my work. The economy got worse, and my regular customers weren't coming by as much as they once did. I started to drain the savings I had built up, and as I got stressed over that, I completely shut off from the rest of the world."

She had to stop again. Her tears were flowing now, and Anastasio tried to help dry her tears. He got up and went to the bathroom and got the tissues. He brought them back to her. She took them and silently dried her tears. She took her time trying to collect herself. She looked at him and gave him a small kiss. He hugged her neck and let her cry on his shoulder for a few minutes.

She pulled her head back and looked at him. She put her hand on the side of his face gave him a slight smile. She dropped her eyes from his and took another deep breath. "My poor mom was so worried about me. She raised me most of my life by herself and didn't like what I was doing to myself. I wouldn't talk to her, and when I did, I was get upset at her because she wouldn't drop the subject of me working too much. She said she wanted to see me happy and didn't just let me work myself to death. She said that work wasn't what life was all about. Of course, she was right, but I just couldn't see it at the time. I stopped talking to her and ignored her calls. I ignored everyone else as well. A few months passed by like this, and one evening I had gone to her house to have dinner with her and watch a few of our favorite shows we had made a habit of watching over the years. In the middle of one of the shows, she just..."

She stopped again and was crying uncontrollably. He pulled her into his chest and rocked her gently as she sobbed into him. He knew there were no words to be said right now and remained silent. It took her several minutes before her breathing evened out, and her body was becoming limp in his arms. He wished there were something to do for her to help her, but he knew that the only help he could give right now was to listen and hold her when she needed to be held.

She started to talk as her face was buried in his chest. "They said she suffered a massive stroke." She stopped again, her crying renewed. "We were laughing at something, and she just started to choke, and I couldn't do anything to help her. I called the paramedics as quickly as I could. They arrived much faster than I expected but unfortunately too late to really be able to do anything. We rushed to the hospital, but they couldn't do anything. She looked awful. "She was in a coma, and they put her on life support." More tears fell from her eyes. "All those machines hooked up to her. My friend Antonio met me there..."

He knew how the end of this story was going to turn out but was patient to let her tell him when she was ready. She stayed in his arms as he rocked her back and forth. He wanted so bad to take her pain away. He didn't like to see her hurting. He felt as though he had experienced it himself. He was sure he felt every emotion she was feeling at that moment. He felt they were as one person now.

"She died a few days later. The doctors said that no matter how quickly anyone could have acted, there wasn't anything anyone could do!"

Marcela stopped again. Her breathing didn't change much this time, and she cried softly. He knew she was emotionally exhausted now. She didn't move in his arms. He just held her there and stroked her hair. He was glad her head was buried into his body because he had tears in his eyes, and she didn't need to see that right now.

He didn't feel her sobbing anymore. Her body was completely limp in his arms, and her breathing seemed to be getting deeper. She was so exhausted! She must have fallen asleep. Slowly, he laid her down beside him, being careful not to wake her up. He slid down in the bed some to get more comfortable. She stirred some but didn't wake fully. She slid down with him but kept her head right where it was on his chest. He moved the covers so she wouldn't get cold under the fan and put his arms back around her. He closed his own eyes and drifted off to sleep next to her.

Marcela was unlocking the door to her house as quickly as she could. She could hear the phone ringing inside. She made it inside and picked up the phone. "Hello?"

"Do you not know how to return calls? I have been trying to reach you for a week! I'm worried about you!"

"I know, I know. You don't have to worry, I'm fine," Marcela said, showing that she was already annoyed with the conversation she knew she was about to have.

"Marcela, you aren't fine. You are working too hard! Why don't you take the day off, and we can go and spend the day roaming around the city, and I'll cook us dinner."

"I don't have time right now, Mom. I have to get this new design right, and I'm the only one at the shop. Why can't you understand that?"

"I do understand, but you are going to kill yourself if you don't stop sometimes and do something else. You need a life outside of work!"

"Fine, I will come over for dinner tonight, but I really don't have the time. I can't take a whole day off. I'll call you when I'm leaving here."

The next thing she knew, she was standing in a hospital room looking down at an empty bed. She knew where she was but was confused. In her mind, her mom was still lying there with some kind of hope. Where was she? Why was the bed empty?

"Hi, darling, what are you looking at?"

Marcela looked, and there her mother was in the doorway. She was dressed in normal clothes, but her face was blurred to a point she couldn't see any feature of her face. The body with the blurred face walked toward her with a subtle grace. Marcela looked back and forth from her to the bed and back again. The bed was still empty. She couldn't understand why. The woman walking toward her was supposed to be in that bed. "How are you out of bed?"

"You know how I'm out of bed!" The woman was right next to her now. Her face suddenly became clear. She looked exactly how she did when she was much younger. There weren't any wrinkles on her face. She was absolutely beautiful, and her smile was radiant. "You need to listen to me now! Don't waste your life on stuff that isn't really important. I want you to be happy. You deserve it. I love you, darling!"

She tried to look her in the eyes, but she wasn't standing there anymore. Marcela was confused and about to leave the room. As she started to walk out, she could hear a noise coming from beside her. She looked over and saw what she expected when she was first in this room. Her mom was lying there with the breathing tube covering her mouth. She ran over to the bed, and her mom wasn't moving. Her eyes were shut, and she looked just as she did the last time she saw her. She started to cry and laid her head on her mom's chest. "I love you too, Mom."

"I love you too!"

Chapter 5

Marcela awoke sometime in the middle of the night. She looked over and saw Anastasio was sleeping on his back. His arm was wrapped around her as her head lay on his chest. The last thing she remembered was telling Anastasio about her mother's stroke. Her mind was still fuzzy, but there was a sense of relief that came over her. This had been the first time she really had talked about what happened. She hadn't even told Antonio all that. She wondered if just talking about what had happened with her mother or if talking with Anastasio about it that made her feel better.

She lay there still so she wouldn't wake Anastasio up. He had been such a great listener. He didn't pretend he could solve the problem or take away the pain. But she felt his compassion and understanding. That was the best thing he could do in her mind. He seemed to be a great man, and she didn't realize it until now, but he's just what she needed. He must have been sent by her mom in heaven.

She wasn't sure how long she had lay there before she fell back to sleep. But the next thing she knew, Anastasio was giving her forehead a kiss. It was now light outside, and she was content with just lying there in his arms. "Good morning, sunshine!" he said when he realized that she was awake.

"Morning!" she replied and lifted her head up to give him a kiss. "What time is it?"

He looked at his watch that he was still wearing from the night before. "It's about 9:00 a.m. How are you feeling?"

"My mind is a bit foggy, but lying here with you makes everything seem to be better. I'm almost afraid to ask, but I don't remember falling asleep. I hope you weren't talking to me, and I passed out on you!"

"No, no, nothing like that! You had explained about your…" He paused to make sure to get the wording right not to upset her, "Mother passing just recently! I think between the days' events, having a few drinks, and the emotional stress you have been going through finally caught up to you!"

"I'm sorry I laid that all on you. I rarely talk about things that don't make me comfortable. But with you last night, I felt different. I felt safe! I think I could've talked about anything with you listening."

"I'm glad I could be here for you! I think you really needed to let it out. I know many times people keep things in for fear that it will make the pain more real. I'm included in that category, but I do know that when I do finally let things out, I feel more relief than anything!"

"Yeah, I guess you're right! Now I know you told me, but I have to ask again, how can a man as handsome, intelligent, and caring be single? I don't get it!"

"Well, I guess God had other plans for me. And right now, I think I see the reason!"

Marcela felt her heart almost jump out of her chest when he said that. Even though she didn't have those thoughts until he said it, it instantly seemed to be the logical answer. She usually would finally talk to her mom about things over time, but now she didn't have her to talk to anymore. Then she had broken things off with Lee basically for the same reason Anastasio broke things off with his wife. Lee was a great guy, but she never really felt totally comfortable talking about things that bothered her. She talked a lot with Antonio, but she still didn't just come out and say things right away even though he always knew when something was wrong. Maybe Anastasio was right. Maybe God had brought them together.

She realized that she was absent for the moment while she was thinking about what he had said. She shifted her body to lie on her side but kept her head propped up to be able to look at Anastasio easier. She wanted to be able to look into his eyes. "I don't know how to explain it, but I felt compelled to take this trip. It was something that I never would have thought I'd ever do. But there was something in my mind and heart that told me I needed this for whatever unknown reason. And after meeting you, I never have felt comfortable with someone so quickly as I have with you. I should feel scared right now, as I don't know where this goes. I mean, you live in Italy, I live in Spain, and here we are in France. But my heart is telling me not to worry about it. That all will be answered!"

They both analyzed each other for a moment, and looking into each other's eyes, they were both thinking the same thing. Neither of them contemplated where this was going to go when they both needed to return home. But he felt it! She felt it! This was meant to be! Neither had any doubt in their eyes, heart, and soul. Neither spoke for a few minutes. They just looked into each other's eyes. His arm was now rubbing her arm as they looked at each other.

Breaking the silence, she gave him a quick kiss and said, "Come on, let's go get some breakfast!"

He looked back at his watch and let out a small sigh. "We can go for a quick breakfast, but I do have a meeting that I can't reschedule. I will try to make the meeting as quick as possible so I can come spend the rest of the day with you if you aren't getting tired of me yet."

She had already forgotten that he wasn't here for vacation. He was here for work. They hadn't discussed when he was going to leave for Italy. She didn't even know when she was leaving. But right now, none of that mattered. She wanted every second with him that she could get. "Are you sure you have time? We can meet up later if that's better for you!"

"No, we have some time. I will just get ready quickly before so I can go straight from breakfast." And with that said, he gave her a small kiss and started to get up to go to his room to get ready. "Want to meet in the lobby in about fifteen minutes?"

"I think I can handle that," she said with a smile.

He smiled back at her, put on his clothes, and left the room. She lay there just few more minutes thinking about the past few days. For the first time since he wasn't physically with her, she felt a bit nervous about the future. They both had to leave for their separate lives at some point. And that time was going to happen way too soon for that matter. She tried to think about other things, somewhat successfully, but the thought kept coming back.

She finally got up and started to get ready. She had already wasted some of the little time she had to get ready. She picked out another sundress that she liked. From the window she could see that it was sunny out and didn't seem to be too cool or hot out thus far. She got dressed quickly, brushed her teeth, and put her hair back in a ponytail since she didn't really have time to try to deal with the tangled mess that it was. She went to the full-length mirror and looked at herself. For the time she had, she was satisfied with how she looked. She grabbed her purse and room key and headed out of the room to meet Anastasio.

Anastasio gave her a few options of places that they could go that were close by. They chose a small café that, like the place she went for lunch before, had outside tables. The weather was perfect again. There wasn't as many people walking about as it was now a Monday, and most people were at work and living their normal lives. She wasn't looking forward to being one of those people when she went back home.

Ever since the thoughts of them both having to leave Paris at some point, she couldn't really get it out of her head. She dreaded to bring it up, but she didn't see that it would ever get easier to bring it up. "Anastasio, I'm not sure I'm ready for the answer, but I'm curious. How long will you be here in Paris?"

His smile faded some, and he looked down for the first time instead of directly in her eyes. Now she was wishing she hadn't asked. She didn't think she was going to like the answer. "Well, I only have a few more days of business here, but I have a few days after that before I need to be home."

The waiter appeared before he could say anything else. They ordered quickly with the anticipation of what else he was going to say. The waiter took their order and disappeared. Anastasio was now looking back into her eyes. "I'm glad you brought it up. I have been thinking about it, but there never seemed to be a good time to bring it up. This isn't something I've ever had to think about. When I travel, I meet people here and there, sure. But never have I met someone that has made me want nothing else in life other than to be with them. I don't have a choice to really stay longer right now, but I am hopeful that in the next few days, if you are feeling how I am, that we can figure out a plan to see each other as soon and as often as possible."

Marcela was relieved that he had thought about this too. She didn't like hearing that he only had a few days left there, but honestly, she would probably need to return home soon as well. She didn't really have the money to spend staying there, and she needed to get back to work. She wanted to say something, but no words came out. What could she say? She had no idea of a good plan as of now.

He saw that she was searching for something to say. He took control and said, "I know this is going to sound crazy, but I've never met anyone that I cared for so much, especially only after a few days. I don't even know how it's possible, but I feel it. So as long as we're on the same page, we will work out something. Deal?" He held out his hand for a handshake, and she shook his hand and had to laugh.

He didn't let go of her hand. He just held on, and now his smile was back on his face. She was smiling as well. Her world felt perfect again, as it had the night they had met. She knew it wasn't going to be as simple as it sounded. Nothing worth it ever was. But he was worth it! And she believed that he meant every word he said.

There was a slight breeze, and she leaned her head back and closed her eyes as the breeze hit her smiling face. When she closed her eyes, she could see her mom looking at her, smiling. She didn't realize it, but she whispered out loud, "Thank you, Mom, thank you!"

Anastasio couldn't hear what she said but knew she said something. "I'm sorry, I didn't hear what you said."

It took her a moment to realize what he was talking about but then realized that she had said that out loud. "Oh, nothing, was just thinking of something."

She was once again saved by the arrival of their food. This morning was quite simple. Both got bagels with cream cheese and assorted fruits. The fruits looked so fresh and inviting. She picked up a raspberry and almost put it in her mouth. But then she reached over and fed it to Anastasio. They both smiled, and throughout the breakfast, they would occasionally feed fruit to each other. At one point, he put some cream cheese on a strawberry, and just before she could take a bite, she rubbed it on her nose. They were both enjoying the playful banter they had going. All her fears and worries disappeared as quick as they had come.

They finished up their breakfast and paid the bill. "I'm sorry that I have to go for now. I'm not sure how long this meeting will take. But I will do the best that I can. Do you want any suggestions of what to do for the next few hours? I know the areas pretty well!"

"I think I will just walk around and see what interests me. I'd prefer to wait for you to do any real sightseeing. Would you mind showing me more when you aren't working?"

"It would be an honor to be your guide. But it will cost you!" he said with a grin on his face.

"Hm, well, I'm just a poor girl lost in this big city. How ever could I repay you?"

"I think we can come to some kind of arrangement. It's now about 11:30 a.m. Just to be safe, would you like to meet back at the hotel lobby around 3:00 p.m.?"

"I'll be there. Good luck with your meeting! Although with your charm, I doubt you need much luck. I can't imagine many people saying no to you."

"If that were the case, I wouldn't have met you. Each year gets harder and harder with all the big vineyards taking over. I do what I can. So I will see you at 3:00 p.m., okay?"

"I'll be there." They gave each other another small kiss, and he was off.

Marcela walked around the streets randomly and found herself in many different boutiques and thought that this was the plan she had had for her own business. But so far, it hadn't quite turned out the way she had planned it. Her shop wasn't in a big tourist area like this, so she didn't get much business from people that weren't locals. These streets were lined with shops for clothing, jewelry, food, home furnishings, and on and on.

She found a few little things she liked, so she treated herself and bought them. One being a silver bracelet that was different than anything she'd normally like. She also found a cute small purse and some sandals she liked. She mostly just enjoyed walking around and taking in the sights. She also got some fresh ideas for some designs she'd like to try to put together for her own shop.

It was now getting close to time to meet back with Anastasio. She really hoped his meeting was going well. He seemed stressed about it, and she knew the feeling of being a small business. It's a fight to stay alive in this modern age. She couldn't imagine if she had to travel all over the place on top of running a company to keep things going. She knew how hard he must be working to try to keep their vineyard going.

She started back toward the hotel. She would have just enough time to put away the things she had bought. She should also take a few minutes to get freshened up. She wished she would've asked Anastasio what types of things he had in mind to do this afternoon to know if she needed to change. She wondered how much more work he had while he was here also. There were so many things she wanted to see, but she really now wanted to experience those things with him.

She made it back to the hotel with about twenty minutes to spare. She took her hair out of the ponytail and did the best she could in the few minutes she had. She decided to put on the bracelet she had purchased. Without knowing what they were going to be doing, she didn't change anything else. She was sure he would tell her if she needed to change. He might want to change himself.

~

Anastasio had made it to his meeting with just a few minutes to spare. On the walk over to the establishment, he tried to focus on how to keep their business. They had been clients now for over a decade, and the original owners sold out this past year, and the new owners were talking with several distributors and export wine companies. He couldn't quite keep his focus though. Marcela dominated his thoughts. He just needed to get through the next few meetings, and he'd figure out things from there. He wasn't sure what, but he believed life would show him the way.

The place wasn't open for dinner yet, but the front door was open for him. He walked in, and he immediately saw a man and woman sitting at a table. He assumed these must be the new owners and walked over to them. "Hello. I'm Anastasio. Would you happen to be Mr. and Mrs. Bourgeois?"

"That would be us. It is a pleasure to meet you, Anastasio. We want to be very upfront with you. We are talking with several companies to see what will fit our needs the best. We understand your company has been the sole supplier here for many years, and your wine is particularly good. We just want to make smart decisions as it's not easy to make profits in this industry these days. But we won't let the quality suffer just to make an extra dollar. So what would you like to show us?"

Over the next hour, he opened several different types of wines from different years. They sampled each one carefully and went over pricing points dependent on the quantity they would order. They seemed pleased with what they sampled and heard. But he had done enough of these meetings that he thought it went perfect only to get a call or message saying that they were sorry to inform him that they had chosen to go with other vineyards.

Anastasio wrapped up his presentation and started putting his stuff away. Much to his surprise, Mr. Bourgeois said, "Are you already planning on leaving?"

He was a bit confused by the comment and said, "I will be in Paris for the next few days seeing different clients—"

He was cut off before he could finish his sentence. "Sit, sit. I'm sure there is paperwork we can do now to go ahead and keep you as our supplier of our wines. You do have stuff that we can sign here today, don't you?"

Anastasio quickly sat back down and opened up his briefcase and pulled out the paperwork he needed. Even though this was a smaller establishment and it wouldn't ensure the future existence of the vineyard, it was a good start. Coupled with the past few days with Marcela, this was proving to be an amazing start to his trip. As the couple filled out the paperwork, Anastasio said a quick prayer to God, thanking Him for the blessings of the past few days. For the first time in a long time, Anastasio was genuinely happy. He felt like superman right now. He was ready to leap tall buildings and take on anything right now.

With the paperwork in hand, Anastasio made his way back to the hotel. He was excited to tell Marcela of the meeting and how well it went. But most of all, he was excited to be back with Marcela. Everything else that life could offer was just a bonus. He felt like he could dance on the way back. He didn't have any headphones to listen to music, but his mind replayed a song, and he walked to the beat in his head.

As he was walking back, all of a sudden, he felt a cramp in his stomach and realized that he really hadn't hydrated enough in the past few days, and now his body was paying for it. He stopped and got a bottled water and continued back to the hotel. He needed to remind himself that he really hadn't exerted himself in quite some time, so he needed to make sure to eat and drink enough. He didn't want to get sick while they only had a few days left together here.

He drank the water quickly as he made it back to the hotel. All the excitement seemed to be taking a toll on his body now. He was a little tired. But he couldn't wait to see Marcela again even though it had only been a few hours. That was about as long as he thought he could take being without her right now. He barely knew her, but he knew two things. First, she was completely amazing! And second, he knew she was the one for him!

He walked into the hotel lobby almost exactly at 3:00 pm., and Marcela was standing there waiting for him. She hadn't changed her outfit, but she had let her hair down. He didn't care which way she did her hair or what she was wearing for that matter. He found her absolutely stunning in her natural state. They smiled at each other, and he walked up to her and gave her a kiss. Rocco was standing behind the counter now, and the folding table was put away. He gave them both a big smile, and they both smiled back at him.

"So tell me, how did your meeting go?" she asked.

"Let's just say we have something other than our meeting to celebrate tonight!" he said with a beaming smile.

"Oh, how wonderful! I didn't know you'd know so quickly. The way you made it sound, you wouldn't know right away. But it's great news!" She wrapped her arms around him and gave him a big hug. As she was hugging him, she could feel his skin was hot and sweaty. It was a little warm out now but not that warm. "Are you feeling okay? You're very warm."

"Yeah, I'm okay. I just haven't been drinking enough water, I think. And you have kept me quite physically active in the last few days," he said and pulled back so he could look into her eyes. "What would you say we take a few minutes to let me rest, and then I thought maybe I could take you to some of the gardens in the eighteenth district and find somewhere pleasurable to eat? After that, we will see what we feel like doing. How does that sound?"

"You're my guide. So I go where you go. Do you want to rest alone, or do you want me to come with you?"

"And here I took you for an intelligent woman. Of course, I want you with me if that's okay with you. I don't want to sleep or anything. Just rest a bit. So my place or yours?"

"Decisions, decisions! Let's go to your room this time. You need to put away your things anyways. And you can tell me about your meeting if you like. You will have to tell me how I need to dress. I hope I have something suitable," she said as she remembered her lack of selection of clothing.

"Sounds like a good plan to me." He led the way up the stairs to his room and opened the door for her. She knew it was silly, but the small gestures like that made her fall for him even that much more. Things like that had seemed to have gotten lost in the past decade. But it said a lot about the character of a person. Once they were in the room, she went to the far side of the bed and lay down on her side as he put his things away. His room was pretty much identical to hers. As soon as he put away his things, he looked over at her, and she patted the bed for him to come lie next to her.

He removed his shirt and left his jeans on and lay in the bed next to her. As soon as he was lying there, she told him to lie on his side facing away from her. He was confused why she wanted him to do this, but he did it without any questions. When he was on his side, he felt her hands make their way to the outside of his neck, and she started to massage the area. He didn't realize that he was tense before this, but now he realized he was, and her hands felt great. He closed his eyes and let his mind relax with the soothing feeling of her hands on him.

After about twenty minutes of her massaging his neck and shoulders, she cuddled up behind him and put her arm around him. Having her so close felt incredible. He never wanted this feeling to end. He reached up and took her hand into his and then brought her hand to his lips and kissed it. Then he just held it there for a few moments longer. "Thank you. I didn't even realize how tense I was. That was just what I needed!"

"I think we both got what we needed!" she said, shocking herself by her statement. But she did mean it. He was what she needed in her life!

He turned in the bed to face her. He studied her face and looked into her eyes, as he usually did. He couldn't get enough of looking deep into her soul. "You are truly an amazing woman, Marcela! I don't know how all this came about, but I know it was meant to be. These past few days, I've had more happiness than I can remember ever having in my entire lifetime." And he meant every word he said. "What do you say we go see some gardens and then we can come back to change into something else for the evening?"

"I'm ready whenever you are."

He reluctantly got up and put on another shirt. He went and checked his face and hair to make sure he looked presentable. He came back into the main room, and she was up and straightening herself out. When they both were ready, he grabbed the room key and led the way back out of the room and hotel.

They made their way to the Renoir gardens. It was late afternoon now, and being a weekday, it wasn't too busy. It was so beautiful, and she saw instantly why artists came to be inspired. There was so much history here. Anastasio had only been there once many years ago, so it was pretty unfamiliar to him as well. It was nice that they were almost experiencing this as new to them both. They walked hand in hand. He was in a playful mood now it seemed. It was cute to see the kid side of him. He was simple, yet complex. He could go from a serious businessman to a kid in a park without blinking an eye. He would be good for her! She had been way too serious for way too long now. She didn't allow herself to let loose like this. It felt amazing to be living like she didn't have a worry in the world!

They spent about two hours going through the gardens and taking in the beautiful sunshine. Seeing the beauty of the garden made their senses go into overload. The day—well, the past few days—had been perfect in her mind. They both were getting hungry, so they decided that they should go back and get ready for the evening.

They decided it would be quicker and perhaps safer if they showered and got ready in their own rooms. If they were together, she doubted that they would even make it out of the room to make it to dinner. She didn't really care where they went, if they went anywhere at all, as long as they were together. But he insisted that she was on vacation, so she should get out and see the sights. Plus, there was still great weather outside, which allowed them so many options. Even if they spent every minute of the time they had left to see the city, they wouldn't even get to see half of the things.

"How long do you need to get ready?" he asked.

"I probably need about forty-five minutes if that is okay with you."

"Perfect, would you like to meet in the lobby, or shall I escort you from your room?"

"I think we should meet in the lobby. I think if you come to my room, I may pull you into the room, and we wouldn't go anywhere at all!" she said, half joking.

"Well, that sounds tempting! But I wouldn't be a good host if I kept you in the hotel your whole trip. So I will play the part of the perfect gentleman and meet you down in the lobby in about forty-five minutes. Okay?"

"I'll be there!"

They gave each other a quick kiss and headed to their rooms. Marcela showered and again thought about the shower they had taken together. She could definitely get used to that. What was it about his hands that felt so different? She could touch her body in the exact same spots, and it didn't even remotely feel the same. She didn't stay in the shower long. She wanted a bit more time to get ready and apply some makeup that she didn't use very often. She wanted to look the best she could for him. After she was happy with her makeup, she picked out a white dress she had. She put lotion on most of her body. She didn't have much in the way of a tan, but with this lotion, it made her look darker than she really was. She found a white thong-and-bra combo that worked with the dress she had. Then finally she put the dress on. It flattered her body but wasn't flashy. Satisfied with how she looked, she changed out her purses to the new one she had bought when she was out and headed down to the lobby.

~

Anastasio also showered quickly, and he still felt a little off, so he lay down for about fifteen minutes after his shower to try to rest some just in case they were out late. He hoped that he wasn't coming down with a cold or flu. He only had a few days left to spend with Marcela before they had to part, and he didn't want to miss a minute of it. He had several bottles of water in his room and made sure to drink one while he got ready. He found a gray pair of slacks and a blue button-down shirt that he liked. Unlike Marcela, Anastasio was quite tan from spending so much time outside. The colors fit his complexion well. He was normally clean-shaven, but Marcela had mentioned to him earlier that she liked a little bit of beard growth, so he decided not to shave and let it grow out some. Once he was ready, he sprayed his favorite cologne, Tom Ford. Marcela had also mentioned that she loved the way it smelled on him. He was all set to go. He checked the room to make sure he wasn't forgetting anything and left to meet Marcela down in the lobby.

They had decided that they were going to have dinner in the central square area. There would be several choices once they got there. Most of the restaurants displayed their menus outside, so they could look at several menus and decide what sounded the best to them. They planned to keep it pretty casual, per her request, as she didn't have much to wear in the way of going to the nicer places. That was something she was going to have to fix tomorrow. They hadn't made any plans yet, but she wanted to be prepared for anything.

He made it down to the lobby just moments before she made it down. As he watched her walk down the stairs, he was again amazed by her natural beauty. She didn't have the look of that of like a model, but he found her more attractive than any model he could think of. And getting to know her, she just became more and more attractive in his opinion. Although he didn't like the thought that she had been having a rough time with life in the last few years, he was selfishly happy that he was the benefactor of it now. He was the one that got to kiss her, hug her, and now become an important part of his life. He liked to think of the possibilities that lie before him with her.

As she made her way down the stairs, she saw Anastasio standing there, waiting. She couldn't get over the way he looked at her each time he saw her. She couldn't remember the last time someone constantly looked at her like that. At first, it made her blush. But now she was starting to get used to it, and it made her feel more self-confident. It also made her feel something good inside of her that she couldn't explain. She was incredibly happy with life now. And Anastasio was the reason for that!

He looked fabulous as usual. The way his shirts hugged his body in the right places, she wondered if they were tailor-made for him. He was very fit to begin with. And he had great facial structure that made him very handsome, like a young Cary Grant. It didn't hurt that he had his charisma either. She still couldn't comprehend why he was single. She couldn't imagine any woman meeting him and not wanting to spend the rest of their lives with him. She barely knew him, and she could safely say that she hoped that she would be that person that did spend the rest of her life with him.

He was smiling at her, and when she walked up, he gave her a kiss, and then he whispered in her ear, "You look absolutely radiant!"

It took her by surprise, and she found herself blushing. He now pulled back far enough to look into her smiling eyes. "You don't look so bad yourself!" she said. She wished she was better with words but that was the best she could come up with at that moment. But it didn't say enough about how she really thought about how he looked.

Before they started to make their way out of the lobby, Rocco stepped around the counter and had a camera in his hand. He didn't say a word but gestured for them to pose for a photo. Anastasio looked around and decided that it would be best if they stood in front of one of the paintings hanging in the lobby. Rocco took several photos of them, and then Anastasio insisted that Rocco take a photo with each of them. He had known Rocco now for about ten years, and he would almost consider him as family. There were many days that he and Rocco would sit and talk for hours about life experiences, and Rocco proved to be incredibly wise. Anastasio knew he could trust any advice Rocco gave him.

Now that the photos were done, they headed out and caught a taxi to central square. He was glad that Rocco had took the photos. He had been so caught up in all the moments that he had completely forgot to take photos. Now he wished he had thought of it when they were in the gardens before. But he would remember from here on out. They sat hand in hand as usual as the taxi made its way to the square. It was a pretty short trip, and they had the taxi just stop in a totally random part. He knew they were going to be walking around looking at menus anyways, so they didn't need a specific location to stop.

They walked down the sidewalk and peeked at several different menus and crossed the street and looked through menus on the other side. They finally decided on a steak house. They had the option to sit in or outside, and since it was lovely outside, they chose to sit outside again. So far, the weather was cooperating very well with her on this trip. The only rain they had seemed perfectly timed for when they were inside or that incredibly bold moment Marcela had while they were dancing. She smiled to herself, thinking maybe her mom was already pulling some strings for her. This was exactly what her mother would've wanted on Marcela's trip.

They were seated right away, and Anastasio was greeted instantly by some people that apparently worked there. Their conversations were short, and he explained that this was one of the places their vineyard supplied wine to. He didn't choose to eat here because of that. It just happened to be the place that sounded the best out of the choices they found. He had only eaten here a few times, and from what he had had before, the food was particularly good. They picked up their menus, and immediately Marcela almost squealed in delight. The menu was in French and English as well. She didn't need Anastasio to be her interpreter for reading the menu at least.

Without any instruction from Anastasio, a waiter appeared with a bottle of wine and presented it to Anastasio. He smiled, and the waiter opened the bottle and poured a sample for him. He tasted it and let out a little chuckle. He nodded in approval. "I better like it. It's one of ours!" he explained to Marcela. The waiter filled her glass and then his and set the bottle down and disappeared as quickly as he had appeared. Marcela was looking forward to tasting his wines. Not that she knew anything about wine. But just knowing that it came from his family, she was betting that she would enjoy it. It also was just another thing she could start to learn about who he was. And she wanted to know everything she possibly could.

He picked up his glass, and she did the same. "And what shall we toast to tonight?" he asked her.

The words came out of her mouth without her even realizing what she was saying. "To a beautiful beginning of a lifetime of something that will forever change our lives." She was happy with what she said, which surprised her because she was the type that got shy when talking about personal feelings. Just saying that without being embarrassed or shy meant something that Marcela wasn't sure she ever really had in a relationship. It meant she was in love!

"I can drink to that!" They put their glasses together and took their first drink.

She might be biased since it was a wine that his family made, but this wine tasted especially good to her. She had always enjoyed a glass of wine but normally couldn't tell the difference between a cheap wine versus an expensive bottle. This, she could say, tasted exceptionally good, and Anastasio should be proud of what his family was producing. She would have a lot to learn as she literally knew nothing about wine. But she sensed she would enjoy learning just about anything that had to do with Anastasio's life.

As Anastasio listened to her toast, he wasn't sure that he could have said it any better. And if he was the one giving the toast, he was sure it would've been something remarkably similar. As he took his first drink, he knew there was no turning back now. He knew without a doubt he wanted Marcela to be not only in his life but for her to also be a major part of his life or their life, he thought. He couldn't believe what was happening. He had always believed in true love and soulmates and things like that. But he wasn't sure that he would ever actually have those things in his life. As if a light switch of his life was turned on, all was clear and bright now. These things did in fact exist and existed in his life.

They drank in silence for the moment, but as customary, they looked into each other's eyes as they drank, and they both knew they were thinking the same thing. No words were needed for this right now. Both their lives changed in that very moment! It was a peaceful and relaxing sensation. Neither had realized how much power love had until now. Love wasn't something that could be controlled! Both had tried with other partners to try to force feeling love, both without success.

Anastasio broke their silence after a few minutes. He reached across the table and held his hand out for hers. She smiled and held his hand in the middle of the table. "So did you see anything on the menu outside that really stood out to you, or were there several options for you?"

"There were a few different selections I saw that sounded good. What about you? I know you've been here before. Did they have something that you are craving for again, or are you going with something new?"

"To be honest, I'm not sure I remember what I had here before. I think I've only eaten here once. I have been here several times, visiting with the owners to sample wines that they were choosing between. But I think tonight I am craving red meat. I will see which steak sounds the best!" He picked up the menu with his other hand. This menu was convenient because it was just a one-sided list of selections. This meant he could continue to hold her hand, and she could do the same.

They both ordered steaks and enjoyed the wine and the company of each other. The ambience was lovely. Even though it was crowded, the noise level was very low. They could talk with each other without having to raise their voices. So far, it seemed he was mindful of thinking of things like that. It made it so much easier to get to know each other. Most dates she had been on before had been to places meant to impress her, but they were loud and didn't allow for her to really get to know anything about the other person.

She thought for a moment, and suddenly she had the desire to learn about his family. "If I may ask, tell me about your family. I want to know about how you grew up and became who you are today." She picked up her wine and watched his face. She didn't notice any hint that he didn't want to talk about it.

He took another sip of his wine and set it down. He put his elbows on the table and rested his chin in his hands. "Well, that's a question that could take days to answer. But I will give you the short version. I am an only child. My mom, Patricia, and my dad, Christian, got married very young. My dad was twenty-one when they got married. Mom was twenty. They had me a year later. I don't think I was planned, but life has a funny way of working out like that. I grew up helping out any way I could in our vineyard. I always enjoyed it and had hopes that one day it would grow into a bigger vineyard and have lots of wines and workers, but even in the best times, we stayed about the same size. It provided for us pretty well until just recently. It's getting harder and harder to find buyers and compete with the larger vineyards with their low pricing. But my father is a good man, an honest man. He had gained a lot of respect throughout his years in the business. That plays a role in keeping some of the business we've had for a long time.

"I did well enough in school and went to a local university so I could help him with the vineyard. He's gotten older, and I know his hope is for me to take over the family business as he did from his father. But the way things are going, I don't think the business will survive much longer. I try as hard as I can, but I'm fighting a losing battle. But I do it for my father. I see the pain in his eyes when we talk about losing the vineyard. It's all he has ever known. It's pretty much all I've ever known as well, but at least I finished at the university, and I will have some options when that day comes. But I will help him as long as I can.

"My mom, I don't really know what I can say about her. She's a tough lady. She's a proud woman, and she pretends that the problems don't exist. She just keeps telling us to work hard, and it will all come together. But we are trying as hard as we can. I know she means well, but she's going to have to come to the reality that the dreams aren't going to happen. And that's okay. The world is changing, and not everything stays the same. I worry about her though, but I think she will manage it in time."

He took another drink of wine and started again. "As I told you before, I got married young as well. She was a nice enough person, and it seemed right at the time, but I think we were meant to be friends and not try to have the romance. We still talk here and there, and she's now remarried and seems genuinely happy now. And I'm happy for her!

"I've mostly avoided dating since then. It's not that I didn't think a relationship was for me or anything like that. I was just focused on trying to help my dad out and not get sidetracked with other things. That is, until I met you. Now it seems my life has completely changed in a matter of days. I couldn't be happier about it actually. Working all the time isn't what life is supposed to be, but I think you already know that!"

Their waiter arrived with their entrees and placed it in front of them. It smelled and looked delicious, like everything she already had been this whole trip. They both cut into their steaks and ate the first bite. It was even better than it looked. His face showed that he was clearly pleased with what he was eating.

They were mostly quiet while eating. The waiter would come by and refill their wine and brought a new bottle when they finished the first one. The wine did complement the steaks very well. She knew she had a lot to learn about all this stuff, but she didn't have any doubt he would be there to teach her. She liked the thought that she didn't question the future with him, although there should be so many questions given the circumstances.

They finished their meals and contemplated desert and didn't decide against it. They still had some wine left, and their bellies were full. She asked some more questions about him growing up, and he happily answered everything she asked. He thought to ask about her childhood as well but thought that was a subject that might be too painful for her to think about right now. He'd ask when the time felt right or when she just offered the information.

Anastasio still didn't quite feel himself but didn't let it show. "Would you like to call it an early evening? I have a meeting in the morning, but I figured after that, we could do one of the tours of the city down the river and see the Eiffel Tower. I've never taken one, but I hear there are quite nice ones that include lunch and dinner and really show you a lot of sights."

"I would love that. Are you sure have time to spend all day away? I don't want to keep you from work that you need to do!"

"Please don't worry about that. I have made sure all my meetings are set, and what free time I have around that I'd prefer to spend with you." He was looking into her eyes as he said this, and she could tell that he was being very sincere.

"Okay, it's a date, then. Will you allow me to pay for dinner?" She was pleased that he seemed to want to spend as much time with her as she did with him.

"You can if you beat me to it!" he said as he winked at her.

She smiled thinking she could finally win this battle. She waited patiently for the waiter to return, and when he did, she asked him for the check. He looked at her confused and said, "I'm sorry, but the bill has already been taken care of." He looked at Anastasio, and he smiled.

"I guess you will just have to take me out some other time," he said with a wink.

"How did you..." She didn't even need to finish the sentence.

Anastasio let out a laugh and said, "I gave him my card when we first came in and told him to charge it when we were finished. I knew you were going to try, so I figured I'd beat you to it."

She shook her head and had to laugh as well. It was a clever move. She would have to remember that.

He stood and held out his hand for hers. "Shall we talk a little walk before we head back?"

"I'd love to. It's such a nice evening out."

She took his hand, and they left the restaurant and walked around the square for a bit. He started to feel a little tired again, and so they found a cab back to the hotel. He sat hand in hand with her through the ride, but he remained pretty quiet. They were back at the hotel in a flash.

As they were going through the lobby, he asked if she'd like to stay in his room this evening. She was happy to. So they split at the stairs for her to get the things she needed and for him to get the room ready for the both of them. He was hoping she'd say yes to his room tonight.

When he got into his room, he made sure everything was ready for the morning meeting and went to get ready for bed. His stomach was still giving him some trouble, so he took some medicine he had gotten from a doctor back in Italy when his stomach wasn't doing well. He guessed it was coming from the stress of everything. Once he had taken the medication and brushed his teeth, Marcela knocked on his door, and he let her into the room. It looked like she was all set.

She was wearing the cutest white cotton shorts and tank top to match. Her hair was pulled back. She had brought some clothes down with her for the morning. He took off the rest of his clothes and pulled back the covers to the bed. They both climbed in the bed and lay next to each other. He loved being able to just look into her eyes, put his hand on her face, and stroke her hair, face, and back. She closed her eyes after looking at him for some time and found herself relaxed enough to fall asleep even though she wished that she never had to sleep. She wanted to feel his touch as long as possible.

The last thing she remembered was him kissing her forehead and saying, "I love you, Marcela! I truly do."

She didn't hesitate for moment nor did she say it because of the way she was feeling at the moment. She replied, "I love you too, Anastasio!" She said it because she truly meant and felt it. She was always unsure if she was feeling love in life or if it was something else. This time it was clear. It was love! And she was loved back. It was the best feeling she had ever known. This was what she was thinking as she fell asleep to his touch.

Chapter 6

They slept through the night holding each other. Anastasio's alarm went off at 8:00 a.m., and they began to stir. She was so comfortable lying there in his arms. She could stay like this all day, she thought. He had his arms wrapped around her, and it was difficult for him to even move to turn off his alarm. He didn't ever want to let go of her even for a second. But life unfortunately didn't work that way. He had a meeting this morning, but after that, he could spend the rest of the day with her. That made things somewhat better. And it was nice to miss someone sometimes. Even if it's only for a few hours. Some people wanted to get away and be alone. He didn't understand that!

He reluctantly let go of her and turned off his alarm. He turned back to her, and she turned to face him. "Good morning," she said and kissed him on the lips. She meant it to be a short kiss, but he kissed her back with a passion that she would never get enough of. He hadn't intended on kissing her like that. It just happened. Before he knew it, they were clawing each other's clothes off. Within seconds, she had his boxers off, and he had her tank top and shorts off. Without breaking their kiss, he entered her, and she received him eagerly and had her hands around his hips pulling him in deeper and faster.

The encounter only lasted a few minutes. But it was intense, passionate, and full of love. He rolled off her, and they both were trying to catch their breath. He looked at her, and she knew what he was going to say and beat him to it. "Go, get ready! You have a meeting you need to get to. And then you have to get back to me so we can spend the day together!"

"I know, I don't want to go, but I have to get ready! It shouldn't take too long though. Then you have to put up with me for the whole day again. Do you think you can handle that?" he said as he was getting up to get into the shower.

"I don't know! I may just have to find someone to take me to breakfast while I'm waiting for you!"

He laughed, and she smiled at him as she lay in the bed, feeling lazy and that she could just lie there the whole time he was gone. He went into the bathroom, and she heard the shower start. She lay there and relaxed and let her mind wonder. What was in her future now? She was sure he was going to be a part of her life now, but how? Would she pick up and move to Italy and pick grapes all day? Would he move to her and have to travel all the time to try to keep his family's vineyard alive? Normally, thoughts like this would worry her endlessly, but now she knew everything would be answered in its right time.

He was out of the shower quickly and went to the closet and pulled out a pair of black slacks and another blue button-down shirt. This one was a lighter shade of blue than the one he wore last night. He got dressed and asked her what she planned to do for breakfast while he was gone. He continued to get ready, and she wasn't even sure how long it was going to take her to get out of bed. She felt like she could sleep more and wouldn't mind him climbing back in bed with her, but she knew they had plans for the day that they both were excited about.

"I'm not sure. I may just find a local café and have a bite and come back and get ready. How do you think I should dress since we will be gone all day and evening without the chance to come back here to change for the evening?"

"Well, I figured we will dress like we would for the evening. Being on the river, it will be a little cooler, so we shouldn't get hot during the day. And then this evening, we will be dressed appropriate for the things we will be doing. From what I was told by Rocco, they allow time for shopping and things like that, so if we need anything, we can get it while were out. Sound like a good plan?"

"How did you get to be so wonderful?" she asked, smiling at him.

"Years of being bad!" he said with a wink.

She couldn't imagine him ever being bad. She wondered if he ever did have a bad side. Everyone had something. She knew her mood was often everywhere, and without meaning to, she would take it out on other people. "I seriously doubt that!"

"I've had my moments," he said and finished doing his hair. He started to collect the things he needed for his meeting. "I figure the meeting will take me about two hours. I will grab something to eat on the way. So please remember to eat even if you order something in. We will have some time when I get back, so don't feel rushed to get up and get ready. You are welcome to stay in bed as long as you want. I wish I could be in it with you. I've gotta run. I'll come knock on your door when I get back. I will miss you!" He leaned down and gave her another passionate kiss, this time not allowing it to sidetrack him for too long. He pulled back and smiled at her. "See you soon!" And with that, he opened the door and headed out.

Looking at the door, she said, "I'll miss you too!" even though he was already gone. She wondered if she would ever get used to him leaving even if it was just for a few hours. Eventually the reality of life would be back, and they would both have things they had to do and be apart many times, especially with him having to travel for work. She closed her eyes and imagined him still lying there beside her, and she could smell him on her pillow. She loved his scent. When they would have to part, she wanted to take something of his to keep when he wasn't around. She hoped that wouldn't be too long or often, but that was a bridge that they hadn't crossed yet.

Anastasio made it to his meeting with plenty of time to spare. He stopped and got a croissant and a cappuccino. He sat and enjoyed the fresh morning air and was still smiling from the events of the morning. He couldn't imagine anything could take away his smile or feelings that he had right now! He felt like he was living in an old-fashioned movie where the man and woman fell in love right away, were dancing in the rain, and were not letting anything in life stand in the way of a love that was meant to be. He finished up his breakfast and headed over to his meeting.

He was greeted by the owner promptly when he arrived. Unlike the previous meeting, he had met this person before. He was young and trying to make a name for himself. He was nice but always to the point and seemed to be in a hurry even when he knew there was nothing else he had to be doing right at that moment. "Good morning, Anastasio! Would you prefer to talk in my office or at a table out here?" asked the man.

"Whatever is most comfortable for you would be fine with me."

He led him to a table that would generally seat four people. He sat on one side, and Anastasio sat on the other. Anastasio started with thanking him for taking the time out of his day to meet with him. He reached into his bag and took out several different bottles of wine. He always carried wineglasses as well even though every place he went would have them. He wanted to be as professional and make meetings as convenient as possible for his potential clients.

He pulled out several glasses to taste the different wines. He carefully presented each wine and opened each one to let them breathe properly before they would taste them. He also placed a plate of coffee beans on the table to cleanse their palates between each tasting. Coffee beans had always been a great way to hit the reset button on your senses and get a fresh smell and taste of the different wines each time. Now he had everything in place.

Over the next hour, they sampled each wine as Anastasio would give information, like what kind of grapes were used, the vintage, and all the pertinent information that would help the clients make decisions on selecting wines. Each vineyard had their own sales reps and tactics to sell their products. Anastasio was no expectation to that. He felt he was more genuine and tailored his presentation to meet what each individual client might need to see or hear. He could do that because he didn't have as many accounts to see and prepare for as these other guys. He felt sometimes that gave him an advantage, being able to be personable. And he was that!

But the advantage that it gave him with certain clients was a disadvantage with other clients. He felt this was one of those clients. This one wanted to be on top of whatever he was doing and wanted wines that people knew from commercials or seen out and about, not wines that might be better and cost less, and they didn't recognize the name of the wine. He could feel it all through the meeting that this man wasn't really listening to what he was saying, but he kept on to at least give it his best shot.

He started to wrap up his meeting, and the owner kept quiet during that time. He could never read people like this. He preferred to have some kind of indication of what the other was thinking, but his face and lack of words told Anastasio nothing! This always worried him some, but all in all, what could he do even if they gave him any indication right then? He needed yeses to keep the vineyard going! And they needed that answer from most of the clients he was seeing. Too many *no*'s would mean that they would have to cut costs somehow after they had already cut out what they could.

He acted like it didn't matter though. It wasn't good to show desperation to a client. That definitely never helped with making the sell. Anastasio politely said his goodbyes, and the owner promised to get back with him in the next few weeks. Anastasio, would have, of course, contact him before then and thank him for his time, and many times, that would spark the answer that they had already came up with.

But now the meeting was over, and now he could focus on something he never thought would be more important to him than keeping their vineyard in business. His focus was now back on Marcela and what the future could possibly hold for them. Over the past few days, he had thought of a few different ideas he could toss around with her and get her thoughts. And it was very possible she had ideas of her own. He was somewhat scared of starting to plan a new future, but the positive far outweighed the negatives. His mind was made up. They were going to be together! The question was where and how soon.

~

She got out of the bed after about thirty minutes of lying there. She didn't want to go back to her room wearing what she had worn down to his last night. Even though she had never run into anyone in the halls yet, this would be the time she would. She didn't think he'd mind if she borrowed one of his shirts to wear back to her room. She went to his closet and found a pink button-down shirt that she liked and put it on and loved the way it looked on her. She was careful not to wrinkle it as he had brought it here for a reason. She assumed he was planning on wearing it. She put her shorts back on and headed out to her room.

She got to her room and looked at herself in front of the full-length mirror, wearing his shirt. She really liked it. She could see wearing his shirts around the house. In movies she had seen, she always found it sexy when women did this. The men seemed to think so too. She would have to make sure to tell him to bring extra shirts when he visited for her to wear for him when he was there. Of course, she would buy some other things that he would enjoy seeing her wear as well. But the shirts were a must!

She took it off and hung it up in her closet, careful not to wrinkle it, just as she did when she was wearing it. She couldn't imagine he would get upset about her wearing it, but she was still considerate and wanted to keep his things exactly how they were. She took off her shorts and looked in the mirror again. She wasn't unhappy with the way she looked. But now that she had someone in her life, she was going to try to exercise a little more and tone up the best she could. She knew she wasn't the type to dedicate her life to the gym or running at early hours of the morning. But she wanted to look the best she possibly could for him!

She went and turned on the shower and came back out into the room and looked through her clothes. She didn't really like what she had. She looked at the clock and knew she had a little time. She quickly went and turned off the shower and got dressed in a pair of jeans and T-shirt. She wrote Anastasio a quick note saying she would be back shortly, and she would come to his room when she was back. She would put it on the outside of his door when she left. She left the room quickly and went downstairs and left the hotel in a hurry.

She went back to the boutique she had bought the other dress from and found Jacqueline, the owner, there again. They smiled at each other, but Jacqueline could tell that she was in a rush. "Let me guess, the date went well, and we need to find you something for today?"

Marcela was still out of breath from rushing to the store, and all she could do at the moment was nod.

Jacqueline disappeared for a moment and returned with a bottle of water. Marcela's face lit up with delight, and she smiled at her, opened the water, and quickly drank about half the bottle. "Oh, thank you, Jacqueline. You are a saint! Yes, the date, well, let's just say it hasn't ended yet. And today we are going on a tour of the city, and we will be gone all day, so I need something that will be good for the day and the evening."

"Oh my! When you have more time, you must tell me about this date. Do you know if you are doing the tour by bus or the river tour?"

"We are doing the river tour, but I know we will be stopping in the city several times, and then we will get to see the Eiffel Tower. I guess you know of this tour?"

"Oh yes, it's a good one! There's so much to see, and it rushes over some things that you will want to come back to see later. But it will give you a good idea what you'd really like to spend more time seeing and what isn't as important. Now let's find you an outfit that will leave this man not wanting the date to end yet again. While we do, you better get to talking! I must know about your last few days now. I've been curious since you left here and wondered if I'd see you again!"

Jacqueline didn't wait for her to answer but started leading her around the store, picking up things and holding them to Marcela, and then without a word, she would put it back and search for something else. After several attempts, she had a few dresses picked out. During that time, Marcela did her best to tell her about the adventures of the past few days. As she was telling Jacqueline about everything, she tried on the different dresses as quickly as she could. She didn't want to make them late. Jacqueline mostly listened to her telling her about the dinners, the block party, the dancing, and every little detail Marcela shared, only stopping her to ask her an occasional question.

The last thing Marcela tried on was a cream-colored skirt and a slightly darker blouse that flattered her body. She thought it was perfect and came out and showed Jacqueline. The joy on Jacqueline's face said it all! Marcela wished that Jacqueline lived in Barcelona and could be there to help her with her whole wardrobe. She might have been a little older, but she was up on the latest fashions. And she was able to do it on a budget at that. She was truly godsend! Marcela needed all the help she could get with the tight budget she had.

Within minutes, Jacqueline picked out the perfect matching set of panties, bra, garter, and stockings. Marcela had never worn things like that, but even though she hadn't tried it on yet, she already felt sexier just knowing she had it now. She couldn't wait to put it on and, later that night, show Anastasio her new additions to her wardrobe! She paid for the things and promised Jacqueline once again that she would return before the end of her trip to shop for a few things. She felt like she could really be friends with her. She thanked her and rushed back to the hotel as quickly as she had rushed to the boutique.

When Marcela turned onto the street to the hotel, she saw Anastasio just a few feet in front of her. She quickened her step and came up behind him and put her hands over his eyes and said, "Guess who?"

He stopped walking, surprised by this. He let a laugh and said, "Oh, I can't believe it. Mother Teresa has finally come to visit me?" He turned around and still had a big smile on his face. "Oh, it's not Mother Teresa? Well, this is even a more pleasant surprise! I didn't expect to see you here. Are you visiting Paris?" he asked with almost a straight face.

"You are silly! I had to run out and find something to wear for today. I'm glad I'm not late getting back! How was your meeting?" she asked as she gave him a kiss.

"It was a meeting!" he said and gave her a shrug. "I can never read this guy, so we'll see what happens over the next few weeks. What did you get?"

She put the bag behind her back and playfully pushed him away. "You will just have to wait and see, won't you?"

He laughed and shook his head. "Come on, let's go get ready and enjoy the day. How long will you need? I will be ready pretty quickly!" They started walking to the hotel together as they talked.

"How much time do I have?" she asked.

"About an hour. Maybe a little more. Is that okay?"

"It's perfect!" she said as they entered the hotel. "Okay, I will go get ready. I will come down to your room when I'm ready. Will that work?"

"Sounds good to me! I look forward to seeing what you got there!" He gave her a kiss again, and they headed up the stairs. "I'll see you soon!" he said, and they went their different ways.

He got to his room and immediately went to his closet. He had an idea what he was going to wear and went straight for the pink shirt that Marcela had borrowed. He looked closely for it, and when he didn't see it, he was confused. He was sure he brought it. He even remembered seeing it the other day. He then realized that there was an empty hanger, and that wasn't there before. He then knew that Marcela must have taken it this morning when she left his room. He almost picked up the phone to call her room but got a better idea.

A few minutes after she got into her room, she heard a knock at the door. She looked at the room, and it had been made up yesterday, and since she hadn't slept there that night, she didn't see that housekeeping would need to clean the room again. But maybe they were there now to check the room. She opened the door and was surprised to see Anastasio standing there. He had the same smile on his face that he usually did. "So I think you may have something I want!" he said.

"Oh really, and you think you can come up here and just take what you want?" She wasn't quite sure if he was there for her or for his shirt. But the question worked for either answer.

"I'll take only what you want to give!" he said, playing the game right back with her.

"Well, mister, you better be talking about your shirt. Because for now, that's all you have time to take!" She liked playing this game with him.

"Then I'll take it! But we'll have to discuss later plans!" he said as she went to the closet to get his shirt. She was just wearing a white silk robe. He was having a hard time not coming in, shutting the door, and forgetting the day's plans.

She interrupted his thoughts, brought his shirt to him, and said, "I'm sorry, I forgot to tell you I borrowed this this morning. I needed a cover-up when I came back to my room."

"I figured as much. No problem. I was just planning on wearing it today. Otherwise, I wouldn't have come for it." He took the shirt from her and raised his eyebrows. "I'll let you get to it, then." Reluctantly, he turned and went back to his room.

She loved these flirtatious moments they had. It was so unlike her to flirt, but she liked the way she was around him. She felt confident, sexy, and desired. And she felt like with him, she would continue to feel that way without him physically with her. He made her feel a way that she didn't know she could. Now she understood when people said sexy was a state of mind. And it really was!

She started the shower and unpacked the new outfit she had just bought. She was excited to see his face when he would see her in it. She laid everything out on the bed and then made her way into the shower. The hot water felt great on her body, and she tried to be as quick as she could be in the shower this time so she could take her time to get ready for a whole day and evening out. She was planning that they would take a lot of photos, and she wanted to look the best she possibly could. These were memories that she would take with her for the rest of her life!

He made it back to his room and started the shower. He got in and thought about the meeting for a moment and didn't have a good feeling about it. He put it out of his mind and thought about what they had planned for the day. He had never been on this tour, and he was really looking forward to experiencing it with her for the first time. He finished his shower pretty quickly and got out and dried off.

She finished her shower and wrapped her body in a towel and her hair in another. She was going to let her body dry naturally as she started to apply her makeup. She paid close attention to her eyes and lips. She thought they were her best features. Once she was satisfied with the work she had done, she unwrapped her hair and started to dry it and brush it out. Her hair wasn't too thick, so it didn't take a long time to do. And thankfully, there wasn't much humidity, and her hair was cooperating nicely.

He stood in front of the mirror and made sure his eyebrows weren't too long and trimmed his beard down a little. She said she liked it that way, so he was going to do his best to keep it that way. Next, he did his hair and moisturized his face. He normally didn't take this much time and care, but he felt like today was especially important and wanted it to be done right. Even though his shirt and pants were already pressed, he quickly went over them with an iron and put on his boxer briefs, shirt, and then his pants. He found a pair of black socks and put them on and then his only pair of black dress shoes he had brought. The only thing left was to put on her favorite cologne, Tom Ford. He sprayed it on his neck and some on his shirt. He felt like he was all ready to go.

She put lotion on her body and covered everywhere she could reach. She put on her new lingerie piece by piece and was stunned on how well it fit her and how sexy it made her feel. As she slid on the stockings, they felt so smooth with her legs just being shaved, and with the lotion, her legs felt amazing. Now she understood women that spent a lot of money on this type of stuff. She never really had, but now she felt it was going to be important in her new daily life. She stood in front of the mirror for a moment to admire how nice it looked. She picked up the blouse and put it on and buttoned it up. It was pretty formfitting, and the top button she buttoned was a bit lower than she usually would have chosen. But again, she was finding herself in all kinds of new situations. She put on the skirt and zipped it up in the back and tucked the blouse into it. She looked back into the mirror, and she felt complete. She was amazed at the way she looked! She sprayed on some perfume and was ready to go.

He was sitting on his bed waiting for her when there was a knock on his door. He was excited and nervous at the same time. He opened up the door and was instantly speechless. He wished he could have seen his own face. He knew his jaw must have been hanging down to his knees. He already thought she was beautiful, but now standing here in front of him, she was one of the most beautiful women he had ever laid eyes on. He finally was able to mumble out a few words. "Marcela, you are stunning! I don't feel like I do you justice at all!"

"Thank you. And don't be silly! You are a very handsome man, and you know it. And for at least today, you are my handsome man!" She stood there looking at him, waiting for him to react.

He was still in shock but realized that she was standing there waiting on him to do something. "Shall we start this adventure? I think we will have an amazing day."

"I expect it's going to be one of those days that will replay in my head for the rest of my life, so yes, I'm ready to start our adventure!"

He put his hands on her hips and looked straight into her eyes. "Trust me when I say this. It won't only be replaying in your head for the rest of your life. And second, I hope that I am your man for much longer than today!" He leaned in and gave her a kiss that lingered just a bit. He pulled back and stepped out of his room, and he held out his arm for her to take. She did, and they made their way down the stairs and out of the hotel.

Anastasio had called Bernard previously, and he was waiting patiently outside the hotel, waiting for them to arrive. He smiled when he saw them and gave both of them the customary hug and kiss and then opened the door for Marcela. Anastasio walked around to the other side and got in. In very broken English, Bernard said, "You look more beautiful than the stars and the moon!" He held her hand until she got into the car, and he closed her door and got into the driver's seat. Marcela couldn't believe that he said that. There was nothing wrong about what he said. She just couldn't believe he had learned how to say that.

Once again, Bernard needed no instructions. He started darting through the streets, as he and Bernard made some small talk. Marcela enjoyed looking at all the scenery passing by them. Anastasio held her hand as he usually did and would occasionally give her hand a small squeeze, and she would look over at him, and he would give her a kiss, a wink, or just a big smile. They didn't talk a whole lot on the drive to the meeting place for the river cruise. The drive was relatively short before they were at the Seine river. She had seen photos of it and even heard songs about it, but this was the first time she saw it. She couldn't wait to see all the sights the river would lead them to.

Bernard stopped in front of the office they needed to check in at, but before he left, Marcela held her camera out for him to take a photo. He happily took the camera and lined them up with the cruise ship behind them and took a few photos. She then asked to take a photo with Bernard and then Bernard with Anastasio. As soon as the photos were done, she gave him a kiss on the cheek, and he smiled brightly at her and returned to his car and left.

They walked into the office and checked in. They signed some waivers and were led to the cruise ship. When they were boarding the ship, there was a professional photographer there taking photos of each person or couple that were taking the cruise that they could purchase at the end if they chose to. They took a few photos there and boarded the ship. They took their time walking around the ship to get familiar with where everything was and where they might want to sit at different points during the tour. It wasn't a big ship, but it was perfect for what they were doing. It had seating inside with lots of windows and an upstairs area of seating that was out in the open. There was a bar and tables on both levels to make it convenient to eat and drink wherever they chose.

They still had about thirty minutes before the cruise was to depart down the river with the final stop being the tour of the Eiffel Tower. They decided to go to the bar on the upper level, and both ordered a glass of champagne. It seemed like a special occasion, so champagne seemed appropriate. They toasted to the wonderful day ahead of them and took a drink. The taste was refreshing and light. They walked around a bit more and settled on leaning on a railing. They looked around, and Anastasio pointed out the very few things he knew about the area. All this was going to be just about as new for him as it was for her. There were constant announcements in several languages saying that the cruise would start shortly.

No longer worrying about her reaction, he decided to ask her about her family and childhood. "So you know a little about my life now. What's your story? I want to know everything I can about you!"

She thought for a moment where to start and began, "Well, you know that my mom just passed. She was an amazing person. She was always happy. Even when I knew she wasn't, she wouldn't let it show. She loved life and tried so hard through all my years to get me to appreciate life and the beauty of it. Of course, I always listened to her and believed her but never really acted on it. I always thought, if I can just get past this part, I can start to slow down and enjoy the things in life that are important, like friendships, relationships, travel, and things like that. But it seemed once I got past one thing, I always had something else planned to take its place. She would be very proud of me right now, being on this trip and being here with you.

"My dad left when I was young. He had found another woman and decided that's where he wanted to be. So he left us and ended up getting married to the other woman. He wasn't really present in our lives much in the beginning. He made an effort here and there, but mostly after a couple of years, he was just someone that we once knew. It was hard at first, but then I realized we didn't need him. My mom did the job of both parents. I was the only child and, for the most part, very well-behaved. I did well in school. I was never into drugs or drinking. I had good friends. I didn't date a lot growing up, but that was by choice. I have always been comfortable being by myself.

"My mom was an accountant, but I didn't really get the math gene from either of my parents. I understand it and am decent with numbers, but I was always drawn to being an artist. I wasn't sure what exactly that would be, but by chance, I had designed a few small jewelry pieces, and many people would comment on them and ask where I got them. When I explained I made them, several suggested I should be doing that for a living. I was almost done with the university, and when I graduated, I decided to give it a shot. Things started off great. I got a lot of customers quickly. The economy was good at the time, and lots of people were buying things. You know about the last part of that story.

"I met my best friend, Antonio, and we hit it off instantly. Antonio is gay, and I think maybe that's what made us so close so quick. There wasn't the pressure of someone liking the other and trying to get involved in a romantic relationship. I wasn't ready for anything like that at the time. Well, I have to admit, I thought I still wasn't. But someone you may know may have changed my thoughts about that.

"I told you about Lee. We dated for a few years, but he never really stood a chance. He's a really good guy. I feel bad for not being the person he needed, but I just wasn't there. I found everything else in life more important. It wasn't fair to him, so I finally broke it off. He wasn't surprised by my decision. In fact, I think if I hadn't, he probably would have shortly after. We still talk. He has found someone else now, and he seems incredibly happy. I'm happy for him as well. He deserves someone great in his life.

"Other than that, there's not much to tell. Nothing amazing and nothing terrible to report until now! I have found someone amazing in my life as of a few days ago. You may know who it is." She didn't realize that she had been speaking without stopping through the whole thing. Anastasio had stood there, listening to her patiently.

"All that sounds reasonable, and I understand how life can get away from us. I have done it at times as well. My dad never really offered a lot of advice on how to live. He just led by example. My father is a good man. He did his best to provide for us. He was always there when I needed him most. I knew I could count on him for anything I needed. He would always take his time listening to me. Sometimes he could offer advice that would solve whatever problem I was experiencing. Sometimes he would just listen, and that was enough.

"My mom, she is the complete opposite of how your mother was and my dad for that matter. She has told me since I was barely old enough to work that I needed to always focus on work, and that's what kept life going. For a long time, I listened and thought she was right, but then I saw life wasn't supposed to be only about work. There should be time for other things. Love, family, spending time enjoying what you like to do. None of us know when our last day is going to be. So why spend every day thinking that down the line you can slow down and enjoy life. You may not make it that far, and then you get so conditioned to being that way you always think when you have opportunity to slow down, you don't!"

The ship started to move, and an announcer came on the speakers that were placed all around the ship, welcoming them and giving them an introduction to the tour. This message was repeated in several languages. It explained that there were audio devices you could get that would guide them through the whole tour in whatever language they needed. Marcela and Anastasio decided that they didn't want to use the audio devices. They would look at all the architecture of the buildings, bridges, and other monuments they would pass along the way.

She was definitely already camera happy. She was taking photos of the ship, bridges, and everything else she thought was interesting. She took photos of Anastasio, and he took photos of her, and they got others to take photos of them together every chance they got. She couldn't imagine that she could ever forget all these things in her mind, but she would always have these photos to look at and smile. She thought about how many photos they would take over time. She always liked photos but seemed to always forget to take them in the important moments.

A little after about two hours into the cruise, they served lunch, and they chose to sit downstairs to eat as Marcela hadn't spent much time in the sun, and he didn't want her to get burnt by the sun. They talked about the sites they were seeing and just small things about each other's lives. They took their time eating and enjoyed each other's company. They met some random people here and there from all over the world visiting, just like she was. That was the nice thing about going to trips like this. Most people were from other places and usually very friendly and willing to share their experiences.

Shortly after lunch, the ship docked, and they disembarked and walked around the area. There were lots of little shops and cafés. They looked through a few shops and finally stopped and got some ice cream and sat in the grass next to the river. The whole scene was so surreal. She really felt like she was in a movie. That brought the movie *An Affair to Remember* to her mind. They wouldn't be going to the Empire State Building but an even more famous place, the Eiffel Tower. Was she Debra Kerr and he Cary Grant? Would they promise to meet on the top of the Eiffel Tower at some later date to be together forever? It was a nice romantic thought and gesture, but she didn't want to wait long to be with him again. And she sure hoped he wasn't engaged to be married, only to leave that person to be with her. She laughed in her head at the thought and looked at him and smiled. He was her Cary Grant!

They sat there a little longer, him sitting behind her and being her support with his arms wrapped around her. She really didn't want this to ever end. After today, they only had one more day together. They had yet to talk about future plans, but she had been thinking about it, and she knew he was too. She was scared to bring it up but knew they needed to soon or the curiosity would kill her. She didn't have a clue what the answer was. But honestly, she would do just about anything to be with him. If she had to move to Italy and learn another language, different work, or whatever, he was worth it!

It was time to go again, so they started their walk back to the ship. They boarded the ship again and chose to sit inside for a little while to get out of the sun again. It was another pleasant day with very little cloud cover. It was great to have such a beautiful day like this, but her skin would suffer if she tried to stay outside all day. She didn't think to bring sunscreen. And she liked the way she felt and smelled. She didn't want the smell and feel of the sunscreen on her body. She still felt just as sexy now as she did this morning when she saw herself in the mirror. It helped that every time she caught him looking at her when he didn't know, she could see the desire in his eyes. That made her feel more confident and special than she ever felt.

They passed bridge after bridge, each one beautiful in its own way. There were so many historic buildings they passed, and she got photos of all of them, some with both of them in the photo, some with just one of them. She was glad they lived in the digital age. If she were using the old film cameras, she couldn't imagine how much film she would've needed just for today, much less the whole trip. She was smart enough to bring several memory cards to make sure she didn't run out of room. Anastasio only had his phone to use for taking photos and was taking plenty himself. But she promised to share all the photos she took with him as well.

It was now getting later in the afternoon, and they went back up to the upper level. The city looked so beautiful. The Eiffel Tower could be seen in the distance, and she couldn't wait until they were up there looking down on such a beautiful city. And this tour had it to where they would be up there right about sunset, so they would get the view with daylight but also at night with the lights of the city. She knew it was going to be a spectacular sight. There would be dinner there also.

The tour would end there, and they'd be free to walk around and do whatever they wanted after that point. She looked forward to seeing the Eiffel Tower from the ground, all lit up in all its splendor. She had no idea what they would do after the tour, but she didn't care as long as she was with him. She actually wouldn't mind going back to the hotel and making love to him until the sun came up.

They were now at the very front of the ship, and he was now standing behind her. He took each of her hands in his and lifted her arms out like in the movie *Titanic*. She knew right away what he was doing, and she loved the cuteness of it. He whispered in her ear, "Do you trust me?"

She had to laugh, but it felt nice, and she saw the scene in her head. He then told her to close her eyes, and she did. She could feel the wind hitting her face, his body against hers. She felt safe, free, and most of all, she felt loved. She wished that it were a movie, and she could see what this looked like from somewhere in front of them.

She was visualizing it, and it was beautiful. He kissed her lightly on the cheek. And at first, she thought she imagined it, but he whispered softly, "I love you, Marcela!" She then realized it was real. She was amazed that he really felt the same way that she felt for him.

She let go of his hands and turned to face him. She looked up into his eyes. "I love you too, Anastasio!" She really did. She loved him. And he loved her in return!

He took her face into his hands and kissed her deeply. Every time she thought their kisses couldn't get any more passionate, she would be wrong! This kiss made her literally feel like she was going to melt on the spot. She swore their lips were one, not two. Their moments were fluid and easy. Her heart felt like it was going to explode. Her body tingled from the top of her head to the tips of her toes. She wished that he could make love to her right there, right then. Every fiber of her body wanted him. She could tell he wanted the same thing.

They must have been kissing for at least five minutes. He finally pulled back, still looking into her eyes with an intensity that could make anyone do anything he wanted. They were both out of breath. She felt that any moment he might start kissing her again. His hands were still on the sides of her face. She didn't think her heart could take another kiss like that at the moment. He finally slid his hands off her face, down her shoulders, down her arms, and to her hands. He grasped both of them, and his look became less intense. Neither of them said a word. There were no words that could ever make this moment better than it already was. It was absolutely perfect! Now that her face was pulled back a little from his, she could see that people had collected around them, each of them looking at them and commenting to one another. One older couple smiled at her, and she got a little shy and smiled and looked at Anastasio, then eyed the crowd behind him. He turned and looked at the crowd. He had forgotten a world existed with other people until now. He smiled at the crowd and, without thought, gave a small bow to make it feel a little less awkward. It worked! Some of the people laughed and clapped for them. She had to laugh at this too, and she now felt more comfortable too. Not that it really mattered. She wouldn't have traded that moment for anything in the world.

He let go of one of her hands and led her through the crowd. She could still feel everyone's eyes on them. They made their way to the bar and decided on a glass of red wine. The cruise was getting close to the end, and the Eiffel Tower was in perfect view now. They took their wine and stood on the side of the ship that was closest to the Tower. It was such a surreal moment seeing it so close up and with Anastasio by her side!

A couple walked up to them and started talking to them in English. They asked where they were from, and they both replied their respective places. The Americans were from Chicago. They briefly exchanged their stories, and the American couple couldn't believe that Anastasio and Marcela had just met a few days ago. The Americans, Michael and Cindy, were in their late forties. They said they had been married now for twenty-five years. This was their anniversary present to each other. Their story wasn't far off from what Anastasio and Marcela were currently experiencing. They had met and had married within months of meeting each other. They had two children, Stephen and Kristina. Both were now in college in the US. They were a lovely couple. They asked Anastasio and Marcela if they would care to join them for dinner. They said they would be happy to join them for dinner. They talked a little more and then split apart but promised to find one another for the dinner that was also part of the tour.

The cruise docked at its final destination, and everyone got off, and the photos that were taken at the beginning were being offered for sale. They found their photos and thought they turned out nicely. Anastasio bought a package, which each of them would have a large photo and a few smaller photos that came in a nice album. Marcela knew exactly where she was going to put this photo in her home. She had the perfect place.

The group was led to the Eiffel Tower and were taken around the line of people that weren't part of tours or packages and went straight up to the second floor of the tower. The view was even better than they both imagined it would be. They took their time walking around and seeing the views from different vantage points. The sun was setting now, and it was beautiful! Her camera was getting more use today than it probably got in the whole time she had had it.

The sun went down quickly, and nightfall came. All the lights in the city were starting to light up and made the view even more spectacular. They held onto each other while looking over the city. Different people from their group would come by and say hello, ask for them to take photos of them, and offer to take photos for them as well. It was a truly pleasant experience. She was happy they were part of this tour. Normally she didn't like tours that much since you had to comply with their timelines and do only the things that the tour offered. But she couldn't imagine how long they would've had to wait in line to get up there. And would they have gotten the timing right like it was now? She didn't think that would have come easily. Everything was so well organized!

As they were looking out over the city and alone again, Anastasio was again standing behind her with his arms wrapped around her. She thought this must be his favorite way of holding her. And she certainly didn't mind it! "Have you ever seen the movie *An Affair to Remember*?" he asked.

She couldn't believe how much their minds thought alike. "Yes, I was actually just thinking about that earlier today. Why? Are you going to ask to meet me here in six months?" she asked, half joking.

"Would you want to wait that long to see each other again?" he said, hoping he knew the answer already.

"I would prefer sooner, but I don't know what your plans are and how busy your schedule is."

"Well, I just thought of the movie while we were up here. But no, I don't want to wait that long to see you again. I have actually been thinking about it a lot over the past few days, trying to think of different scenarios that might work. Let me know what you think of this one..."

She was excited and nervous to hear his proposal. She was glad he brought it up and silently prayed that he had a plan that they could actually arrange and work out relatively easy and with as little time apart as possible. She was silently jumping up and down in her mind.

"I have to go home the day after tomorrow, and I have some meetings set up over the next few weeks that I can't change. But I was thinking, what would you think if I moved to Barcelona to be with you there? You could continue doing what you love, and I could still help my father with the business by doing what I do mostly now, which is visit clients or potential clients to keep the business running. I know it won't be easy for him at first, but he will manage. I would have to travel quite a bit, but we would be together. What do you think?"

Marcela tried extremely hard to hold back the tears of joy she had but couldn't. She turned and faced him. He could see her tears and wasn't quite sure what to think for a second until she said, "Oh, Anastasio! You would do that for me, for us?" She was now hugging him tightly, and he now knew the tears were that of joy and not sadness. She was squeezing him so tight that he was having a hard time breathing.

"I'd do anything I needed to do to be with you! I know we've only known each other a few days, but nothing has felt more right, more real in my entire life. I know we are meant to be together, and I want to make that happen. And I think you feel the same way too!"

"I do, Anastasio. I have been thinking about it over the last few days as well. I didn't know how to bring it up or what the solution was. All I knew is that I wanted to be with you. Are you saying that you think you can move in a few weeks after your meetings?"

"If that's all right with you, I would love to!"

"I couldn't think of anything more perfect. Are your parents going to hate me for you going away to be with me?"

"My dad probably won't say much. My mom, it will probably take some time for her to come around, but in the end, it's my life, and they will be happy as long as I'm happy!"

"I couldn't ask for anything more. Thank you, Anastasio. I love you!"

"I love you too! Now it's about that time we are supposed to meet Michael and Cindy for dinner. I know you're happy, but your face doesn't look happy at the moment with tears streaming down on it. Why don't you take a few minutes to collect yourself, and we will go and meet them for dinner."

"Oh, you're so right. My makeup must be a mess! Please just give me a few minutes, and I'll be right back."

She walked away and found the women's restroom and freshened up her makeup. She was in shock! She couldn't believe what he had just proposed. She felt like he just asked her to marry him. Even if he did, she would've said yes in a heartbeat. She probably would've said yes to anything he had asked of her as long as it meant they were going to be together. She was happy with the way she looked again. She took one last look and went back and found Anastasio. It looked like Michael and Cindy had already found him.

She walked up and slid her arm into his. Anastasio looked at all of them and said, "Shall we go to dinner now?"

Michael was the first to answer, and they all agreed to go. They made their way to the restaurant. There were tables that were reserved for their group, and they were seated promptly. A bottle of champagne was brought out as it was part of the package, and the waiter poured them each a glass and presented them with their menus.

Michael lifted his glass, and the rest followed. "To new friends, a beautiful day in a beautiful city, and to a life full of love and happiness!"

Anastasio thought the toast was pretty perfect. They took a drink and reviewed their menus. Anastasio and Marcela decided that he was going to get a steak, and she was going to get lobster, and they were going to split their meals to enjoy their own version of surf and turf. Michael and Cindy both chose pasta dishes.

Marcela asked what they did for work, and it turned out that Michael was a teacher in a high school, and Cindy was also a teacher in middle school. They had met in college and been together ever since. Since they were both teachers, they only took one big trip a year and a few weekend trips here and there. Both seemed highly intelligent, and as it turned out, Michael had quite the sense of humor and, throughout the meal, had them laughing at different stories he had from his life. They were happy that they had been asked to join them for dinner.

Michael also asked about their careers, and each explained what they did. Anastasio also brought up their new plan for him to move to Spain, and Michael said he thought it was a great decision that he doubted he would regret. Michael was in the same mindset as they were. When you loved someone, you would do anything for them. And love had no timeline. He explained that he knew people that had known each other for years and got married and divorced soon after, and he knew people that knew each other for days and married and had never spent a day apart since. It was all about how willing you were to be flexible and considerate of the other person. Anastasio loved the conversation and the thoughts that Michael and Cindy had about relationships and love.

Their entrées came and went quickly. With the great company and conversation, time was flying by! They were now on their second bottle of champagne, and all four of them split one big desert. They really enjoyed themselves. The day had proven to be more than either of them ever could have dreamed of. She didn't think that it could've been more perfect than it had been so far, and it wasn't over yet.

It was getting later now, and Michael and Cindy had planned on going to a lounge at their hotel, which was close by, and invited them to join them. After a brief conversation about it, Anastasio and Marcela politely declined as they now planned to head back to their hotel. They paid the bill and exchanged information and promised to stay in touch. As they left the restaurant, they gave each other hugs and best wishes.

As they were leaving, Anastasio called Bernard, and within minutes, he was there to pick them up. He opened the door for Marcela as always, and then they were off back to the hotel. Anastasio had his arm around Marcela, and they both knew what was to come next. When they got back to the hotel, they knew that there would be no resting. Each of them still had that fire and desire that they had just a few hours before on the ship.

After about thirty minutes, they arrived back at the hotel. They decided on her room for the evening, and both went directly there. As soon as she had the door open, they were kissing frantically. She stopped and gently pushed him on the bed. She had a smile on her face, and she started slowly unbuttoning her blouse. Anastasio was very aroused now and had a hard time sitting there waiting. But she looked so amazing, so sexy.

She finished unbuttoning her blouse and slowly took it off. She reached back and slowly unzipped her skirt. As she was pulling it off, she half-turned, and Anastasio was getting an amazing view of her body. He could feel his heart pounding, and sweat started to form on his forehead. She slowly pulled the skirt off and turned around slowly for him to take it all in.

She had never been so confident and never thought she would be putting on a show like this, but it felt great and so natural with him. She took her time standing in front of him. She finally pushed him back on the bed some and straddled him as he was sitting the bed. She wrapped her arms around his neck and started to slowly kiss him.

As they were kissing, he started to unbutton his shirt and got it completely off without breaking their kiss. Once his shirt was off, she pushed him back to where he was now lying completely down on the bed. She stood and unbuckled his belt and unbuttoned his pants. She slid down the zipper on his pants. She reached down and removed his shoes and then his socks. She came back up and tugged on his pants, and he lifted his hips to help her remove his pants. He would have thought she did this all the time with the ease that she did this with.

She could see he was completely hard inside his boxer briefs, and that turned her on even more than she already was. She removed his boxers and took him into her hand as she made her way back up the bed and started to kiss him again. Without removing any of the lingerie she was wearing, she pulled the panties to the side and put him inside of her. She was already so turned on she didn't need any foreplay. And it was apparent that he didn't either.

She slid up and down on him and broke their kiss, and she sat straight up so she could look at him and he could look at her. He loved the way her body looked. His hands roamed all over her body and constantly found their way to her breasts. He could see she was in ecstasy, and before he knew it, she was having a very intense orgasm. Seeing and hearing her put him over the edge, and he started his own orgasm that didn't seem like it was going to end.

After that, he flipped her over onto her back on the bed and slowly took off her lingerie piece by piece. He started with her bra, then released the garter belt and slid the stockings off her legs slowly, and he kissed her legs as he did. It was so erotic and pleasurable for both of them. He finally took her panties off and entered her again and kissed her neck and lips with the intense passion of this afternoon. For hours, they found themselves trading off who was leading and were in all kinds of positions on the bed, on the floor, against the wall, and finally, in the shower as both of them were now pouring in sweat from the hours of intense lovemaking. They were getting exhausted, and each time they were making love, it got slower and slower.

After they finished making love in the shower, they helped clean each other up and got out of the shower. He dried her off and then himself. He found an extra sheet in the closet and put it over the bed to help not lie in a wet bed. They lay down facing each other. They were past the point of exhaustion. They had no idea what time it was and didn't care. He didn't have his first meeting until 11:00 a.m. and had already set his alarm on his phone earlier between the bouts of lovemaking.

He was stroking her face and hair, as he loved to do each night as they were falling asleep. He had never felt passion like this and was sure she hadn't either. It was the single most incredible day of his life. The combination of all the day's events couldn't have gone better. As they were drifting off to sleep, she said, "I love you. Thank you for such a wonderful day!"

"I love you too. And thank you for giving me a reason to want to be a better man every day and something to look forward to each time I open my eyes." They both shut their eyes and were asleep within minutes. They were still facing each other, and his hand rested on the side of her face. His last thought before sleep was that he hoped he could show her how much he loved her each and every day.

Chapter 7

Marcela woke about the time the sun started to rise. She was still exhausted and figured she couldn't have been asleep for more than a few hours. They were still facing each other, and his hand was still resting on the side of her face. It made her feel safe, warm, and loved. It was amazing that they were so tired that neither of them had moved at all until now.

Careful not to wake him, she turned around slowly and put her back against his chest and lifted his arm and put it around her. He started to stir a little and nuzzled her neck with his face. She thought she felt a small kiss but couldn't be sure. She was trying to be as still as possible not to wake him even more. She closed her eyes again, but instead of sleep, her mind turned to the events of the day before, mainly the part of him standing behind her telling her he wanted to move to Spain to be with her. It all felt like a dream. If he wasn't lying right behind her, she wouldn't be sure if it was really true or just a dream. She laughed silently to herself. It was a dream no matter how she looked at it really.

She felt Anastasio's arm move and this time was sure she felt a kiss on her neck. She was holding his, and he squeezed it lightly. She took it as a sign that he was checking to see if she was awake. She squeezed back and heard, "Good morning, sunshine!" He kissed her neck again.

"Good morning! It's early. You need to get some sleep. You have a meeting later."

"You're right, but since we're already awake, maybe we should take a few minutes to say good morning, and then we can take a little nap."

He didn't give her time to answer, and he didn't need to. She could feel that he was already ready, and she turned her head, and they started to kiss as he entered her from where they lay. His hand made its way up to her breasts, and he massaged them as they made love once again. She couldn't even begin to remember how many times this would make in the past eight hours. It didn't matter. It all felt amazing, and she didn't want it to stop. If it hadn't been for complete exhaustion, she was sure they wouldn't have stopped when they did.

They stayed in this position, and he moved his other hand down and started to rub her as he was inside of her. Their pace picked up, and within minutes, she was panting and almost let out a scream as he led her to another orgasm. She could feel his pace quickening as well and then could feel him pulsing inside of her. She loved the way it felt, and it brought her to another orgasm. She couldn't explain why things were so intense with him, but it was something she had never felt before. She suspected that she wouldn't feel it quite like this with anyone else either.

He stayed inside of her, and they continued to kiss for a few more minutes. "Okay, now I think we can take that little nap now," he said and nuzzled his face back into her neck. Within minutes, they were both back to sleep.

It seemed like no time had passed, and his alarm went off. It wasn't easy to open his eyes this time. With the window open, the sunlight was bright, and it took a few minutes for him to get adjusted to it. Marcela barely moved. He kissed her on her cheek and got out of the bed as quietly as he could. He got up and put on his clothes from the night before. He went to her side of the bed and gently touched her face. She opened her eyes and looked up at him. "I have to go get ready for my meetings. I have two today, so I will be gone longer than I wish I had to be. I just wanted to ask you before I go. Since this is our last night together here, I have two different ideas of what we could do, and I want you to choose. I was thinking either we can go to see the show at the famous Moulin Rouge or have a quite night. Which would you prefer?"

"That's a really tough choice! I like the idea of both! What would you prefer?"

"Well, I'm with you. That it is a tough decision. But I don't know when we'll be back here. So I was thinking maybe we would go see the show? It would also be great to have private time with you, but we're already here, and neither of us have seen the show. And I'll be right back to you within a few weeks. We will have all the private time we want. What do you think?"

"I think I like how your mind works! That sounds like a perfect plan! It's just hard to believe this is our last day together here. I don't really want to think about that right now."

"I'm sorry! It's hard for me too. But it will all be worth it. I have to go get ready. And you need to get some more sleep. The dress code for the Moulin Rouge is quite formal. Do you have anything for it?"

"No, I will go out today and find something though! It will be exciting, and I have a place in mind to go to find what I need and see a new friend." She had mentioned Jacqueline to him before, but he didn't really know that they were quickly becoming friends.

"I know your funds are limited. Would you like me to leave you some money to help out?"

"No, no. You have paid for everything on this trip so far. I have spent much less than I thought I would and done so much more than I ever expected! Thank you though. Now go before I come to my senses and drag you back into this bed with me!"

He smiled and leaned down and gave her a kiss. I will call your room when I have an idea what time I will be done. I hope you can get more sleep and have fun shopping! I'll see you soon."

He wanted so much to stay but forced himself to turn and leave the room. He walked back to his room and felt the pain in his stomach again. As like the last time, he hadn't taken in enough fluids and had little sleep. Some water and food should help him feel better.

He got back to his room and took a water from his bag and turned on the shower. He took the water into the shower with him and drank it this time a bit slower than usual. His stomach was really upset, and he had to get out of the shower to get sick. He really didn't have anything left in his stomach, so he mostly dry-heaved for a bit and then made it back into the shower. He really needed to make sure to focus on eating right and drinking enough fluids today. He had to fly home tomorrow and didn't want to feel ill on the plane.

He finished his shower and got ready. He wondered if maybe he had eaten something that had upset his stomach so much or if it was the lack of everything else. He had to change his focus now though to get ready for his meetings. The two places he had to go he had been going for years now and knew them pretty well. He could dress more casual today. Jeans and a nice shirt and sports coat would work nicely.

He got dressed and again made sure his bag was packed with everything he needed. He was all set. He had a little time to spare, so he planned to stop and have a quick breakfast. He figured these meetings should go well and relatively quickly. Then he would need to go find himself a tux for the evening. He had one at home but never would have guessed he would need something like this on this trip. But he couldn't be happier to go and get one for this evening.

He headed out of the hotel and stopped and talked with Rocco for a few minutes. Normally he would spend hours talking with him and his friends, but since he had met Marcela, every second had been spent with her. But he really enjoyed the time he got to spend with Rocco when they had the chance. He had so many life experiences and had lived a very full life, not that it was over yet by any means. He didn't want to think about a time when Rocco would no longer be around. He considered him a friend and would even go as far as to say he felt like he was family. Rocco had always treated Anastasio like his own family.

He started making his way to the first meeting and found a little restaurant he had been to a few times and stopped for his breakfast. His stomach still didn't feel right, but he was hopeful that food would help. A few hours more, sleep wouldn't hurt either, but that wasn't an option today. He found an empty booth and sat himself. There were menus already on the table, and he just wanted something simple that wouldn't upset his stomach more.

The waitress came, and he ordered coffee and scrambled eggs with a bagel. It wasn't much, but he figured it would be good for his stomach. Coffee might not have been the best idea, but he really needed the caffeine at the moment. He did make sure to drink water while waiting on his breakfast and all through the meal.

It only took a few minutes for it to arrive, and he took his time to eat, making sure he didn't upset his stomach more. He not only wanted to feel good for the trip home tomorrow but also for the rest of his time with Marcela. He finished his breakfast and coffee. He declined a refill on the coffee but did have another glass of water before he left. He did feel a little better now but still felt off. Sleep would probably be the most help at this point.

He walked into the small restaurant that he had his meeting with. They were already open for lunch, and there were a few people already seated. He spoke with the hostess, and she went to find the owner. A few moments later, the owner, Tim, came out and shook Anastasio's hand. He led him back to his office and sat behind his desk, and Anastasio sat across from him.

Anastasio varied his presentation from client to client, depending on how well he knew them and what he knew they were looking for. He reached in his bag and pulled out a few bottles of wine that this client didn't currently carry. They carried different bottles of his but was looking to add to the list. They went through the usual process of sampling the wines. Tim seemed pleased with the new selections and asked for the paperwork to commit to start carrying these new wines in addition to what they were already carrying. Anastasio was thrilled that Tim was quick with his decision. It was one less thing he had to worry about, especially now that he was planning on making a move. He wanted to get as much business secured as he possibly could before he left for Spain.

As Tim was filling out the paperwork, they made small conversation as he was filling out the paperwork. Anastasio started to feel sick again and excused himself to the restroom. He found himself getting sick again, this time losing most of his breakfast. He must have eaten something and gotten food poisoning, he thought. He washed his face and luckily had a mint with him and popped it in his mouth. He headed back to the office.

Tim was almost done with the order forms and looked up at him. "Are you feeling okay? You look a little pale."

"I think I may have caught some kind of stomach flu or ate something that didn't sit right or maybe gotten food poisoning. But I am feeling better now," he lied.

"You should've eaten here. Our food is always the best," Tim said with a smile.

He completed the paperwork and walked Anastasio back out to the front. They shook hands again. Anastasio thanked him again for his continued business. Tim nodded in approval and wished Anastasio well and wished him the best on feeling better soon. He walked out of the restaurant with mixed emotions. He was happy that the deal went so well, but now he was getting worried about the rest of the day. And then if he felt like this tomorrow, the trip home would be miserable. He had no intentions of canceling any of the plans for the rest of the day.

As he had hoped, he had extra time before his next appointment. He made his way over to the Moulin Rouge and bought the tickets for the show and dinner for that evening. That left him just enough time to make it over to his next meeting. Again, this meeting was with a client he knew fairly well. He wasn't as sure how this meeting would go, but right now, he just wanted to get through it without feeling or getting sick. He felt okay for the moment.

This establishment was a little bigger. It was a pretty popular spot. The owner here was Dijon. He was a pleasant man, but tough with what wines he preferred to carry. They were always open for lunch, and now it was about the prime time for businesspeople to be having lunch. He was surprised when Dijon set the time for this, but he knew Dijon knew what he was doing. He always seemed to be on top of everything that was going on without showing any stress.

When Anastasio entered the restaurant, he immediately saw Dijon behind the bar. It looked like he was taking inventory. He made his way to the bar, which was mostly empty, and Dijon saw he walk up. He smiled and told him to sit, and he would be with him in a few moments. The bartender walked up and asked if he would like something to drink while he was waiting. He asked for water, and the bartender brought him a bottle of water and a chilled glass. Anastasio chose to use the glass as opposed to drinking out of the bottle since he was in the restaurant.

Dijon finally made his way over to Anastasio and waved him to sit down closer to the end of the bar, so they had more privacy and room to work it. Once they were seated, Dijon shook his hand and asked the usual pleasantries, like how he was, his family, and so on. He was always very polite, and Anastasio understood why his restaurant did so well. He trained all his employees to be the same way. He always had the best staff.

There were only two wines that Dijon was contemplating adding to his collection. Anastasio grabbed both bottles, and Dijon already had his own glasses out ready for the samplings. They sampled both wines. They were both from a special collection, and Anastasio personally thought both of them were exceptionally good. He couldn't tell by Dijon's face what he thought.

When he was closing up his presentation, Dijon informed him that he would order one of the wines but wasn't so impressed with the other. So it was a half win, he thought. Could be worse! The order was also not as big as he had hoped it would be either. But he took what he could get, and any business helped at this point.

Now that his business was over for the day, he could focus on finding a tux for the evening and also finding a bite to eat again since most of his breakfast didn't stay down. He was doing better than expected on time. If all went well with finding a tux rather quickly, he thought he might even have time for a thirty-minute nap. He hoped that would help.

He had a good idea of where to go for the tux. He would find a place that sounded good to eat on the way there. Within a few minutes, he came across the pub that he and Marcela had eaten at just a few nights before. He walked in, and it was pretty busy for the time it was. He was seated right away and didn't need to look at the menu. He knew he wanted their fish and chips. He always enjoyed having that there. It sounded particularly good to him right now. He wanted to order a beer but decided it wasn't the best idea.

The waitress was quick to take his order, and he looked up some places on his phone that sold formal wear close to where he was. He found a few options in case the place he was thinking didn't have what he needed. He thought he might have to rent one since there would not be time to tailor it. But sometimes they sold things like this that were ready-to-wear, so to speak. He always enjoyed getting dressed up. In the last several years, he didn't have many occasions that he had somewhere to be that required it. So this would be a nice treat. He also already knew that Marcela would look stunning in whatever she found.

His lunch arrived, and he ate most of it and was starting to feel a little better. He said a silent prayer for that. He was hoping it would last and that he was over whatever had happened. He made sure to keep drinking water. Water was not his favorite thing to drink, especially during meals, but hard times called for hard measures. He finished the water, paid the bill, and started to make his way to the first clothing store. He said another quick prayer that he would find what he needed quickly so he could get back to the hotel and take in a short nap. He wanted to be as fresh as possible for their last evening together. He wondered how much more sleep she had gotten and what she was doing now. He guessed she was out shopping like he was.

He made it to the store in about ten minutes. The store was empty other than a salesman. Anastasio explained what he was looking for and needed. The salesman apologized, but everything they had was tailor-made, and they didn't have any rentals but suggested another store that Anastasio had looked up on his phone before. The next store was pretty close by. He was able to walk there in about five minutes. Like the first store, there was no one there other than the salesman. He again explained what he needed, and this time he was in luck. They had both ready-to-wear and rentals available. He asked to see the ready-to-wear first.

The salesman was able to tell Anastasio's size very easily. It was something he assumed these people would get particularly good at over time. He showed Anastasio a few different styles and options.

Anastasio picked out four different ones to try on, went to the dressing room, and tried on each one. All of them fit pretty well for not being personally tailored. Out of the four he tried on, he liked the third one he tried on the best. It was the most classic in style, and he liked the fit. He decided on a vest and bow tie. All of it was in black. He needed shoes to match as well, and they were able to accommodate him with that as well.

He was happy with his selections and paid for his items and left. He was only about a fifteen-minute walk from the hotel. It was now about 3:30 p.m., and he didn't really need to be ready until about 5:30 p.m. He remembered to call Marcela's room, and as he expected, she wasn't there. He left a message that said he was heading back and his plan. He told her that he would come up to her room at 5:30 p.m.

When he made it back to the hotel, he said hello to Rocco, and Rocco asked him if he and Marcela would have any time to talk with him before they left. He told him that tonight wouldn't work but would talk to Marcela, and he would see if she would want to in the morning before Anastasio left. Marcela had a flight planned for later in the day. He questioned Rocco what he wanted to talk about, but he just smiled and said, "You know me, I like to talk, and I have nice stories to tell you."

Anastasio agreed that he would talk to Marcela and let him know before they left for the evening. He was quite curious what he wanted to talk about. Rocco had never requested for him to take time out of his day to talk with him. And why did he want Marcela there? This certainly should prove to be interesting!

He made it to his room and took off his shirt, shoes, and socks. He meant to take off his jeans, but when he lay down and set his alarm, he dozed before he even had the chance to. He set his alarm to go off in forty-five minutes. That should be perfect timing for him to take his time to get ready. As he drifted off, his mind wandered to different possibilities of what Marcela would be wearing when he knocked on her door.

~

Marcela could barely keep her eyes open. She grabbed her phone and set the alarm for a few hours later. She had a feeling if she didn't set it, she could sleep all day. She closed her eyes again. As she lay there, she thought about everything that had happened over the past few days. She couldn't believe the trip was getting close to ending. She saw images of the past several days as she was going to go back to sleep. The image of him when she first ran into him flashed into her mind many times as she was falling asleep. His eyes burned into her soul. She fell asleep as he was looking at her.

Her alarm woke her, and she turned it off. She lay there for about another fifteen minutes before she finally got up. She was hungry and knew she also needed time to find something to wear for this evening. She was going to go back to see Jacqueline and hoped she could help but didn't remember seeing anything in her store that was formal. But it would be a good starting point.

She got up and decided to skip on taking a shower for now. She would just get ready quickly, and after her shopping was done, she would take her time showering and getting ready. She went and brushed her teeth, brushed out her hair, and pulled it back into a ponytail. She washed her face. She didn't need any makeup for the afternoon. She found the last of her sundresses she had packed. She put the dress on and found some sandals to go with it.

When she was ready, she found her purse and room key and headed out the door. She would find something to eat for a late breakfast or early lunch and then make her way to see Jacqueline. She was hoping this would go as easily as it had in the past few times of shopping. Could she get that lucky? She knew that if anyone could help her, it was going to be Jacqueline. Even if she didn't have anything, she guessed that she would know where Marcela could get something appropriate for the evening.

Rocco waved at her as she left the hotel, and she waved and smiled back to him. She had gotten incredibly lucky with the weather on this trip as it was another beautiful day out. Springtime normally meant a lot of rain, but each day, it had been sunny and beautiful out when she needed it to be. Her mom was definitely watching out for her, she thought.

She figured she would eat at the café she had on her first day there since she knew exactly where it was and how to get to Jacqueline's shop from there. The café was only a few minutes walk from where she was. With as hungry as she was, the café would be perfect. It was simple, good, and quick.

She got to the café and found an empty table outside with ease. There were more people here than before but still a pretty quiet scene. She sat facing the street, as she liked to do. The same waitress she had before came to her table and welcomed her back and gave her a smile. She gave her a menu and asked if she would like any coffee. She nodded and thanked her. The waitress left to get her coffee, and Marcela looked through the menu to see what sounded good to her today. She was honestly so hungry almost everything she saw on the menu sounded good. She had yet to have the beignets that France was so well-known for, so she decided that she would try that now with some fruit.

The waitress returned with her coffee. Marcela indicated that she was ready to order, and the waitress took down her order and left her alone again. She looked around at the people at the tables around her and made up stories for them all and laughed to herself. She then turned her attention to people walking by and did the same thing. She wished Anastasio was there to play the game with her. She wished he was there also just because she loved being with him.

After a short wait, the waitress returned with her food. She asked how her trip was going. They talked for a few minutes, and she told the waitress about the different things she had done. She didn't get into too much detail about meeting Anastasio. The waitress seemed impressed by all the things she had done and seen in such a short time. She left after a few minutes to let Marcela enjoy her beignets.

Marcela was quite impressed with how good the beignets were and would have to learn how to make them for herself at home. She had always loved to cook but didn't do it as much as she would have liked to. She always worked too late, and since she was living alone, she didn't cook on a regular basis unless her mom or friends came over. She would have to cook more now, and with everything that had happened in the last few weeks, her life had and would be changing quite a bit. Things that seemed so important to her before didn't seem so important now. Some of it she learned on her own. But most of it came from meeting Anastasio and trying to take in how he viewed life. He was much like her mother, and she knew they were both right.

She finished her breakfast and felt much better now. She could use a little more energy, but all in all, she felt pretty good and ready for the rest of the day now. The waitress brought her check, and Marcela paid the bill and thanked her. It was time to go shopping now. She couldn't remember the last time she wore something formal. She was normally very conservative with the way she dressed but liked to dress up when the opportunity arose, which in her life was just about never.

She made it to Jacqueline's shop after a short ten-minute walk. As always, Jacqueline was happy to see her. They gave each other a hug. "You know, I was just thinking about you this morning! I was hoping I'd see you again before you left," Jacqueline told Marcela.

"Oh, thank you. That's so nice to hear! I think I have thought about you every day since I had the pleasure of meeting you. You have been so kind and helpful! I'm afraid I need your help again. I'm not sure if you will be able to, but you have been amazing so far."

"Sure, honey. What do you need?"

"Anastasio and I are going to the Moulin Rouge tonight, and I need something formal to wear. I don't know if you carry anything like that but figured if you didn't, you may know where I can go to get something for this evening. I'm sorry that every time I see you, I need something immediate. I really appreciate you!"

"I don't have a lot in the way of formal, but let me show you what I do have. And it's lovely that you are getting to go to the show. I haven't been in years. It's such a historic and wonderful place! You will have an amazing time. Now let's find you something to make you part of the history and make you look amazing for it." She led Marcela to the back of the store, where she had mostly picked out the lingerie for her. She saw that Jacqueline did have some things and was hoping that, first, there was going to be something she liked and, second, that it would fit her. She was pretty average in size, but with formal wear, things were usual more custom fit.

Jacqueline was going through dress after dress that either didn't seem right for the event or wasn't the right size. Jacqueline didn't seem fazed by the lack of success, but it was worrying Marcela. She only had hours until she needed to be back to the hotel to get ready. She went through her whole inventory and didn't come up with anything. She led her back to the front of the store and went behind the counter and picked up the phone. She called someone unknown to Marcela and was speaking quickly in French. From what Marcela could tell by one side of the conversation she could hear and the expressions on Jacqueline's face, it seemed like good news. Jacqueline finished the call and explained to Marcela that she had a friend that owned a women's formal wear store not far away.

Much to Marcela's surprise, Jacqueline said that she would take her over there and to just give her a few minutes to collect her things and lock up. Marcela protested that she shouldn't close the store for her, but Jacqueline wasn't going to change her mind. Marcela couldn't believe how nice Jacqueline was to her from the beginning. She barely even knew her, and here she was closing her store to help Marcela. Jacqueline was truly an amazing person!

On their way over to her friend's store, Jacqueline asked about her life, about who her mom was, and what her plan was now. Marcela told her about the news that Anastasio was planning to move to be with her in a few weeks. She thought Jacqueline was going to fall over when she heard the news! She stopped walking and looked at Marcela. She thought she was going to say it was a bad idea or something, but instead, she gave Marcela a huge hug and expressed how happy she was. Marcela was worried about telling people, that they would think it was too rushed. So getting this positive response was a relief.

Jacqueline finally released her and started to walk again. She asked all kinds of questions, like was he planning to live with her, how much he would be traveling, etc. Marcela admitted that they hadn't discussed all that, but she knew they would get it all figured out in time. Marcela had already started to think about some of that stuff. She figured he would move in with her. And she was more than okay with it. She didn't think he would want to live apart, but she was sure they'd talk about it when things calmed down.

It was a short walk, and they arrived at another store that Jacqueline led her into, and they were immediately greeted by a woman about the same age as Jacqueline. They hugged and kissed, then Jacqueline introduced them to each other. "I want you to meet my new friend, Marcela. Marcela, this is a very good friend of mine, Darci. She is actually the person that got me started with my own clothing store. She has taught me all I know." Jacqueline was speaking in English now, so Marcela could understand what she was saying.

Darci gave Marcela a hug and kiss and said, "Welcome, Marcela! It's a pleasure to meet you. And Jacqueline is too kind. She teaches me just as much as I've taught her, if not more. So I hear you are in need of a dress for the show at the Moulin Rouge tonight?"

"Yes, I know it's very last minute. But I'm hoping to find something suitable," Marcela answered back to her.

"Don't you worry. We'll get you taken care of!" She spoke in French to Jacqueline again, and she replied, and then they were off to the other side of the store. Marcela followed along behind them. She had a feeling they were going to be tossing things at her from every direction. She could see scenes from different movies where the person was trying on lots of different outfits and showing off the outfits to people that would nod or shake their heads, like they did in the movies.

It didn't quite end up like that, but she did try on many different dresses. She liked the personalized attention she was getting. She wasn't used to that. She either shopped online or bought the same things over and over. She really appreciated what they were doing for her! And she was lucky that it was a weekday, and there wasn't currently anyone else in the store shopping. So far, there were a few that they all agreed on, but she was still trying different ones. It gave her peace of mind though, knowing that she at least had one she liked.

She was down to the last one. It was a dress that she never saw herself wearing. It was deep blue and made with lace from top to bottom. Most of the back was bare, and even the parts that were covered were mostly see through. It was full-length and fit her body perfectly.

It was elegant and sexy all in one. Before she showed the ladies, she made sure that the dress at least covered the areas that shouldn't be seen, and it did! The designer had done an amazing job with this dress. It was absolutely perfect!

She walked out of the dressing area, and both the women were talking and didn't see her at first. Marcela purposely made a noise that caught their attention. They both looked over at her at the same time, and she swore she could see both their jaws drop. That made her smile, and she knew without words that this was the dress for her. Both Jacqueline and Darci jumped up and came over and looked at her. They made her turn this way and that way, and both exclaimed how stunning Marcela looked. They made her feel like a princess going to a ball!

Darci started bringing different accessories for Marcela to try on. She tried on several different pairs of earrings, necklaces, and bracelets. Marcela was a little worried that she wasn't going to be able to afford all this but didn't say anything. She would deal with it once they found the right combination. She also knew that Jacqueline knew of her financial situation and didn't think she would suggest things that she couldn't afford. The frenzy kept on for about thirty minutes before everyone was satisfied with the complete look.

Marcela looked at herself in the mirror, and for the millionth time on this trip, she was amazed at the transformation that was taking place. A week ago, she imagined herself walking through Paris in jeans and a T-shirt, and now here she was dressed up for the third time this trip, each time even more out of her usual comfort zone. She had no idea at the start of this trip that she would be reinventing herself. But she liked it! No, that wasn't the truth. She didn't like it. She thought again. She loved it! She needed it!

It was time now to change back into the clothes she was wearing and figure out what the damage was going to be. Jacqueline helped her out of the dressed and again told her how beautiful she was and that it wasn't the dress that made her beautiful but that it was Marcela made the dress beautiful! Marcela had to blush at this comment. When she was out of the dress, Jacqueline excused herself to allow her to get dressed. She took the dress and accessories with her as she left the dressing room.

Once she was dressed, she looked at herself in the mirror. Even though the clothes she was wearing now were the same, she felt more confident, more beautiful! She knew that she was now standing taller, and she had a different feel about herself now. She liked feeling this way. She hoped that she would continue to feel this way after she got home and was back to her regular life. She needed all these change in her life from here on out!

She came out of the dressing area, and both the women had made their way to the counter. Marcela came over and nervously asked how much everything was going to be. Darci wrote everything down and was talking with Jacqueline in French again as she was figuring the total. She finished writing and talking with Jacqueline. "With everything, it is two hundred euros."

Marcela thought she must have heard wrong. There was no way all this could only be two hundred euros. "I'm sorry, did you say two hundred euros for everything? That can't be right."

Darci shot a glance at Jacqueline and then back to Marcela. "Yes, that's right. Is that okay?"

Marcela knew something odd was going on, but right now, who was she to argue? She needed that dress, and everything they had picked out with it went perfectly with it. "Yes, it is more than okay. Thank you so much!" She pulled out her credit card, and Darci finished up the transaction. She put the dress in a bag that covered the whole thing and the accessories into another bag and handed it all to Marcela.

They thanked one another, and Darci again gave her a hug and wished her a wonderful evening. She said she better take photos and send them to Jacqueline for her to see. She said she could use the photos to sell more of the dresses and wanted to see how she looked with Anastasio. They said goodbye, and Jacqueline and Marcela started walking back to Jacqueline's store. Marcela asked her how this was so inexpensive. Jacqueline wasn't going to lie to Marcela and told her that she got the dress at her cost. And as a gift, Jacqueline bought the accessories for her.

Marcela almost didn't know what to say. She was nearly in tears! Everyone was being so nice to her in a time in her life when she needed it the most. She knew that she had really made a new friend and was sure they would be a part of each other's lives as long as they lived. This whole trip, from the taxi driver to Rocco to Anastasio to Jacqueline, had been a blessing that she never knew she'd get. She knew she would thank God every day for what He had done for her. "I don't know what to say. Thank you, Jacqueline! You didn't have to do that. You have done so much for me that I will never forget."

"You are more than welcome, dear. And don't worry, you can repay me by inviting me to visit you in Spain sometime. And if you ever come back or have friends come, send them my way to do some shopping!" They were now back to her store, and she unlocked the door. Marcela was ready to tell her goodbye, but Jacqueline opened the door for her and asked her, "Can you please come in for a minute?" Marcela followed her back into the store, and Jacqueline took her to the section where the lingerie was. "Well, we have to match stuff with the dress again, right? Can't go out only half dressed!" she said with a wink.

Marcela let out a laugh and followed her. "You've got a deal!" she replied. They picked a beautiful blue thong and some different stockings. The dress didn't need a bra, so Marcela thought they were done, but Jacqueline picked out one anyways. She explained that she might not need it for tonight but would appreciate having it later. Marcela saw her point and appreciated her thoughts. She was starting to get a nice collection of beautiful, matching lingerie.

She was ready to pay for the collection, and Jacqueline said it was part of her gift to Marcela. She was again without words and gave Jacqueline a long hug. "Thank you for everything you have done for me. I will never forget you, and you have an open invitation to visit me anytime! I will do my best to make it back here and come see you. And when I need any clothes, you are going to be my first call. I promise to keep in touch, and I will send you photos. I have your number and email from your card. You are an angel in disguise. I will miss you and your kindness, Jacqueline!"

"I will miss you too! I will be happy to hear from you anytime! And believe me, you will be seeing me again. I need a vacation myself, and I haven't been to Barcelona. You will have to show me around. And I'd love to see your store and your lovely designs. Keep in touch, my dear! And most importantly, enjoy your life every minute that you possibly can. You deserve it! Your smile is so radiant and infectious that it will light up other people's lives around you! Now it's time for you to go get ready. Have a wonderful time. Tell Anastasio hello from me. He's a very lucky man!"

"I promise will keep in touch. I don't like goodbyes, so I will say, until next time!" She gave her one last hug, took the dress and the bags, and left the store. She felt a little sadness come over her, leaving her new friend. But she knew that they would remain in touch. For now, she needed to get back to the hotel and start to get ready. Tonight was going to be another wonderful night! She could feel it.

~

Anastasio's alarm sounded, and he shut it off. He lay there a few minutes, waking up. The nap seemed to help. He felt energized, and his stomach no longer hurt. He started to think where he had left off when he fell asleep about the evening ahead of him. He was getting excited about seeing her, wondering what she would be wearing, what the show would be like, and so on. He heard the show they were playing was very entertaining! It would be a wonderful experience to share with her.

He got up, and he knew he had plenty of time to get ready. He was still being mindful that he needed to keep hydrating and found a new bottle of water and started drinking. He took his tux out of the bag that it was wrapped in and laid it out. He was happy with what he had found! It was a very classic look and fit his body perfectly. When he was home, he would have it altered a bit to fit even better, but for tonight it would do just fine.

He started the shower, and before he got in, he looked in the mirror and trimmed his beard again. He checked for any stray hairs on his eyebrows, nose, and ears, all the places hair shouldn't be growing. That was one of the fun parts of getting older. Hair stopped growing where it should grow and started growing in places where it wasn't wanted. He generally kept up with these things on a regular basis. But these special occasions, he wanted to look the best he possibly could.

He thought he got everything taken care of that needed work and jumped into the shower. The hot water was invigorating and woke him up even more. He could feel his mood getting better and better by the minute. Not that his mood was ever bad today, but every minute that went by, it meant it was a minute closer to being with Marcela. The thought of that made him extremely happy! He caught himself singing in the shower, which he couldn't really remember when he had done it last.

He took his time washing every part of his body. He washed his hair and then just spent time standing there, letting the water cascade down his body starting at the base of his neck. It was so relaxing that he felt he could stay in there all day. He realized that much of his life he rushed things, and although he had a decent balance in life, he generally didn't take the time to do little things like this. That was something he planned to change in the future. It was time to not only enjoy the big things in life but to also do the little things that really made life special.

He finished his shower and went through his usual ritual of getting ready. He dried off, brushed his teeth, fixed his hair, and all the other little things he liked to do before he got dressed. He still was a little early, and he didn't want to put on the tux to sit around and let it wrinkle up before it was time to go. He found a pair of athletic shorts and put them on.

He went to his briefcase and found the calendar. He looked at his meetings over the next couple of weeks. He was looking to see when the most opportune dates would be to make the move to Spain. He hadn't asked if she wanted him to move in with her or for him to get a place of his own. They would need to discuss that soon, so he'd plan extra time if he needed to find a place as well as spending time with her and learning the area. He was hoping that he would be living with her! He liked having her sleeping next to him. He wanted her to be the last person he saw before sleeping and the first person he'd see when he woke up. He loved the thought of that.

He found a few different areas that could work, and he would talk to her soon about it. He didn't know if they'd have much time to talk about things like that tonight. But if not, they could talk about over the phone when they had time to really talk about the important things. Moving in together was always a big deal! He memorized the different dates so he could discuss it whenever they had the time.

He sat and thought about different ways to tell his parents. He figured his father wouldn't say much about it. He knew his dad loved and cared about him more than life itself. But he was a simple man and grew up in a time that men expressing emotions was considered weak. Even though he didn't always offer the words, he knew how he felt about him and knew that if he ever needed anything, he would be the first to be there to help.

His mother was going to be the tricky one! His whole life, she would try to convince him to do things based on what she felt was best for her way of thinking. When he went to college, she told him he was wasting his time because running the vineyard required more hard work than any degree would give. His family needed him there. But he managed both. When he started to date seriously, she would tell him that he was losing focus and dating could come later. The family business needed his help, and that's where his focus should be. When he announced that he was getting married, his mom pulled him aside, of course, after expressing to both of them how happy she was for them. She told him he was too young, and it was a mistake. His family needed him there. If his girlfriend—she refused to use the word *fiancé*—really loved him, she would be understanding and wait for him. The girl was just being selfish and didn't know what taking care of a family meant.

He usually let the words go in one ear and out the other. He was expecting this reaction from her as she had done very similar things all his life. He got married as planned. In front of others, she could convince the world that she was so proud and happy for them. But in private, she would make comments to both of them that she didn't agree with their decision and didn't treat his wife very well. His wife got used to it, and later when they would be alone, they would laugh it off. He knew it hurt his wife even though she didn't say it. But his mom was stubborn, and he knew it was pointless to argue with her. She wasn't going to change.

When he told his parents that they had decided to get divorced, she tried to seem concerned and upset that things weren't working out for them. He knew secretly that she was happy that he would be focusing more of his time there instead on making his own family. His grandmother died when he was very young, so he wasn't sure if she was the way she was because she grew up that way or if she was just like that. He knew she loved him and didn't intentionally try to hurt him with the things she did or more often didn't do. And he loved her as well! He just wanted a different life for himself than she wanted. He knew most families went through this.

He shook the thoughts of his parents from his head. He would figure out the best way to tell them in time. He would have to carefully think about it. It wasn't something he could solve in the next ten minutes. He knew his life was going to be with Marcela, and he would be there as much as he could for his family. He believed in family, but it was time for him to create his own family with someone special. He had no idea if he or she wanted kids, a lot of small details, but those things didn't really matter right now. As long as he had her, his world would be right.

He put his calendar back into his briefcase and slowly started to get dressed. He put music on as he got ready. The thoughts of his family had taken his mood down a little, but now that he was back in real time, his mood immediately started to change back to where it was. He was excited about spending the evening with Marcela. It was going to be special! That he knew for sure. He had a sudden thought of being married to Marcela and laughed out loud. He was glad he didn't have a ring because he thought he'd have an extremely difficult time restraining himself from asking her to marry him at any moment. She would probably think he was crazy if she even knew he had the thought in his head.

He put on his shirt and then put his pants on. Luckily, the shirt was perfectly pressed before he left the store. He went to the bathroom mirror to tie his bow tie. He normally had ones that were tied before, but this one was the real deal. The salesman had taught him how to tie it before he left. It took him a few tries, but he finally got it right and liked the way it looked. He was happy to finally learn how to tie one himself. It just felt a little more elegant than having one that was tied already. He had always liked to pay attention to the little details, such as this. He wanted every detail to be perfect.

He put on the coat and made sure everything looked exactly how it should be. He really wanted perfection tonight! He knew these things wouldn't matter to her. She loved him for who he was. But because he loved her, he wanted to give her the best of him that he could possibly give. He planned to spend every day showing her that she was important to him and would do things that wasn't in his normal plans to show her that. He, of course, would tell her he loved her. But it was more than that. He would show her every day that he loved her. Whether it be a big or small gesture, he would make sure that he did something daily.

He put on his shoes last, and now his outfit was complete. He was happy with the way he looked. He again wondered what she had found to wear for this evening and couldn't wait to see her. He knew no matter what, he would find her beautiful and would be pleased with everything about the evening. He was all ready to go, got his wallet, sprayed on his cologne, and got his room key to go to her room.

~

Marcela got back to her room and was excited about how the day went. She never expected to find something so amazing to wear and the unexpected gifts she had received from Jacqueline. She had always believed that people like Jacqueline existed in life but had rarely met people that were like her! She had such high expectations of people, she figured that's why she had only a few good friends in her life. But she'd rather have less friends that were true than to have lots of friends that weren't kind and loving to her and other people. She needed genuine people in her life!

She took the wrapping off the dress as she hung it up. She looked at it for some time. It was an amazingly beautiful dress, and the wished she knew who the designer was. His vision was incredible. Being an artist herself in a sort, she found the beauty in other people's work. Whoever this person was that designed it, she wanted to study them and perhaps get inspired to design something of her own that struck her as beautiful as what these other people created.

She looked at the dress and the detail. The designer had been careful to think of every little detail, like making sure everything that was supposed to be covered was covered, letting things be seen that were appealing to the eye. It had a beautiful design, and the material was perfect for the type of dress it was. And the designer thought of an average-sized woman wearing this instead of a model-sized woman that could fit into anything. As a designer of her jewelry, she paid attention to the smallest details. When she got home, she planned to research this designer and see what else he had to offer. The designer was careful with the seams and seemed to pay attention to the little details that most didn't really care about. She just looked at every little detail that the designer put in. These were things she really enjoyed looking at.

She went and turned on the shower and got in. She took her time soaping and shampooing her hair. She shaved her legs and the other parts of her body that she wanted to be perfect. During the shower, she thought about Anastasio. The questions that Jacqueline brought up about if he was going to be living with her and other plans that they hadn't talked about came into her mind. She had no idea that he was thinking the exact same thing at that moment. She knew her friends would be concerned that she wanted him to just move in after a short period of knowing each other, but she trusted him. He was kind and loving! She could tell he had a heart of gold. Even though she couldn't say that she could read people especially well, she knew he was real. She hoped her friends would be happy for her and trust her judgment. She wasn't one to just jump blindly into anything. Well, until she booked this trip. But she felt that she should trust what her heart was telling her. She'd jump, but she didn't think she'd fall. He would be there to catch her, hold her, and keep her safe.

As she was finishing up her shower, her thoughts turned on what tonight would be like. In her mind, she envisioned how she looked in her dress and imagined Anastasio in a classic black tux. They would catch the attention of many people watching them walk by. It would make her feel glamorous! She would be in the arms of such a handsome man, and she would be standing tall and proud. Both would have genuine smiles on their faces that would show the world that they couldn't be happier than they were at that moment. She looked forward to having photos wearing the dress and being with Anastasio, another memory that would never fade from her memory.

She got out of the shower and wrapped her body and hair to let them dry. She started on her makeup, like before. She couldn't remember the last time before this trip that she wore makeup, and now it seemed to be a daily thing. She still didn't think she really needed it for everyday life. When she was back home, she was sure she wouldn't really use it unless it was a special event. And she knew he wouldn't mind. He seemed quite pleased with how she looked without it. He seemed to like her for who she was, not who she could be.

She finished her makeup and put lotion all over her body. Her skin was so smooth, and the lotion's scent smelled good. She put on new lace thong. It was beautiful and actually extremely comfortable, which many times the best-looking lingerie wasn't the most comfortable. She looked in the mirror and turned this way and that. It was flattering to her figure! Meeting Jacqueline was truly a miracle, she thought. Never would she have been able to find the things that she helped her with. She would have to design her some jewelry to at least partially thank her for everything she had done for her. She could probably spend the rest of her life doing things for Jacqueline, and it still wouldn't be enough. She very well could've been the person that possibly helped her start the relationship that anyone would envy having! That was something that was priceless.

She went and dried her hair and did her hair. Again, it was cooperating nicely and turned out exactly how she wanted it to. She had put it partially up and had strands hanging down on both sides of her face. Her mother had taught her that many years ago. It always reminded her of her mother's favorite actress, Audrey Hepburn. Her hair always seemed perfect! She was beautiful and had such grace. Her mom loved watching her films and always said that she wished she had her confidence and attitude. But to Marcela, she might not have the looks of Aubrey, but she had everything else. She was kind and quick with a witty line, and even though she was no model, she carried herself with confidence. If her mom had chosen to meet another man after her father left, she could have found a thousand men that would have happily spent the rest of their lives with her. Her mother was her idol and hero. She felt sad she was gone but now felt that her mother was still guiding her along. The only difference now was Marcela was ready to listen and act upon it.

Now that her hair was done, she went and put on the stockings. With how fitting and long the dress was, it would be near impossible to put them on after putting on the dress. As she put on the stockings, she noticed they were a little different than the ones she already bought. They had a thick black line right in the middle of the back of the stockings. She liked it but wondered if she would have the guts and confidence to wear something like that out in public, where she could see people she knew. She was such a conservative person and didn't wear these things, especially in public. Her whole life was changing on a daily basis without her even realizing it until now. She really liked feeling like this. To have a real reason to smile, to literally stop and smell the roses, and to feel confident, sexy, desired. There couldn't be a better feeling in her mind!

She slowly put on the dress. She still couldn't believe she found something so perfect and how absolutely perfect this dress looked and fit. Jacqueline had told her that she made the dress look beautiful, but Marcela wasn't quite that confident yet. She thought the dress made her! It seemed like life was completely on her side, and she didn't think she deserved it but was happy with what life was handing her right now. She would continue to pray and thank God for these small blessings she was getting.

Once the dress was on, she looked again in the mirror. She couldn't believe she was looking at herself and not watching some fairy-tale movie. She laughed and thought that she was now living in a fairy-tale movie. She had the dress, she had the man, and now she was going to a show. Sure, it wasn't a ball like the movies, but they'd be dressed up. There would be dancing, and everyone would be dressed up for the show. She was hoping that she wouldn't lose her love to only find him again later, like in many of the fairy-tale movies. But the rest of it seemed perfect.

She found the bag that had all the accessories. She put on the necklace and earrings. They really were the perfect complement to the dress. She put on her watch and the bracelet she had found with the Jacqueline and Darci. Each piece complemented the other pieces perfectly. She again thought of the movie *Pretty Woman*. She was going from wearing clothes that didn't really do her justice to feeling like she was a girl being transformed in the movie.

She was dressed now and had put on all the accessories that were meant for this dress. Everything really complemented one another. Although she wished the stones in the necklace were real diamonds, they still shined and looked elegant. The bracelet that she had gotten and the watch she already had made everything look perfectly in place. She wished she could dress up and look like this every day. She knew that wasn't realistic but wanted to look the best for Anastasio each and every day. She wanted to offer him all the best parts of herself even if he didn't ask for it.

She looked at herself in the mirror again to make sure she was happy with how she looked. Everything seemed in place, and she was more than happy with the way she looked. She kept looking in the mirror and was unsure that she would ever top how she looked tonight. She knew her camera had had its use over the past several days, but tonight was special, and she know there would be a lot of photos being taken again.

She felt like she was finally completely ready. She knew that he would be up soon to get her, and she couldn't be more excited. It wasn't the show that made her so excited. It was the fact that starting from here on out, she was really starting her life wish someone that she could have only dreamed for! She hadn't experienced life with someone that she wanted romantically in her life, like Anastasio, but she was ready for the good and bad that came with it. She couldn't think that Anastasio could be bad to her, but life was life, and she wasn't dumb enough to believe that they wouldn't go through their share of hard times.

She found the perfume she was looking for and sprayed it on her wrists and neck. She sat on the edge of her bed and waited for Anastasio to knock on her door. She was excited to be with him. She had the nervous butterflies in her belly, but more than anything, she was excited to see him, hug him, and kiss him. She was very curious to know what he would be wearing for the show, but she knew he would look perfect. He seemed to always care about how he looked in front of other people. She thought more about what their evening would consist of but was being as patient as possible. She was just waiting on the knock on the door from Anastasio and the start of the life both of them wanted.

He knocked on the door, and after a short wait, she opened the door. When she answered the door, once again he was amazed on how she stunning she looked. He knew she would look beautiful, but this, this he didn't expect. She looked like a movie star about to go down the red carpet. As she looked at him, she was thinking the same thing about him. They didn't know it yet, but a lot of their thoughts happened at the same time. It wasn't something they had talked about yet but would come up in the future.

He opened his mouth a few times without words escaping. Finally, he said, "You look amazing! Like a movie star ready to walk down the red carpet." He felt like he and his outfit didn't do her justice, but her look suggested otherwise. He looked her up and down. He couldn't believe she could possibly look any more beautiful as she did now. She had to smile at his comment for several reasons. First, he had thought the same as her. And second, that he seemed so pleased with the way she looked. More than pleased really! She looked amazing, and he felt lucky that she was his date for tonight, if not for the rest of his life.

She looked at him and felt that he looked at straight out of the movies as well. "You look amazing yourself. So, Mr. Handsome, are you ready to escort me to the show?"

"I'd be more than honored to escort you anywhere! May I escort the most beautiful woman in Paris to the Moulin Rouge for a show this evening?"

Even though he had said something similar with his words and thoughtfulness, she was still amazed by the way it made her heart skip a beat when he said sweet things. "It would be a pleasure and honor to have you escort me to me the show." She didn't have to say another word. She just took his arm and closed the door behind her.

As they were leaving the hotel, Rocco caught Anastasio's attention and gave him a look that was a reminder that he wanted to talk to them before they left. Anastasio would have to remember to tell Marcela that Rocco wanted to talk to them both before they left to go home. He knew she would have questions that he didn't have the answers to, like why he wanted to talk, etc. He still wondered what Rocco wanted to talk about himself. But it's the first time that Rocco requested something like this, so he figured it would be something important.

Bernard was waiting for them outside as usual. He smiled at them both and gave Marcela a look that said everything that words couldn't. She blushed, and he opened and took her hand to help her into the car. She could feel his eyes on her but not in a creepy way. She knew the dress would draw attention, and she had to try to get used to it. She usually didn't like to be the center of attention, but with the mood she was in, she thought she might enjoy the attention tonight.

Bernard got in the car, and they were off to the famous Moulin Rouge. It was very close to the hotel, but with what she was wearing, it wasn't the type of dress and heels that one wanted to walk blocks to get to where they were going. Plus, it was nice to see Bernard again. She wasn't sure if she'd see him again or not, and even though he didn't speak any language she understood, it was nice to see his smiling face. Even Bernard had dressed up more than usual. She guessed that Anastasio had told him about the date, and he wanted to dress the part for them.

Within minutes, they were in front of the Moulin Rouge. There were many people walking in all dressed to impress. Most of the men were in tuxes, some in the occasional nice-looking suit. The women were in their elegant dresses, some very elaborate, some conservative, but all looking their best. She was excited to be in the company of Anastasio and be a part of a big part of history here at the Moulin Rouge.

Bernard opened her door and helped her out of the car. Anastasio walked up and put his arm out for her to take. Before she did, she gave Bernard a kiss on the cheek and gave him a big smile. He gave a big smile in return, and she then took Anastasio's arm. She was grateful for the new people in her life. She really didn't think she could ever forget any of the people she had met from this trip. Everyone played a part in what was being the first chapter of the rest of her life. No matter how little that part was, everyone was important!

From the outside, it was just like she imagined it. The windmill was spinning slowly, and the building was old and looked like it was well maintained. Just to be in the presence of such a historical place made her feel more than she thought she would. She imagined seeing all the people when it originally opened walking in, all dressed up, not knowing that they would be part of history. She suspected it was different back then. A different type of excitement. She imagined the men dressed up and coming alone. The women dressed up, ready to meet the men. The excitement of the art of dancing they had back then. For the most part, that art had been mostly lost over the years. She was sure it was different now, but in her mind, she could see it all.

They walked in, and there are many hosts and hostesses that were ready to show everyone to where they would be seated for dinner and the show. They were shown to their table. Looking around, she didn't think there would really be a bad seat anywhere in the place. But she was quite pleased where they were seated. They were just off center of the main stage. They were close enough to be part of the action but far enough away to catch everything that was going on. She expected that it would probably get pretty crazy.

The waitress brought them the menu and left them to let them look over their menus. They both decided that they wanted to order a specialty cocktail that they offered. There were only a few options on the menu to eat, but all of them sounded delightful in their own way. They made their choices, and the waitress came and took their order. People from other tables were engaging them in conversation, and everybody seemed so happy to be there. It was so easy to get caught up in all the excitement.

The waitress brought their drinks and took their order. Anastasio was quick to make another toast, "To an amazing trip and the start of a wonderful relationship. Being part of history and creating our own. Our last night in Paris, but we'll always Paris in our hearts! Here's to us!" he toasted. They took their first drink, and it was very refreshing. It was hard to believe that this was their last night there, but what he said was true. They would always have Paris!

They decided that since they had already ordered, they would walk around a little to see the whole place. As they walked around, they met different people, and many women would stop her and compliment her on her dress. She could feel the men checking her out as well but were well-mannered enough not to stare or make comments that were inappropriate. Anastasio stayed close by her as they met different couples from all over the world. Everyone seemed just as excited as they were to be there.

They had made their way around the place, stopping to take photos here and there and deciding to go back to their table and taking their seats. Shortly after, their appetizer came, and they ate and drank while still being greeted by others who were still settling in. They were both smiling, laughing, and having a great time. She was glad they decided on doing this instead of just spending time alone. She hoped that they would have years to spend time alone. Coming to a place like this didn't come along every day.

The show started with dancers and loud music. Everything was done with such high energy. Even though she was just sitting there watching, she really felt that she was a part of it. Their entrees came in stages as the show went on. They ate, drank, and shared food and comments about the show. The food was incredible, as everything else had been so far. The dancing and music were amazing! She wished she knew how to dance like that and wondered if Anastasio knew how to dance to things like this also. He seemed very well versed in many things. She wanted to ask but didn't want to have him thinking that she wanted to dance. The dancing they did on the first night was more than she usually did. Seeing that her dress put a lot of attention on her, she didn't want to embarrass herself in front of others with trying something like that.

They finished their food and had ordered more drinks. They ordered desert that was an amazing chocolate dish. It went along perfectly with their drinks. As the show progressed, the patrons were asked to be involved more and more. There were now many couple out dancing and singing along to the music. It was quite the scene! The whole experience was so surreal! She wondered where people learned how to dance like that.

Anastasio looked at her, and she knew right away what he was thinking. She shook her head and said, "Not on your life!" But he pretended not to hear her. Before she knew it, he was standing in front of her and took her hand. She looked up at him, and just the look he had on his face, she couldn't resist. She no longer felt the fear she just felt moments ago. With him, she was invincible. He took the camera off the table and asked another couple that were sitting close to them to keep an eye on it for them. They asked if he would like them to take some photos of them while they were dancing and told them to feel free to take as many photos as they wanted and thanked them.

He led her to the dance floor, and they started with some very basic steps. He seemed to really know what he was doing, and even though she had no clue, she didn't have to. He led her perfectly. Every few minutes, he would throw in another move, and she would turn, spin, and twist any way he led her to. She was having so much fun! She couldn't get the smile off her face and was now so happy that she didn't protest coming to the dance floor. It was an experience of a lifetime!

After about twenty minutes of dancing, they both were getting a little sweaty and needed a break. They went back to the table, and others commented to them how wonderful they looked on the dance floor on their way back to the table. She was so happy that it had her laughing for no reason at all. The man that had her camera gave it back and said that he thought he got some good shots of them. They sat and looked through the photos, and they did have some great photos. They thanked the couple again for taking the photos for them.

Each day had been completely different, and each day she was extremely happy. She didn't realize how many different ways that she could be happy. She was now seeing that happiness came in all sorts of ways. All she had to do was allow life to happen instead of trying to control it. It would be hard for her to learn to do this on her own but knew with Anastasio by her side, she would learn to really live her life to the fullest.

The show was now winding down, and it was getting a little later in the evening now. Anastasio's flight was leaving around 9:00 a.m., and that meant that he would probably have to leave the hotel by about 6:00 a.m. to ensure that he would make his flight on time. She didn't want to think about tomorrow yet, but it was there in the back of her mind now.

The waitress brought them their check, and he paid the bill. He asked her if she wanted to dance more or see anything else there, and she declined. They had some other people take more photos of them together inside and outside of the Moulin Rouge. Part of her didn't want to leave, but the other part was getting tired, and she wanted to spend some time alone with him before they parted ways in the morning.

He made a quick call, and Bernard showed up within minutes. She was going to miss this guy even though she really didn't know anything about him. She did know he was kind and loved the smile that he always had on his face. She reminded herself to ask Anastasio if she could hire him to take her to the airport tomorrow. She was half-thinking to leave when he had to leave, but that would leave her at the airport for about five hours before her flight would leave. She would think about that more later.

When they were on the way back to the hotel, Anastasio remembered that Rocco had asked if he could talk with them both, and he told Marcela about it. She agreed that she would, but just like Anastasio, she wondered what he would possibly want to talk to them both about. Anastasio said he would prefer the morning to do it if she was up to it. She again agreed.

By the time they had finished talking about it, they were back to the hotel. She asked Anastasio to ask Bernard if she could hire him to take her to the airport. He spoke with him and said Bernard said it would be an honor. They discussed the time that he was going to be there for Anastasio and then back for her. They all hugged, and Bernard left them to have the rest of their evening together.

They walked into the hotel, and Rocco had the folding table set up and was sitting there instead of behind the counter. The other men that were usually there, weren't there. He was just sitting there alone looking through what looked to be a photo album. He looked up when he saw them and smiled the big grin he always had. But his eyes looked different. If Marcela wasn't mistaken, there was a sadness in his eyes.

Anastasio looked at Marcela, and they knew that they should sit with him and now talk about whatever he wanted to talk about. Anastasio pulled out a chair for her, and she sat and then he took his own seat. Rocco looked at them both and put out his hands for them to both to hold. They each took one of his hands. Marcela shot Anastasio a quick glance that said she was worried about Rocco. Anastasio had the same look in his eyes, but they sat there and waited for Rocco to say whatever it was that he wanted to tell them.

They were sitting there a few minutes before he said anything. He finally spoke, and they were shocked, not about what he said but that it was in English and very good English at that. Anastasio had known him over ten years and not once had heard him say anything in English. Whenever someone had said something in English to him, he would just smile and go along his way as if he didn't know what they were saying, just like Marcela had met him.

"It was August of 1943. Germany had control of most of France. I didn't live in Paris at the time. I lived with my family in the farmlands. I wasn't home when they came to our home. My family was helping some others hide from the Germans, and somehow they found out, came to our home, and I assume they questioned my family. My dad wasn't one to give in to anyone. I believe this was one of those times.

"When I returned home, they were all laying on the floor, and I knew instantly that no one was alive. The family they were hiding were also among them. I was only seventeen at the time. I was in shock and had so much anger in me! Anger in what the Germans had done, anger that I wasn't there. Not that I could've changed things, but it was my family, and I wasn't there. It was a pain that burned deep into my heart. My father, my mother, and my two little sisters.

"My father was a simple man. He loved his family. He provided for us. He cared deeply for us. He would have done anything for us, for anyone really, just like he did for the family he was hiding and protecting. That proved to be the death of him. But it was who he was and who he taught all of us to be."

He opened the photo album up and pointed out photos of his family and separate photos of himself when he was younger. Marcela had tears in her eyes already. Anastasio did also. Rocco didn't have any tears but sadness in his eyes. His hands were shaking some. He told them about each photo. When it was taken, the names of each person in the photos, and then he continued his story.

"I wasn't home because a few years before this, I had met a girl in Paris that was American. Even though we were both just kids, we met, and although we couldn't see each other all that often, I came to her any chance I could get. I didn't tell my family as there was no way that my father would have let me go into Paris by myself. But we were in love! That day was one of the days that I told my father I was running some errands, and I really was going to Paris to see Marisa.

"We had spent the day together running around the city. We had promised that when we could get the nerve to tell our parents, we would marry and be together forever. But her parents were extremely strict people. They believed she was too young to date and knew nothing of me. They were actually in the process of going back to America. We didn't know how we were going to do it, but we weren't going to let anything tear us apart."

He stopped, and Marcela could tell that he was trying to hold back his emotions. She looked at Anastasio, and she could see that he was getting emotional, just like she was. She gave Rocco's hand a gentle squeeze, and he kept his head down but let a single tear drop. He breathed in deep and composed himself and started again.

"After hours of standing over my family, I got scared that the Germans would come back for me. So I ran as fast as I could back into the city. I knew I couldn't see Marisa, but I didn't know what else to do or where to go. For two days, I walked around the city. I had to steal my food, and I slept in the streets. But I didn't care. I was set to see Marisa after that two days. She was all I had, and I was going to do anything to see her.

"When I finally met up with her, I told her what had happened, and she was horrified by what I had gone through. She went back to the flat they had and found some clothes that I could wear. She also got into her father's safe and took enough money that we could flee somewhere together and would be able to eat and find a place to lay our heads. She left her home for me and didn't tell her parents.

"We married a few days later. The way she looked at me each time, it told me that she would do anything for me, and she knew I'd do anything for her. We wanted to be able to tell her parents, and I wanted their blessing as that was the way I was raised. But we knew they would not approve of anything we were doing. I knew this was hard for her, and I wanted ever so badly to change that.

"Over time, we both found work. I worked at a meat packaging company, and she started to nanny for couple. The family she worked for knew of our situation, what had happened with my family, and then her leaving her family. They were a kind and generous family. If they disapproved of what we were doing, they were exceptionally good at hiding it.

"After she was working for them for about three months, they invited us to live with them. They knew even with both of us working, we were struggling to make ends meet on a daily basis. We believed they were angels sent from heaven to help and protect us. They became the family that neither of us had anymore. We were blessed to have them!

"Shortly after, they were killed by an explosion that the Germans had set off. We weren't sure what we were going to do. We were devastated. First, my family, then losing hers, and we found another family, and they were now gone too! Well, the parents, that is. We had their baby with us when it happened. We weren't sure what else we could endure.

"A few days later, there was a knock at the door, and we were sure that was the end of us living in the flat that the family had. We immediately thought we'd have to find our way again. But God was great to us again! It was the attorney that the family had. We had no idea that they had put us in their will as they didn't have any family left. They left us their flat, some money, and custody of their child. Her name was Penelope. In a split second, we went from the thoughts that we were going to be homeless, hungry, and losing another whole family to having our whole world change.

"We decided to sell the flat as we didn't need such a big place. And the money they had left was limited, so we knew we'd have to make changes to keep going. So the flat sold, and we now had to find a place. Guess where we moved? We moved right where you are staying. This hotel was for sale, and because of the German invasion and control, the owners sold it to us for almost nothing. God was again in our favor!

"We didn't have many guests over the next year. But we had enough money to keep us going, to eat, and to raise the child that was left to us. Having that little girl was a miracle that we didn't know we had. When things had gotten better years later and the Germans were gone, we tried to have a child of our own and couldn't."

He looked at us and smiled. The sadness seemed to be replaced with something else now that she couldn't place. Her mind was spinning with the story of his life. How could anyone be that strong to go through so much and keep going? She had only lost her mother and felt completely lost it until she met Anastasio. She couldn't image going through anything remotely as bad as Rocco had gone through. They stayed silent, waiting for Rocco to continue.

"We were married for sixty-six years before Marisa passed. We didn't spend one day apart and never wanted anything else other than to be together and make each other happy. We never had much other than this hotel. We didn't get to travel the world or do many things that people think they need to be happy. Our happiness was in each other, not searching endlessly for it in some foreign land.

"Our daughter passed a few years before my wife from leukemia. It was hard on us, but we still had each other. After my wife passed, I hoped that I would follow shortly after. Each night I prayed that God would take me home to my wife, but every morning I would wake. I prayed this same prayer for probably close to two year, and for those two years, I kept waking up just the same. It finally hit me that God wasn't going to let me die just because I wanted to. He decides when that is, not us!

"It took me a long time to find my way again! But I haven't spoken any English since my wife died. People tend to talk too much. I don't believe you always have to. Look into someone's eyes, and it will tell you everything you need to know if you really pay attention!

"So the reason I wanted to talk to you both is not to tell you an old man's sad story. I am now ninety-four. In all my time of paying attention to people, I haven't seen that look you two have for each other since the last time I looked into Marisa's eyes. It is written in you! You belong together. Remember that life isn't always easy, and things, people, money, friends will come and go. But you two will remain. I wanted to share my story because I believe you will have a happy story, like mine. Sure, I lost so much in life. But I had one thing that not everyone is given. I was given a love that will never die. My story is a happy one! You control what happens from here. Make your story a happy one!"

He squeezed both their hands to signal that he was done with his story. They were both at a loss for words, but neither of them let go of his hands yet. Finally, Marcela was able to speak, "May I ask, do you know what happened with Marisa's family?"

"Ah, yes. They apparently looked for us for a few years and finally gave up. After about ten years, she would make little comments about her parents, and I knew that she missed them even though she didn't say it. It took me a few years, but I found them in America. I wrote them a long letter and explained everything. Within a few weeks, they showed up at the hotel and were so happy that she was alive and doing well. If they were upset with either of us, they didn't show it. I think they were just happy to have their daughter back. They visited us each year. They finally passed on, and she didn't have any siblings."

Marcela had such a mix of emotions that she didn't know how to feel. But then she looked into Anastasio's eyes, and all the confusion went away. She saw that look that Rocco was talking about. It made her smile and feel even more love for him than she already felt. She was so happy that Rocco had taken the time to tell them his story.

"Thank you for sharing that with us, Rocco. You have known your share of tragedy and overcame it all. You are an inspiration! It means the world to me that you see that in us. I can feel it. I didn't know that it really existed before I met Anastasio. I think we will be working on a story to someday share with a young couple, like you just did. We will be sure to come see you as often as we can or at least keep in touch. You are part of our story! Without your story, the beginning of our story wouldn't exist!"

Rocco stood up and walked around the table. They both stood, and they all hugged for a good amount of time. Anastasio felt that he was getting the same blessings in his life that Rocco did. He was still shocked that he had no idea that he knew how to speak English, but it was a wonderful surprise for the night.

"Now I don't want to hold you two up. I know you both leave tomorrow. I hope you have a plan in place because nothing else in your life will ever matter like this does. I won't say every day will be perfect, but your lives will be happy ones!"

"Thank you, Rocco. Thank you for being who you are. You are a very special man. God bless you!" Marcela said as they finished their hug.

They said good night to him, and they made their way to her room. After hearing his story, their emotions were on a different note now. It wasn't sadness or anything negative. It was an intense feeling of love. They hugged as they shut the door and stayed that way for quite a bit. He pulled back and looked into her eyes. "He is right! Nothing else matters. I love you, Marcela. Let's continue our story!" He then kissed her passionately.

Their kiss stayed intense as they slowly undressed each other. He couldn't be sure, but he didn't think their lips ever parted from the moment they started to kiss until they were done making love. They made love passionately, slowly, lovingly. It was amazing how the intensity kept rising each day between them. It was such an incredible feeling.

When they finally broke off their kiss, they just held each other. It was late, and they were both tired. He asked if she wanted to talk about the details of what they were going to do next. She told him that they could do that after they were back home and had time to think about how all of it needed to happen. Right now, she just wanted to look at him and feel their love for each other.

They looked at each other for some time before they drifted off to sleep. Marcela dreamed of the story she had just heard from Rocco. She felt like she was Marisa and lived her life. The dream was so real. She didn't wake once before Anastasio's alarm went off.

Chapter 8

They both slept peacefully and woke to Anastasio's alarm. He purposely set it earlier than he needed to give them time to talk, pack, and get to the airport. They hadn't made the decision if she was going to leave with him or if she was going to stay later because her flight was so much later than his.

He gave her a kiss good morning and smiled at her. He loved her being the first person he saw when he opened his eyes. She smiled back and said, "Good morning! How did you sleep?"

"I slept like a baby. I was hoping I was going to be able to stay up longer and watch you fall asleep, but everything was so peaceful when we were holding each other, I fell right asleep. How about yourself?"

"I slept well too. It's funny, but I dreamed about Rocco's story last night. I was the girl, Marisa, in his story. It felt so real, like I was really there! I'm so happy that we got to talk to him. So you really didn't know he spoke English?"

"I didn't have a clue! Even when we speak in French, occasionally he would talk a lot, but overall, he never one to talk very much. It was quite the surprise. And his story, wow! I mean, I can't imagine all that he experienced. The things he went through, the time he lived in, I can't imagine even one single thing that happened to him, much less the everyday struggle they went through. I always thought of Rocco with high regard, but this put him in a place in my heart that I will never be able to forget!"

"It's really amazing what people can go through and endure, isn't it? We think we know pain and hurt until someone comes along like Rocco, and we realize that our lives are so easy compared to some of the others out there!"

"It's all perception Marcela. The pain we know is real! It's what we know. And until we go through something better or worse, those are the things we know. Your pain, my pain, your love, my love, are real to us, because it's what we know. Until something else happens, it's as real as anything he has been through. I mean, I hope neither of us ever go through some of the things he has gone through, other than one thing. The one thing being the love he knew!"

"I think we are starting to know that now! Do you think we can live a life like that? Love each other that much that nothing could come between us? You won't tire of me?" she said playfully.

"I can't imagine ever being tired of you! And I sure hope we can live a life like that. I will do my best to show you every day what you mean to me. I will never intentionally hurt you and want to make your life better each day, not worse!"

Marcela gave him a long, soft kiss. "I know you will take good care of me. And I will do that for you as well. Everything that is important to me is in this bed right now!" she said and gave him another kiss.

He kept looking into her eyes and smiling at her. He thought she was the most incredible woman he had ever met. He never thought he'd be love struck like he was now. He needed to think of something else or he was never going to be able to get out of the bed and onto the things that needed to be done. "So have you decided if you are going to the airport with me, or are you going to go later and maybe get a little more rest?"

"I think I'll go with you. It may seem silly, but even getting to spend the few extra minutes in the car with you is worth sitting at the airport bar, drinking my sorrows away!" she said with a big smile.

"Okay, would you like to take a shower with me, then I can go pack and you do the same, and we can meet up after?"

"Sure. You know you're spoiling me! I don't know if I will remember how to shower myself when I'm not with you!"

"Well, then my sinister plan is working! You can't live without me!" He laughed and got up. "Come on now, I have hair to wash, and you don't want me to have to rush washing that amazing body of yours, would you?"

Even though she was very tired, and it was very early, she jumped out of bed and followed him to the shower. He started the shower and they both got in. Even though it had only been a few times, they had their ritual down. He washed her body and hair, and then she did the same to him. Of course, they kissed and get handsy, but they got done what needed to be done. They weren't in a huge hurry, but also didn't have time to do more than be flirtatious and tease each other. That was going to make the next few weeks without each other harder on both of them, but they didn't care.

After they were both dried off, he put on the shirt and pants from the night before. He grabbed the rest of his clothes and gave her a kiss. "It will take me about thirty to forty-five minutes to get ready and packed. What about you?"

"I think I will be closer to the forty-five minutes. Would you like me to meet you at your room?"

"No, why won't we meet in the lobby? If Rocco is there, I'd love to talk to him just a few more minutes more before we leave. He caught me by such surprise last night, I didn't even know what to say!"

"Okay, I'll see you down in the lobby soon!"

He gave her a kiss and was out the door. She looked around the room and tried to decide where to begin. She would pack as her hair dried a little bit. Then she would get ready. It was just a flight home, so she planned to just throw her hair back as usual and wear something comfortable. She started to fold her clothes. She left out what she was going to wear home, a pair of jeans, a T-shirt, and she had a sweatshirt she would carry, in case it was cold on the plane, like it usually was.

She picked her new dress off the floor. She looked forward to going through the photos from last night. She wasn't sure that she would ever look and feel as she did then. It was one of those rare moments in her life that she wished would happen more, but that's not how her life generally worked. But now, after meeting Anastasio, she didn't know what to expect. She folded it up neatly and started to place her clothing on her bed.

She put her suitcase on the bed and started by putting her shoes on the bottom of the bag and then other items. After about fifteen minutes of packing, she was done, outside of the things she needed to finish getting ready. She checked the closet, under the bed, and all the places she could imagine some piece of clothing finding and her going home without.

She went into the bathroom, brushed her teeth, dried her hair, and pulled it back in a ponytail. She looked at her face and decided that she could use a little concealer to cover up the blue shade under her eyes from the lack of sleep she had gotten. She had gotten lucky that her eyes weren't puffy underneath. She also added a little lip gloss. She didn't look glamorous like last night, but certainly good enough to fly home.

She packed up the rest of her stuff and still had about ten minutes to spare. She sat on the bed and closed her eyes. She thought about everything that had happened over the past week. She thought about how nervous she was getting on the plane and how the taxi driver was annoyed with her but was helpful. She needed to remember to call him and thank him for what he had done for her. She still had his number that he had given her. She thought about coming into the hotel and the way Rocco looked at her and showed her the room she was in now and the confusion of not knowing anything.

She stood up and went over to the window. The sun was just starting to come up, and she looked out over the street and buildings. The lights that were strung across were still lit up, and she smiled thinking about the block party they had attended, the dancing, the rain, oh, the rain. And then the person she didn't know she had inside of her came and took over, and she took a man she barely knew to her room and made love to him all night. She wished she knew of a place like this in Barcelona that she could escape to with Anastasio to relive their first moments together. But she guessed that they would have so many new moments that they would never run out of things that would be special to them. But this would always remain the closest to her heart, as it was the beginning of them. The start of a new life for her.

She shut the window, got her bag, and made her way to the door. She opened it and started to walk out. She was just about to shut the door and decided to take a photo of the room. During her time here, she hadn't thought to take a photo of the room, but now it seemed important. She took a few photos, but she knew that no matter how long she lived and what happened in her life, she would never forget the way this room looked. What seemed so small and unimportant ended up being one of the most memorable things she had experienced up until now.

She finished taking pictures of the room and closed the door and started making her way downstairs. She didn't want this time to end but was looking forward to the next chapter of her life. She thought of her dream and of Marisa and could see her and Anastasio growing old together like that. She had to laugh at thinking of them growing old together. She never thought she'd be one of those women that thought about things like that. She lived her life day by day, not really thinking about the future before now.

~

Anastasio got to his room and took off the clothes he had put on to leave Marcela's room. He found a pair of jeans and put them on. He went and brushed his teeth and did his hair. He put on a polo type of shirt, found some socks, and put on his shoes. He didn't need anything else out to be on his way home.

His stuff was pretty organized, and packing for him was easy. He traveled so much that it was almost second nature for him. He knew the order of how he liked everything packed. He knew the order in which he checked the room for stuff that he may leave behind, like phone chargers and things like that. He knew he had everything he needed. He wasn't quite ready to leave, but he was ready for the next few weeks to be done so he could be with Marcela as soon as possible.

The only thing he didn't pack was the pink button-down shirt she had worn back to her room earlier in the week. He wanted her to have something of his, and she seemed to really like it. He sprayed it with some of his cologne. He folded it and put it in a little bag for her. He looked around and knew he had everything. He normally didn't linger, but he took a few moments to take in everything and remember their time here.

He left the room and headed downstairs. As always, Rocco was behind the desk. He wondered if and when he ever slept. He couldn't remember a time when he would come or go from the hotel and Rocco wasn't there to greet him. He already had so much respect for Rocco, but after the talk they had last night, his own view of him changed. He looked up to him and knew he was wiser than most anyone he ever met.

Just after a few moments after he got downstairs, he heard her coming down the stairs. She joined him by the counter, and Rocco came around and stood with them. He gave them each a hug and asked that they come visit him sometime. He smiled at them with his big smile and escorted them to the front of the hotel and held the door open for them.

As soon as they walked out the door, Marcela remembered that she hadn't paid for the room. Even though Rocco had told her to give whatever she felt she could, she didn't want to leave him upset that maybe she didn't pay enough. "Rocco, I haven't paid you for the room yet." She started to open her purse, and he stopped her.

"To know that my story led to this hotel and on to your story is payment enough for me! Please let me know how you two are doing until the next time we see each other."

She still wanted to give him money but knew he also may be offended by it. So she just gave him another hug and kiss. "Thank you, Rocco! Your story is inspiring, and I can't imagine anything stopping us from making our own beautiful story."

Bernard was there waiting and immediately came and took their bags. He looked Marcela and pointed to her bags. She nodded that she was going now, and he could take her bag as well. They said one last goodbye to Rocco. She hoped that they would be able to come back soon and spend more time there. This was the beginning of them becoming an us, and she would never forget a detail. She took a photo of Rocco standing in front of the hotel.

They all got in the car, and Rocco stood there and waved at them as they drove off. Marcela wanted to look back but didn't. Everything in her life now was looking forward, not backward. She would look for the reasons to do things instead of not doing things and live instead of just filling space and time. She had become who her mother was and wanted her to be within a matter of days. She smiled and knew that her mom was watching from above and was proud of her.

Bernard stayed quiet on the drive to the airport. Anastasio took her hand in his and gave it a kiss. She looked at him. She couldn't tell if she saw sadness or happiness in his eyes. She guessed that her eyes probably showed the same thing. She wasn't ready to not be by his side but knew that soon he would be by her side forever. But goodbyes were never easy for her! She needed to break this train of thought. "So what is the first thing you will do when you get back home?" she asked to get her mind on other things.

"Call you and make sure you are behaving and not flirting with some stranger at the airport?" he said jokingly. She would actually probably still be waiting at the airport when he arrived.

"You know me! Maybe I can introduce you to the new guy and you can have a new friend!" she joked in reply.

"Seriously, I will go home and tell my father of the good news of the meetings." He never called on his trips. He liked telling him in person what had transpired. Technology was great, but something about being able to look someone in the eye and talk with him still meant something to him. "Then I'm not sure. Not that I'm a child and need permission, but I have to think about how I'm going to break the news to my mother and father about my future plans. My dad will likely be happy for me, and I can't see him saying anything negative. I'm sure he'll worry about what will happen with the vineyard, but I will reassure him that I will still be very dedicated to keeping things going the best I can.

"My mom, she's a whole other thing. She won't be happy about me leaving. She will come around in time, but I'm sure it won't be pleasant in the beginning with her! I will have to think of the best way to break this to her. She will try to find ways to keep me there. She's never wanted me far away."

"Are you sure you are making the right decision? If it's going to hurt your family, I can come to you! I don't want to make things hard on you and your family. I don't have any family around. I really don't mind coming to you!"

"No, I don't want you to give up your life. I wouldn't mind getting away. I can work from anywhere, and I don't want you to have to give up your life. I don't have many friends there, and I'd love to be where you are. Our love is what matters, not where we are! Everything will be okay in the end. You are what matters. Nothing else!"

She didn't have any words. They were still looking at each other, and she knew he was serious and meant every word he said. She loved the man he was. She loved the way he made her feel as if nothing were more important in life other than her. She felt the same for him. She didn't care where they were, what they did, if she was with him, the world would seem right. He was amazing man, and she would do anything for him. She knew he would do the same for her.

They were getting close to the airport now. Her heart was beginning to race. Although she knew the goodbye would have to come eventually, she wasn't ready yet! Her palms got sweaty, and she started to fidget. He gripped her hand, and she looked back at him again.

"Don't be sad, this isn't goodbye! We will talk every day, and in a few weeks, I'll be looking into your beautiful eyes again! It's hard for me too. But I know where I'll be soon. I will be in your arms. You will be in my heart and mind until those few days pass!"

She, again, didn't have words. She knew anything she'd say would make her cry. This was a happy time, not sad. She buried her head into his neck and held on to his hand. She hoped to feel his touch every day. She had thought the phrase "you complete me" was silly until now. Now she understood what it really meant. He did complete her!

They arrived at the airport, and they all got out of the car. Bernard got the bags out of the trunk as they waited. She wanted one more photo of them all together. She found someone to take the photo of all of them. It was time for Bernard to leave, and they all hugged and said their goodbyes to him. He gave a big smile to Marcela, got in the car, and left.

Reality was really starting to set in. She wasn't ready for this! But she remembered when she was coming, she wasn't ready for that either, and she saw how that turned out. They went to his ticket counter first and checked in and they took his bag. Then they did the same for hers. Luckily, they were flying out of the same terminal. They went through the security checkpoints and customs. They had about two hours before his flight was to leave.

They found a restaurant that was open, and they sat at the bar. They both ordered a morning drink and some breakfast. Both of them were quieter than usual, as neither of them were ready to part from each other. He broke the silence and asked, "So now that you know what my plans are for when I get home, what will be your first things you will do?"

"My friend will be picking me up from the airport, and I assume he'll want to go to dinner. I'm sure he will have lots of questions about you. He knows me better than I know myself sometimes. He will be shocked that I have met someone and all that has happened over the last six days. I'm sure he will be thrilled for me but will want to know everything about you. He's a great guy! He will be in my corner until the day either of us don't have a breath left in us. I think you guys will get along very well. He's very laid-back like you are. He's just protective of me!

After that, I will go home. I would love to say I'd unpack and get everything organized, but I think I will probably go home and just try to relax for the evening. It will be hard being home and not knowing that my mom won't be around to talk to." For the first time in days, she had tears in her eyes.

He took her hand into his and kissed it gently. "I know it will be very difficult for you! Please know that you can call me at any time if you need or want to talk. I really don't care what time it is! Is it possible your friend could stay the night or even a few nights to help you?"

"Yeah, he could, and he would for me! But I will have to face being alone at some point, I might as well start now. Only time will make it better, I hope anyways. And soon you will be with me. That will help things. But I know it will be hard for a while. This isn't really the time to talk about things like this, but we haven't talked much about the details of you coming to Barcelona. Would you like to live together, or would you prefer your own place? Please don't answer if you're not ready to!"

"Well, we will discuss it, but I'd love to live together. But if you aren't ready for that, I have no problems getting my own place. I just want to be close to you! Whether that's living together or close by you and seeing you when we can, I'll do it! I'm open to what you feel comfortable with!"

"I'd really like if you stayed with me! I know we've only known each other for several days, but there is just something about you. I trust you. I want you. I need you. I desire you! I would love for us to live together. I don't have a mansion or some lovely country home that I imagine you live in now. But it's home for now. You are more than welcome there!"

"I could care less if he lived in a shack or a home that could fit a whole country. You are what's important! They say home is where the heart is! My heart is with you. So I don't care about the other stuff. I will provide for you the best I know how and love you!"

She squeezed his hand and looked into his eyes. Her tears were still in her eyes. He leaned over and kissed her forehead. "I know things will be difficult for you. I am here for you in any way I can be for you! I hope you know that!"

"Thank you, Anastasio. I know you are here for me. And it really means the world to me. Truly! I have a few good friends that are there for me. But having you, that means more to me than anything! I love you!"

"I love you too!"

Their breakfast arrived. They ate in almost silence again. It was hard for both of them to leave one another. It was going to be a long few weeks for them. Neither of them wanted to think or talk about it. But it was hanging there in the air. He wished he could just hop on the flight with her and be with her from this moment on. But that, unfortunately, isn't how life works. They had lives they had to return to. In time, they would be together. But at this moment, it wasn't easy for either of them.

They ate their breakfast and finished their drinks. It was getting close to time for him to get to his gate and board his flight. He settled the bill, and they walked slowly to his gate. He wished he could just skip this part and fly home with her. But he had to live in reality. It would only be a few weeks! He would be busy with work and getting prepared to move. It would go by quick, and he would be back with her.

They got to his gate, and they were just starting to board the plane. She didn't want to see him leave. They were holding hands, and he turned and looked into her eyes. "It will only be a few weeks. But we'll talk every day, and we'll be together soon! Will you call me when you arrive in Barcelona? You will be on your flight when I get home."

"Of course, I will! Will you call and leave me a message that you arrive as well?"

"Sure." He gave her a big hug and kiss. "I have to go. We'll talk later tonight. I wish you a safe flight. I look forward to talking to you later."

She gave him another kiss. "Have a good flight! Now go before I kidnap you!" She gave him a playful push toward the line of people waiting to board the flight.

"I'll talk to you soon. I love you!"

"I love you too!"

He showed his ticket to the agent and turned and looked at her one last time before he disappeared down the ramp to the plane. She took a deep breath and went and sat on a seat by the window and stared at his plane. She wished she could see through it and watch him until he was actually gone. It had only been a few minutes, but it already felt like days. She guessed that the next few weeks would feel like a lifetime!

She sat there until the plane was pushed back and started to make its way to the runway. She slowly walked to her gate. She was feeling very mixed emotions. She was sad that he was gone. But she could still feel his eyes looking into hers. She didn't think that she would ever not be able to envision that. The thought made her smile as she made her way to her gate.

She sat at her gate, wondering what he was thinking about. She tried to make her time productive and think about what she was going to tell Antonio. She thought about little things like cleaning out her closet and dresser to make room for his clothes. She had no idea how much stuff he had, but they would deal with whatever needed to be done about that when it came up.

She thought about her work, and she was inspired to design some new things after meeting Jacqueline. She was hoping she could come up with something special that she could make for her as a small token of appreciation. She also had some other ideas that she thought she could put together.

Before she knew it, it was time for her to board her flight. She guessed he was probably about halfway home now. Her flight would be about five hours. She got lucky and had the row to herself and was able to spread her stuff out and start to draw out some ideas for the new designs. She tried to keep her mind busy. But every few minutes, he would enter her mind, and she would see his face and smile. The thought made her smile! She couldn't wait until they landed, and she could hear his voice.

She kept busy with her work until the pilot came on the speaker and told them it was almost time to land. She packed her stuff back up. She looked forward to checking her voice mail and hearing his voice. And she was also extremely excited to see Antonio and share all the excitement of her trip. She thought about going home to an empty house and thought that maybe she would ask Antonio to stay over. But she also thought that she needed to just do it on her own and start her healing process. She'd decide later, she thought.

The plane landed, and she immediately turned on her phone and called to check her voice mail before there was even an indication that she had one. There were two messages. The first was Antonio. He said he'd be by the baggage claim area and for her to call him when we got in. The second was Anastasio. "Hi, baby! I just landed and you have been on my mind the whole flight. I hope your flight is going well. Call me when you get the first chance. I love you!"

She decided to call Antonio first and let him know her flight was in and she'd be there as soon as she could. He said he was there and ready to see her and hear all about her trip. She rushed him off the phone so she could make the call she really wanted to make. She dialed Anastasio's number, and he answered on the first ring.

"Hi, baby. How was your flight?" It was so wonderful to hear his voice! Her smile widened, and she closed her eyes for a moment and imagined he was sitting right beside her, touching her hand, talking to her.

"My flight was fine. I had the whole row to myself, so I laid my stuff out and tried to work some. How about yours? I assume you made it home with no problems?"

"Yes, I got home a few hours ago. I got home and talked with my dad about what happened with the meetings. My mom was out until just a few moments ago. I don't have anything I really have to do tomorrow, so I plan to talk to my parents about everything. Is your friend still picking you up?"

"Yes, he's here. I plan on taking him to dinner for picking me up and so I can share the past week with him. I know it will sound silly, but I already miss you!"

"It's not silly at all. I was actually just thinking the same thing. I was just sitting here with my phone in my hand, waiting for your call. I feel like a teenage boy again. Waiting on the call from the girl he really likes. Only in this case, the woman I love!"

"You are too sweet! Do you know that?" She didn't wait for an answer. "I'm about to have to get off the plane and go through the drill I'm sure you know all too well. Can I call you after I get home after dinner? It might be kind of late and don't want to wake you if you are tired!"

"I'll be here. Don't worry about what time it is. But don't worry about calling me if you are tired or your friend will be staying with you."

"I will call you! I wish I could talk to you from now until I fall asleep. But I'll have to settle for later."

"Okay, I wish you a wonderful dinner with your friend, and I will be here whenever you are done and can talk."

"Sounds perfect! I'll talk to you soon!"

They ended the call, and she made her way off the plane. She made it to her baggage relatively quickly and found Antonio waiting for her. She was happy to see him, and he looked happy to see her as well. She made it to him, and they gave each other a long hug. To people around her, they probably would think that he was her boyfriend or husband. She did love him but not in that kind of way. His hugs always made her feel warm and happy.

"I'm happy you are home! You look great! And it looks like you got a little sun!"

"Thank you! Yes, the weather was amazing there, and I spent a lot of time outside. Are you hungry? I'd like to go to dinner and tell you again the trip!"

"You already knew we were going to dinner. And you know that I am always ready to eat. And you know I want to know everything about your trip!"

She gave him another short hug. "It's good to see you!"

Her bags came shortly after, and they walked to his car. He was talking to her about random stuff. She knew he would save the questions about the trip until they were at dinner. He always really paid attention to every word she said. That was one of his best qualities. He always paid attention to the small details and really cared about what she had to say. She noticed that he was that way with everyone she knew of. He was just a genuinely caring person and cared about his friends like they were family.

She suggested they eat at a tapas restaurant that they both always enjoyed. It was true that he was always ready to eat. She was the same way. They were both food lovers. At this place, they could order many different dishes and enjoy eating and having a drink or two. And of course this time, they would talk about her trip. She really couldn't wait until she got to tell him everything.

He seemed pleased with her suggestion of where they were going to eat, and they made their way to the restaurant. It wasn't too long of a drive. They were both in a great mood. He put on music, and they found themselves singing along and laughing. He would purposely change some of the words to make the songs funny. He was glad she had met him years earlier. She was an important part of his life.

They got to the restaurant and were seated right away. They didn't even need to look at the menu. They pretty much always had the same dishes. They ordered beers and their food. It was now that time to talk about her trip. He looked at and said, "So tell me about your trip! Did you have fun?"

She hadn't really thought about where she was going to start, so she just started from the beginning. She told him about almost turning back and going home at the airport, to the flight and her dream on the plane, then told her about her taxi ride. He laughed at her when she told him about that part. He could see the driver's face in his mind. He had to think she was crazy!

She then told him about getting to the hotel and how nervous she was. She told him about her encounter with the owner and how she didn't have a clue what was going on with how much she was paying or anything. She almost didn't even believe the story she was telling. It was so crazy and unlike her. She could tell he was surprised by what she had done. His mouth was already hanging open, and she hadn't even gotten to how she met Anastasio.

Their food came, and they picked different foods and put them on their plates. As they started to eat, she told him about how she met Anastasio. Antonio looked like he was going to fall out of his seat as she told her about meeting him, going to dinner, and then the block party. She told him in detail about the wine and the people she met.

She suddenly got really shy about telling him about the rest of the night. To him, it was probably going to sound irresponsible and stupid of her. But she always told him everything. They were enjoying the food, and she wanted to tell him everything. She built up her courage and started with telling him about dancing with him. She told him about dancing in the rain and his face said everything he was thinking.

He couldn't believe what she was telling him. In all the time he knew her, he had never known her to do anything even remotely close to what she was telling him. He had so many questions but would wait until the end to start all his questions. He just listened and sat there in shock. He hadn't decided if it was good or bad yet, but it was shock, none the less.

She told him about taking Anastasio to her room, and she didn't get into lots of detail with that part but told him that they were intimate. She felt a little embarrassed to tell him about that part. She got through it though. Her shyness of telling him about having Anastasio in her room and being completely intimate. She had gotten through the hard part, so the rest was going to be a piece of cake.

Over the next hour and a half, she told him about the rest of the week. The people she met, the things they did, and how happy she was that she took the trip. She looked at him and smiled. "So there's one last thing I need to tell you. Anastasio is coming to live here with me in a few weeks!" She stopped talking and waited for his response.

He sat there for a few moments before he first spoke. He wanted to choose his words carefully. "I'm sorry, I'm just in shock here! Are you telling me, that you, Marcela, did all these things? Where is the Marcela I knew a week ago?"

She wasn't sure if he was happy or upset with her story. "I'm still me! I just finally opened up the way you and others wanted me to. Do you think I've lost my mind?"

"I'm just really surprised. I mean, I'm happy for you! You deserve to be happy more than anyone I can think of. You seem to be sure of how you feel about Anastasio. I don't want to doubt you, but are you certain you two are in love and it wasn't just a great feeling to have someone and infatuation instead of love?"

"I believe it without a doubt in my mind!"

He looked at her and then gave her a big smile. "Then let me be the first to congratulate you!" He got out of his chair and gave her a hug. "I'm incredibly happy for you! You deserve to be in love and have real happiness!"

He sat back down, and they continued to talk about the trip. He asked lots of questions, and she felt all the worry about how he would take it go away. She knew he was sincere in being happy for her. They finished up their drinks, and it was starting to get late. "Are you ready to get out of here and get home?" he asked.

"Yeah, I think that's probably the best idea. I'm not really looking forward to going home, but I have to face it sometime!"

They asked for the check, and she grabbed it before he could even try to take it. He knew better than to try to argue with her and let her pay for the dinner. "You didn't have to do that but thank you!"

"It is my pleasure. Thank you for picking me up and listening to my rambling!"

"You never ramble. I'm so happy for you!"

They left the restaurant, and he drove her home. They talked about what she was going to do in the few days and if she was going to be all right being alone. She assured him that she would manage, and she would call him if she weren't. He would always be there for her, and she knew that! She also had Anastasio to lean on if she needed it.

Her thoughts turned to calling Anastasio again, and her fear of going home started to fade. She enjoyed her time with Antonio, but she was looking forward to hearing Anastasio's voice again. She didn't even care what they talked about. She just wanted to feel close to him in any way possible.

They got to her house, and Antonio helped her inside with her bag. He didn't stay for long but made sure she was doing okay before he left. She thanked him again for picking her up and for his friendship. He left, and she got comfortable and opened a bottle of wine. She would forever now look at wine differently after meeting Anastasio. She would pay attention to the different styles and try to learn as much as she could about the different wines. She poured a glass of wine and sat in the chair in her living room and called Anastasio.

She called him, and he answered quickly again. He sounded tired when he answered though. "Hi, there. How was your dinner?"

"It was great, thank you. Did I wake you?"

"No, I was just catching up on some reading!" He was reading, but he wasn't feeling well either. His stomach was bothering him again. But he had the next few days to relax and recover from the trip. "Is Antonio still with you, or did you go home by yourself?"

"I decided to come home alone. It will be hard for a little while I'm sure. But I'm a big girl. I need to be able to do things on my own."

"I understand. Anything I can do to help?"

"You already are! Just hearing your voice makes me happy and brings a smile to my face. I look forward to seeing that cute face of yours again very soon!"

"You always bring a smile to my face too. Why don't you get some rest? What do you have planned for tomorrow?"

"I plan to sleep in a bit, unpack, and hopefully go to my shop for a little while. I had a few ideas on the way home I'd like to start working. What about yourself?"

"I think I'll sleep in too. I want to organize my calendar and start seeing what the best dates are to make this move happen. Then when my parents are around, I am going to break the news to them. I'm sure my mother will have all kinds of questions and suggestions to change my mind. I know it will take her time to come to terms with me leaving the area, but she'll come around at some point!" He really wasn't looking forward to talking with them. He knew his dad would understand and be happy for him. He always trusted Anastasio's decisions. His mother was a whole other story.

"Are you sure you're up for that? Is your mom going to hate me for taking you away?" She really didn't like the idea of anyone he was close to not liking her. She didn't want to cause any problems with his family either.

"Don't worry about her. She's harmless! It will take some time, like I said. But once she gets to know you, she'll see that we make each other happy, and she'll come around. She isn't as bad as I make her sound. She just has her own ways and her own thoughts."

"Well, do what you think is best! I hope she does like me sooner rather than later though!"

"I think it would be impossible not to like you! Okay, get some rest! Do you mind if I call you tomorrow night? I think we both need some rest now."

"I'd love for you to call anytime you can. Get some sleep, and I'll talk to you tomorrow."

"Will do. You can dream about me until then!" he said and laughed.

"Good night, you!"

"Good night!" She hung up the phone and sat in her chair for a while, sipping her wine. She thought about him talking with his parents. She didn't like the idea that his mom wasn't going to like her. She didn't want to feel like she was taking him away from anyone.

But after they talked about it all, it did make the most sense. She would think of ways to ensure his mom knew she would be good for him. She would do whatever it took to win his parents over.

Chapter 9

Anastasio didn't sleep well all night. His stomach was giving him problems. In addition, he was stressed trying to think of the best way to talk to his parents. He knew his mother's reaction wasn't to be a good one. He wanted to put it out of his mind as he could tell the stress of it was making his stomach feel worse. But it sat there, lingering in his mind as he lay there restlessly. All he wanted to do was sleep. His thoughts would come easier with rest and feeling better.

He found himself getting up several times to get sick throughout the night. He knew if he could just get to sleep, he would be better! But the hours continued to pass without sleep. He tried to think about the conversation with his parents he was going to have again. He just couldn't keep focused for more than a few minutes at a time. The only comfort he found was thinking about Marcela. He imagined she was beside him there now. He closed his eyes and could see her face, her eyes burning into his soul. He could feel her touch on his face and the softness of her skin. He could smell her scent when he breathed in. The thoughts of her relaxed him but unfortunately not enough to get him to sleep.

Before he knew it, the sun was beginning to rise. He finally decided to just get up and get his day going. Sleep was not going to come! And maybe by busying himself with work, the pain in his stomach would go away. Hopefully later in the day, he could get a nap in. He really wanted and needed sleep. He thought of Marcela and hoped she was sleeping well. He wanted to call her and tell her good morning. But he didn't want to wake her up or for her to know he was up all night for that matter. He thought it best not to call her until later that afternoon or evening.

He got up and took a long shower. He let the water run over his shoulders to relax him as much as he could be feeling so sick. He missed having her with him, but this was how real life worked. Even when they would be together for the rest of their lives, they wouldn't be together every day especially when he had to travel for work. But he liked the thought of every moment he could anyways.

After he finished his shower and got dressed, he went downstairs and made breakfast. He could hear his parents stirring, so he decided to make them breakfast as well. His mother was normally the first one up, and she often made breakfast for them. It was nice when he could return the favor. Besides, he liked to cook. When he was married, he was the cook in that relationship and loved every minute of it.

He made scrambled eggs, bacon, home-fried potatoes, and toast. He found fresh oranges and made fresh-squeezed orange juice. He also made coffee. He wasn't much of a coffee drinker, but his parents, especially his dad, had to have it in the mornings. As long as he could remember, his dad had never missed a breakfast. It was never something like cereal or something you just picked up and ate. His mother made breakfast every morning without fail.

He was almost done making breakfast when they made their way to the kitchen. His mom was the first in the kitchen and commented, "Wow, what a surprise! So nice of you. You shouldn't have troubled yourself though. You just got home. I would've made breakfast!"

His dad just smiled at him and said, "Good morning!"

"Morning to both of you! And it's no problem, Mom. I was up early and thought I could make us breakfast. Please, sit down and enjoy!"

Being the mother that she was, she didn't just sit down. She made him sit as she brought everything to the table. She poured the juice for all of them and coffee for herself and his dad. She finally sat down, and they all began to make their plates up and start to eat. His mom raised her eyebrows and said, "You did a good job! You trying to take over around here?"

"Of course not, Mom! You can't be replaced! Just was up and wanted to do something nice for you!"

"Who said anything about replacing me? You know there is no one that can replace me! So does your father!"

His dad didn't even look up from his food at her comment. He continued to just eat. His dad tended to be a sarcastic man, and his comments would get him in trouble. So most of the time, he decided to stay quiet until a time she wasn't around. She didn't particularly like his sense of humor. He had the same sense of humor his father had. When they were alone together, they could joke all they wanted in good fun. His father loved his mother, and he loved them both. They were simply different in ways, like anyone else was.

His mom broke the silence. "How was your trip? I'm sorry I missed you last night. I was at one of my friend's house visiting, and I lost track of time."

"The trip went well. I already told Dad, but the meetings went well. I'd say better than I expected. I actually have some ideas that I thought about while on the trip that I want to talk with you both about later."

"We're already here. What ideas do you have?" she asked before his dad could even react.

"I'm not completely prepared to talk about it yet. I still need to work on some details, but if you two have time maybe before or after dinner, we could talk then?"

"Okay, Mr. Secretive! I will make dinner tonight, and after dinner, we can all talk," she suggested, not even bothering to ask his dad if that was okay with him.

They continued to eat now in silence. He was happy that his mom didn't ask any more questions for now. He really didn't want to get into anything until later. He needed time to get his schedule together, figure out a good date for him to transition, and come up with answers to objections he knew she was going to come up with. He was going to have a busy morning and afternoon.

~

She had finished her glass of wine and went and got ready for bed. She took the shirt that Anastasio had given her and chose to sleep in it. She loved the way it looked on her, the smell of his cologne on it, and just the fact that it was his. She didn't remember falling asleep or any of her dreams. She felt rested and was surprised by the ease she went to sleep in her empty house. Normally her mom would come and stay the night a few times a week. Her clothes were still in the bedroom she always slept in. Marcela woke after a nice, long night of sleep.

She took her time getting out of bed. She went into the kitchen, thinking that she would have to go to the store this morning to get some food. But it appeared her thoughtful friend had done that for her before she got home. She couldn't believe she hadn't noticed it last night when she opened the wine. She would have to thank him for his consideration. He had gotten her fresh fruit, juices, milk, and all the things she would need to make some meals. She was hungry, and she couldn't have been more thrilled by the surprise.

She made some instant oatmeal with fresh strawberries and some juice. She sat at the bar in her kitchen and watched some news on the TV as she ate her breakfast. She had ignored the rest of the world for the last week. She had no idea what was going on in the world now, and it was nice to get caught up a little bit. As she was watching, she thought of Anastasio and was wondering what he was doing at that exact moment.

She finished up her breakfast and cleaned up the kitchen. She found her phone and called Antonio. "I can't believe you! Thank you so much for getting the groceries for me. I didn't even notice last night and thought I was going to have to go to the store this morning, and I got such a nice surprise when I really looked in the kitchen!"

"It was my pleasure. I knew you'd be getting home late and didn't want you not to have food to eat! Did you sleep okay? How was your night?" he asked.

"I actually got a lot of sleep, and everything was okay last night. The house is quiet, and it's going to be hard, but I'll be okay. I did better than I ever expected to last night. I had opened a bottle of wine, thinking it may take that to keep me okay, but I had one glass, and I was fine. I didn't even really need the glass. But it was relaxing."

"That makes me feel better. I was worried about you last night! I wanted to call to make sure you were okay but didn't want to wake you if you were sleeping!"

"You know you can call me anytime! You're never a bother! Are you still planning on going to your shop today?"

"Yes, I will probably go in a bit. I need to unpack and shower. Then I will head over there for a few hours I think."

"And did you get a chance to talk to Anastasio last night?"

"Yes, we talked for a short while. We will talk again tonight!"

"Good! All seems to be in order then. Call me later? Maybe this weekend we can do lunch or dinner?"

"Sounds good to me. If you want, come over tomorrow night, and I'll cook. We'll eat, drink, and find some good, sappy movie to watch!"

"It's a date. Is about six o'clock okay?"

"Perfect. See you then!"

"Until then, have a wonderful day! Let me know if you want me to bring anything!"

"Okay. See you tomorrow!"

Anastasio got on his laptop and started to go through his schedule. In the past few years, he was pretty loose with his schedule. Most of the time, he didn't have too much of a reason to keep a tight schedule. Business was slow. He was home with his parents trying to help in any way he could. That meant that he left a lot of schedule open. He wanted to be able to really help and be there for his family. But things were going to change now. He'd still be there for his family no matter what, but Marcela was where his heart and mind was. And he hoped she was going to be his family.

He made calls and changed some meetings around to give him a week gap in his schedule. He thought that should be good enough to get to Barcelona and settle before he had his next meeting. He would have to travel several times in the next few months to different countries to either try to retain their business or get new business. He would go back to the vineyard here and there for a few days to help his father with whatever he could. He wasn't just going to leave his family behind because he was moving to Barcelona.

He kept himself busy most of the morning and early afternoon. His stomach was still giving him issues, but he pushed through it. He would go to the doctor in the next few days and get checked out. He assumed the stress, even though it was good stress, was causing the problems. In addition, he really hadn't rested in the last week. He didn't think there was much the doctor could do other than telling him to get rest and reduce his stress. He had been a healthy person most of his life and didn't think that was going to change now.

He pressed on and continued to call, make future appointments, and arrange his schedule. God was on his side as everyone he called either agreed to the changes or confirmed their original meetings. Even the potential clients seemed to fit his schedule perfectly. He planned it the best that he could. He now had a solid nine days off. That was more than he expected and was happy with the results. He wanted sufficient time to move and get settled before moving, and he was getting the time he needed.

The next call was to his doctor. His doctor scheduled him into his schedule a few days later. He was happy about that part but not happy that he even had to schedule an appointment. It was likely he had some kind of stomach flu or food poisoning that would just take a few days of medications, and he would be as good as new in a few days. He would be back to himself in no time.

He finished up with his calls and emails for work and closed his computer. He put the dates of where and when he had meetings and when he was off into his phone calendar. He also wrote it onto a regular calendar to have it in writing when he was leaving to give to his parents. He knew his mom would ask him over and over again about when he was leaving and try to make some kind of plans during that time to keep him there longer. He wasn't going to let that happen!

After he wrote everything out, he thought about how he was going to sit them down and tell them about the trip, meeting Marcela, and falling in love with her. The thought of falling in love with someone so quickly still surprised him, but it was that way with her! She had taken him completely by surprise! He would tell him about his decision to move to Spain to be with her. He knew this would take his mother by complete surprise!

He made up a schedule that he could give them. It said when he could be there helping them, when he was at meetings, and when he'd be home with Marcela. He liked the way that sounded. "Home with Marcela!" Even though he hadn't seen her house, been there yet, or moved there, his heart was already there. She was his home now! He needed to find the words to be able to explain to his mother.

He planned to remind her that his mom and his dad met and married fairly quickly. He knew she would say it was different back then, and it didn't work like that anymore. But the whole truth of it was, relationships have always worked the same. Love was the same now as it was two hundred years ago. Social acceptance and things like that had changed. But you couldn't help falling in love when it's really there! It didn't seem to matter whether you knew the person for ten years or ten days; the heart knew. Over the years, people had just thought that we had gotten smarter than our hearts and think we could control it. It's likely that's how love got really messed up, trying to control something that you couldn't!

And he wasn't a kid anymore. He shouldn't even have to explain his actions. But he learned to respect his parents from the time he was little, and this was part of a sign of respect. He would talk to them, listen to what they had to say, and tell them what he decided. He was sure his dad would understand and really wanted whatever would be best for Anastasio. His mother did really care about him, but she wasn't going to let him go easily.

He decided to lie down for a bit and try to rest a little more before doing the rest of the things he needed to do. He realized that for the first time in a long time that he was a little stressed. There was the stress of talking with his parents and planning the move. There was also the stress of not feeling well for several days now. And there was the good stress of starting something new and the excitement of it! It all was taking a toll on him, and he needed more rest. He wanted to be able to think clearly when talking with his parents tonight. He closed his eyes, and luckily, it didn't take long for him to fall asleep.

~

Marcela made it to her store around eleven o'clock. She wasn't planning on opening up the store to the public. She just wanted to start working on the few ideas she had worked on while on the plane on the way home while it was still fresh in her mind. The ideas were simple enough. If she worked hard on it for a few days, she could probably get the close to what she wanted. It would take time to perfect it after that, but soon she thought she could have a couple of nice pieces inspired by her new friend Jacqueline.

After being gone for the last week, it felt a little strange to be back there, but it was her comfort zone. For years, this was all she really knew. She had often wondered before she met Anastasio if she'd ever balance her life out and work less. Now she knew without a doubt she'd balance her life in an instant! She couldn't imagine a day going by that she wouldn't want to rush home a hurry to be back with him.

She thought for a moment about Anastasio's work schedule and wondered how often he'd be out of town and for how long. She didn't want to think about ever coming home without him there! It had only been a day now, but she already missed him, like she never knew she could miss someone. She realized at that moment that again she hadn't really been thinking of her mother. How had he done that to her? Before the trip, she thought that the trip would be boring and that she would sulk and not enjoy herself. And then when she had to come home, she thought that she would be a mess without her mother being around. But here she was now, thinking of him with a smile on her face, looking forward to her future for the first time that she could remember.

She busied herself with her designs, and the time started to fly by. Before she knew it, it was getting close to evening. She made more progress than she had expected. She had more inspiration in her than she had in a long time. She wanted to take advantage of this time! She knew when her mind was like this, she created things easily, and that didn't always happen. She was happy that she was able to work and accomplish so much today. She didn't know if she was going to be able to concentrate, but she really was able to.

She figured she would work for a few more hours, then go home and find something to make for dinner. She knew Anastasio would be calling at some point during the evening. That brought another smile to her face. She missed his face, his smile, his intense look he gave her, and his conversations! She replayed them all in her mind time and time again, like rewinding a movie you had seen over and over.

She put her focus back on the pieces she was working on. As she worked, she smiled at the recent memories of meeting Jacqueline and Rocco and everything she had done and all the people she met in Paris. She hoped that she would be able to go back sometime soon and relive it all. That week had marked the beginning of the rest of her life. There were so many uncertainties in her life after her mom had passed. But Paris proved to her that life kept going, and everything did happen for a reason! With those thoughts in her head, her hands worked the metals, and the pieces started to come to life.

After a few hours of restful sleep, Anastasio woke up. It took him a few minutes to gather his thoughts and get out of the bed. He couldn't remember his dreams, but he knew they were peaceful, and for the first time in several days, he felt rested. He lay there just a bit longer before finally getting up. He wanted to have some more time to think about what to say to his parents before he headed downstairs. It was getting close to getting dark outside, so he knew it was getting awfully close to dinnertime.

He felt calmer about talking with his parents now that his mind was rested. He sat at his desk and checked his emails and phone for messages. There was nothing there of importance. So he shut down his laptop and decided to send Marcela a quick message. He wrote, "Hi. I'm sorry I haven't called yet. I was just trying to finish some things up, and I will be having dinner and talking with my parents tonight. I will call you after. I'm thinking about you!"

He put his phone down on the desk and went and freshened up. After he brushed his teeth and brushed his hair, he changed his shirt and headed downstairs. He was nervous but was ready to get this part over with. He tried to believe that he could convince his mom that this was a great choice and would be good for all of them. He was going to give it all he could to make her understand his decision.

He made his way downstairs and into the kitchen. He could smell the food from the stairway. When he entered the kitchen, he saw his mom standing in front of the stove stirring the pasta sauce he had grown up loving so much. She had the best sauce that he had ever had, and that wasn't just his opinion. Every time he had a friend or girlfriend over, they couldn't seem to get enough of it. He knew his mom took pride in everything she made, especially her sauce! He considered himself a good cook, but he couldn't cook the way she did. He had tried tirelessly to make it how she did, but with no success.

He walked up behind his mom and gave her a kiss on the cheek. "It smells amazing as usual, Mama."

She smiled and said, "Thank you. Will you set the table for us?"

His dad was sitting at the table already, flipping through the newspaper. Anastasio put the plates out and got glasses for the wine and water. He found a bottle of red wine and poured each of them a glass. Once he was finished, he sat with his dad. "Anything interesting going on in the world today?"

"Same old stuff, different day, I suppose!" he replied.

His mom had finished cooking, and he helped her bring everything to the table. They sat and started to fix their plates. His dad put away the paper and took for drink of his wine. His face lit up by the taste and the pride of what their vineyard produced. Without saying a word, they all started to eat. Anastasio was nervous to start the conversation, but he also knew it wasn't going to get any easier, so he decided to start. "I wanted to talk to you both about something that happened to me on my trip."

His mom looked up at him with concern. "What happened? Are you okay? I knew something was off but wasn't going to say anything!"

"Yes, I'm okay. I'm more than okay! In fact, I'm happier than I've ever been." He took a deep breath as his parents looked at him. "I met someone! It was completely unexpected, and when I first met her, I didn't know that anything would come of it, but it did. We spent quite a bit of time together for several days, and she's truly amazing!" He paused for a response from either of them.

His mother was first to speak, "Oh, that's lovely! I'm so happy you had a good trip!"

His dad looked at him with a look that said he knew there was something else. He knew it was more than just meeting someone on the trip. For him to bring it up, it meant there was more to it. His father chimed in, "She must be a very special woman."

"Yes, she is! Her name is Marcela. She is from Barcelona. She was in Paris for vacation, and she was staying at the same hotel I always stay at. She had never been to Paris before, and we got to know each other and spent my remaining days there together before and after my meetings." He stopped again knowing that his mom was going to have questions or comments.

His mom forced a smile and said, "That's really wonderful! Do you think she will come to visit you here? If she had such a good time with you, she will make the time to come see you!"

"Well, that's what I really wanted to talk to you about. I know it may not seem rational, but we fell in love." He knew this probably sounded crazy, but it was the truth. He started again before he could be interrupted. "We have talked about things, and I have thought about different ways we could be together, and we have decided that I will move to Barcelona to be with her!"

Without hesitation, his mother spoke up rather harshly, "Anastasio, you barely know her! Don't be ridiculous! You can't fall in love over a few days. And if she really loved you, she would understand that you need to be here helping your family. We have kept this family business alive for you! And she wants you to up and walk out on it and us?"

This was the reaction that he was hoping to avoid, but he knew his mom wouldn't take it easily. "Mom, she is not the one who suggested it. I did! I'm not walking out on anything or anyone! I still plan to do what I'm doing now, just from somewhere else. And have you ever known me to just jump into a relationship? I never have! I may not have been successful in relationships before, but I know what I feel now is real. And remember, you told me that you and Dad met and married very quickly. How it this different?"

Just as he thought before, she said, "That was a different time, Anastasio! Things don't work like that now. Love takes time to come. You were married. You should know that! In the beginning, it always seems like the best thing you've known. But as time goes on, you find out how you really feel!"

His mother always knew what buttons to push to get him frustrated, but he wasn't going to let that happen this time. "Yes, I know that things can take time. You're reasoning doesn't make since though. We do live in different times than when you and Dad met. But finding love and being in love with someone hasn't ever changed. When you feel it, you have to grab ahold of it. I know what I feel is real!"

His mom wasn't going to let go so easily. "I'm not telling you not to see her again. But moving right after meeting someone is not the way to go about it! You haven't really thought this through."

His dad broke his silence and not to the liking of his wife. "I'm happy for you, son! I want nothing more for you than to find someone that makes you happy!" His smile and words were genuine.

Anastasio looked at both of them. He didn't want this to turn into an argument, but he was determined to stay firm with his decision. "Thank you, Dad!" He looked at his mom and continued, "I have made my decision. I will continue to do my sales calls and do what I can to keep our vineyard alive. I'm not walking out on you, her, or anything. I love her, and I want to be with her!"

His mom looked away from him and stopped eating. She took her napkin off her lap and threw it on top of her plate. She shook her head, stood, and left the table without another word or looking at either of them. She walked out of the kitchen, and he could hear her going up the stairs to her bedroom. She was being very dramatic to try to prove her point.

It was an awkward silence for a moment before his dad took his hand. He held his hand and looked into his eyes. "Don't you worry about her. It will take time, but she will come around. I'm happy for you, son. You mom loves you, but you know she isn't so great with any changes when they first happen. Give her some time! I love you!" he said and kept holding his hand and looking at him. He now understood where he got his intense look from. His father had the same look that he guessed Marcela saw in him.

He gave his dad's hand a tight squeeze. "Thank you, Dad! I love you too!"

They finished their meal in silence. Anastasio wished it had gone better with his mother, but he expected a reaction like this. He wished she could know what his heart felt, and then she would understand. Maybe it was how she felt for his dad when she had met him. He knew he had his work cut out for him to get her to see what he did. But it would be worth it!

Anastasio took the dishes from the table and washed everything. His dad had retired to the living room to watch some television. His mom had not come out of her room to come downstairs, where she always sat with his dad. He was hoping to talk to her more but wasn't going to go find her to do it. He sat in the living room with his father for some time but then decided to go upstairs to call Marcela.

Marcela had just walked in the door as her cell phone started to ring. She got her phone from her purse and immediately saw that it was Anastasio. She got a big smile on her face and answered the phone. "Hey you! How are you?"

"I'm doing okay. I missed you today!" It wasn't just words. He really did miss her! He was happy to hear her voice. "Did you go into your store today?"

"Yes, I actually just got home. I think it was a very productive day! What did you do today?" All day she had tried to imagine what his home looked like, where he spent most of his time, and what his normal daily routine was like.

"You mean other than thinking of you?" He didn't wait for an answer. "I contacted my clients to try to consolidate my meetings a bit more efficiently. I was still pretty tired from the trip, so I took a nice nap. Then I had dinner with my parents. I told them about my plan to move."

"And how did that go?" she asked, wondering how they reacted.

He gave a little laugh. "It was about what I expected. My dad seemed happy for me. My mom, that's another story. She didn't take it so well. She will come around though!"

"Oh, baby, I don't want your parents to hate me!" she said as she suddenly felt rejected.

"They don't hate you. My mom is just, how can I put this lightly, she has her mind made up before you even tell her what's going on. My dad was totally supportive. It will take time with my mom. Let her get to know you, and she'll see what I see. She just doesn't know you yet!"

She still felt rejected but knew that she genuinely loved Anastasio and would do anything for him! "Okay, so are you still planning on coming in a few weeks?" She was scared to hear his response and immediately regretted asking.

"Of course, I am! There is nothing that can stop me!"

She still felt that something could go wrong, but she trusted him. "Okay. I just don't want to make things difficult for you!"

"Everything will work out. You'll see!" he said with conviction, although he did have some doubt about his mom. Surely, she would come around before too long. At least he hoped!

For the first time since she met him, she didn't know what to say. Her heart hurt a bit. She searched for something to say. Finally, she came up with the most basic response. "Okay."

He could feel the doubt in her words. He didn't want her to feel bad or question if he was going to follow through with their plans. "Everything will be fine, I promise! Don't worry too much about her. She's just very set in her own ways." He knew his words weren't going to help too much, but he meant them.

They talked for about another hour. Without either of them realizing it, they avoided the topic they just had for the rest of the time they talked. The conversation didn't seem forced, but it lacked some of the passion they had previously. Neither of them had avoided anything in their conversations before. They were now in unchartered waters. But one thing was for certain, they both knew how that felt for each other. Reluctantly, they decided to end the conversation and agreed to talk the next day.

They said goodbye for the evening, and Marcela thought about calling Antonio. She decided against it as she didn't want to talk or think about Anastasio's mom coming between them. She trusted Anastasio, and that was what mattered. Plus, she was going to see Antonio tomorrow, and if she really was bothered still, she would talk to him then. Better in person than by phone!

She made herself some chicken and rice. She still had some wine leftover from the night before, so she poured a glass. She thought about turning on the television but decided to listen to some music instead. Music always made her think more clearly. She wanted to clear her head and relax. For starters, she started with Stan Getz and the album that had "Girl from Ipanema" on it. It was a beautiful song and always put a smile on her face.

She finished her dinner and poured another glass of wine. She changed the music to something more upbeat and found herself dancing by herself as she did the dishes. Her idea of putting music on was doing her better than she expected. She was not only dancing, but she was also singing along, and her mood was instantly changed. She felt carefree again, as she did when she was on vacation. That was a feeling she wanted to feel more in her life. She vowed to herself that she would stop worrying about things she couldn't control. All she had to do was believe!

It was still early, so she decided that she would start working on her closet to make room for Anastasio. She didn't know exactly how much room he would need. She assumed he had lots of clothes. He seemed to be well-dressed and fashionable. She didn't think she dressed bad by any means, but she thought she could probably learn from him. Just being with him made her want to always try to look better and care just that little bit more. The thought made her think of an older movie where the female was a great influence on the male's life, and he said she made him want to be a better person. That's the way she felt with Anastasio. He made her want to be a better person!

After about two hours, she was finished with what she could do with her closet. She thought she had made significant room for him. She would work on her dresser later. She assumed they would probably need to buy another dresser, but she would wait for him to be there before buying anything. It was funny, she thought, how quickly you could change from being completely independent and making all your decisions by yourself to wanting to make decisions with someone else.

She kept the music on and kept the wine flowing. She was no longer thinking about what Anastasio had said and was back to thinking the way she was before their conversation. She loved him, and he loved her, period! He made her happy. She couldn't remember the last time she danced by herself and enjoyed an evening alone as she did now. But she felt anything but alone. She knew he was with her even if he wasn't there.

The wine was now really taking an effect on her. She was getting tired, and she could feel that she was almost drunk. She shut all the lights off in the living room and kitchen and turned off the music. She brushed her teeth and got ready for bed. She had a feeling that she would sleep very well. As she climbed into bed, she thought about which side of bed he slept on when they were together and immediately made sure she chose the side that he didn't before. Maybe it didn't matter to him, but she wanted to get used to not being alone. There was two of them now, not just her.

~

When Anastasio set his phone down, he felt bad! He wished he could've have lied to her about his mom's reaction, but he wouldn't do that. He wanted to start this relationship with complete honesty and not hide anything. Well, almost anything! He hadn't told her that he was feeling bad, but it was unlikely anything of importance. He loved her and wouldn't ever keep anything important from her.

He wanted so badly to call Marcela back and to tell her that none of the stuff his mom thought mattered. But he didn't. He knew how he felt for her and had been honest with that. He really wanted this relationship to be based on trust and love. Nothing else! He would be sure to reassure her every chance that he got. That wasn't going to be the easiest to do, but he would do his best.

He went back downstairs, and his dad was sitting there watching television. His mom was not in sight. After about twenty minutes, his dad turned the volume down and turned to face Anastasio as he sat in his favorite recliner. "Don't worry about your mother. She means well. She has never dealt with change very well. But she loves you very much. Both of us want what's best for you. Give her some time to come to terms with it. It was a surprise to us. A week ago, this woman didn't exist in your life. You are an adult, and I have always trusted you and will always give you my support. So will your mother! Perhaps you can bring the Marcela here sometime soon. I'm sure your mother will see what you see then." His dad offered a big smile.

"Thank you, Dad. You're right! It would shock me too, I guess. I will talk to Marcela and see what her schedule is like. You will love her! I hope Mom will too. And thank you for everything you've always done for me. I love you!"

"We love you too!"

Chapter 10

Marcela woke up earlier than she expected. She decided to go into her store and continue to work on her new projects. She decided that she would also open the store for a few hours. She was hoping that since it was a Saturday, she would get some customers to come in. She hadn't spent as much money on her trip as she expected, so she wasn't hurting for the money at the moment. But it would be nice to get things going again. She wanted to have a more successful business. With her new attitude toward life, she thought she could really make it happen and without killing herself to do it. She would just have to work smarter rather than harder.

She picked up her phone and decided to text Anastasio. It was later where he was, but she hoped he was still sleeping. She didn't want to wake him, but she wanted to let him know that she was thinking about him. She wrote, "Hi, hon. I decided to go into work for a little while. I will call you after. I hope you are sleeping well. I miss you!"

She went and put the coffee on to brew while she took a shower. As much as it would be nice to be on vacation forever, it was also nice to get back into a routine. Although she was going to change many things, like how much time she spent working and spending more time with people that mattered to her, she did like much of her routine. She enjoyed the sense of stability it gave her. On the days she worked, she normally did the same things. Get up, put the coffee on, take a shower, have some breakfast, and get ready to go into her store. Today would be no different besides the fact that she didn't plan to spend her whole day there. Weekends were her busiest times, so she wouldn't always work only a few hours, but today she planned to make it a short day.

Her shower was quick, and she had her coffee with a bagel with cream cheese and some fruit. She got ready and put on some jeans and a short-sleeved blouse. She got her purse, and her phone, and headed out the door. She glanced at her phone, and she had a text waiting. She got excited, hoping it was from Anastasio. It was! He wrote, "Hi, baby. You must have been reading my mind because I was about to text you when I got your message. I didn't want to wake you either. I miss you too! I'll be around, so call whenever you want. I love you!" She couldn't wait to see him again. *Soon,* she thought!

She loved this time of the year. The weather was warming up but not too hot yet. It was going to be a great time of the year for Anastasio to move there. They could go to the beach, go to different places by train or car, and visit the many different attractions Spain had to offer. She couldn't remember the last time she did any of that. It was usually when relatives came into town. And other than her mom's funeral, that hadn't happened in a long time. It was going to be nice to do those things again, especially with him!

She got to her store and opened everything up. The streets seemed to be busier than in the previous weeks, and she was glad she had decided to come in and open the store up. Her new projects were sitting there, waiting to come to life. She started to work on them again. She had several people come in and browse what she had out. Most were tourists with the occasional repeat client. Between working on the new things and paying attention to the customers, her day was going by very quickly. She made a few good sales and got a lot done on her designs as well.

Before she knew it, it was getting pretty late in the afternoon. It was amazing the difference being happy made on how fast her day went. She also noticed an increase in her sales even though she was open less hours today. She attributed it to her positive energy. She interacted with the customers with more ease and was more comfortable than usual. Not that she was ever negative or uncomfortable. She would have to pay attention to the next several days ahead to see if the trend stayed that way.

It was time for her to close and get ready for Antonio to come over. They were going to cook dinner, talk, and likely watch a movie or two. That was a typical night for them. She wanted to have time to stop by the store to get some things to cook. She knew he loved seafood, so she was going to get lobster to steam, spinach, and potatoes to bake. She also wanted to get some more wine, cheese, and crackers. She hadn't eaten lunch, and she was looking forward to eating!

On her way to the grocery store, she called Anastasio. She knew Antonio would be over shortly after she got home and wanted to have a few moments to talk with Anastasio while she was alone. Antonio wasn't the type to get upset if she was on the phone, but she still felt it was rude to be with friends and be on your phone also. Plus, she had wanted to call him all day but didn't get too much of a break between working on the projects and the customers coming in.

When she called, it went straight to his voice mail, and she left him a message. He was probably working with his father or busy doing other work. She knew he would call him back. She drove to the store and found the stuff she needed relatively quickly. She called Antonio to let him know that she was going to be home soon, and he informed her that he was already on his way. He had a key, and it wasn't unusual for him to come over before she was home sometimes. He was a great and trustworthy friend. She looked forward to him and Anastasio getting to know each other as well. She suspected they would get along well. Hopefully she was right about that! They were important to her life in their own way.

When she got home, Antonio had already poured some wine for himself and her as well. She hugged him and went to change her clothes. When she came back, she prepared the cheese and crackers. They chatted while she made the lobster and sides. He tried to help her, but she told him to relax and enjoy. He asked about Anastasio, her work, and random other thoughts that came up. She asked about his life, and as usual, they were enjoying each other's company. They had dinner and settled in to watch a movie.

She heard her phone beep, indicating she had a text message. It was from Anastasio, and she smiled instantly. He wrote, "Hey, hon. Sorry I couldn't get to the phone earlier. You are probably with Antonio now. I am still tied up. I will try to call you later tonight or in the morning. I'm thinking about you!"

She hoped that they would be able to talk after Antonio was gone, but she wasn't sure what time that would be or what Anastasio was tied up with anyways. She replied, "Okay. Yes, I'm with Antonio. We just had dinner and are going to watch a movie. I can't wait to hear your voice. I love you!"

She put her phone away, and they spent the next several hours watching two movies. Antonio admitted that he was getting tired. She was as well. Since he had several glasses of wine, they decided it was best for him to stay in the guest bedroom. He used it quite often when he would come over. They said good night, and both retreated to their rooms. She got ready for bed and checked her phone as she lay down. Still nothing from Anastasio. It wasn't like him to go this long without talking with her. She hoped he was okay. She put her phone on the nightstand and closed her eyes to sleep. She fell asleep very quickly.

She woke up several times and checked her phone. Sometime in the early morning, she heard her phone beep. She cleared her eyes and read the message, "I'm so sorry I couldn't talk last night. I hope you are sleeping well. I will call sometime this morning. I love you!"

She was relieved to hear from him. She had begun to worry during the middle of the night. She didn't know what was going on, but she was sure he would tell her when they talked. She thought for a moment what to write. She decided to keep it simple, "I hope everything is okay. Call anytime you like! Get some sleep, mister!"

Now that she knew he was okay, she was able to fall back asleep. She slept peacefully for about another three hours. She woke up, brushed her teeth, and headed for the kitchen to make Antonio and herself some coffee. When she got to the kitchen, she saw that she had been beat to it. Antonio was making eggs, bacon, and toast.

He looked up and smiled at her. She smiled back and said, "Good morning!"

He handed her a cup of coffee and asked, "How did you sleep?"

"I slept okay. How about you?" she asked.

"I was out like a light! I hope you are hungry. Let's eat!" he said as he made their plates up.

They spent the next hour together, eating and talking. He had some plans for the afternoon, so he excused himself and left shortly after breakfast. She wasn't sure what she wanted to do today. She thought about going into the store again but decided against it. She still hadn't heard back from Anastasio, and she wanted to busy herself to distract her thoughts. She got online and looked up what was going on the area. She found an outdoor art fair that wasn't too far from where she lived. It was an outdoor event, and the weather seemed pleasant. She got ready, and headed out to go to the art fair.

For several hours, she looked at different art while walking around. The fair was well organized, and the day turned out more beautiful than she expected. She loved looking at the different pieces and artists. Being a designer, she could really appreciate all different types of art and creativity. Some pieces moved her, and she thought about buying a few but thought it best to save her money. Plus, she had no idea what kind of art Anastasio liked. It didn't make sense to buy something right now.

After she left the fair, she stopped and ate a late lunch. She wasn't very hungry but knew it was best to eat something. She wasn't ready to go home yet. There was still no call or message from Anastasio. At the end of her lunch, she decided to message him again. "I'm getting worried about you! I don't want to bother you if you are busy. Please just let me know you are okay."

She got in her car and headed toward the beach. It was such a nice day out. She wanted to take advantage of it before she went back to work tomorrow. As she was parking, her phone began to ring. She looked at the number, and it was Anastasio. She was excited that she finally was hearing from him. "Hey, stranger. You okay?" she asked.

"Yes, I'm sorry I haven't been able to talk until now. We had a family emergency that came up yesterday. I hope you know how much I missed you!"

Just hearing the words *I missed you* made her heart beat faster. She instantly felt better. She turned off the car and got out to sit on the beach while she was going to talk to Anastasio. "I missed you too!"

They talked for the next hour or so. It felt good to put her feet in the sand and talk to him. She felt the tension that she was feeling building up fading as she was relaxed from just hearing his voice. It wasn't too crowded out. There was a slight breeze that made it perfect for her to enjoy the rest of the afternoon out. Their conversation was light but nice. She told him about the evening with Antonio, about going to the fair, and about her day at work the day before. As usual, the conversation flowed with ease. She could talk to him all day and not get enough. She'd never been like it in her adult life. Maybe back in high school when she liked a boy. She never imagined she would want that now.

She wanted to ask what had happened with his family but knew if he wanted to talk about it, he'd bring it up. It was just a few days ago that he didn't press her to tell him about what happened with her mom. She just hoped everything was all right with his parents. She especially hoped that whatever was wrong didn't stem from the news that Anastasio gave them. That was her biggest fear at the moment. But his side of the conversation seemed casual, and he didn't seem to be stressed about anything. They even discussed the move a little bit. She had told him about cleaning her closet and the plan to get another dresser.

After they got off the phone, she sat there sitting in the sand a little bit longer. Listening to the ocean, the slight breeze, and the conversation with Anastasio washed away all her fears. And she felt sincerely happy! She thought about her mom some more. Her mom used to love to go to the beach and sit, just watching the ocean and clouds and just relaxing, like Marcela was doing right now. The thoughts of her mom didn't make her sad this time. She finally understood the life her mom wanted for her. She didn't realize how unhappy she was in life. The thought of everything that was happening in her life now made her smile. She imagined her mom sitting beside her, enjoying the day with her.

She reluctantly left the beach and headed home. It had been a wonderful weekend. But she wanted to do a few things around the house and make it an early evening so she could focus on work and get everything ready for Anastasio's move. She would do it bit by bit each night after work. She knew she was going to also be busy with work, finishing her new projects. She was inspired and was hoping that she would be able to come up with some more ideas in the near future. She wanted to take advantage of the time she had for the next few weeks before he was there. She wanted to spend as much time as she could with him when he moved there.

After she got home and cleaned up, she prepared her dinner. She watched some television as she ate. Then she got her notebook and wrote down the things she wanted to accomplish this week at home and at work. She liked being organized and having a plan that she could stick to. Throughout the night, she found herself daydreaming about Anastasio being there with her. She hoped the next few weeks would go by quickly. She couldn't wait to see him, touch him, smell him and have all her senses filled by him.

She finished making her list for the week. She cleaned the kitchen and got ready for bed. It had been a nice and productive weekend. She was happy about that. Hopefully the week would prove to be just as good as the weekend. She sent Anastasio a good-night text as she lay down. She still had a little more energy that might make it difficult to sleep, so she picked up a book that she had been reading before her trip. She liked to read before she went to sleep. It calmed her. It didn't take long until she drifted off to sleep for the night.

After a peaceful night of sleep, Marcela woke up and was about to start her normal routine of getting ready for work when she saw a message from Anastasio. He had sent it shortly after she had messaged him when she was going to sleep. He had told her good night and that he missed and loved her. She started her coffee, took a shower, got ready for work, and ate a little breakfast. She sent him a message saying good morning and to wish him a good day. She then made her way into her store.

She spent the day mostly working on her projects, finishing one of her designs. It was the one she had made for and because of Jacqueline. It was perfect, she thought. She couldn't wait to send it to Jacqueline. Jacqueline would surely like it. She imagined seeing it on her and what she would be wearing with it. She had the feeling that Jacqueline, even though a bit older, had particularly good fashion sense. After she made a few more like it, she would send one to her. She was glad she got her contact information before she left. Hopefully she would have time to make several pieces in the next few days.

She spent the morning starting to create clones of the piece she had just finished. She had the other designs to work on but decided to do one at a time now. It was easier to make several of a particular design at a time. Being a Monday morning, she didn't have any customers coming in so far. It allowed her to focus on the task at hand. Several hours passed with her engrossed in starting the new pieces. It helped that she wasn't constantly interrupted by customers coming in. Of course, she wanted to have more customers to make more money, but right now, she wanted to be able to focus on what she was doing.

The morning flew by, and she decided to grab some lunch before it got too late. There was a deli just around the corner from her store that she went to quite often. She brought her lunch most days as she was the only one in the store, and she didn't want to be closed if a customer came by. That was the biggest downside of having to let the two salespeople go. She always had to be at the store, skipping most lunches and dinners as well. While most people were off on the weekends, that was the busiest time for her, so she couldn't skip those days.

She got a sandwich, chips, and drink to go. She would eat the lunch in the store just in case someone came by. With no luck on a customer coming in, she was able to eat in peace. After finishing her lunch, she started back on her project with having the occasional customer coming in. Luckily, the few that came by ended up buying several things. It wasn't every day that she had the success that she was having today. Between Saturday and today, she found more success than usual and again that it was probably linked to her newfound attitude.

The afternoon went on much like that. Customers came in randomly and ended up buying random things. All the people that came in were new customers, and luckily, almost all were locals. She hoped to make them customers for life. She had been taught that successful businesses like hers depended a lot by having repeat customers. They all seemed to like her unique pieces that they couldn't find in an ordinary chain jewelry store. She hoped that many of them would return to buy more stuff. She made sure to get their contact information to let them know of any new pieces that she would make and any kind of sale or event. She felt it was important to not only have new customers but to also have more repeat customers.

Before she knew it, it was time to close up and go home. She had a very productive day and was happy with the sales. She made a lot of progress on making more pieces. It would be nice if every day would be like today and last Saturday. She decided that she would have a sale soon to show off the new pieces that she thought that many of her customers would like. Most of her customers would at least come in to see what she had to offer. Of course, not all of them would end up buying something, but they generally showed her support by coming by.

She made her way home, happy with her success in making headway on the projects and the sales that she had made. She hadn't tried to talk with Anastasio thus far, and he hadn't reached out to her either. She had lost track of time and didn't mean to let the whole day go by without responding to him. She sent him a text to say hello and tell him about her day. She also told him that she would try to call him after she had dinner. She hadn't asked what his schedule for the day was, so she didn't want to interrupt him if he was working.

On her way home, she stopped by the store and bought some stuff for dinner. She also picked up some things to eat for the rest of the week. She liked to bring her lunch to work and didn't have much in the house to easily make for her lunches. After about an hour of shopping, she thought she had everything that she needed for the rest of the week. She got back in the car and made the rest of her way home. Her house was pretty close to the store, so it didn't take her long to get home.

She took the groceries in the house and turned on the television to watch the news and see what was happening in the world. She liked to stay informed of what was going on, not only in the areas around her but what was happening in the world as well. She made a simple dinner and ate it while watching the television. There was nothing particularly appealing going on in the world that she hadn't already known about, so she changed it over to watch a movie.

As she sat on the couch, she tried to call Anastasio. He didn't answer, so she left him a message. She poured herself a glass of wine and sat on the couch and watched a movie. She found herself checking her phone on a regular basis even though her sound was on. She wanted to make sure she hadn't missed a text or call from Anastasio. As she was watching the movie, she was also waiting to hear from him. She had made it most of the way through the movie, then she caught herself dosing off. She didn't realize until now that she had worked awfully hard today, and it was taking a toll on her now.

At about 9:00 p.m., she decided that she was going to bed. She was more tired than she had initially thought, but she knew that it was going to be hard to fall asleep as she was getting worried about what was going on with Anastasio again. She got ready for bed, and as she usually did, she continued reading the book she had. Even though she knew her phone hadn't notified her of a message or a call, she kept checking it anyways. She decided to send him another massage before she fell asleep for the night. It wasn't long before she fell asleep as she was reading her book.

Marcela awoke to her alarm at about seven the next morning. There was still nothing from Anastasio. She wondered what was going on with him and didn't know if she should worry or try to reach out to him over and over. She didn't know what to think. Maybe he had gone to bed early, or there could be many different reasons he hadn't reached out to her. Unfortunately, she couldn't think of very many right now. She thought that she really didn't know him well enough to know how he would communicate with her while they were apart. Some people didn't like to use their phones too much. Until the last few days, they were together and didn't need to talk by phone or text. She took a deep breath and tried to shake the negative thoughts from her head.

She started her usual routine. As much as she tried to push thoughts about why he hadn't said anything, they stayed in her mind. As she was getting ready for work, the thoughts continued. Why hadn't he messaged her or called her? Should she be worried that his mom had talked him out of moving to Spain and he was scared to tell her? Was there something else going on? When they had talked yesterday afternoon, everything seemed fine, and she didn't question anything. But now she couldn't get the negative thoughts out of her head. She wondered if she should bring it up the next time they talked. She didn't want to seem possessive or the type of person that needed him to be in contact nonstop. This was something she really needed to think about throughout the day before she made decisions that might make him think that she was the type of person that needed constant attention. The last thing she wanted to do is to scare him off.

She got ready for work and made her way to the store. She couldn't help thinking about what she was going to say or do about the way she was feeling. She couldn't help but get a sinking feeling in her stomach. As much as she tried, it stayed there in her mind, like chains around her neck. She felt like it was hard to breathe and think clearly. She tried everything, from listening to music to making a list in her head of what she needed to do. But it seemed nothing could take her mind from him. She decided that she needed to come up with a way to ask him about his lack of communication when she talked to him that didn't make her seem needy.

The drive didn't take long, and she still hadn't come up with how or what she wanted to say to convey her concern. She opened up the store and tried to focus on her projects that she had been working on while waiting for new or previous customers. She didn't expect to be too busy on a Tuesday morning. If things stayed the way they usually did, there wouldn't be many people coming in, so she could focus on the work she wanted to work on and finish.

The morning didn't go as well as the last time. She tried her best to focus, but thoughts of Anastasio kept creeping in her head. No matter what she did or tried, she couldn't take her mind off him. During the morning, she decided to text him, and about an hour after that, she called him. There was no answer, and she left him a message, "Hey there! I haven't heard from you since yesterday afternoon. I'm getting worried about you again. Please call me when you get this."

The rest of the morning went by with no word from him. She didn't have any customers come in, and it made the morning slowly drag on. The work on the new pieces didn't go well with her mind not being able to focus on the task at hand. She put off the work on the projects for another time. Feeling the way she did, she knew that nothing was going to turn out the way she wanted it to. She started feeling the same feelings she had when she had lost her mom. Her heart hurt, and nothing seemed right in the world again. But she knew one word from him would make her feel right again. He had a hold of her heart, and only he could make it feel whole.

She ate her lunch in silence in the store. She had made a sandwich and brought some fruit this morning. The food seemed tasteless and made her sick to her stomach. She wasn't able to eat much of it. Time seemed to be standing still. She just wanted to close up the store and go home and curl up into a ball and cry. All the feelings of her mom, Anastasio, and everything she failed at before came crashing down in her mind and heart. But she was strong. She wasn't going to close up and break down. As hard as it was to breathe, she did. As much as her heart hurt, it kept beating. As hard as it was to put one foot in front of the other, her legs still worked, and she didn't fall over. She wondered how long that was going to last. Was this the beginning of the bottom falling-out? Was this life repaying her for being so cold, out of touch with people, and only living for herself? People said karma was a bitch! Was this karma knocking on her door?

The afternoon went on much like the morning did. The only difference was that she had some customers come in. She didn't sell anything, like she did over the weekend. She couldn't put a smile on her face and act like all was right in the world. She knew that the vibe she was putting out to the people was a direct result of them not buying anything, and they all seemed to want to leave in a hurry. She didn't even care about any of that. All she wanted was for Anastasio to walk in and look at her in the eye and hold her. That would make everything in her world right again. But she knew that wasn't going to happen. At best, he would call or text her. She didn't know how that would make her feel, but she assumed it would make her heart not shatter into pieces.

It was time for her to close up the store and head home. As hard as it was to be there all alone, she knew being at home would be even that much worse. She thought about calling Antonio to come over, but she didn't want anyone around other than Anastasio. He was her life now. He had made her feel invincible! Now she felt like she would crumble at any second. If he called now, would she snap right back to how she felt yesterday afternoon when she was sitting on the beach talking with him? She guessed she wouldn't. She didn't know why she was hurting so bad. It had only been a day since they talked. Anything could have happened, and he wasn't able to talk. But she felt it in heart that something more was happening. She couldn't explain the feeling, but her heart and mind were screaming at her.

She arrived home and couldn't even remember any of the drive there. She didn't bother to listen to the radio or make a call to anyone. She was now on autopilot. All she wanted to do was lie on the couch or in her bed and cry until she fell asleep. Why was life so cruel at times? It didn't matter. She was in control of everything for so long. Now she wasn't in control of anything. Life would go on no matter what happened. The world could be so wonderful. Birds chirping, a beautiful day, a song that made her want to dance, the smell of roses, the laughter of child, the smiles that you could see come from the heart. But it also had a brutal side. It could twist and turn and give you the feeling you were being stabbed. The cold winter days, the cruelty of people, wars, the hollowness of people's words. Of course, the world couldn't have one without the other. But right now, she felt the sadness that life was handing her.

The evening hours seemed to go even slower than the day did. She turned on the television but had no clue what she was watching.

It was just images on the screen. She contemplated making dinner but knew she wouldn't be able to eat any of it. She checked her phone every so often to see if there was word from Anastasio. There was nothing. She tried to call him a few more times with no luck. She tried to sound like her world wasn't breaking apart when she left him a couple more messages. She knew her words didn't come out right, and she knew that when he listened to the messages, he would hear the pain in her voice. She hadn't decided if that was a good or bad thing.

She found herself dozing off and on throughout the evening. She didn't have the energy or the will to move off the couch. She had no idea what time it was nor did it matter. The television stayed on, but the volume was now off. She didn't care to hear anything and wasn't in a place that she could pay attention to anything anyways. Food still didn't sound good, and she didn't feel hungry. The only thing she felt was pain and sadness. Even though it had only been a day since they talked, she felt it in her heart that he was gone. Just as fast and easily as he came, he was gone. If asked, she wouldn't be able to explain how she knew, but she was sure that he was gone.

Why had she opened herself up to a complete stranger? She should have known better than to fall in love with someone that she really didn't know. Also, he lived in another country! Why would she expect someone to leave their home to come to her? She thought about that last question and knew she would have moved in a heartbeat to be with him. Did she somehow push him away? She really felt that he had been the one to offer the things that they had decided on. But maybe she was pushing him without meaning to. She hoped she would have the answers but felt that she might not ever know.

She wasn't sure what time she had fallen asleep for good for the night, but she knew it wasn't a peaceful sleep. She had dreams of Anastasio, each one of them with different reasons why he wasn't talking with her. He was married, he was a player, his family had changed his mind, and on and on. Each dream felt so real and equally as painful as the others. The pain from each one was just as real. She was hurting and felt like her life was now over. Not that she thought she'd die, but she could feel her heart dying inside. She would go through the motions of living but likely wouldn't feel anything ever again.

She made herself get up and go through the motions of getting ready for work. Every little thing she did made her think of the moments she had shared with him. She could see the images clearly in her head. She could see them showering together, having coffee, getting ready for the day, and eating breakfast. It was an endless motion picture playing in her mind. There was one image that kept popping up that she couldn't shake. It was the day she had met him. She could see the intensity in his eyes and the way her heart almost leaped out of her chest. Now it felt like her heart wasn't leaping but hiding inside her chest.

It seemed that every task she did was ten times harder than it was the day before. She had to force herself to eat a little breakfast. She drove to work without even knowing that she was going there. She was on autopilot for everything, it seemed. She couldn't tell you any part of what she did. All she could recall were the images in her mind playing over and over. Even now the images wouldn't stop even for a minute. It was like he had been a part of her life forever. She didn't have one thought about her mother, Antonio, anybody, or anything else. Just him!

It was almost pointless to be at work. She couldn't even think about working on her projects. The customers that came in, she couldn't muster the energy to smile or tell them about the things they were looking at. She might as well have locked the door and sat there in a daze. But she had to try. She couldn't just close up and go home. She wasn't wealthy and needed work to live. If she were rich, maybe she'd choose to stay at home. But she knew she needed a distraction from her thoughts if it were at all possible.

She skipped lunch as she knew she wouldn't be able to eat. Nothing seemed like they would go back to normal. *Even time couldn't heal these wounds*, she thought. They say that all pains lessened over time. She couldn't imagine this pain would ever go away. For the first time in her life, she had really opened up her heart. Now she was paying the price. Her life wouldn't only go back to the way it was before; it was also going to be much worse. She no longer had her mom, and now she had lost someone she genuinely loved.

She forced herself to stay at work for the rest of the day. She checked her phone over and over. She didn't want to call or text him anymore. Well, that wasn't completely true. There were many different things she wanted to say to him. Some of it loving, but mostly, she wanted to vent! She wrote so many different texts but never had the courage to send them. She wanted to call, but she couldn't face the disappointment of him not answering or responding. If she pretended he didn't exist, maybe she could start to breathe on her own again. Who was she kidding? She was lying to herself.

She finished her day at work and closed up the store. Just like when she came to work, she drove home without the radio or knowing where she was. If she hadn't driven this a billion times in the past, she was sure she would get lost. But she could probably drive this route with her eyes closed. To be honest, she wasn't sure that her eyes were open half the time. All she saw were the images of them. Even though she wanted to think of anything else, she couldn't shake the thoughts.

Once she was home, the night was much like the night before. She ate but couldn't tell you how it tasted. She turned on the television but couldn't tell you what was on. She had no idea what time anything happened or what time she went to sleep. Everything was just a blur to her. Time seemed to be cruel to her. She wanted it to go by much faster, but it didn't. The hours went by, and each hour was harder and harder on her. She couldn't believe all this was happening to her.

There was still no message or call from Anastasio! She couldn't stop looking at her phone, hoping that she would see a call or message from him. She knew the answer before she even looked as her sound was on, and her phone was right next to her. She couldn't decide what she wanted. Was it good for him to call or text now? Did she want to hear that he didn't want to be with her? Was it all a game to him? There were a million questions that she could ask, but all of them led to the same answer. He wasn't with her! He wasn't contacting her. He had disappeared with no explanation. She thought about calling him and texting him, but she did still have her pride, if nothing else. She didn't want to be the person that obsessed about someone even though she loved him more than she had loved anyone.

She made it to her bed, unlike last night. Now that she wasn't hearing from Anastasio, she found herself thinking of her mother now. All her thoughts she found were all on the negative things that had happened in her life. She thought about all her past failed relationships and how she was the one that always left them. She couldn't remember many times in her life that she was the one to be left. She was too good at saying goodbye to people in her life. Finding Antonio was a miracle. He put up with her when she was difficult, which was most of the time. Her ex was also still one of her good friends for some reason that she couldn't explain. She hadn't been so nice with him at times when there was nothing he did wrong. She had to count her blessings with the people that were still in her life. But there was only one person she wanted right now. And he wasn't there for her. Her heart was sinking more than she knew was possible.

Her sleep wasn't peaceful again. Dreams of her mother and Anastasio dominated her night when she was actually asleep. She no longer could tell when she was asleep or awake. Her thoughts and dreams occupied her mind. She didn't want to think about either of them right now. She wanted her heart to just stop beating. How long could one feel this way without their heart just stopping? She felt that she was a good person. But in the last several days, life was really handing her a bad hand. Most of her life she had made her own way. She found that her unhappiness was caused by her own self. Until her mom and Anastasio, she couldn't remember ever losing sleep about someone. She thought she was too strong and independent for things like this preventing her to sleep or do anything. She knew that her mind wasn't going to let this go for a long time. She would have to find something else to occupy her mind and time.

Marcela woke up the next morning without feeling that she slept at all. She felt spent, and her mind and body were exhausted. She couldn't even begin to guess how long she had slept. All she wanted to do was lie in the bed or lie on the couch and feel sorry for herself. It was the first time that she really felt true love in her heart. And now her heart was broken. Not just broken, it was shattering. She didn't even know if she would be able to pick up the pieces off the floor. All she could think about now was her mom and Anastasio. And not the good parts! She thought about her mom's death and Anastasio not contacting her. She couldn't think of anything else at the moment.

It took her longer than usual to get ready for work as she kept finding herself lost in thought. While showering, she had moments that she was just standing there, letting the water run over her body. When drinking her coffee and having breakfast, she didn't feel hungry, and the thought of eating or drinking anything seemed like she would get sick if she ingested anything. Everything she did or tried took much longer than usual as she couldn't focus on anything but thoughts of Anastasio. She wanted desperately to hear from him. Even if he told her what she was already concluding, she at least wanted to hear it from him.

She made it to work just a little bit later than she usually did. She wasn't sure how she wasn't later since everything had taken so long for her to do this morning. Antonio had called on her way to work, but she let it go to voice mail. She didn't want to be asked about anything she wasn't ready to answer. He was very in tune with her, and he would know something was wrong if he heard her voice. She didn't want to talk about things right now. She needed time to think and compose herself before she talked to anyone she knew. She wasn't particularly good at hiding things she felt.

The morning continued about the same as when she was getting ready. She didn't even try to work on her projects. She just sat in silence waiting for customers to come in or her heart to stop beating. She didn't know which one would be better for her. Time seemed to be standing still. Every time she looked at the clock, the time didn't seem to go as fast as it should. All she wanted was for time to pass to lessen the pain she felt. She felt bitter from the cruelty of life and how it didn't care what she was feeling. It let her feel pain over and over and made time go by faster when she was happy and slowed down time when she wasn't. Shouldn't it be the other way around?

Again, there weren't many people that stopped by in the morning to browse or buy anything. She wasn't sure if it was a good or bad thing. She didn't want to see or deal with anyone right now, but she couldn't afford to not have customers in the near future. This only made her stress even more than she already was. It seemed that nothing was going to go right this week. She wished she could just close up her store, go home, and just lie around doing nothing for a week or two. But that wasn't realistic. She couldn't afford that. And she needed to distract herself as much as possible.

She spent the afternoon getting ready for the sale she was having in almost two weeks. She really needed the sale to be successful. The relaxed state she was in just a few days ago had come and gone. For the first time since she opened her store, she had finally thought she could balance her life between work and her personal life. But now she wanted to just dive into work and not think anything about her personal life. The last thing she wanted was to be home by herself and have time to reflect on the bad things in her life. Distraction was her best defense she had to not deal with reality.

Antonio had called her and texted her several more times during the afternoon. She was always good about responding to him quickly, but now she was avoiding him. She didn't want to answer any questions about what was going on or lie to him about what was on her mind. Of course, he would be there for her no matter what! But she didn't want to feel more stupid right now. Telling him what was happening would make her look irresponsible. She couldn't avoid him forever, but for now, she didn't want to discuss anything with anyone, including him. All she wanted was silence and to grieve over everything that was going on. She just lost her mom and now the love that she thought would be in her life forever.

It was time to close up again and go home. She closed everything up and drove home. She decided that she needed to call Antonio back as he wouldn't stop calling or texting if she didn't answer. The last thing she wanted was for him to show up at her house asking questions. She had to think for a few minutes to come up with answers that weren't flat-out lies but not reveal the whole truth. She didn't like to lie, especially to someone so close to her. But she really didn't have any answers yet anyways. Just the fact that Anastasio had fallen off the earth and from her. She stopped going over the same questions and answers in her head and finally dialed Antonio's number.

It rang a few times, and Antonio answered, "There you are! I was just about to call you to make sure you weren't stuck under a large object!" he said, laughing.

She tried to come up with some witty answer but couldn't. Instead she said, "Hey! I'm so sorry that I haven't been able to talk lately. With designing the new pieces, normal work, and trying to get the ready for Anastasio's move, time has completely gotten away from me. How are you? Did I call at a bad time?"

Just by her tone and not giving some kind of silly response, he knew something wasn't right with her. But he generally never had to push for her to tell him what was going on. "I'm pretty good. I just finished up myself and heading over to Lee's house for dinner. Do you want me to ask him if you can join us? He hasn't seen you for some time now. I'm sure he'd love to see you!"

"I wish I could! But I have to get the house ready for the move, and honestly, even if someone wasn't moving in, the house still needs a deep clean. I have so much stuff there that I don't need or even remember why it was there in the first place. I need to go through my mom's stuff and do something with all her clothes. Also, with the sale at work coming up, I need to try to get a couple of pieces I'm working on done so I can have them ready for the sale I'm having soon. Can I take a rain check?"

"Of course. I'll tell him you said hello!"

"Please tell him I'm sorry that I can't make it over…even though he didn't technically invite me. We will all make a plan very soon. But enjoy your evening, and we'll talk some other time!"

He wanted to ask something to get an idea what she was avoiding talking about, but now was not the time. "Sure thing. But make sure you eat and not just work throughout the night, like I know you're good at. And please tell me you at least have wine to make it more enjoyable!"

"Thanks, Antonio! I will, and I do. Wouldn't dream of working on the house without a glass or two of wine. Enjoy your evening. I love you!"

"We love you too. I'm here if you need me." He ended the call and knew there was a lot she wasn't telling him. He suspected it has something to do with Anastasio as her voice sounded flat, as it did for so many years. He hoped he was wrong, and maybe she was just stressed by everything she had to get done. But deep inside he knew what the problem was.

She made it home and was happy she was able to get off the phone so fast. She knew she didn't sound convincing even though what she said was true. The house needed a lot of work that had been put off for a long time now. It shouldn't matter if Anastasio was going to be moving in or not. Now that she put her mind to it, she knew she could get it done. The sale for the store would also be here before she knew it, and she wanted to be as organized as possible. Her excuses had worked for now even though she had the idea that he knew something was up. He always knew!

She also needed to get over to her mom's house at some point soon to get everything sold, take things that meant a lot to her, and get rid of everything else. There were already offers on the house. She was hoping to get at least what was still owed on the house. Since the economy was not good, this was not the best time to try to sell as house since the values were so low. She knew that she wouldn't make any money on the house but needed to sell now because she couldn't afford two house payments. Her goal was just to break even on selling it.

Her evening started just like the last two did. She still found herself lost, staring into space at times, but she was trying to keep her mind busy. She knew she couldn't just lay there for the rest of her life. She came up with a schedule of what she was going to clean in the house day by day. She also came up with a plan of what needed to be done for the store to be ready for her sale. All the while, she checked her phone, hoping for something from Anastasio. She couldn't tell if she was more mad or sad that he had stopping communicating. She guessed it would be sadder as she couldn't tell her heart that she didn't love him anymore. In theory, she would not want to listen to his excuses and not give him any chances. But she knew if he called, her heart would probably melt all over again. She did the best she could to keep her mind on other things than on him. This meant not changing anything in the bedroom or living area. She would keep her dresser the way it was. She mostly worked on the guest bedroom that her mom used and the second bathroom.

The house wasn't huge but certainly not small. When it was originally built, it was made with eleven rooms. Almost all the older homes were designed like that. Each room could barely fit a bed and little stuff in it. The purpose was to keep the family together during family time instead of disappearing into each of their rooms avoiding others. She had thought to buy a smaller one before she found this one. It was just going to be herself, and she didn't need a lot of room. So Marcela decided to buy this one. It was already converted into four bedrooms to make the rooms spacious and comfortable. Marcela had the master bedroom and bathroom. Her mom had a room of her own. She made another room into an official guest bedroom, and the other guest room was more of Antonio's room. The last room was made into a makeshift office and shop for her to work on stuff for work at home.

It was just only a week ago that she thought that these rooms might actually be filled with her children. She liked to imagine what they would look like and what they would like to do. Would she have boys or girls or both? And now even though her life was far from over, it felt like that dream was coming to an end. She didn't know if she'd be able to trust someone with her heart again. That's the way it needed to be for her now. She needed it to make things easier for herself to get back to some kind of life now that her mom and now Anastasio were gone. She would live until she died and nothing more. She would build up a fence around her heart over a few days to ease the pain into something else, like not feeling at all!

The rest of her week went on like this. She felt completely numb and had no desire to see or talk to anyone, even Antonio. He had always been so good to her that she felt bad avoiding him. She was sure he already knew the reason, but he let her have her space as she needed it. He was protective of her. And it wasn't the part of telling him what was going on that she was avoiding. It was that she felt that if she didn't tell anyone, it didn't exist! But if she talked about it, it became very real again. So she became the person she was before the vacation. Only this time, she didn't have her mother to push her in the right direction.

Chapter 11

She had her sale, but it didn't go very well. She was fumbling around with everything and having a hard time concentrating. The clients that she had before that came in didn't seem too thrilled with what she had. The new customers seemed turned off by the negative energy she was putting out. It turned out to be a disaster, but she couldn't feel any more sorry for herself than she already felt.

Throughout the next several weeks, Marcela couldn't tell you when she did something, why she did something, or if she did anything at all. She tried to refuse to see anyone when she wasn't at work. She kept breathing even though there seemed to be no reason to breathe at all. At first, the hours seemed like days, the days seemed like weeks, and the weeks were unforgiving. Just a few days after Antonio had called her, he showed up at her house before she got off work and let himself in. From the looks of her place, it was apparent that she was hurting. There were dirty dishes all over the counter and in the sink. Laundry hadn't been done, her bedding almost falling off the bed. He was sitting and waiting for her in her living room when she got home. "So is there anything you'd like to talk about?" he asked as he purposely looked around the room.

She just looked at him and couldn't get the words out of her mouth. He came to her as she just stood in the doorway, unable to move, and wrapped his arms tightly around her. It was just in time too because the weight of the world seemed to bear down on her when she saw him and could no longer live in this fantasy world that Anastasio was no longer in. Her knees buckled, and she wept like she hadn't ever before. Everything hit her at once! Every person that treated her bad, every person's death in her life, and every failed relationship were all crashing down on her at once, and she lost control of her emotions for the second time in just over a few weeks, the first being with Anastasio just a mere few weeks ago.

She couldn't tell you how long she stood there, and she couldn't find the strength to move out of his arms. She guessed that he had to hold her up the whole time. After some time, he finally guided her to the couch and sat her down. He sat on the floor in front of her so he could look her directly where they could see each other when she could find the strength and courage to open her eyes. He just sat there holding her hand, waiting for her to speak first. He didn't care if it took all night. She would eventually start talking and let everything out. There was nothing more important to him at this moment. He would sit there and wait even if it took days.

After about thirty minutes, just that happened. It took her some time, but she recounted everything that had happened from the first encounter to when she didn't hear from him. She had to pause a lot because it was very painful for her to talk and think about. There wasn't anything she left out. Well, almost everything. She was so upset that she even found herself talking about not being able to function at work, the sale turning out not being so great because she had no interest in dealing with people, and the death of her mom, and the list went on and on. But Antonio sat there patiently, listening and taking in every word. He was truly an amazing friend to her. And she appreciated that he was a person that would truly listen to her and let her deal with things without trying to always offer a fix to the issues. He was always good like that.

For the rest of the night, they talked about everything that was going on. He knew she needed to eat, so he made a simple dinner for them to have. He thought about pouring some wine but assumed she didn't want any as there were dishes of every kind sitting out, but there was no wine bottles or glasses. They ate in silence before they continued talking about what had or, moreover, what hadn't happened. Even though Antonio didn't generally trust people quickly, especially ones he didn't know, he was even in disbelief that this was happening to her. He had gotten such a good feeling about this guy from everything that she had told him. Something just didn't make sense. And Antonio planned to figure out just what didn't add up. He had never searched anyone, but he was going to find out exactly what was going on. His best friend deserved that!

For the rest of the night they talked. He didn't tell her about his new-formed plans to find him and to find out what was going on. If and when he found him, then he would give him a piece of his mind! He wanted Anastasio to know and to feel how bad he had hurt Marcela. He wanted Anastasio to answer for why he did this to her. He had met some inconsiderate and bad people in his time, but this really made his blood boil. No one could hurt his friend like this and get away with it. From that moment on, he was plotting what he was going to do. He cared about nothing more than the day he would be face to face with Anastasio!

It had gotten late as she wrapped up telling him everything that had happened. He almost had to force her off the couch to get ready for bed. They both were tired and worn out after all the emotions that had poured out of Marcela. She had been holding this in for weeks now. He got her to bed, and she couldn't even keep her eyes open anymore. He wasn't far behind her in that matter. Usually he would either go home or sleep in his guest bedroom, but tonight, he felt that he should stay right there with her. He got ready for bed and joined her.

When he climbed into bed, he put his arm around her instinctively. He doubted that she even realized what she was doing, but she grabbed ahold of his hand and held him close to her body. He ached for the pain her heart was going through. He didn't think twice about holding her as tight as he could without waking her up. He wasn't sure if he was going to be able to sleep as he was thinking of the moves he was going to make, like in a game of chest, that he would do to get to the truth of what was going on. He wasn't going to let her down. She meant the world to him!

Antonio was seriously worried about his best friend. She was hurting more than he had ever seen before. He thought she was having a rough time when her mother died, but it was nothing like this! He wanted to keep a close eye on her and be there for whatever she needed. He was spending most of his free time with her. He also enlisted help from Lee and a couple of their other mutual friends. He would find a way to get her out of this slump. He would do whatever it took to see her happy again.

He talked with Lee several times, and they both wanted to help. Their first concern was making sure she was eating and getting to work. They knew she wasn't making enough to survive, but they were doing what they could to help her. They did grocery shopping, made sure she paid her bills on time, and kept an eye on her every evening when she wasn't working. They watched comedy movies that were funny but didn't involve any kind of romantic relationship that could upset her. That wasn't such an easy task as most comedies nowadays were romantic comedies.

They went through her phone to find the numbers she had for Anastasio. When they called his cell phone, there was never any answer. It just went to voice mail. When they called his home number, there was either no answer or his mother answered and said he no longer lived there. She wouldn't offer any more information and was quite rude each time she answered. But they didn't give up on trying to contact him. They called every day hoping that either someone else would answer or she would finally give up and tell them how to contact him.

But their efforts offered no fruits. They were blocked at every turn. Each time was either no answer or his mother became more hostile every time they called. If it weren't for the love they had for Marcela, they would have just given up. And giving up was not an option! Their friend was hurting, and they would do anything to find the truth and help her get through this pain she was in. It would just take more thought than they originally expected. It was time to hire someone to help them find Anastasio and find out what was going on.

They wanted to get answers and needed help in doing so. They decided that hiring a private investigator was the right answer, and they wouldn't let Marcela know what they were doing. She wouldn't agree with what they were planning to do. But they wanted to find out the truth, and second, they wanted him to know the pain she was in because of his actions. They wanted to make his life as miserable as they could possibly make it for him. He hurt their friend, and he was going to pay for that! They vowed to not quit looking for the truth, no matter how long it took or how much it cost them.

After they carefully researched investigators, they chose a couple that they thought seemed reputable, and they made appointments to go see them. The appointments went well, and they picked an investigator that really impressed them with his success in the past finding people and getting all the information that was asked for. His name was Alejandro, and he had been an investigator for fourteen years after leaving the police force. His fees were something they could realistically afford as well. He was confident that the case would be quite simple and should be completed quickly. They paid the retainer fee, and Alejandro assured them that he would keep them updated with anything he was able to find out.

Antonio and Lee took turns on keeping an eye on Marcela. They didn't want her to be alone when she wasn't working. She kept telling them that she was okay, but they knew better. She was hurting, and more depressed than they had ever seen her. She wasn't eating, she had lost interest in doing anything, and she seemed zoned out every time they saw her. They were worried about her driving and her overall well-being. They were determined to make her feel better, no matter what it took.

They were getting more worried about her because there were several times that they called her store or stopped by, and she wasn't there. When they asked about it without saying that they had stopped by, she told them that she couldn't answer the phone because she had customers, out for lunch, or several other excuses. They didn't like that she wasn't being honest with them, but they knew she was going through so much that they didn't want to make things worse for her.

Their hope was that little by little, she would get better. They knew these things took time and were ready to be patient with her as she coped with everything that was going on. They wished that they could just wave a magic wand and make everything better for her right away. It was unbelievable that someone could be so cold and didn't care who they hurt along the way. As much as they tried to understand what was happening, they couldn't think of any good reasons for the lack of consideration. It would be interesting to hear what he would have to say about it. They couldn't think of any reason for what he has done to Marcela! He was going to pay!

After a week of waiting for any answers, they finally got a call from Alejandro. He asked them to come in, and he would go over what he had found out. They confirmed that they would come in the following day. Both Antonio and Lee were very curious of what he had found out. They wished they could drop everything they had going on to find out that day, but it would have to wait until the next day. It had been hard to keep what they were doing from Marcela, and it was going to be even harder to keep whatever news they were going to get the next day. So many thoughts were going through their heads, each plotting what they planned to do with different scenarios that they could think they would get.

Lee spent that evening with Marcela. He cooked her dinner, and they sat and watched a movie. He tried to start a few different conversations that led nowhere. So now they sat in silence. It might have been for the best not to talk very much as his mind was distracted by the thoughts of Anastasio. He tried everything he could think of other things, but he couldn't for very long. He knew it wasn't even close to what Marcela's mind was going through, but he now understood a little bit of what she was feeling.

After the movie ended, she looked completely exhausted. He helped her get to bed and went back out to the kitchen to clean the dishes from cooking and having dinner. As he was cleaning, he sorted through her mail to make sure all her bills were paid on time. There was a big envelope that she hadn't opened from some insurance company. He opened it, thinking maybe it was some bill or something important that might need to be paid or immediate attention. There was a letter to Marcela explaining that they were the life insurance company that her mom had with. Marcela was listed as the sole beneficiary and that there was a check for the full amount that her mom had left. The check was for $500,000. Lee gasp when he read that and saw the check. No longer would Marcela have to stress about her daily finances since she wasn't doing well at work lately.

He left her house to head home and had left her a note to read the mail that he opened. He didn't say what he had seen. On his way home, he called Antonio to let him know how the night went and the news of the insurance check she had received. Antonio was elated of the news from Lee. They had previously talked about how each of them would contribute to help her financially if things didn't pick up for her. Antonio didn't make the most money in the world, and Lee was saving for his wedding that was coming up in a few months. They finished the conversation with when they were going to meet to go to see Alejandro.

Antonio found it hard to sleep with everything that was going on. It was a lot to digest at one time. He tossed and turned, and when he did sleep, his dreams were about finding out where Anastasio was and what he did when he found him. He also dreamed about Marcela being happy again and how the money made her stress disappear. He finally gave up on sleep early in the morning and got up and headed into his office early. He was leaving early to see the investigator so he could use the extra time to get things done.

He got to the office about two hours earlier than usual. With no one in the office yet, he found that he got a lot more done than usual. He thought that he should do this more often. He would get so much more than what he was currently getting done. Luckily, his mind was on work this morning versus what he was thinking about all night. The meeting with the investigator was set for 3:00 p.m., and he wouldn't be returning to work for the day. He called Lee to make sure that he was going to be on time for the meeting with Alejandro. Everything was all set for the meeting.

He left work after a very productive day and met Lee at his house. They rode together to the investigator's office. On the way, they talked about the great news of the insurance money that Marcela had received. Neither of them had talked to Marcela today and didn't know if she had looked at Lee's note or the mail from the insurance company. They were so focused on the meeting that they were heading to that they didn't try to talk with Marcela. They decided it was best to talk to her after the meeting and when she was off work. For now their focus was on the meeting they were about to have.

They got the office about ten minutes prior to their appointment. The secretary told them that it would be just a few moments before they would be seen. They sat in the waiting room, and Lee asked Antonio if he thought that private investigators really needed a secretary and needed a waiting room. How many people hired investigators enough to need a waiting room? It wasn't long before Alejandro called them into his office. They were eager to find out what he had uncovered.

He welcomed them into his office, and they sat, eager to hear what he had found. They sat, and Alejandro didn't waste any time getting to the information they wanted. He started by saying that it wasn't what he expected to find. After careful research and the help with a few people, he found out that Anastasio was in the hospital and had cancer of the stomach and esophagus. He was currently in the hospital, but they would release him soon. There wasn't much they could do since he didn't have any insurance that could pay for the doctors he might need to get better. For all purposes they knew, Anastasio wouldn't live very long in his current condition. He had found out right around the time that he disappeared from existence as far as Marcela was concerned.

It was not what either of them had expected. As mad as they were at Anastasio before, it was erased by the news they had just received. They felt bad for the guy and now understood why he had stopped contacting Marcela. They would probably do the same thing. He was protecting her from being even more hurt by the news they had just found out. Neither of them had even thought of something like this. He hadn't played her like they had thought. Perhaps everything he had told Marcela and said he had felt was real. Perhaps he was actually a good guy but was trying to shield the truth from Marcela. Perhaps he knew she would not care about his illness and would insist on being there for him. He was just protecting her from being hurt even more.

They left his office in utter disbelief. Neither of them had imagined this in the thoughts they had. The walk back to Antonio's car was almost in complete silence. Once they reached his car, they started to discuss what their next move was. Was it best to tell Marcela about what they had found out? Or was it best to leave it as it was and let time heal her wounds? Both seemed to be the wrong answer. The question now was, what would they tell or not tell Marcela? They decided that they needed to tell Marcela what they had found. It was the right thing to do. They weren't sure if it would help or hurt the situation, but they were her friends, and they would not hide the truth from her any longer. The question was, how would they tell her? They decided to just do it that night together. They didn't have any kind of script or real way they planned on telling her. Whatever came out at that time, they would just go with.

Antonio and Lee met again at 6:00 p.m. They wanted to be at her house before she got home from work. They planned to make her dinner, and afterward, they would start the conversation that neither of them wished to be having. It was better than if they had found out that Anastasio was just leading her on the whole time. But it was still going to be exceedingly difficult to tell her. They knew that as much as she was hurting now, it was probably going to get worse for the short term. They hoped it was the best thing to do in the long run. What else could they do? They had found out what was going on, and they were hiding it from her. They didn't feel it was right to continue to keep their findings from her.

Marcela hadn't had the best day as the customers that had come in didn't stay long and didn't buy anything she had to offer. When she pulled into her driveway, she saw both Lee and Antonio's car. It wasn't unusual at this point to see either of their cars there. But to see both of them there at the same time hadn't happened in some time. She immediately wanted to drive off to some unknown destination. The day she had was enough for her for the whole day and evening. She just wanted to go inside, change into some comfortable clothes, and zone out for the evening. She knew now that that wasn't going to happen.

She walked into the house, and Antonio and Lee were cooking dinner together. They had some music playing in the background. They smiled and greeted her with hugs and a glass of wine.

She excused herself to go change. She didn't really want to leave her room, but she knew it was best to get whatever was going on over with. She expected it was going to be a long night ahead of her. She washed her face and braced herself for what was to come.

When she came out to the dining area, the table was already set with the food that they had made. They all sat, and Lee poured some wine for all of them. It was a dish she liked very much. It was simple but very tasty. Pasta with chicken and broccoli in a butter garlic sauce. She sat, and they did right after her. Antonio put portions on each of their plates. She sat and was nervous about what was to come. She couldn't remember the last time she saw both of them together at the same time other than the days after her mother had died. She suspected it was going to be a long night indeed.

After dinner, it wasn't a comfortable feeling for Antonio and Lee. As much as they had thought about what they were going to say in the last few hours, it was harder now that Marcela was right there in their face. Each time that one of them thought they had grown the courage to say something, they would back down thinking that it wasn't the right decision to tell her. They started to second-guess their decision to tell her about what they had learned. Nothing seemed right regarding what was going on. It was harder to do in person than what they thought when she wasn't right in front of her. But it had to be done! They kept giving each other glances to see if one of them was going to start the conversation.

Finally, Antonio took a bold first step and started the conversation that no one wanted to have. It wasn't going to get any easier, so he decided to just dive headfirst into what was going on. "Marcela, we need to talk about something serious. I know you are going through the hardest time of your life, but we can't hold the truth from you."

She looked at him in a questioning face and also looked at Lee to see what his face showed. His face confirmed that whatever Antonio had to say was serious. She had no idea what was going on, but she wasn't really prepared for a lecture or a speech about how she should be living her life. Why else would they both be there and wanted to talk about something serious? She saw Lee's note this morning on the table but didn't read it as she waited to the last minute to get ready for work. There was a small possibility it was about that, but she seemed to think it was unlikely. She finally said, "What is it?" It was with much less conviction than she meant as it came out in a weak and unsure way.

Antonio looked at Lee and took a deep breath before starting. "Marcela, we know how rough the last several weeks have been for you. We just want to help you in any way that we can." He looked at Lee, a bit nervous about going on, but he knew he had to. They had come this far. He just needed to get it out. "I don't want you to be upset with us, but you may be. Just know that we had only the best intentions for you."

She looked at him, then to Lee, and didn't say a word. But the look she gave them said it all. She was clearly upset. "What did you do?"

This time Lee took control of the conversation. He felt emboldened at the moment. "We hired an investigator to find Anastasio. We wanted to find him to know why he did this to you! You might not like that we did it, but we did. We love you!"

She looked back and forth between them. Her mouth was now wide open, and it was hard to tell if it was anger or disbelief or somewhere in between. "What do you mean you hired an investigator?"

Lee started again. "We just wanted to find out what was going on. You can hate us all you want for doing it. But we did it in the best interest of you."

Marcela's eyes were wide open and now tearing up. "Who told you to do that? I don't care why or what he is up to. I don't want to know! I don't want to hear his name or what he did or what he's doing..." She put her head in her hands to keep the tears from showing.

Antonio started to talk again. "I know this is hard on you. It's hard on all of us! Even though it didn't happen to us, it kind of did. You know we love you and would do anything for you, just like you would for us. We think you deserve an answer for what happened. We wanted to know as well. You were so happy, then you were destroyed by what happened. We couldn't just sit here and do nothing while you were hurting."

She lifted her head just enough to look at them. She shook her head and said, "Well, go ahead, then! Tell me why the man I fell in love with didn't want to be with me." Tears were streaming down her face now.

Antonio and Lee looked at each other to see who was going to tell her this part. Lee took the lead. "It's not as simple as that. Marcela, we don't think he chose to not be with you. He's, he's…"

She was looking at him very intently now. "He's what? Married? He's not who he said he was?" She was going to keep going but Lee interrupted her before she could.

"Marcela, he's sick!" It came out harsher than he meant it to. He took a deep breath and started again. "Marcela, he has cancer and is in the hospital. He has been there since about the time that you stopped hearing from him."

"You talked with him? How is he? What are they doing for him?" she asked as her head was now spinning.

Antonio answered this time, "No, we haven't tried to contact him. We just found out today. We didn't like keeping what we were doing from you. And when we found this out, we thought it was best to tell you now."

She felt like she couldn't breathe. The man she loved was in the hospital with cancer! Was life really that cruel to take her mother, let her find love, and have him taken away from sickness too? In an instance, she was no longer mad at Anastasio but at God! This just wasn't fair. She needed a break from life right now. She was dizzy and unable to speak. She was glad she was sitting because she didn't think her legs could hold her up. She wasn't sure if the chair would hold her much longer now. Maybe the floor would be better for her anyways. She could curl up into a ball, and maybe her heart would stop beating. That's all she wanted right now.

She did just that. She rolled off her chair and curled up on the floor. Antonio was the first one to her. He didn't say anything to her. He just sat next to her and put his hand on her back and rubbed it to let her know she wasn't alone. He looked at Lee, and they silently communicated about what to do or say next. But for the moment, silence was probably best. They were in shock when they heard the news. It had to be a thousand times harder for her. He wished he could take away her pain. She didn't deserve what she was going through. He'd give anything to make it different. But all he could do is be there for whatever she needed, just like the he did in past several weeks.

After about fifteen minutes of rubbing her back, he pulled her head up and put it in his lap. Lee handed him a napkin from the table, and Antonio wiped the tears away from her face. Within seconds, her face was completely wet again. He felt so bad for her! He broke the silence and said, "I know it's hard. We don't know everything yet. Let's see what's going on. Maybe things are better than they seem now. Doctors are incredibly good these days. I'm sure he didn't want to worry you about his health, so maybe he thought this was the best thing to do."

It took her a little time before she tried to talk. It came out almost as a whisper. "Why is this happening?"

He stroked her face and said, "I don't know! I'm sure in time everything will be understood. Even if we don't see the light at the end of the tunnel, we're here for you and always will be!" He knew his words weren't going to help her right now, but it was the best answer he could give.

She was visibly shaking, and she couldn't control her tears. She looked up at Antonio and cleared her throat. "There is no light! Do you remember asking me why I was gone from work several times? Well…" It took her another minute to get out what she was trying to say. "I'm pregnant! How is there light?"

Antonio and Lee looked at each other, then back to her. They were surprised yet again! This time Lee spoke first, "How long have you known?"

"A few weeks now," she said.

Now things were adding up. This is why she slipped away from work. It also made sense that they never saw wine bottles opened, they never saw her drink lately, and she hadn't touched the wine they had poured for her at dinner. "I know nothing makes sense now, but I'm sure you'll get everything figured out in time. We're here to help you any way we can," Antonio said.

Marcela didn't answer back and closed her eyes. It wasn't too long before she fell asleep. They were sure that she was emotionally drained. He didn't try to move her. He kept stroking her face and hair. He and Lee quietly discussed what their next move would be. They felt they needed to find out more about what was going on with Anastasio's health now. They weren't sure if Alejandro would be able to find out Anastasio's prognosis, but they would get whatever information they could. They owed that much to Marcela.

They sat there for about an hour before they decided to wake Marcela and get her to bed. When they woke her up, she could barely open her eyes. Lee was stronger than Antonio, so he picked her up and carried her to her bed. He didn't try to get her changed. He just laid her down in the bed and covered her up. He was sure she fell asleep as soon as her head was on the pillow. They hadn't discussed who was going to stay with her for the evening. They would figure it out. They still had more to talk about before either one of them left for the night.

Quite happy with Alejandro's job on finding Anastasio and getting the information that he did, they were confident in having him dig more into the situation. Hopefully he would be able to come up with the answers they were searching for. They only hoped the answers would be positive and that somehow everything would work out for Marcela and Anastasio. They felt awful for the both of them. Even though they didn't know Anastasio, they were quite sure that he was going through a very tough time too. It couldn't have been easy for him to make the decision to stop contacting Marcela. They had no reason to now think that he didn't love her. It was probably that same love that made him make the choice he had made.

They called and left a message for Alejandro to call them back when he had the chance. Lee decided that he would stay with her for the night. Antonio looked exhausted, and Lee knew that he had gone into work early. He was very thankful for Antonio! He was a really good friend to her. He was a good friend to him as well. He said his goodbyes to Antonio and gave him a big hug before letting him go. Even though it wasn't them specifically going through all this, it was emotionally draining on them too.

After Antonio left, Lee made his way into the second bathroom and found a new toothbrush, brushed his teeth, and went to the guest bedroom and lay down. Normally he slept very well when he was there. But he knew tonight his senses were on high alert. He didn't want to not hear her if she needed him. He also wanted to keep a close eye on her. He knew her depression was very real. He didn't think she would do something stupid, but he was going to make sure she knew she wasn't alone. He was seriously worried about her. They didn't know exactly how she would take the news that they told her. He guessed he probably would have reacted in a similar way. She was stronger than she thought she was. He couldn't imagine having to go through everything she was going through.

He woke several times throughout the night. Each time, he went and checked on Marcela. She hadn't moved from the position he had left her in. He knew she was exhausted but thought she might wake and be restless. That wasn't the case. He heard her alarm going off around 6:00 a.m. and wished he would have thought of checking it during the night so she could just sleep without any interruption. He didn't expect that she would feel like going into work today anyways. He hoped she would sleep in and get the rest she needed.

He walked into her room, and she was starting to sit up. She looked dazed and confused, so he walked over and sat on the bed next to her. Her eyes were still red and swollen from all the crying that she did the night before. Her stare was blank. She didn't seem to really be looking at anything but only looked at one spot. She didn't turn to look at him or try to say anything. He knew that there wasn't much she would want to say at this point.

He went over and sat on the bed next to her. "Hey there! How are you feeling?" he asked as he put his hand on her knee and rubbed it gently.

Without looking his way, she said, "I'm alive, I'm breathing, but I'm not sure why."

He wished there were something he could say that would erase her pain. "I know! I wish I could take away your pain. I know it's hard to see it now, but your life will go on. It has to! You will have someone amazing to care for someday soon. I know you will find your happiness. It will just take time."

She looked away from him now. "And what am I supposed to do in that time? I just feel numb! The world no longer makes sense to me. I guess this is my punishment for not living life how I should've before now. I took everything and everyone for granted! I don't know how I'm supposed to take care of anyone. I can't even take care of myself right now!"

"That's not true! You are an amazing person, Marcela! How long have I known you now? Eight years or so? I can't think of a better person that I have met."

"You shouldn't think that. I was with you and didn't treat you right in our relationship. I took you for granted. And here you are! Why?" She looked straight into his eyes and kept going, "You should run as fast as you can!"

He looked back at her with the same intensity that she was looking at him. "It wasn't the right time for you, and I wasn't the right person. They say everything happens for a reason, right?" As soon as he said that, he regretted it.

"Exactly! Everything happens for a reason." She again looked away from him. She didn't say anything else. She didn't have to. She did have a point. He didn't know how any of this was going to turn out any more than she did. He thought it best not to say anything else at the moment. He just kept rubbing her leg and stayed silent.

It wasn't long before she started to get out of the bed. He didn't really want to let her up, but he wasn't sure her intention. Maybe she needed the bathroom or wanted just to clean up. He would wait and see what her intentions were. He would try to convince her not to go to work if that's what she was planning. He knew he couldn't stop her, but he would do what he could to keep her home for the day.

She went into the bathroom and started the shower. She felt very weak but didn't think that anything was going to change that. She had eaten before she had heard the news, so she shouldn't be too weak from that. It was about the only news worse than him not wanting to be with her. She cared more about his life more than she cared for her own. He really was the man she thought he was! He deserved to live, and she deserved the pain she was going through. He didn't deserve what was being handed to him. She didn't know what to think. It was the worst possible news she could think of.

She got in the shower and held on to anything she could so she wouldn't fall. The last thing she wanted was for Lee to come storming in and having to pick her up off the floor. In fact, she didn't even remember how she got off the floor last night. All she really remembered is hearing the news that they had told her and then waking up to her alarm. She had no idea what happened between those two times. She had the same clothes on when she woke as she had on yesterday. She only hoped that she didn't do or say anything that she would regret later.

Lee was pacing outside the bathroom door. He wanted to just barge in and make sure she was okay. But he knew she also should have her privacy. He even called Antonio to ask his advice of what he should do. Neither were sure of the best action to take. Lee decided to wait in her room until she was out of the shower. He wanted to stay in her room just in case he heard her fall or if she needed him for any reason. He was definitely in unchartered waters now. This was the first and hopefully the last time that he experienced something like this.

It was about thirty minutes later that he heard the shower turn off. He stayed attentive to sounds coming from the bathroom to ensure she was okay. He figured she would be weak after everything she had gone through last night, this morning, and everything she experienced in the last couple of weeks. He couldn't even begin to imagine the pain she was in right now. If the same had happened to him, he didn't think he would even be able to get out of bed for months. He wouldn't be able to eat, work, or do anything. She was stronger than she knew.

It wasn't too much longer before she came out of the bathroom. Her eyes were still swollen, but she looked better than she did when she woke. She didn't say anything as she went to her closet to get some clothes. She disappeared back into the bathroom with her clothes. Lee wanted to protest as he knew that she planned to go to work. If she wasn't going to work, she wasn't the type to get dressed right away in the morning. He knew her well enough to know that. He would try to stop her when she came back out. Maybe she would allow him to take her to breakfast. After that, he would figure it out. He had already decided that he would stay with her instead of going to work today.

She came back out dressed as she usually did when going to work. She avoided looking at him. He was sure she did it because she knew he was going to try to convince her not to go to work. She knew him just as well as he knew her. She walked out of the room and went into the kitchen to find something to eat. She was hungrier than she usually was. She knew Lee had followed her into the kitchen but still ignored that he was there. She didn't mean it to be mean, but she didn't want to talk about anything that they had talked about last night.

She found some fruit and poured a glass of orange juice. She chose to stand by the island in her kitchen and not sit down. It was easier to avoid being questioned than if she was sitting next to him. She finally looked at him. She was happy when he only looked at her and didn't say anything immediately. She knew the look he was giving her though. The silence wouldn't last much longer.

"Are you seriously thinking you are going to work?" he asked as he went to pour himself an orange juice.

"Why wouldn't I? I need the money," she said without looking at him.

"I assume you didn't look at your mail that I left a note for you to read." He walked around her and found it sitting in the same place he had left it. The note was still on it. He picked it up and placed it on the counter in front of her. "You need to look at this."

She tried to walk around him, but he blocked her. She had never seen him like this. She knew he was serious and immediately retreated to the counter and picked up the mail. She opened the envelope and started to read the letter that Lee had read previously. She had to read it twice! Now tears were streaming down her face again. She couldn't even turn the page to read anything else or see the check. Her hands were shaking.

She didn't know how many more things could come up. Yes, she should be happy about receiving the money, but it made all the memories of her mother come flooding back. First, she had to deal with her mom passing, then the loneliness that made her decide to go on the trip and all the uncertainties that came with that. Then meeting Anastasio and thinking her mom would be proud of her for finally opening up her heart and mind. She fell head over heels in love with him. She let herself be genuinely happy for the first time in her life that she could remember. She made plans for her future that didn't only consist of work. Then the whole deal with Anastasio not contacting her and feeling that he didn't want her. Finding out she was going to be having his baby. Finding out that he was sick. And now her mom still taking care of her because she couldn't do it herself. She felt like a child now. Even in death, her mom was still doing it! It wasn't the best feeling to have.

Lee could see that she was crying and shaking again. Now he felt bad for making her look at the mail. He thought it would be a good thing for her. But on second thought, he could see why she was very upset. He went over to her and hugged her from behind. She put her hands on his arms and allowed him to hold her. She didn't feel like she was going to crumble onto the floor this time. But she liked the closeness that he was offering.

She was glad that he wasn't trying to talk to her as she wasn't sure if she had the ability to understand anything right now. She just held onto him tightly. She knew it was ultimately good news that she just got. All was hard to see right now. She just wanted to feel sorry for herself and wallow in her misery. As much as she wanted to move, there was no way she was going to work now. There was no way that she could drive right now. And she was going to be even more worthless than before as she knew her mind was going to be on everything that happened.

He waited a few more minutes before asking if she wanted to sit on the couch. She didn't speak but nodded. He helped her out of the kitchen and into the living room. He sat her down and sat right beside her. He carefully chose his next words to her, "I know it's a lot to take in! But your mom loved you, cared for you, and was responsible enough to not put the expenses of her funeral on you. She also wanted to make sure you'd be okay in the future. Now you will be able to take your time to make the designs you always dreamed of without the worry of day-to-day finances. And now it won't only be you. You have to take care of another person before too long. I know it will take time to take this all in."

She didn't answer him back again. She just sat in silence trying to control her emotions. She didn't enjoy being such an emotional wreck in front of everyone. It was better that it was Lee and Antonio there, not anyone else. They were more understanding than anyone she had ever met in her entire life. She was truly grateful for having them as friends. It was still nice having Lee as a friend, as many couples that break up didn't remain friends. And as much as she didn't want to admit it, he was right about it all.

Her tears had stopped, and she just felt numb again. She didn't know if she could feel anything ever again. Her heart had enough pain in the last two months to last a lifetime. She knew now that her wish to die wasn't going to happen. Life was going to keep going! And it would punish her for not appreciating life before now. She would go through the motions of living, but she would only be filling space until life was done with its cruelty!

She tried to think about the happiness a baby might bring to her. But every time she imagined how the baby would look, all she could see was Anastasio's face. She wasn't sure she could bear it. She already missed him so much. Why couldn't he get better and be part of the new family she was going to have? She wondered how the child would feel after getting a little older about what happened to their dad. She didn't want to think about having to explain everything and bring up the whole deal over again. Life was going to be a serious challenge!

Chapter 12

Anastasio couldn't find sleep. His stomach was becoming more and more painful, and he found himself getting sick for several hours. He knew now that this was something more than food poisoning or lack of rest. He saw blood each time that he got sick. He decided it was best to go into the emergency room to get checked out. He wasn't going to be able to sleep anyways. It was the right choice to make.

He woke his parents up before he planned to leave. He told them that he would let them know what was going on when he knew. Neither of them was about to let him go to the emergency room alone. They didn't have much experience with him being sick to the point that he needed to go to the emergency room or even the doctor. He grew up with an extremely healthy body. He protested that it wasn't necessary in the middle of the night for them to come. He probably wouldn't know anything until the morning anyways. They told him that they were coming, and that was that!

The hospital was a bit of a drive from their home. By the time they arrived at the emergency room, it was about 3:00 a.m. Luckily, there weren't too many people waiting to be seen. He had heard horror stories from other people that the wait seemed to be forever when going to the emergency room. He only ended up waiting for about an hour before they called him and showed him into a room. Since he was not feeling well and in a lot of pain, he was happy with the short wait. All he wanted was to find out what was going on and to start feeling better again very soon.

Once he got in the room and got changed into the lovely gown they provide, the nurse came in and started an IV on him. She asked exactly what had brought him in, how long had it been going on, his previous medical issues, and his medications, and it seemed the list wasn't going to end. After what seemed forever, the doctor came in and asked the same question the nurse had asked him. Not feeling well, he was annoyed that he had to repeat everything over again. His mom kept making noises that showed frustration in the process they were going through. She even started to chime in and told the doctor to please start doing any tests that needed to be done right away.

The doctor told him that he was ordering a CT scan, a few x-rays, and routine blood work. For the next hour, he was poked to give them his blood and start an IV, had x-rays done, and did the CT scan. He was exhausted, but with everything going on, there wasn't going to be any sleep for him. They did give him some pain and nausea medicines that were helping the pain and keeping him from getting sick as much as he was before they came. His mother was already driving him crazy with asking him how he was feeling and if she could do anything and kept calling the nurse to see what was going on. He kept telling her to be patient, but that was like trying to tell a dog not to wag its tail. He wished now that he would have come to the hospital without waking them and dealt with them in the morning.

His eyes were getting heavy as the drugs had kicked in, and the beeping of the machines were making him drowsy. His dad was sleeping already, sitting up in his chair. He swore that man could sleep through anything, possibly even standing up if he needed to. His mom was off somewhere, probably trying to find his nurse or doctor to continue to annoy them to make sure they knew we were still there. He figured that by bothering them so much, they probably were going to purposely make them wait longer. That's what he would do in that case.

He wasn't sure how much time had passed when the doctor came back in. He was in and out of sleep. Every time he was actually sleeping well, his mom would wake him to ask how he was. The doctor asked if it was okay to talk about results with them in the room. Of course, he said yes. His mother would throw a fit if she wasn't allowed to hear what was going on. His doctor looked either very somber or very tired or maybe a combination of both. He sat down in the only chair left in the room. Anastasio knew now that he wasn't going to like what he was going to say.

The doctor looked at Anastasio with an intense look. "I'm not going to sugarcoat this! Based on your blood work and the CT scan, it looks like you may have cancer of the stomach and esophagus. We will need to biopsy both to know more. It's why you have been getting sick and not feeling well. I'm so sorry to have to tell you this! I know it will take you time to process what's going on. I will leave you to talk with your parents, and I will come back in about thirty minutes, and we will talk about the next steps you need to take. Again, I'm sorry to have to give you this news!"

Anastasio couldn't even answer the doctor as he left. He really couldn't even process the information that he had just heard. He couldn't have cancer! He was only thirty-eight. He didn't smoke, drink too much, or eat bad things. He was a pretty healthy person. He didn't exercise as much as he would've liked to, but he was still very fit. He wanted to think the tests were wrong. But the doctor had said the blood work and the CT scan had shown otherwise. How could this be? He wished that he could have another answer, but he already knew that the doctor likely had it right.

His mom and dad were now standing next to him. His mom held his hand. She had tears streaming down her face. "Oh, Anastasio!" She stopped speaking. She was overwhelmed with emotion. She wanted to say more but couldn't seem to catch her breath.

His dad took over. "Son, we will do whatever it takes to get you better! Let's see what we have to do to get you past this. You will be fine, I know it!" He didn't have anything else to add. He just walked to the other side of the bed and took his other hand in his. There were tears in his eyes as well.

Anastasio had never seen his father cry. His mom now had her head on his chest, weeping loudly. He didn't feel so encouraged at the moment, seeing them cry. He was so numb that he couldn't even cry now. He still couldn't think straight or say anything. He was lost! He was glad now that he wasn't alone when he got the news. As hard as it was to see his parents like this, he needed them. He thought of Marcela and wished she was there with him.

Marcela! He hadn't thought about how she would take the news until that moment. She had just lost her mother. She would be devastated by the news! Even if he got better, it was going to be extremely difficult for her and him for that matter. He would probably have to cancel his move. He would need to be with his doctors, and his mom didn't work, and his dad worked lots of hours in the vineyard. It would be easier for them to take care of him. Maybe she could move to Italy until he got better if that was even possible. He didn't know anything about stomach and esophagus cancer. This was going to be one of the longest mornings of his life.

The doctor came back when he said he would. His parents had finally found their composure. Anastasio was still in complete shock and hadn't spoken yet. His parents were standing behind him on both sides of the bed. His father went back to his chair to make room for the doctor to talk to Anastasio. The room wasn't very big, so there wasn't too much room for multiple people to standing on either side. His mom stayed by his side, holding his hand. She was squeezing his hand very hard now. Her palm was sweaty. He guessed she might be more nervous than he was.

"I know this is very hard for you all! It's hard for me to come in and talk with people that don't get good news. You have choices to make. First, we can admit you, and tomorrow morning, they can do a scope that goes down your throat to biopsy the areas and give you more specific answers than we can here in the emergency room. Then they can give you more information, maybe run some more tests, and go from there. Second option, you can go home and do this as an outpatient. It will be slower than if we admit you. I know some people don't like to be in hospitals, so I understand if you don't want to be admitted. I will give you some time to talk with your family and decide what you'd like to do. Before I go, how is your pain and nausea? I can have the nurse bring you more if you need it."

For the first time in half an hour, Anastasio finally spoke. "I'm okay for now, thank you." He didn't feel any pain now. His whole body was numb. If someone cut off his leg or arm, he probably would have no idea it happened unless he saw it.

As soon as the doctor left the room, his mom said, "Honey, we will get you admitted and get everything done right away. I will stay here with you. You shouldn't waste any time! I don't know why they have to wait until tomorrow to do that scope thing. We will try to get them to do it today!"

"Dad, can you get my phone?"

"Why do you need your phone right now?" his mom asked.

"I need to call Marcela and talk with her about what I should do!"

"This is a family matter. If she loves you, she will understand that! Besides, what are you going to tell her? You don't know everything yet, and you will break that girl's heart!" she said sharply.

"I can't just not call her!" he said just as sharply.

"Let's get you admitted, and we will talk about that later. Right now, your focus should be on getting these tests done. You will have time for all that later."

His dad looked confused on what he should do. He had Anastasio's phone in his hand but was still sitting in the chair. Anastasio wanted to argue but knew it was pointless. When his mom was like this, there was no changing her mind. She always had to get her way regardless if it was right or wrong. Most of the time she had the best intentions. At other times, she just wanted things that would benefit her. He looked at his dad and, in a soft and deflated voice, said, "It's okay, Dad! I will call her later." He stayed silent again until the doctor came back in.

"Have you had time to discuss this and make a decision?"

Before Anastasio could try to answer, his mom blurted out, "He will admit!"

The doctor looked at Anastasio for confirmation. He had seen this too many times where the patient didn't want what the others wanted. Anastasio just nodded to the doctor. He didn't have anything else to say right now. His mind was on Marcela now and what he was going to say to her. He would have to think of how to break the news to her! He hadn't even told her he was feeling so bad. She was probably going to be upset that he didn't tell her before now. And even worse, she was going to be devastated by the news. He wasn't looking forward to telling her!

The doctor shook his hand, wished him good luck, and left to start the paperwork to have him admitted. His mom kept holding his hand. He wasn't sure if it was going to be good or bad to have her there with him every day and night. She generally drove him crazy when he had to spend just one whole day with her. He really could use some alone time to think about the things that were going on. He also wanted to think about what he was going to say to Marcela. He couldn't leave her in the dark. He loved her! He didn't want to hurt her, but what else could he do?

About an hour later, he was moved into the room that he would be staying in. He didn't know how long they would keep him. And other than the scope, he didn't know what other tests he would have to do. He hoped he would be able to go home soon but really had no clue what was going to happen. For the first time in his life, he was scared! It was the worst timing he could think of.

The rest of the morning was spent telling nurses of his medical history, if he took medications, and answers to what seemed like an endless line of questioning. There was a couch in his room that his mom had already lay down on. She was sleeping, but he still didn't have time to think about things without any interruptions. Each time he tried to focus on it, someone else would come in and give him this or that. This was the first experience he had in the hospital, and now he understood what people meant that you can't get rest in a hospital.

Around noon they brought him lunch, but he really didn't feel like eating. His nerves were still shot, and the pain and nausea medications made him feel tired and made his brain foggy. He gave his lunch to his mom as she refused to leave the room to go get lunch. He was very tired and found himself in and out of sleep for the next few hours. He wanted to be able to figure things out, but it was impossible being drugged like this. He hoped the sleep would help.

A few hours past, and he felt a little better when he woke up. His mom was watching TV when he woke. She saw him moving and turned off the TV and came over to the bed and sat on the edge of it next to him. "How are you feeling? I hope the TV didn't wake you."

"No, not at all. The sleep helped! I still feel quite drugged, but I guess that's going to be something I'm going to have to get used to while in the hospital."

"Maybe they will start giving you less medicines soon. Are you hungry? Want something to drink?"

"I'm okay for now, thank you!"

"I wish they would start the tests today. I don't know why they have to wait until tomorrow!"

"Mom, it's Sunday. Unless it's a matter of life or death, they will wait for the regular doctors to be back tomorrow. It's only one day."

"Is this not a matter of…" She couldn't finish her sentence as she turned her head away.

"They can't fix this in a day. Can we please talk about something else?"

She composed herself and turned to him. "Yes, I'm sorry! I think there is something we need to talk about though. I know you aren't going to want to talk about it, but it's something I've been thinking about while you were sleeping. We need to discuss what you are going to do with Marcela."

No, he didn't want to talk about it, especially with her, but he was too drugged to fight her. Besides, she wasn't going to drop it until he let her talk. "What is there to discuss?"

"Well, I was thinking about it. I think you need to let her go! It will be easier for her in the long run. I know how you think you feel about each other. You only have known each other a short time. You need to focus all your energy on getting better. You will find someone even better when you are well!"

"I'm sorry, Mom, but I can't do that! And I've been around for many years and never found someone even close to her!"

"I know you think that now. But think of that poor girl! You could ruin her life if you don't get better!" He tried to speak, but she put up her hand to finish. "We have to unite as a family to help you get through this. You wouldn't be able to go see her anyways. Please listen to me. I know you don't think I make the right decisions sometimes, but I have always tried to do the best thing for you!"

"I know you have! I appreciate it. I really do! But I don't think what you are saying is the best thing to do. We love each other!"

"Okay, let me say it another way. If you genuinely love her, you will let her go. Think about it. It is the best decision. Do you really want to hurt her more than you need to? It is the right decision."

He didn't answer her after that. What could he say to change her mind? There wasn't anything, so there was no reason to keep trying. He just closed his eyes and tried to relax. He wanted to think about what he should tell her and do now, but he was still too drugged. His mom didn't move from where she was sitting. He guessed that maybe she was waiting for him to open his eyes so she could talk more about things he really didn't want to talk about right now or possibly ever! Soon he drifted off to sleep.

His dreams were filled with dealing with doctors, being sick, his parents, and Marcela. Each time Marcela was involved in the dreams, it wasn't good thoughts. She was crying and cursing God for him being sick. She was so broken up over the news! One dream, she took her own life from learning of him being ill. There were bad dreams about him wasting away and not getting better. And each time he knew all he had to do was wake up to end the dream, but he couldn't!

Several hours passed, and when he woke, his room was empty. He didn't see his mom anywhere. He was very sweaty and felt completely exhausted still. He tried to erase the dreams out of his head, but he kept reliving each one. He never had dreams like this and guessed it was from the drugs and the conversation he had with his mom. He was very upset and wanted to forget the dreams forever. He had a sneaking feeling though that wasn't going to happen. He saw now that he was going to have to think about the things he didn't want to even as drugged as he was.

He didn't want to admit it, but maybe his mom was right. Maybe letting her go was the best decision. If he wasn't going to get better or if it took a long time, that would ruin her life, just as his mom had pointed out. And he couldn't ask her to come live there until he got better as he first thought. She would have to get up her whole life on a chance that he would get better. He couldn't do that to her! Not with all that she had been through in her life. But what was he going to tell her? He had to have some kind of reason for breaking things off with her. He didn't want to lie or hide things from her more than he already had. She did deserve better than that. This wasn't going to be easy no matter how he did it. And he hadn't even begun to think about what that was going to do for himself. He couldn't believe how fast his world could be turned upside down. But he didn't care about what happened to himself currently. All he cared about was Marcela!

His mom came back in about an hour after he had woken. She must have gone home because she had changed and had a bag with her. She asked him again how he was feeling, and he told her he was okay. He was far from okay, but he didn't want her asking a million questions! She sat on the edge of the bed again and rubbed his lower arm. "Your dad will be up here in a little bit."

"He doesn't need to come up here. I know he must be tired and needs to do things."

"He doesn't need to. He wants to! Besides, he's going to bring us leftovers from yesterday so that we can all eat together."

He put on a fake smile and didn't protest anymore. The pasta did sound good now that he hadn't eaten since the day before. The thoughts he just had were still lingering in his head. He almost decided against it but finally just asked, "Mom, I guess you are right. It wouldn't be fair to her. But what do I say to her? I don't want to lie to her!"

"I have thought about that, and I think the best thing is to just not contact her anymore. It will only make things worse for both of you!"

"Wait, what do you mean? I shouldn't say anything to her? That seems a bit harsh! She may think awful things or that I had an accident or in the…" He trailed off knowing that his last statement was where he actually was, the hospital. "She will look for me. She's not just going to accept that I am gone out of her life."

"I'm sure she will. But over time she will stop. But you shouldn't contact her or text her or reply to anything! We can ask that the hospital not provide any information to anyone about your health or that you are even here. She will get over it in time. And so will you! You have your family here with you. That's all you need for now. Be strong, for you and for her!"

He wasn't sure that was the right answer, but he didn't have a better one at the moment. So for now, he would leave it be. Besides, he had no idea where his phone was or if she had taken it home to keep him from trying to talk to her. He suspected she did. He asked his mom to turn on the TV. She was still standing beside him, so he scooted over and told her to lie down next to him. She smiled and laid back with him. She patted him on his thigh and told her everything was going to be okay.

About an hour later, his dad showed up. He looked much better than he did in the morning. He must have gotten the rest that he needed. He came over and gave Anastasio a kiss on the forehead. He couldn't remember the last time his dad did something like that. He knew both his parents must be very worried about him. He worried about his dad mainly! He wasn't getting any younger, and the stress from the decrease in sales had him worried quite a bit. Now this wasn't going to help!

He smiled at his dad, and his dad winked back at him. That was their thing. Anastasio remembered when he was very young, his dad had some clients over, and they were touring the vineyard. They were walking past Anastasio as he was playing in the yard. His dad looked over and gave him a big wink. He couldn't have been more than four or five, but he never forgot that. After that, his dad would randomly wink at him, and it always brought a smile to his face. It still worked to this day! It's funny that some of the smallest things meant the most to you in life. Most of the big things in life he could barely remember. Wasn't it the good things you were supposed to remember and not the bad?

His mom pulled everything out of a bag his dad had packed for their dinner. Just then, a nurse came in to give Anastasio his scheduled medications and to checked on him. His mom never missed an opportunity to feed someone. She insisted that the nurse take some for herself. She politely declined, but in the end, she left with a plate full of food. All Anastasio could do was laugh silently to himself. His mom fixed them all with plates and poured them all a glass of wine. Anastasio said that he shouldn't drink with the medicines, but she pretended not to hear him. She even had his dad bring candles she could light. It was nice to have them there and to eat with them. It made things seem a little more normal. He'd take it even if it was just for a short time.

They all watched TV after dinner. His mom and dad sat on the couch together. It was amazing that no matter how different they were, they were great together! He never understood it, but it was so nice to see how they were with one another. It made him really believe in lasting love and that sometimes opposites did attract. They were certainly polar opposites of each other. He found himself watching them more than the TV. His dad was holding one of her hands, the other wrapped around her neck. He always envied them, and now even more so. He might never know what that was like again. He only had it for a brief moment.

He was lost in thought about Marcela when his dad announced he was going home for the evening. He said he'd return in the morning. Although Anastasio knew the answer, he told his mom she should go home as well. Nothing was going to happen overnight anyways. Of course, he wasn't going to win that battle either! His dad gave him another hug and walked out. His dad was a good man! He was worried about what this was going to do to his dad's stress level and health.

Shortly after, the nurse came with another round of medicine. She told him that these would make him very sleepy. She looked over and saw the empty wineglass, gave him a look, then just proceeded to give him his medicine. All he could do was smile at her and silently said thank you. The nurse just smiled back at him. He had completely forgotten to have his mom take the glass away. But this was Italy after all. He was from a vineyard! It should be expected.

The nurse wasn't kidding about the medicine making him sleepy. No more than five minutes could have passed between getting the medicine and his eyes beginning to shut. He was a bit worried about what dreams he was going to have. But there was nothing he could do to stop the sleep from coming. He told his mom good night as his eyes were shutting. The last thing he remembered was feeling a kiss on his cheek and hearing something but was too tired to make it out.

He was awoken a few times during the night by another nurse getting more medicine. He wondered how much medicine they were going to give him. He hadn't even begun knowing everything that was going on yet. He asked for something to drink. The nurse told him he couldn't have anything to eat or drink until at least the scope was over. They were now giving his medicine through his IV line. They took effect immediately, as opposed to the medicine taken by mouth earlier. They put him to sleep even faster. Each time he woke, he knew he had been dreaming something but never could remember what. He didn't know if that was a good or bad thing. But given what had happened during the afternoon, he thought it was probably a good thing.

He was again woken up at 6:00 a.m. because they needed to take him down to get his scope done. He was glad they were doing it so early as he really wanted something to drink. And he would likely be getting hungry soon because he didn't eat very much the day before. His mom was ready to go with him, but they told her to wait in the room. The scope wouldn't take very long, and they would bring him right back up when they were done. The doctor should arrive shortly after that to explain any findings and any tests they wanted to order and tell them more about the particular cancer that they expected to confirm. She wasn't happy that she couldn't go, but she couldn't change it.

When they got downstairs, he signed a bunch of paperwork that he didn't even bother to know what all of it was. They told him what everything was, but his mind was still focused on the good chance that he had cancer. He met with the anesthesiologist, the doctor performing the procedure, and the nurses that would be in the room. They told him that the procedure would only take about thirty minutes. He would be asleep for it, but he would be awake very shortly after. There were minimal risks with the procedure, and he had nothing to worry about. Nothing to worry about. That's easy to say when you weren't the one that just found out he probably had cancer!

They took him into another room, where they were doing the procedure in. Everything seemed be going so quick that he couldn't keep up with what they were doing. They had him lie on his side and put something in his mouth that kept it open for the procedure. They told him that he would be getting sleepy now and to count backward from one hundred. The last number he remembered was ninety-four, and that was it. The next thing he remembered was waking up in his own room.

His mind was even more in a fog than before. He saw his mom and dad there but shut his eyes again. He woke a few times for just a few seconds and went right back to sleep. He was exhausted! He woke up when the doctor that did the procedure came in to talk to them. He explained the procedure to his parents, which they listened intently. Then he told what he had saw. "There were several concerning areas that we biopsied. There no bleeding at this time. I'm surprised he didn't have any symptoms sooner. It will take a few days to get the results. In the meantime, the oncologist will be coming by any time now. I saw that he scheduled for a PET scan this morning. So we will keep you with nothing to eat or drink by mouth until we know what tests will be done today and if they require you to be NPO."

He left, and within minutes, the oncologist came in. He introduced himself as Dr. Lin. He seemed like a very kind and knowledgeable man. He explained the blood work that he was going to order, the other various tests that they would do, and what to expect if the tests came back positive for the particular cancer they were thinking he had. He told them that Anastasio should be able to go home in a day or two. He would be able to tell him more once the tests results were back in. They would do everything as quickly as possible as doctors knew that no one wanted to be in the hospital very long. That was the understatement of the year, but he was happy that the doctor was on top of things and that he was going to do it as quickly as possible. As tough as his mom was to please, Dr. Lin had done the near-impossible task to appease her. He gave them some papers that explained some things about stomach and esophagus cancer. His mom had nothing to add or ask before he left the room. That in itself was a miracle!

It wasn't long before the nurse came back in to take more blood. Soon after that, he did the PET scan. None of it was painful, which he was happy about. The pain medicine was taking away the pain that he was experiencing before. He still felt foggy, but now it was much milder than the day before. Now the reality of what was going on was hitting him. He was scared, and even though his mom and dad would be there, he felt more alone than ever felt.

Later in the afternoon, he was done with the tests for the day, and his mom had gone home to change, and she said she would be back around dinner time. She told him that they would bring dinner again and asked if he had any preference what she could cook for him. He told her not to worry about him as they brought breakfast, lunch, and dinner. But his mom would have none of it. She wasn't going to let him eat the hospital food for every meal. If she would go home for more than a few hours a day, he was sure she would bring him food for every meal. She would likely remind him of what she did for him if he mentioned Marcela again. At first, it would seem she was doing it out of kindness of her heart. But after all was said and done, she would always do the same thing! It was all about her, not the person that she was doing it for.

He got up and looked around the room to see if his phone was around there. He wanted to see if Marcela had called and text, but he already knew she did. Of course, his phone wasn't there! He knew his mother didn't want him to have the chance to talk to her. Perhaps his mom was right this time, but he had feelings for Marcela and wanted to see what she wrote, how she was doing, what she was thinking about. He couldn't just turn off his feelings for her. It was probably best that they had taken his phone. He doubted that he could resist the urge to call or text her. He missed her so much!

He spent the rest of the afternoon trying to come to terms with his new illness. He had never really dealt with anything like this before. He assumed he was getting used to the drugs they were giving him. Each time, he seemed to be in less of a fog. He really couldn't focus on anything now outside of thinking of Marcela. He didn't want to let her go. He wasn't sure which was going to be harder to deal with, having cancer or losing Marcela! He was second-guessing his decision to not contact her, but he was going to try. He didn't want to hurt her any more than was doing now!

His mom and dad came back, just as promised. Their attitudes seemed to be more upbeat now. His dad came over and put his hand on his shoulder and asked how he was feeling. He told him he was okay. He then told him what tests he had done today. His mom unpacked the dinner and got it ready for them again. It was a different nurse than the night before, and she had made the mistake of coming in when they were having dinner. She left with more food than all the nurses could eat. As usual, they had wine, but this time he would remember to put it away before the nurse came back in. He didn't want to be in any kind of trouble.

They did the same as the night before. They watched TV for a few hours and chatted some. Anastasio found himself getting tired early. It had been a long day! It was a shorter day than he would have if he was working in the vineyard, but the stress of everything was taking its toll. He asked him mom to please go home with his dad. The answer was a no and with a look that said it wasn't a discussion. He said goodbye to his dad and called for the nurse to bring in the drugs that he took last night when he went to sleep. He also needed to get a pillow and stuff for his mom. He hoped he would sleep as well as he did the night before.

The nurse came in with everything they needed. She gave him the IV medicines and informed him that he didn't have any new procedures for the next day as of now. So if he needed anything to drink or eat throughout the night, he could just call the nurses' station, and they would get him whatever he needed. She left, and Anastasio got settled in for the night. He said good night to his mom quickly because if the meds were going to work as fast as they did the night before, he would be asleep within a few minutes.

He woke, and it was already starting to get light outside. He didn't remember waking up during the night at all. His mom was still sleeping, so he just lay there in silence until his doctor came in. He asked Anastasio how he was feeling, and Anastasio said that he was doing okay. His mom woke when they started talking and immediately came over to make sure she didn't miss anything. The doctor had quite a lot to tell them about what the tests showed. The blood work had come back indicating exactly what the emergency room had already had. The PET scan showed that he had cancer in the esophagus and stomach but, at this point, nowhere else. The biopsies would take another day or two to come back. He asked if Anastasio would like to go home that day. The answer was definitely a yes! He told him that it would take a few hours for him to get the report in the computer and for the nurse to discharge him. He said that he was leaving instructions and referrals for different specialists to make appointments with. He also gave his information if Anastasio wanted to continue to see him. He shook his hand and left.

His mom seemed pleased that he was going to be able to leave within a few hours. She was probably happy to not have to sleep on that couch again. She was never one for traveling or staying outside of their home. He couldn't ever remember a time that she didn't sleep away from his dad. His dad was able to stay at home when Anastasio started doing all the traveling for work. That left his dad at home to work in the vineyard every day. They always talked about going on a vacation, but work always took over. And lately funds were getting tighter because of the decline in business. He knew his mom and dad really needed to get away! He wished things were better. And now with his health, he knew they weren't even thinking about getting away with was going to happen anytime soon.

As promised, they left the hospital a few hours later. They had to drop off the prescriptions that needed to be filled and went home after that. He needed to call the doctors once he got home to set up the appointments he needed to get scheduled. He had formulated a new plan. If he somehow beat this quickly, maybe he could find his way back to Marcela! He just hoped that first, he could beat this, second, he could make his way to her, and third, she would still want to be with him. He knew many things had to go exactly right to be with her again. But she was worth the challenge!

The next several weeks weren't as easy as he originally had hoped. The doctors that he needed weren't covered under his insurance. When he researched success rates between doctors, there was a vast difference between the ones that his insurance covered and the ones that weren't. His dad told him to go to the better doctors anyways and that they would figure out a way make it work. Anastasio knew better than that! His family had worked so hard to make ends meet. He wasn't going to let them lose everything for him. They had intense arguments about it, but this time, it was Anastasio that walked away not giving in. His parents couldn't make him go! Depression had set in knowing that his life was all but over now. All he was doing now was waiting for death to come.

The phone would ring here and there, and his mom would always rush to get it and was quiet once she answered it. He knew she was hiding things from him, but every time he would ask, she would just brush him off, telling him it was a wrong number, spam, or some other thing. He knew not many people had that number and was suspicious of what she was up to, but there wasn't really anything he could do about it.

He was surprised by how quick he was declining. Each day he was getting sicker. He was losing weight faster than he could count it. Even with the meds, he was getting sick more often, and the pain was increasing. Each time he looked in the mirror, he looked like a different person. His face was pale, his eyes sunken, and his face hollow. He was glad no one was around to see him like this. Some friends would ask to come by, but he always gave them the same answer, "Maybe tomorrow or next week."

After about a month, he was placed in the hospital. There wasn't a lot they were doing for him. They were just trying to keep him comfortable. His parents rarely left his side. As bad as he felt for himself, he felt worse for them. He could see the pain in their eyes, hear it in their voice, and feel it in every hug or touch. He knew the family business was seriously suffering, but he was too weak to fight them. This was the way it was going to be. At least the time should be short now.

Chapter 13

Marcela had a new attitude now! With the information that Alejandro had collected, her plan was to do everything she could to save the man she loved! Every day all her focus went to researching doctors, talking with them, seeing if there was any place better for him to get better help, and so on. She had collected the insurance money and only spent what she needed to survive. She went into work each day, but she no longer cared about if she made sales or not. She was on a mission. Mission Anastasio, that was!

She had finished the project that she was doing inspired by Jacqueline. She mailed it to her, and a few days later, she got a call from an overly excited Jacqueline. They talked for some time. When she asked about Anastasio, Marcela gave her a brief summary of everything that happened. Jacqueline asked if Marcela would let her come visit to do whatever she could for her. Marcela declined and told her she could come visit once Anastasio was better. She wouldn't be good company to anyone right now. But she did promise to call her and update her as often as possible. It was good to talk to her again. Maybe one day she would get to see her again.

At first, she thought Antonio and Lee wouldn't like her plan, that they would try to discourage her from following through with what she was planning. She was wrong! They knew how important he was to her. If that was what she wanted, they were going to help her in any way possible. They were extremely helpful with helping her research everything and coming up with a solid plan of how this was all going to work. If they doubted her, they never showed it. Each day after work, they would all meet at her house, have dinner, and discuss what each found out each day.

They also made sure she was eating right and made her own doctor appointments to ensure she was doing the best she could during her pregnancy. She wasn't showing much yet. If they didn't know she was pregnant, they would not be able to tell yet. But she would lift her shirt sometimes when they asked, and they could see the small swelling of her belly. They were excited about becoming the child's godfathers, which Marcela had asked them to be.

After a couple of weeks of intense researching, reaching out, and talking with some of the doctors in the field, they finally had a core group of doctors that would have the best chance at successfully curing Anastasio. The doctors that they had decided on were Dr. Lin, oncology/surgery; Dr. Golden, another great surgeon; and Dr. Saddler, a gastroenterologist. The beginning stages could prove to be the most challenging for the fact that Anastasio was not in the hospital at that time. They didn't know how to get him to go the doctors that they had found. But God was hearing them. Anastasio was admitted again, and things became much easier for the doctors they hired to do their job. The doctors that they encountered and liked were all willing to see him there in the hospital and see what could be done there. There were no guarantees, of course, but they would do everything they could for him. It would likely take most of the money she had, but that didn't matter one bit to her. She would give anything to save him! She would even give her own life for his.

The doctors were instructed not to tell him where the money was coming from. Only that there was a donation in his honor. He would likely question them about that, and they came up with only two real objections he could come up with. The first being that someone sicker than himself or someone else should be the recipient of such a wonderful gift from God. Of course, he wanted to get better! He just didn't want to take money away from those that could die if they didn't receive treatment. Hopefully he would be able to get better with the doctors he already had.

If he did get better, she wasn't sure how or if she was going to approach him. She wasn't trying to save his life for herself. She wanted him to have a chance at living a full life and to get better very soon. That was all that mattered now! She would take each small victory that she could get. And perhaps if he was cured, he would make his way back to her. She fantasized about him coming back and being an amazing dad to their child. She wasn't sure exactly how she would tell him about being pregnant if he did contact her again. If he didn't try to contact her, she wouldn't try either way, and she would raise their child by herself.

Antonio and Lee both agreed that she should tell him what she was doing for him, tell him that she was his hero just as much as he was hers. She had no intention of doing that though. She had played all her cards. Now it was time for him to participate in the game. He seemed like a winner in life, not just moments here and there! He had been winning all his life. She didn't want to take credit! All she wanted was for him to get better and get to enjoy rest of his life. Perhaps that would mean he would find her, they could be together, and they would start a new journey that included her. If her prayers were going to come true, he would make his way back to her! That's all she could hope for, and she only wanted the best possible life for him. She prayed that he would get better and find his true passion in life. She didn't have a selfish bone in her body. Everything she was doing was just to save his life. The rest was just a hope that she had.

~

Dr. Lin came in to check on Anastasio. He had just received a few calls from a few doctors inquiring of Anastasio's status. He told them that things didn't look good in his current state. They told him that they were going to start treatments on him as soon as possible. Dr. Lin was more than happy to hear the news. He had grown somewhat fond of him over the past several weeks. He wondered where the money came from but didn't ask. He told Anastasio of the news. His parents happened to be away when he got the news. His first thought is that his parents had done something crazy to get the money. He thought maybe they sold the vineyard. But their sheer surprise and his emotions overcame him from regardless of what had transpired. When they returned, he would have to question what they had done to make this happen.

His parents returned shortly after the doctor left. Anastasio could hear them talking outside of his room. Overhearing the conversation between the doctor and his parents, they seemed just as shocked as he was! They didn't know who gave the money and honestly didn't care! Their boy had a chance at living a full life. He could hear them talking about who might have done such a thing, but the doctor couldn't tell not only because of patient/doctor privilege but also because he honestly didn't know.

The next morning when Dr. Lin came by doing his rounds, he was accompanied by two other doctors that introduced themselves to him as Dr. Golden and Dr. Saddler. They each explained their role and what they were going to try to accomplish. Since the cancer hadn't spread at this point, there was a decent chance that they could change his course. No matter how small, it was still a chance! Anastasio was overcome with emotion. He had all but given up at this point, waiting for death to take him. But each day, he laid there not to die and only to think about the time he spent with Marcela in Paris. It was the truest love he could ever know!

A few minutes later, he met the doctors he heard in the hall. Dr. Golden was a middle-aged man that walked and talked with such confidence that he immediately felt better about his illness. Dr. Saddler was a woman, also in her upper forties. Both smiled at him and introduced themselves. They took turns on explaining what was going on happen next. Anastasio was overwhelmed with emotion as each of them spoke. He had all but given up hope that anything positive was going to happen. They seemed pretty confident of their odds. Nothing was a guarantee, but he liked his chances with the new addition of doctors!

Over the next few weeks, it was a real struggle. Radiation made him even sicker, but he had some newfound hope. His mom was there each day to help him with whatever he needed help with. Even her attitude was much better. He no longer felt that she was doing things only for herself. She only cared what she could do for him. His dad would come each day after work. He would have dinner with him, but Anastasio couldn't hold down much food yet. They would help him eat whatever he was willing to try. They longer sat on the couch watching TV. They would sit on either side of his bed, and they would do different things, like playing cards or games or talking about the latest gossip that his mom would hear or about different childhood memories they had. Anastasio loved hearing about their childhood as well.

He was extremely weak, but he was doing everything they asked. He now had a hard time walking, and the therapist would come twice a day to try to get Anastasio up and moving. She was a witty woman that used her humor to encourage him. She could tell that before he was probably a fun person to be around. Of course, he'd make his remarks to make the staff laugh as he knew no other way of life. Little by little, he was able to do more. Small victories, he told himself. Small victories!

~

Marcela got reports daily from his doctors of his progress. Some days it was positive, other days not as encouraging. But she wasn't going to lose hope! She knew Anastasio. Sure, not his whole life, but she knew he was a fighter. She could see it in his eyes each time he looked at her. She could still see it now, like it was burned into her brain permanently. She wished she could see him walking and doing more things as he fought for his life. He was a survivor! He didn't know how to fail. He knew how to get what he wanted! He didn't have to lie or steal to get it. People saw his determination and gave him their trust. That's hard to come by these days.

Every day, she kept an eye on his progress. It was going much better than anyone expected. All the doctors were amazed by how the treatment was going and his general attitude through it all. He was upbeat and, each day, seemed to grow stronger. She was so happy to hear how he was progressing but sad not to be able to be by his side. She didn't think he would approve of what she had done for him. She wanted to reach out to him but decided that wasn't the best thing to do. If he wanted to talk with her, he would reach out to her. It was still hard to just remain silent. She still loved him with the passion that she did the day she had to leave him.

The doctors gave her encouraging information regarding his health. He seemed to be making improvements each session. Even the scans were coming back better and quicker than anyone had expected. It looked like the treatment plan was working! That was all she could ask for. She always said prayers for him many times a day even though she couldn't pray beside him. She didn't want him to know that it was her that had brought the doctors. In her mind, it wasn't her that was helping, but it was God. God made everything possible for her to pay for the doctors. She couldn't take the credit for that. She was sure he questioned where they came from but would probably never guess it was from her. God had given her the gift of which she received and paid it forward to see another life saved instead of spending it on stuff that would never really matter.

Anastasio was going to live! It would take some time and a lot of rehab, but he would live. According to the doctors, they believed he had an incredibly good chance to fully recover. When she started this, the odds seemed stacked against him. She wanted to hug the doctors and never let go. But she had to stay away from him to let him focus on getting better. If she was close to him, she wouldn't be able to resist staying away from him. She had a plan and vowed to stick to it. If he got better and came to her, she would know he was her one true love!

Life was life, and fairy tales were fairy tales. Which one did she have? Did she have a fairy tale or something real or a combination of the two? All she cared about these days was Anastasio's health and well-being and being as healthy as she could for the baby growing inside of her. She didn't think that she could love someone again if he didn't come back to her. It would be hard to deal with, but she would survive. She had to if for nothing more than their child! She knew she was doing the right thing and couldn't be selfish in a time like this. Her heart was breaking over all that was going on. She wished she could understand why life could be so cruel and difficult.

She spent the next few weeks trying to concentrate on work. She had to keep up her shop now that she had spent the insurance money on the doctors treating Anastasio. Luckily, her attitude was a bit better, and it was reflecting on the sales she was making again. Her business wasn't booming by any means, but she was at least making enough to pay her bills. Her new pieces were also a big hit. Several of her existing clients had bought or placed an order for them. It took time to make the pieces, so some of them had to wait for her to make them. Her business wasn't like the big stores that had mass production. Each piece took time. But along with that, each piece was unique in its own way.

It was going to take every ounce of restraint not to contact him. That's all she really wanted to do! She missed talking to him. She missed the way she felt when they talked. No one had ever made her feel that way. She doubted anyone else would make her feel that way in the future. After this, she didn't think she would even let anyone be able to get close to her. He had been a blessing and a curse all in one. How could anyone else compare to how he had treated her? She knew the answer. No one!

～

After just a few months of treatment, Anastasio felt like a new man. He couldn't believe how he went from not having a prayer in the world to being so close to being rid of the cancer that had devastated his life just months before. He wasn't totally in the clear yet, but all signs pointed to him being a healthy man very soon. The physical therapy was also paying off. He was back to walking more and being able to take care of himself. He had always been an independent person, and that was hard for him to let others take care of him. That being said, his parents were a true blessing to have around. He only hoped that if and when they needed help, he would be able to repay them for what they did for him.

He tried to find out where the donations came from, but as much as he tried, he got no closer to finding out who he so desperately wanted to thank. He didn't know how much all his treatment was costing, but he knew it wasn't something he would have been able to afford. If he knew who was helping, he would spend his life trying to repay that debt. The one thing he really wanted to know was, why him? There had to be millions of people that needed the kind of help that he got. He didn't feel that his life was worthy of what someone had done for him!

He thought of Marcela often. He wasn't sure now if he had made the right decision to not contact her. He tried to talk to his parents about it and got very mixed responses. His dad told him to do what he felt was right in his heart. His mom said that even though he was doing better, he needed to stay focused on getting better and recovering. If and when he was cleared, he was still going to be needed there to help out. Marcela had likely moved on, according to his mom anyways. He still found it fascinating how polar opposites his parents were. He also knew that defying his mother would make life for everyone a lot harder than it needed to be! As good as she had been to him during this whole process, she could still make his life miserable if she chose to.

He had an appointment to go in and see Dr. Lin to get the test results of his latest scans and blood work. Things had been improving ever since all the doctors were working together to try and cure him. His mom wouldn't let him go alone, not that he was really supposed to drive anyways. He wished it could have been his dad going with him rather than his mom. But his dad did need to tend to the vineyard since they were still losing business by the week. It was not an easy time for any of them!

On the way to the appointment, he was able to avoid much conversation with his mom. He knew that any serious conversation would be about how he needed to stay focused on getting better and helping his parents keep up with the business. It seemed that was the only things she had talked about in the last several weeks, and he was tired of hearing the same story over and over. His mind wasn't on any of that at the moment. Like his mom, his mind was on one thing. That one thing was Marcela!

After a short wait, Anastasio and his mom were called by the nurse. Most of the visits were in a room that he was examined in, but this time, they were led into Dr. Lin's personal office. They took their seats, but Dr. Lin wasn't in there yet. He office walls were filled by framed degrees, certificates, and awards that he had gotten over a successful career as a doctor. Anastasio was certainly glad that he had gotten lucky to have such an amazing doctor!

Dr. Lin came in after only a few minutes of waiting. Anastasio stood and shook his hand, and Dr. Lin made his way around the desk and sat down. He pulled a file out of a pile that was sitting on his desk. He was hard to read if he was going to give good news or bad news. Anastasio was prepared for either response. He would do whatever the doctor told him to do. Even if he wasn't better now, he felt that he was going to be very soon.

Dr. Lin opened the file and said, "Anastasio, you must have an angel in your life!" He looked at Anastasio and raised his eyebrows and then continued, "The results of all your tests came back, and there isn't a trace of cancer found in your body!"

Anastasio couldn't breathe for a moment. His mom was now clutching his arm with such a grip that it was actually hurting his arm. He looked at Dr. Lin, then to his mom, then back to the doctor. "I don't even have words! I never expected to hear those words after how it all started. It was truly a miracle!"

"It really is! I was hoping for the best from the beginning but didn't expect such a fast and successful recovery! I'm immensely proud of your strength and courage through all this. I know it wasn't easy for you! But there has always been something in your eyes that said that you wouldn't give up!"

Even though he knew the words were not enough to express how he felt, he just said, "Thank you!"

His mom's grip had loosened now, and she stood and almost ran to the other side of the desk. She wrapped her arms around Dr. Lin and was sobbing loudly. She was muttering something that Anastasio couldn't hear from this side of the desk but assumed it was something like thank you over and over again. She didn't let go of Dr. Lin for what seemed an eternity. When she finally released him, his shirt was wet from the streaming tears from his mother.

They left his office shortly after. They scheduled more appointments to keep an eye on things. The doctor wanted to be cautious of anything returning. And if it did, they wanted to catch it early. His mom was still crying, and he wasn't sure that she was going to be able to drive. She dismissed his attempts to let him drive home. They sat in the car for a few minutes before she was able to get her composure before they started their way home. Her hands were visibly shaking, and she looked almost nervous the way she was jumping around. He was glad they were in the car and not at home. He knew she would've been all over him as she did with the doctor just moments ago.

The ride home was filled with his mom talking extremely fast and with more excitement than he ever remembered seeing. She kept asking him if he could believe it. He answered the same way every time. "No, I can't!" was his response each time. He was now thinking of Marcela and how now he could try to figure out a way back in her life. He knew it wasn't going to be easy after what he had done. He would also have to deal with his mom but didn't care about that now. He was well again, and he knew what he wanted and needed to do. He was ready to face whatever challenges standing in his way!

When they arrived home, his mom basically ran from the car into the house. She was screaming before she was in the door for his dad. "He's healed! Anastasio is healed! Honey, honey…he's healed!" she was screaming over and over.

Anastasio took his time making it into the house. His mom was nowhere in sight now. He guessed she was running around looking his father. Although he wanted his dad to know, he wanted some time alone to get through the shock of the news he had just gotten and to think about his next moves. He was serious about trying to make his way back to Marcela and into her life. He knew he had hurt her and that it might take some serious work to get her back. But she was worth it!

He made it into the living room, where his mom was talking to his dad frantically. His dad's mouth was open and his eyes wide. Anastasio could see tears in his eyes too as he looked over to him. He stood slowly and unsteadily and held his arms open to him to come over and get a hug from his father. He was happy to see his dad as he embraced him. Anastasio was now starting to cry as well. He held onto his father for quite some time.

They all sat down, and Anastasio slowly went over the encounter they had with Dr. Lin. His father praised God for his recovery. Everyone was in disbelief over the news. It didn't quite seem real yet! All that they had been through over the past several months, it all paid off! It seemed too good to be true. The adrenaline was still coursing through his veins. He didn't know that could happen by just hearing words. Well, that wasn't quite true. He felt that adrenaline when Marcela told him that she loved him! He needed to feel that again!

~

Marcela got to the airport with just minutes to spare. She had a customer come in just before she was supposed to leave for the day. As luck would have it, he wanted to see almost everything that she had in the store. For the past several days, there was only minimal business. Now that she had somewhere to be, she got someone interested in buying things from her. As soon as he left, she followed him out the door and rushed to the airport.

She made it to the baggage claim just as Jacqueline made her way through customs. She smiled when she saw Marcela standing there and made her way quickly to her and gave her a big hug. It was so good to see Jacqueline again! When they had made the promise to see each other many months ago, she wasn't sure that she would ever see her again unless she made her way back to Paris. She was surprised to get the call that she had planned to come visit. And it wasn't just to visit but to visit her in particular. She planned to visit for a week, and Marcela had started planning for that the moment after they hung up the phone.

When Marcela got the call, she was finally happy about one thing in her life. As much as she didn't want to think about Paris and what had happened there, she couldn't help but to smile when she thought about how she felt when she was with her. It was a piece of time that she would never forget and forever changed her life. Even though it was hard to see now, it was the best five days of her life. Maybe a few days with her would make her feel some kind of happiness even if it was short-lived. She didn't think it could make her worse at least.

Jacqueline didn't know much about that had happened over the last few months, and Marcela filled her in the best she could on the way from the airport to her house. It wasn't a conversation that she planned to have in the car even though she knew it was going to come up. She tried her best to answer the things that Jacqueline asked. Jacqueline realized her mistake of bringing it up while they were driving. She changed the subject to lighter things. Marcela asked if she was hungry, and she said was starving. Marcela offered to stop at her favorite tapas place, and she said she would be happy to eat whatever she suggested.

While they were at dinner, Marcela started talking about what had transpired without any questions or statements from Jacqueline. At first, it seemed that she was reciting from a paper she had written for a class. After talking about if for about an hour, it seemed she was really talking from the heart. Jacqueline reached out for her hand several times as she was talking to let her know she was there to comfort her. She wasn't going to tell her, but it was the only reason that she came to Barcelona now. She was worried about her friend. Even though they didn't know each other very well, she considered her a good friend. And friends took care of their friends. Plus, it was getting very hot out. She needed a vacation!

After dinner, they made their way back to Marcela's house. Marcela knew Antonio was waiting there for them to return. He wanted to meet her friend and vice versa. Jacqueline was pleasantly surprised when Antonio came up and gave her a big hug. She knew right away that they would get along just fine. Once they started to talk, it was like they were old friends. This was going to be a fun vacation even if it was to cheer someone up from something so terrible. She would've liked Antonio even if she just met him out on the street. He was exactly her speed!

After they got acquainted, Marcela broke the news of her being pregnant. Jacqueline almost knocked Marcela over when she gave her a hug. She made Marcela lift her shirt, and she put her hand on her belly. Of course, it was too early to feel a kick or anything, but she was ecstatic to feel it anyways. Marcela brought some champagne out for Jacqueline and Antonio to toast with. Marcela had to settle with toasting with water. It was going to be a long time until she could drink anything.

It was a fun, unexpected night for all of them. Jacqueline and Antonio both had a way of making things seem not as bad as they were. The champagne flowed between the two of them, and the conversation happened with ease between all of them. Marcela found herself smiling and laughing for the first time in a long time. She was happy that Jacqueline had made the trip to visit her! She was exactly what she needed right now. Having Antonio there too was very nice. It was two people that could make her feel better in a time like this. She thought that she should've invited Lee as well, but they had six days to all get together. She was sure that that was going to happen for in the next few days for sure.

It was around midnight when they all started to wrap up the evening. Everyone was tired from the long day of work and visiting with one another. Antonio was going to stay the night as well since he had been drinking all night. Jacqueline was going to be staying in the guest bedroom, and the third bedroom was the room Marcela's mom used to use. Marcela felt comfort in the fact that he was there and that Jacqueline was right there too. She thought that if Antonio, Lee, and Jacqueline were there together, they would probably stay up all night talking and laughing the night away. She was looking forward to having all of them there.

She got ready for bed and said good night to everyone. They were both planning to go to work in the morning. Antonio would work his normal day, and she would only work in the morning. She wanted to have time to spend with Jacqueline. She wished that she didn't have to go into work at all while she was there, but she needed to bring in at least some money to keep up with her bills. Her mind turned again to Anastasio for the first time since dinner. Antonio and Jacqueline didn't bring him up. Marcela guessed that was probably the best course. If they did, then she would've been thinking how she wanted him there with her now.

Once she was able to fall asleep, her dreams were filled with being with Anastasio again. Some were good, and some were not so good. She wished all the dreams were of them being together and of him not being sick anymore, and they were happy! She wanted that more than anything now. Hopefully her wish would come true! Her first wish had come true with Anastasio getting better. Now she just needed him to stay healthy and to come back to her.

~

Just like Anastasio did with organizing work, he made a detailed plan to go see Marcela again and win her back. He had the best plan he could think of. He was going to find her friend Antonio, whom she had told him about. He knew his last name, so it shouldn't take much to find him. Once he found him, he would call him and talk to him about what had gone on for the last several months. Hopefully he would be receptive to helping him try to get her back. And who knew, maybe Antonio would have some insight on things he could do to try to improve his chances of getting her back. It had to work! He didn't want a life without Marcela in it.

Once he found Antonio and started to put his plan into action, he would talk to his parents. He knew his mom was going to give him hell about it, but it no longer mattered to him at all. She was the reason that he wasn't with Marcela now! He wasn't going to let her run his life and decisions anymore. She would just have to get used to the fact that he was an adult and needed to make the decisions that were important to him. He firmly believed in family! But that also meant that at some point he would start his own family. He needed that! He wanted his parents to have grandchildren and accept the changes life brought. He knew his dad would support him completely. Even though it was going to be rough on his mother for a while, he knew that his parents would make great grandparents.

Then based on any help from Antonio, he would go to Spain and start the next phase of his plan. That was the part that scared him the most. He had no idea what Marcela would think when he saw her for the first time since they left Paris. He planned to sit her down and explain everything to her from the time that he first felt sick to his mom suggesting that he stop talking to her and to what was currently going on. He wanted to be completely honest with her. She deserved the full truth if she was going to take him back. Hopefully she would be understanding and want to still spend the rest of her life with him. He wanted to try every day to make her life better, not worse.

He spent the evening tracking Antonio down. It wasn't too hard with the new way of finding people. All you had to do was spend a little money for internet records of known addresses, phone numbers, and emails. As he was doing that, he wondered about the calls that were coming to his parents' house. His mom was acting strange after some of them. When he asked her about it before, she always said it was a wrong number or that it was telemarketer. But he knew she wasn't telling him something. He would remember to ask her about it at another time.

For now he had his plan in place. It was getting late, so he would start trying to contact Antonio the next day. He was a bit nervous about it all as he lay down to go to sleep. He also had excitement as well! With all the thoughts and scenarios coming and going from his mind, he found himself restless and unable to sleep right away. He was exhausted mentally but knew either his life was going to be amazingly happy or it was going to be lonely, and he doubted he would be able to love someone else. In the short time they had together, it meant more to him than anything he had ever known. She was the reason he was able to fight his illness. He was grateful for whomever donated the money to help him, but he knew a lot of the reason he got better was because of the love he had in his heart for

Marcela. He finally fell asleep from mental exhaustion. His dreams were filled with thoughts of being back with Marcela.

~

Jacqueline insisted on going to work with Marcela. She said she wanted to see her shop and what she had in there and see how she made her jewelry. Marcela thought it was more that she didn't want her to be by herself. The morning went by quickly as she was showing her around the shop and showing her some of the things she was working on. She didn't have many customers come in, so she was able to show her everything pretty quickly. She also knew that the rest of the day would have been most of the same, so she had no problem closing the store for the day around lunchtime.

They had a quick lunch, and Marcela drove her around some of the city that she thought that Jacqueline would be interested in. She wanted the day spent showing her some of the things they could do while she was there and coming up with a good schedule that would fit everything in and allow Marcela to alternate opening the store in the morning and afternoon. She couldn't afford to be closed every day. And more than that, she couldn't just open in the morning. Mornings were usually slower than the afternoons.

They drove around for a few hours, and they ended close to the beach. Jacqueline asked if they could stop there for a little while. This was her first time to see the ocean in person. They walked along the ocean and then sat in the sand while Jacqueline watched the waves roll in and roll away. There was a nice breeze, and the sun was out. It was a perfect day to sit there and not be too hot or cold. They sat there until the sun was setting. They probably would have stayed longer, but they got hungry. Also, Antonio and Lee were coming over in about an hour. So they reluctantly left the beach and started to head home, have dinner, and spend the rest of the evening with Lee and Antonio. She hoped that it would be as fun as the night before. Even though she didn't say anything to Jacqueline, her mind was on Anastasio most of the day, and she needed the distraction.

Jacqueline insisted on helping her make dinner. It was a simple pasta dish that had chicken and broccoli. A few minutes after they started work on dinner, the boys got there. Marcela introduced Lee to Jacqueline. Right away she knew that is was to be another good night. Jacqueline had such a wonderful personality that made everyone feel like family right away. It felt like they all had spent years together with the banter they all had going. As they did the night before, they opened a bottle of champagne and switched to wine after that. Marcela missed having a glass or two of wine but knew she couldn't do that. Antonio seemed happier than the night before, but he said that nothing out of the ordinary happened while he was at work. She didn't know that wasn't true at all!

Again, the night went by quickly, and everyone was getting a little tired now. Lee and Antonio both had a lot to drink, so they were going to stay over again. Marcela told them, the boys, that they had to share a room since she had another guest. Everyone would probably fall asleep right away with all the drinks they had. And it was weekday, so Antonio and Lee needed to be up early. Marcela was taking time off in the morning and working in the afternoon, so she didn't have to be up as early as them. But she wanted to be up early enough that she and Jacqueline could go visit some sights.

They all went to bed, and Marcela was happy that she was able to fall asleep quickly. She didn't have Antonio to hold on to her to make her feel a little bit better. Being so exhausted, her dreams were on random things that she had experienced with Anastasio. Some were about things that had never happened yet. In one of her dreams, Anastasio had a daughter, but Marcela wasn't there. It was rare that she dreamed something that she wasn't actually in. She knew Anastasio said he didn't have any kids. And he didn't know she was carrying his child. Dreams could be so strange at times with how it could mix different things that were and weren't happening.

Anastasio hadn't slept much when it was time to get up. It was earlier in Spain, so he didn't want to call too early. Besides, he usually helped his dad in the vineyard in the mornings that he was there. It looked like a beautiful day out. When he was in the hospital, he didn't have the energy or desire to be outside. It was depressing being inside all the time. Now that he was better, he wanted to take advantage of all the things he took for granted before. He never once thought that one day he might never get to be outside again.

He tried to stay calm through breakfast with his parents. He was counting the hours before he could call the number listed for Antonio. If the number didn't work, he would email as a backup plan. He really wanted the conversation to happen over the phone. Emails could seem to be very cold and not personal. He wanted Antonio to hear the sincerity in his voice. He knew that would mean more than anything. He only had one chance to get this right. He wanted everything to go well. He needed it to!

Breakfast was over, and he was walking through the vineyard with his father. His dad seemed like he didn't notice things at times, but he was always paying attention. While they were walking, he asked what was on his mind. Anastasio shouldn't have been surprised, but it caught him off guard. He hadn't rehearsed his speech that he was preparing for when he was going to tell them what he was doing. He was relieved that he waited until then to ask. It was going to be a hundred times easier to talk to his dad about it than with his mom.

Once he started telling his dad everything that he thought, his dad stayed silent to let him say everything he wanted to say. Anastasio was sure that he intently listened to every word he said. They were still walking through the vineyard, but Anastasio found that he was talking and wasn't paying attention to anything else. They stopped walking at one point, and they sat in a grassy area, and Anastasio kept telling him what his heart felt. He didn't mean to, but he even told him about what he thought about his mom telling him to not contact her and how he felt about her trying to control him all his life. It was his dad's wife. But his dad just kept listening and didn't interrupt him.

It took about an hour for him to get everything out. His dad didn't say one word as he did. He felt better now that he had at least told one person. He loved his dad and all his family. He didn't want to hurt anyone's feelings. His mom was who she was. He didn't really think that she didn't want the best for him. But she continually made suggestions until it made him eventually think that her decision was right. He was worried that his dad would be upset after telling him what he thought about what his mom had done all his life.

Once he was finished, his dad finally spoke. He looked Anastasio right in the eye. "Anastasio, you've been an amazing son! You were never any trouble. You always helped here when needed. You've kept this vineyard going with your ability to keep and bring in new clients. They like your personality! All we want for you is happiness. I know your mother does things that will keep you helping us. But you need to live your life for you. I want you to be happy! Your mother will come around eventually. I love you! I love your mother like no other in my life. Now go get the love of your life back! Go be the man you were meant to be!"

They hugged, and they started walking back to the house. Anastasio felt better now, but when he got back, he knew it was time to call Antonio. As tough as his mom was, he figured Marcela's best friend would be even tougher! The closer they got to the house, the more nervous he got about the call. He felt like a teenager calling a girl he liked for the first time. But this was more than asking a girl to the movies. This was the rest of his life that was hanging on the line!

They got back to the house, and his dad gave him a wink. No words were needed to be exchanged. It was time to get the love of his life back! This was the first step in doing that. He rushed upstairs not to see his mom. He knew that she would see that he was distracted and ask all kinds of questions. He wasn't ready to have that conversation yet. There were other things that had to go right before he would talk to her. He needed all his focus and energy to be spent on a hopeful conversation with Antonio.

He got to his room and found Antonio's number. He took a deep breath and dialed the number. There was no answer, but the voice and name on the voice mail were the same he knew to be Antonio. He wasn't sure if he should leave a message or what to say. But there was no time to decide. So he left a message, "Hi, Antonio! This is Anastasio. I know you probably hate me, but I would very much like to talk to you if you have the time. Please call me back when you have the time." He left his number and ended the call.

He couldn't help pacing the floor and wondering if Antonio was going to call him back. He questioned if he made the right choice to the message or if it would have been better for him to call him back at another time. It was too late for that now! All he could do was wait. If he didn't get a call by evening, he would try him again. He would keep trying until Antonio would take his call. And he doubted that he was ignoring his call. It was a weekday, and he was likely at work. He probably didn't know the number and sent it to voice mail as he was at work and didn't have time for a wrong number or spam.

It was about three hours later when Anastasio's cell phone rang. He immediately knew the number was Antonio's and answered the phone as quickly as he could. He had been waiting for the call but was caught off guard for the second time today. It was likely he had listened to his message just before he called. "Anastasio? This is Antonio. You left me a message earlier."

He didn't say anything after that, and Anastasio was so nervous that he forgot the whole speech he prepared before. He just started just like he did with his dad, "Thanks for calling me back. I know you probably don't want to hear from me, but I would very much like if you will hear me out."

Antonio acted like he didn't know what was going on and said, "I have a few minutes. What do you want?"

Anastasio went through everything that had happened from the day he met Marcela to that day. It took him almost an hour to complete everything that had happened. Antonio pretended that this was the first he knew of any of it. He didn't rush him even though it was a busy day at work. He was happy to hear from him, but he wasn't going to give that away. He wanted Anastasio to prove that he really loved Marcela! If he was going to help him, he wanted to know his best friend's heart was going to be protected this time.

Once Anastasio was done with his monologue, Antonio simply said that Anastasio's idea of coming to Spain might be a good idea. But he didn't know if Marcela would want him back. She was hurt, and he just didn't know if her heart could find love for him again. He had hurt her deeply! He better be sure that he wanted Marcela and that she was the woman that he wanted to be with for the rest of his life! That was, if she wanted him back! He promised that he wouldn't tell Marcela about the conversation. They would talk again soon to figure out when it would be best to come see Marcela.

∼

The rest of the time Jacqueline was there was filled with going to see different sites. Every day was long and exhausting. But it was nice to have her there, and it all kept her mind on other things. Of course, every day she thought about Anastasio and hoped her phone would ring at any moment. But the phone didn't ring. There were no texts, and there was nothing from him. Each time she did get a call or text, she rushed to her phone to see if it was him. No luck! It was usually Antonio or Lee.

Jacqueline's trip had come to an end, and Marcela was taking her to the airport. She wasn't ready to say goodbye yet. If she didn't need to work, she would have asked her to stay longer. She said she really enjoyed the trip and meeting her friends. She would come back as soon as she could to see Marcela. She also suggested that Marcela come see her as well. She even offered to pay for Marcela's flight, and she was welcome in her home anytime.

They said goodbyes at the airport, and Marcela drove back home. On the way home, Antonio called to make sure she was okay. He offered to come over and keep her company. Marcela declined because every day in the past week was full of different events and people over all the time. She just wanted some alone time to keep up on her sleep, and she was feeling somewhat down that Jacqueline, the woman that helped her with her dates with Anastasio, was now gone. It was like Jacqueline was a piece of the puzzle that needed to be solved.

She got home and cleaned the house a bit from having all the company all week. Jacqueline was a very clean person, so there wasn't much to clean. She was just trying to busy her mind to drown out the thoughts of Anastasio. It didn't really work, but she was trying. She almost called Antonio to take him up on his offer. But nights weren't going to get any easier. She needed to come to terms with everything. It had been several weeks since Anastasio was done with treatment, and still there was no contact. It was awfully hard for her not to try to call him, but she wasn't going to chase him down. If it was meant to be, it would happen. She would wait on him. Maybe she would wait the rest of her life.

⁓

After he had dinner with his family, Anastasio sat down in the living room, where his parents were watching TV. He sat down next to his mom, found the remote, and turned off the TV. He turned to his mother and said, "I want you to listen! Please don't interrupt me. You can say what you want to at the end. But I need to say what I need to say."

His mom looked at him with a confused look. She started to say something, but Anastasio put his hand up to stop her. "Mom, Dad, you know how much I love you both. Both of you have always been there for me. I will never forget that!" He looked at his dad and gave him a look that his mom couldn't see that said what he was saying was the first time either had heard.

"You've been amazing through the time I was sick. I couldn't have made it if you weren't there for me. I really appreciate that! I have had a lot of time to think. More than I ever wanted actually! I know how you feel about me leaving, but I know what my heart feels for Marcela. Now that I'm better, I'm going to go to Spain and plead with her to take me back." His mom tried to start talking again, but he stopped her again.

"Mom, please let me talk. I promise you can say what you want when I'm done." He looked at them and continued. "I love her! I don't know if she will take me back. I will never forget her for as long as I live. If she doesn't want me back, I know that it wasn't meant to be. If she will take me back, I want to be with her, marry her, spend the rest of my life with her. I know you think me leaving will kill this family, but I will still continue seeing clients. I will do whatever I can for our family. I just won't be living here anymore if things go well. And even if it doesn't go well, I will be getting my own place. I have lived here long enough. You two need to have your home back to yourselves."

His mom looked at him, at his father, and back at him. Anastasio was done talking now. She wanted to be mad at him, but she wasn't. She took a few moments before she began to speak, "Well, if that is what you want, I will pray that it will be! You go to her! You go get her back. I, we, love you!"

He gave his mom a big hug and then his dad. It went much easier than expected. He was happy about that! He expected to be in an argument for hours with his mom. He didn't expect cooperation from her in the least. Now that that was done, he could focus on getting a flight to Barcelona. He also needed to talk to Antonio again to coordinate the plans he had in place. He was hoping to get a flight the next day and meet with Antonio before he went to Marcela. He was one step closer to her now!

Before he left, his mom sat him down and handed a small ring box to him. "This was your grandmother's ring. When you are sure that you two are ready to move forward, I want you to have this. You don't have to give her this ring, but I'm sure it will have a lot of meaning to you later!"

He couldn't believe what was happening. First, his mom wishing him well, then giving him the ring. He was speechless, other than saying, "Thank you, Mom! I think it is perfect!"

Chapter 14

Anastasio arrived in Barcelona on time and was met by Antonio directly outside of customs. Neither had seen each other before. They had sent a photo of what they looked like and were wearing before his flight to be able to find each other easier. He was grateful that Antonio was helping him so much! When Anastasio talked with him, Antonio listened and offered to pick him up at the airport. Although they talked for over an hour, Antonio wanted to talk with him when he got there. He didn't say whether he thought Anastasio's plan would go well or not with Marcela.

They left the airport, and they were heading to lunch. If Anastasio had his way, he would go right to Marcela. Ever since he made the decision to come to Barcelona, he was anxiously waiting for the time to come. Now that he was so close to her, he wanted it to be like a movie scene where he ran to her and she ran to him too, and they would have a warm embrace. He knew that wasn't going to happen. He also knew what Antonio meant to her, so he wanted any advice he had for him. It was likely he knew what Marcela was thinking and feeling now.

Antonio took him to their favorite tapas restaurant. He didn't tell him that it was one of their restaurants. They sat, and Anastasio looked over the menu. Antonio didn't need to as he could probably recite the menu by heart. The waiter got there after a few minutes, and they ordered several small plates. Anastasio didn't realize how hungry he was until he was reading the menu. His flight didn't offer much in the way of good food. The airlines didn't treat people like they used to.

After they ordered, Anastasio thanked him again for helping him. He was eager to find out what Antonio wanted to talk to him. He looked Antonio and asked, "So what is it you'd like to talk about?"

Antonio smiled and took a drink of his water before he answered. He knew Anastasio was filled with anticipation. It was fun to make him sweat a little. "So you said you were sick? And that's why you stopped talking to her?"

Anastasio hated the fact that he let his mom convince him to stop talking to her. "Yes, to both. I was diagnosed with cancer the day I stopped talking to Marcela. I know it sounds foolish now as I'm an adult, but I let my mom convince to stay silent. She convinced me that whatever pain she went through, it wasn't even close to the pain she would feel if I didn't make it. I thought she was right at the time. But then I realized that she was wrong! That I was wrong! I can't change any of the facts of what I did. Believe me, if I could go back in time, I would have never done that to her!"

Antonio could see the pain in his eyes. It was the same pained look that he saw in Marcela's since that time. Even though the last week that Jacqueline was there she enjoyed herself, there wasn't the light in her eyes that he saw when she came back from Paris. "I don't want to make you feel even worse than you do, but she has been hurt worse than I ever imagined. You have no idea how much I wanted to find you and tell you what I thought of you!" He didn't tell him about everything they did to find him and find out everything he did.

"I know! You have every right to be mad at me! I know it also had to stress you out. All I can do for now is tell you I'm sorry. If she will let me back in her life, I will spend my life proving that I love her more than life itself! You are a good friend to her. That's why I appreciate you at least giving me a chance to explain. May I ask how is she? Do you think she will give me a chance to explain myself?"

Antonio originally was going to make him sweat for some time before letting him know he could talk to Marcela. Now after hearing what he just said, he decided that he was in enough pain and didn't need more. He didn't know exactly what Marcela was going to do when saw him, but he was hoping that was going to happy. "She's really hurt! I know that she thinks about you and misses you. She's been through a lot lately. I will take you there, and then you're on your own! I'm not going in with you. This is between you and her now."

They ate their lunch in almost complete silence. Anastasio was thinking about what and how he was going to say what he wanted to say. And Antonio was thinking about what her reaction was going to be. For both of them, it was going to be very emotional. That's why Antonio said he wasn't going in with him. This was something that should be done in private. He was going to drop him off at her shop. He would have preferred that Anastasio waited until she was home but knew that he would go stir-crazy waiting for that long. And it was a weekday, so he suspected that she wouldn't be busy with customers.

They finished their lunch and were now on the way to Marcela's shop. Each minute that passed left Anastasio more and more nervous. He was fidgeting and looked like he was ready to jump out of the car. Antonio wished there was something he could say to make him calm some but knew there was nothing that would help. It was something that hopefully would be done with very soon. Antonio wanted that for them both. They deserved to be happy. They deserved to be happy together!

Antonio stopped the car just before her shop. He didn't want her to see him parking and see Anastasio. The plan was for him to go into the shop alone. There usually weren't many customers during the daytime hours on a weekday. He was sure that Marcela would close the shop for the rest of the day. He told Anastasio to call him if he or they needed a ride home. He wasn't sure if either of them would be able to drive safely with all the emotion that would come pouring out of them. But he also knew Marcela well enough that she wouldn't want to be around anybody else. Even though he was her best friend, there was some things she kept to herself. Before Anastasio got out of the car, Antonio wished him luck and shook his hand.

Anastasio said goodbye and got out of the car. His hands were sweating, and he felt like he was going to be sick. He knew it wasn't going to get any better, so he just had to do it! This was the moment that both looked forward to, and he also dreaded it the most. He longed to see her face, touch her skin, and hug and kiss her! He didn't know what her first reaction was going to be when she saw him. He had tried to imagine all the different reactions she could have to try to prepare himself for any reaction she might have. Now that he was actually there, he seemed to have forgotten everything he had thought of saying.

He took a deep breath and started walking slowly to the front door of her shop. He opened the door and stepped inside. There was no one in the front of the store, but he heard her voice say she would be right out. It was so nice to hear her voice again! Even though everything about her was burned into his brain, it sounded sweeter than he remembered. The sound seemed to reverberate in his head. There was no turning back now. He didn't say a word and just waited for her to appear. He sat down his bag and stood there waiting for her.

And there she was, the love of his life! Her eyes widened, and her mouth was hanging open, frozen in time. The look on her face was like she had just seen a ghost. She tried to speak, and no words came out. She felt like her legs were going to give out. She had waited for this moment but didn't really think this moment was really going to happen. Here he was, standing before her. Her heart was skipping beats again, like they did when she was with him before.

Anastasio didn't move, but he somehow found some words. "Hi!" It took a moment to keep going. "You look amazing. How are you?" He immediately regretted saying that! Could he have not come up with something better? He had rehearsed this for days. And "How are you?" was the best he could come up with?

She still wasn't sure he was real. He couldn't really be standing before her. "Hello!" That's the best she could do without fainting.

His legs felt like Jell-O. He wanted to run to her, like the movie scenes that he imagined. But he couldn't move or speak. He just stood there staring at her. He couldn't see his own face but knew that he probably had the same expression on his face that she had. He had to say something else or move toward her, something rather than just standing there. This was not a part of the plan he had. Finally, one foot went in front of the other. It was slow, but he was getting closer to her. He wanted so badly to run to her, hold her, and kiss her. He needed to feel her!

Each step got a little faster, and his legs seemed to have purpose now. He didn't offer any words. His mouth still didn't work. He hoped it would when he got to her. He wanted to kiss her more than he ever wanted anything else in his entire life. Every second he was closer to her. She had tears in her eyes. The expression on her face hadn't changed. The only difference was she put her hands up to her face to cover her mouth. He wished he could start running to her even though now there wasn't much distance between them. There were tears in both their eyes.

He finally reached her and wrapped his arms around her just as her legs were about to give out. They both were crying now, and he eased her down on the floor with him without letting her go. Neither one could likely answer how long they were down on the floor huddled together, but it was not a short time. No words were exchanged between them as they were overrun with emotion. The only thing he could manage to do was to stroke her hair. Her arms were curled up on his chest while he kept her close to his body. The only thing he could get out now was, "I missed you so much!"

He couldn't understand what she was saying because it wasn't even a whisper, but it seemed like "I missed you too." She also pointed toward the door, and he knew what she wanted. He stood on uneasy legs and made his way to lock the door. His legs felt stronger now and was able to get back to her much faster than the first time. She was sitting with her back against the wall now. He sat down beside her.

"I missed you so much, Marcela! I know you must be very confused and very hurt. But if you are willing, I'd like to try to explain everything!"

She didn't let on that she already knew everything. She wanted to hear his whole side. It wasn't going to make a difference because she was happy that he was there. It was very emotional, but soon she was sure that was going to turn to more happiness than shock. The first moment she saw him, everything that had happened since she went to Paris rushed back through her mind in fast-forward. She just nodded and looked at him. He had that same intensity in his eyes as the first time she met him. His tears were gone now.

"Do you want to talk about it here, or would you like to go home and talk there?"

She was a bit more composed now. "I don't think I can drive right now. Do you think you can?" She leaned on his shoulder. It was so nice to be with him again. She never wanted to be without him again!

"Yes, I can manage as long as you can tell me where to go."

She nodded again. He stood and offered his hand to help her up. Even though this was exactly what she wanted, it felt so surreal! She wished they were already at her house so they could talk right away. But she didn't really want to talk about things at her shop either. If he was willing to wait and drive her home, she could wait. She was sure it wasn't going to be a short conversation. And they would surely get very emotional with everything he was going to tell her, which she thought she already knew most of it.

It took her a few minutes to gather her stuff and get the shop closed up. She led him to her car, and he helped her in and then got in the driver side. He had remembered that she said she lived pretty close to her work. It wasn't only her that wanted to get home as soon as possible to get this part over with. He just hoped that she could somehow forgive him for the stupidity of his actions! He also hoped that he would remember at least some of what he had prepared to say to her! But something told him that he wasn't to be able to say things as he thought before.

He navigated their way to her house with mostly hand gestures from her to direct him. Fifteen minutes later, they pulled into the driveway of her house. They were quiet on the way home. He knew if he started talking about anything in the car, first, it didn't seem right to try to make small talk, and second, he didn't know if he could talk about anything else until he said what he needed to say. Nothing was more important than getting everything out into the open so she could decide if she could forgive him and moreover want to spend the rest of her life with him. He went and opened her door for her again, and they went inside her house. He hadn't seen it yet, but it looked very homey inside. Just from the living area, it was remarkably close to what he had imagine she would have. He put his bag down by the couch.

"Would you like something to drink?" she asked as he made her way to the kitchen.

"Water would be great, thank you!"

She got two bottles of water out of the refrigerator, and she went to sit on the couch. He followed her back and sat beside her. He left some room between them so he could look at her easier while talking. He wanted her to see the sincerity in his eyes! This was the single most important moment in his life up to this point. It had to work! He really didn't know if he could live the rest of his life without her.

He took a drink of water and looked at her. *Here goes nothing*, he thought. "I want to apologize for everything I have put you through for the last several months. I am not trying to reason anything I have or have not done! I just want to explain. Please don't say anything until I'm done. I need to be able to get through this. When we were in Paris, my stomach was giving me problem. I think you probably remember that."

She nodded, and he continued, "I thought it was lack of sleep or something I ate. Well, what I didn't tell you is that I felt sick after I got home, and it was actually getting worse every day! I couldn't eat very much. Sleep was almost impossible. I went to the emergency room the last day that we talked. I didn't want to upset you, so I didn't tell you when I went. I thought it was something simple that I could take some medicine for and I would get over it very soon."

He took a breath, and she gave him a look that said what she felt for him. She still didn't give away the fact she knew what he was going to say. "I found out that I had cancer of the esophagus and stomach!"

It was like it was the first time she had heard the news. Hearing him say it brought back everything she felt when she learned of what he was going through. Her hand instinctively reached out, and he grabbed it and didn't she let go. He continued, "I wanted to call you as soon as I found out. I wanted you there with me. But then I thought about how you would feel, so I held off. They admitted me to the hospital, and my parents were there for me. I didn't have my phone anymore. My mom had taken it and had my dad take it home. Long story short, she convinced me that it was for the best that I didn't tell you. She said that I would hurt you less if I just never contacted you again. At the time, it seemed like that might very well be the best thing for you."

He took another deep breath. It was hard for him to even think about! But he kept going. "It wasn't expected that I would recover or even live much longer. My family didn't have the kind of money to get the best doctors. I thought, how could I do that to you? My mom kept suggesting that I shouldn't do that to you! I was so lost. After the first few weeks, I got much sicker, and it was extremely hard for me! But then a miracle happened! Just when I had given up hope, several doctors came in and told me they were going to try everything they could for me. Someone had paid them to help me!"

She wanted to tell him that she knew. But Lee, Antonio, and herself had vowed they would never tell a soul what they did! She swallowed it down and looked at him again. "That's amazing!" she said.

He continued, "I couldn't believe it! I had given up, and then here came these experts that I couldn't afford. I thought my parents had done something, like selling the vineyard. But they were just as surprised as I was! I still don't know where the money came from. Anyways, over the next few months, I got better. The doctors were unbelievable! I started thinking more and more that my decision to leave you alone felt wrong. You didn't deserve any of what you were put through!

"So I ended up beating the cancer, and I am in full remission. I knew then that my decision was wrong to not tell you and take the chance of hurting you more! After that, I formulated my plan to come talk to you in person. I felt like you deserved that! I talked to my parents, and my dad was incredibly supportive as I knew he would be. He always has been! But my mom really surprised me when she gave her blessing for me to try to get you back. After that, I found Antonio through a paid finder's site that I used. I knew his full name thanks to you. Funny how something as minor as telling me his name could make things happen!"

She now knew she was looking at him with complete shock! Antonio hadn't said anything about them talking. "When did you talk to Antonio?" was all she said.

"Just a few days ago. Please don't be mad at him for not telling you. I begged him not to! I wanted to come here in person to talk to you."

Still in complete shock, she mumbled, "Oh!" She looked away from his eyes because she was afraid her eyes would give away that she knew something was going on. She didn't know the latest news, but she knew everything else.

"I got the first available flight out, and he picked me up from the airport. We talked for some time again, and he dropped me off at your work. And that brings us to this moment."

Her head was spinning hearing him talking about everything. She felt awful for him! She was even now thinking about telling him what they had done. "Anastasio…"

But before she could say anything else, he got off the couch and kneeled down in front of her. "Marcela, I know our relationship is far from perfect, and I know you probably won't be able to answer this now. But I know what I want in life. I know my life isn't complete without. I doubt I would ever be able to enjoy food. Drinks won't taste the same. Sleep would be difficult. Marcela, what we had and felt in Paris was real. I know you, and I have a connection that not many people have. My life is with you. My life is you! Marcela, I will spend the rest of my life trying to make your life better, not only because you make my life better but because you deserve that!"

He reached in his pocket, and she saw he had a box in his hand. With all that she heard, she wasn't expecting this part! The thought never occurred to her about what she was about to hear. Without even knowing that she did, she put her hands to her mouth again. Her eyes were wide. She wasn't sure if she was even breathing.

"I would be honored if you would make me the happiest man on the planet and marry me! Marcela..." He opened the box, and there was the ring she thought she might never see or wear in her life. "Will you marry me?"

She was overcome with emotion again. But this was different. She was happier than she thought she could be! Even more than when she was in Paris. She put her hands out and pulled his face to bring it to hers to kiss. "Yes, yes, yes, yes! A million times yes!"

She experienced real happiness for the first time since they talked last. She kissed him all over his face. The tears were back for both of them. She didn't want to let go of him. She didn't know he was coming, didn't expect that conversation today, and certainly didn't expect for him to propose. This was going to be a day that she wouldn't forget in ten lifetimes. Their lips found each other, and it was the same passion they had when they were together last. Nothing else could matter in life again. She dreamed of this day so many times to only wake up to being alone and fearing she would never see him again.

He didn't expect that she was going to answer so quickly. He thought he'd spend a lot time trying to make up for the pain he had caused her. And now he was telling her that he had cancer and the miracle of getting better. He hadn't told a soul that he was planning to ask her to marry him. He didn't tell his parents or Antonio that he planned to do it. He wasn't even sure he was going to ask her today. The plan was to tell her about what had happened. If that went well, then maybe a few days after. But he felt it and went with it. He was happy he did!

He was still down on one knee as they kissed, and there was now excitement that replaced the heaviness that was in the air with everything else. He pulled away from her and placed the ring on her finger. He knew the size she was when they were in Paris. While she was sleeping one night, he had a chart that he was able to place one of her rings she was wearing in the evening on before they went to bed. He was hoping it would still be same. It was a perfect fit! "It was my grandmother's! She met her husband during the war. He asked her to marry after only a few dates before he left to go to war."

She really looked at the ring now. When he asked her, she was so surprised that he was asking her to marry him that she didn't even pay attention to the ring. It was beautiful! It was princess cut. If she had to guess, it was at least two karats. Her mind was having a hard time processing everything. When she went to work this morning, she had no clue that she would be engaged to be married to the one man that she loved! Life was strange. At times, it was so good to you. Then it could twist you, turn you, eat you up, and then spit you out. And all that could even happen in one day. But she would take what she was feeling at the moment for as long as she could! She honestly believed that this was just a continuation of what she felt before.

They continued to kiss each other, and now there were smiles on their faces. Their tears of sadness were replaced with tears of joy. He got up and sat next to her again. This time, he sat very close to her. For the first time since he saw her in her shop, he felt like he could breathe again. Every moment that he spent in the hospital with all the tests, treatments, therapy, and the endless thinking that he very well was going to die was all gone in a single minute. Everything did up to this moment was worth every minute of it.

He was now holding her hand, and she kept looking at her ring finger both in awe and disbelief. She was still crying some, but now she had a smile on her face. She wished her mom was still alive to see this and share in her happiness. She knew Antonio and Lee would be incredibly happy for her! They were so very protective of her, but they knew what she felt for Anastasio. And after they learned of his illness, they knew why he did what he did.

It was getting close to dinnertime, and Anastasio's stomach was growling. He laughed as it was so loud that she definitely heard it. He rested his forehead on hers. "Are you hungry?"

She laughed and said, "I think we better get you some food before you eat me! But first, I need to tell you something. Anastasio, I didn't know if I was ever going to hear from you again. That was painful, but there's more to it than that. You're going to be a daddy in about five months!"

He looked at her like he didn't hear her correctly. She just nodded to confirm what he just heard. Then a smile came to his face like she had never seen before. "Marcela! I can't believe it. And I don't mean that in a bad way. I didn't even think about something like that! Do you know if it's a boy or girl yet?"

"No, I have an appointment in a few weeks, and if I want, they will tell me the sex of the baby!"

"I can't believe it! You are going to be my wife, and we will have our own family very soon!"

"Yes, we will! Now back to eating. I know you don't still want to eat me. Let's find you some food."

He laughed again. "That still sounds tempting. But we'll talk about that later. Do you have anything we can cook? Or maybe we can order in? I don't know that either of us should be in public with us crying over and over."

"Yes, we can do either. I have food here. But we can order in too."

"How about we order some food. I don't know that either of us are in the right state to be responsible for using a stove or oven!"

She laughed and nodded. "I have some delivery menus in the kitchen. You can tell me what sounds good to you."

She got up, and he followed her to the kitchen. She opened a drawer and pulled out several menus. He stood behind her and wrapped his arms around her from behind. She flipped through the menus slowly so that he could see all of them. Plus, she didn't want him to move from where she was. It was so nice to feel his touch again. She missed his touch, his scent, the way he looked at her, and the way he made her feel when he was near her. It was like not a day had passed since she was with him. All the negative things that happened were now erased.

They decided on Chinese, and she called and placed the order. They stayed just like they were for some time. She couldn't help looking at her hand. It was a beautiful ring. She would have been happy with a $5 ring. That part didn't matter to her! It was the fact that the man of her dreams had just asked her to marry him. She didn't have her mom to tell or share this with, but she did have Antonio and Lee. She wasn't sure if Antonio knew this was going to happen since he met with Anastasio right before this happened. She wanted to call them and tell them but really didn't want to do it over the phone.

"Do you mind if I call Antonio and Lee and invite them over tomorrow night? I really want them to know. They have been so good to me!"

"I wouldn't expect any less. I know what they mean to you!"

Reluctantly she pulled away from him to get her phone to call them. She first called Antonio and invited him for dinner the following evening. She asked him not to tell Lee about seeing Anastasio. He promised that he wouldn't tell Lee. Luckily, he didn't ask why she was inviting them to dinner. She then called Lee. He had no idea Anastasio was even there, so he'd be really surprised when he got there! He also agreed to come for dinner with no questions.

While she was on the phone, Anastasio went to his bag and pulled out a bottle of wine and a bottle of champagne. He took the champagne and put it in the refrigerator. He looked at her with the bottle of wine still in his hand and motioned that he needed a corkscrew. She went to a drawer where she kept things like that and handed it to him. He realized then that he would need to get familiar where everything was. He wanted to know every little thing he could. Where the utensils were, plates, glasses, cookware, where she kept her clothes, toothbrush, everything!

He opened the bottle of wine and started opening cabinets to find the wineglasses. It only took him two tries to find them. Just from what he saw, there was perfect logic of where she put things. He would have placed them in the same spot as well. He poured a glass and suddenly realized that she was having a baby. She wouldn't be able to drink. He waited for her to finish her calls to take a drink. He originally planned that this was going to be there first drink after he asked her to marry him, so it was especially important to him. He knew it would mean something significant to her too. He decided to pour just enough for her to toast and have just one drink. He was saving this wine for an occasion like this. It was a wine that was produced in 1987, one of the best that his family ever made. He would make sure they kept the bottle and the cork as well as a memory of the day.

When she finished the call, he took her hand and led her back to the couch, and they sat down. They raised their glasses. "I know you can't really drink now. But just a taste won't hurt. To the most amazing woman on the planet! Today marks the happiest day I've had, and I don't doubt for a second that we will build an amazing life together. Happiness will be the foundation of our life, not the exception as many have. I will spend the rest of my life supporting you, loving you, showing you how much you mean to me every single day! To us, Marcela! I love you!"

He was about to take a drink, but she stopped him. "I would like to make a toast as well. Anastasio, forces greater than us brought us together in the most unlikely circumstances. From the moment I met you, you changed my life. You made me understand what happiness really is. For years I thought I sort of knew what happiness was, but I was wrong. And as fate would have it, you showed up again in my life at a time I needed it the most. Just seeing you made my heart skip beats again. I didn't know if I was ever going to see or hear from you again. And I'm happy that I did! I will offer you the same that you will do for me. I will show you how much I love you and support you. I love you, Anastasio! What was it you said to me when I was falling asleep on our first night? I loved you before I even met you!"

They now drank as he held her hand again. He was surprised that she heard him or even remembered that he said that! Their food arrived shortly after. They ate, and it felt like no time had passed between them. Both had smiles on their faces. There was real laughter! The way he looked at her made her heart speed up. It was intense but loving! She knew he would never look at another woman the way he looked at her. She hoped he felt the same from her look because that was how she felt! She would never look at another man the way she looked at him. He was the love of her life!

They stayed up a little while longer, and Marcela showed him around the house so he could get familiar with everything. She had originally thought that she was going to have a full week at work. Now she would feel it out for the near future. She knew she wasn't going in a least tomorrow. They got ready for bed and talked while in bed together. There were many instances of kissing and holding each other. They didn't talk too seriously, like what this meant for his work, when they planned to marry, and so on. All that would come later! Right now, it was just nice to be back together. Maybe they would talk about more when they got up tomorrow.

They were both exhausted from the long day of emotions that they experienced throughout the day. Normally people had to deal with one emotion at a time, not the roller coaster of events throughout the day. There was no need to make love for the intimacy they were feeling. Just being close to each other was all they needed! They fell asleep holding each other. It was the perfect ending to a surprisingly perfect evening.

They ended up sleeping in the next morning. It was a nice change for both of them. She rarely could sleep very long each night and had to be up early for work. For him, he was usually up early for medical treatments or helping his father out in the vineyard. They were already so comfortable with each other that they could finally relax and enjoy life for a day or two before getting back to reality. For today, they were going to keep living in a world that only they could create.

At about 10:00 a.m., they got out of bed and made breakfast together. Just like they had in Paris, they had the easy banter between each other. As they started to eat, Anastasio asked her about how she felt about meeting his parents. He would have loved to meet her mother or father, but that wasn't going to be possible. He wanted his parents to know how amazing she was! He knew that once his mom met her, even though she told him to go get her, he knew she wasn't totally convinced! However, he knew she would fall in love with her.

She was open to meeting them when he thought would be the best time. He preferred sooner than later. He only brought a few changes of clothes as he didn't know what her response was going to be when she saw him. He really didn't expect that he was going to ask her to marry him in the same day. It all just kind of happened, like everything did in their relationship. Why should that have been any different?

After breakfast, they looked at airline prices, and they found some flights to Italy that they could leave in the next few days. They only needed one way as the plan was to drive his car back. They decided to book the trip so they wouldn't lose the fare. Given everything that happened, they couldn't afford to spend too much money or take a long time off work. It was a good time for Marcela because the tourist season hadn't started yet. She didn't get a ton of business from tourists, but it would certainly help. They had to be responsible and think about the future with each other.

It was getting to be early afternoon now, and they hadn't planned what they were going to have for dinner with Antonio and Lee. They wanted to make something nice to tell them about and celebrate their engagement. Anastasio pulled out a bottle of champagne from his bag and put it in the refrigerator to chill. He had come prepared to have reasons to celebrate! They then decided on a seafood delight, which consisted of shrimp, lobster, twice-baked potato, and asparagus. They would go to the store shortly and look for dessert ideas as well. It was going to be nice evening with all her favorite men all in one room.

They made their list, showered quickly, which was hard to do since they were showering together, and went to the store. They bought all the things they talked about and found some apple pie and ice cream for dessert. They also bought some more wine in case the night went long. Marcela decided that since they were going to Italy in a few days, she wouldn't return to work until after they got back from Italy. She would at least stop by there to put up a sign stating when she would return. She also wanted to grab her planner that had all her client information so she could update them with her schedule as well.

They decided to stop by her shop on the way home to do the things he needed to do. That would leave them enough time to start preparing for dinner and to decide exactly what they were going to tell them and when. She didn't want to take off the ring for the rest of her life, so she knew they would see it quickly, so they decided they would tell them right before dinner. She would try to hide her hand as much as possible until they told them.

The doorbell rang, and Marcela was confused for a moment. Antonio and Lee normally just came in. It must have been Antonio as Lee had no idea that Marcela wasn't alone. She opened the door to Antonio standing there. She hugged him while hiding her hand behind his back. She invited him in, and he hugged Anastasio as well. Antonio knew that things must have gone well since he was invited to dinner, and Anastasio was standing there. Also, Marcela seemed happier than he had seen her lately!

Not long after Antonio came, the door opened, and Lee came in. He looked a bit confused at first and caught on quickly. *This must be Anastasio,* he thought. He looked at Antonio, and his look told him that his guess was right. Marcela introduced them to each other, and they shook hands. Marcela gave him a hug, still trying to hide her hand as much as possible. She didn't think Antonio saw it. If he did, he put on a good show of not knowing.

Dinner was getting close to be done, and she knew they would notice during dinner. It was time to announce their engagement. She was hopeful that they would be sincerely happy for her. What they had gone through to find him and tell her what they found, they should be genuinely happy for her. Everything had fallen in place better than anyone would have ever guessed.

Marcela started talking as they had planned together. "So Anastasio and I wanted to invite you over tonight to celebrate our engagement to be married! We haven't set a date yet, but we will in the near future."

Antonio was the first to give Marcela a big hug as Lee did the same to Anastasio. Then they switched congratulations. Anastasio went and got one of the bottles of champagne, opened it, and poured each of them a glass as Marcela was showing them her ring. Anastasio handed them their glasses, and Antonio was the first to toast.

"To my best friend and new friend, I wish you a lifetime of prosperity and happiness. I'm glad I could be part of your celebration!"

Lee toasted next. "Anastasio, you couldn't have found a better woman to spend the rest of your life with! Congratulations to you both!"

Marcela and Anastasio put the dinner on the table, and they all sat. They ate dinner as they talked about the trip she was about to take to his home in Italy. They also asked Anastasio lots of questions to get to know him. When they were done with dinner, they had dessert and wine as they continued to talk. Anastasio felt very welcomed and comfortable with them already. He could see why Marcela liked them so much!

They talked for about an hour more before they started wrapping up. Lee told them that he could take them to the airport for their flight to Italy. They weren't going to see Antonio before they were to leave, so they said their goodbyes before he left. Lee left shortly after Antonio. Marcela and Anastasio cleaned up the dishes from dinner and got ready for bed. They wanted to get a full day in of errands that needed to be done. Marcela wanted to shop for a few new things to wear to Italy.

Before they left, they discussed different dates that they wanted to try for to get married. They first thought about getting married before their child was born but decided against as they wanted more time to plan their wedding. They decided on a date eight months later. The weather would be warming back up, and they had a plan for where they wanted it.

~

They arrived in Italy just after lunchtime. Just his dad came to pick them up. He was waiting by the baggage claim when they came out. He gave his dad a big hug and then introduced him to Marcela. There a little bit of a language barrier as she could understand most of the Italian language but knew very little Italian, so Anastasio had to translate some here or there. Once they had their bags, his dad led them to the car, and they were on their way to the house. Marcela looked forward to seeing where he grew up and see the vineyard. Her only vineyard experiences were when she did the occasional tour she took with her mom.

It took about an hour to get to the house. They made small talk on the way there. She wasn't nervous with his dad. Anastasio always talked about how fond he was of him. But she was nervous about meeting his mom. She was wearing a ring that his grandmother wore. She felt that she might not think she was worthy of her son and wearing the ring. As they got out of the car, she had to take a few deep breaths to calm herself. Anastasio saw knew she was nervous and put this arm around and whispered in her ear that everything was going to be all right.

When they walked inside, his mom was there to greet them all. She went to Marcela before she said anything to anyone else. She kissed her on both cheeks and stepped back a little and introduced herself. She took her hands into her own and looked at the ring and smiled. She hugged Anastasio and kissed him too. They went into the living room, and all sat down. His mom went into the kitchen and returned with a tray full of food. Appetizers, sandwiches, and different cheeses and crackers. She then brought out water, wine, and glasses. They were pretty hungry as they came in right at lunchtime.

They ate while they were talking about random things. Anastasio said that they had a date planned for the wedding. It would be eight months later. He asked them if they could have the wedding there in the vineyard. It was going to be easier to have the wedding there than trying to coordinate his family going to Spain. Marcela didn't have any family left there. Before his dad could say anything, his mom said yes. They would be thrilled to have the wedding there! They were going to tell his parents about the baby at dinner.

Anastasio took her outside to see the vineyard. It was bigger than she expected. It was absolutely beautiful! It would be the perfect place to get married. They walked all through the land and were hand in hand. She was glad they were there. She was no longer nervous. It seemed that his parents liked her. Her plan was to spend as much time with his mom as possible. She wanted her to see that she really did love him love and that she was going to make him happy! She didn't want there to be any question of who she was. She really wanted to get to know his dad too. Since she had no family left, she wanted to be part of his!

They finished their walk and went back inside. His dad was watching TV, and his mom was in the kitchen. She told Anastasio that she was going to go help his mom in the kitchen. Maybe she could also learn some really good homemade Italian dishes. She loved to cook and wanted to be able to cook some of Anastasio's favorite meals. It was important to her to learn everything she could on this trip. The plan was to be there for four days. She needed to take advantage of the time she had. Plus, she wanted to ask his mom if she would like to be a part of planning the wedding.

His mom was making homemade ravioli. Marcela asked if she could help, and she said yes and started to show her what she was doing. They talked as much as they could without Anastasio translating some things. They were making do though. She was really enjoying herself. She didn't see what Anastasio said about his mom not being the nicest person in the world. She seemed very warm and inviting, which was totally unexpected!

Anastasio came in and sat down and poured himself a glass of wine. He was happy to see that they seemed to be getting along just fine. Marcela asked him to translate some to talk about the wedding they wanted to plan. They weren't planning on a big wedding. They just wanted family and a few friends. That was all they needed. Their relationship meant more than a big wedding. His mom was happy to talk about anything she wanted to do! She also offered some ideas as well. It was going to be a lovely wedding.

Once the ravioli was made, they started making the sauce. Marcela was so happy that she was learning so much already. She would have to ask her for the recipes to have at home. That was one thing she hadn't really learned. Her mom wasn't a big cook, and they made simple things usually. She wanted to be able to cook for Anastasio. She knew he liked to cook as well. It would be fun to cook things together.

A few hours later, they all sat down to eat. Marcela wasn't sure if when she was able to drink again. She could keep up with drinking as much wine as they were. It seemed like water to them! She had never been a big drinker. They ate so much food she thought she was going to burst. But his mom kept trying to give more food. Marcela didn't want to be rude, but she literally couldn't eat any more food! They sat at the table for a while longer, having expresso and talking more about plans for the wedding. His dad was usually quiet, and she thought he wouldn't want to talk about it, but he came up with more ideas than his mom and Marcela combined. Anastasio and Marcela had planned to tell his parents of her pregnancy right after dinner.

"Mom, Dad, we have some news to tell you!"

Before he could get another word out, his mom spoke. She looked at Marcela and asked, "Do you know if it's a boy or girl?"

Anastasio and Marcela looked at each other in complete shock. Neither had let on anything about her being pregnant. Even when she refused the wine, she had just said that she was exhausted from the flight and would be asleep before dinner if she drank anything. Anastasio started, "How did you…"

"Son, I may be getting old, but I still know that glow a woman gets only when she's pregnant! Marcela is glowing like a night light!"

Until that moment, neither had noticed the glow. Now Anastasio could see it as plain as day. Marcela couldn't see her own face but thought back to getting ready and seeing herself in the mirror. She assumed the change in her look was from all the excitement of everything that had happened in the last few days. She knew she didn't have that look until Anastasio came back to her!

Marcela spoke this time, "We don't know yet. We can find out in a few weeks at my next doctor's appointment."

They talked a little longer at the table before they adjourned to the living room. They didn't stay up too much longer as they were getting tired. They said good night to his mom and dad and went upstairs to get ready for bed. She was so happy that they made the trip. It was nice to see where he lived, and she hoped that tomorrow she could see what his dad did every day in the vineyard. She didn't want to think anything bad, but they might have to take over the vineyard one day! She wanted to learn as much as possible.

Over the next few days, she spent as much time as she could with both his parents. She learned how to cook new things each day and some of what his dad did in the vineyard. She got to see how wine was made. It was really amazing everything they did on a daily basis! By the time it was time for them to drive back to Barcelona, she was extremely comfortable with his family, and she felt right at home. They packed his car full of his clothes and other things he wanted to have. They said their goodbyes and promised they would come back as soon as they could, and they would tell them what they found out when she went to the doctor next.

Chapter 15

The next several weeks flew by with everything they were doing. Marcela spent her days at work, and in the evenings, they were busy planning their wedding with his mom and dad. They went to her doctor's appointment and found out they were going to have a baby girl! They were so happy! Things couldn't seem to get any better, but it seemed every day was better than the last.

When they found out they were having a girl, Anastasio already knew what she would want to name her. He told her he thought she wanted to name her Paris. She couldn't believe how connected they were as she was thinking that but had never even gave a hint that she was thinking that. Paris was a perfect name for her as she was conceived in Paris, and those several days were perfect! They immediately started buying clothes and changing one of the rooms in the house into a nursery.

The next few months were exciting, going to the doctors and seeing the first photo, hearing the heartbeat, and seeing the changes that both Marcela and Paris were going through. They were so excited for what the near future would bring. Everyone around them were excited as well and offering any help that they might need. Paris was going to have a very loving family around her!

When Anastasio was in town, he helped her in every way that he could. He was traveling about half of every week for the vineyard.

He wanted to be as much help to his family as he could. However, they needed all the money they could get to pay for a beautiful wedding! It wasn't going to be as bad as some wedding cost, but they wanted to have something nice for everyone to remember.

It would be getting close to summer when they would get married. It was going to be outside in the vineyard. His mom was more help than she could've hoped for. She helped with finding bakeries that could do her cake, printers to do they invitations, and a planner to coordinate everything and made sure everything was being taken care of. Marcela thought they wouldn't need a planner to begin with, but after trying to do everything from Barcelona, planning became much more difficult.

She found a dress that she thought was amazing. She would size for it after having Paris. She was only a month away from her due date! During her downtime at work, she made some jewelry to wear with the dress. She really liked the new pieces, and she planned to make some more like them to sell at her shop. Business had picked up again, and like when she came home from Paris, her positive attitude seemed to help with her clients. She had kept up with Jacqueline, and she had promised that she would send Marcela some ideas to wear during and after the wedding.

Anastasio was very involved in the planning as well. Most men didn't get into the planning side, but he showed interest all the way through. He was doing well with his sales, so they were doing very well for saving up for the wedding and honeymoon. They were planning a two-week trip to Paris and Greece! They wanted to go back to Paris because that was where it all started. They'd spend a week there and the other week traveling through Greece. Neither of them had been to Greece before. They were extremely excited about the trip. His parents wanted to keep Paris while they were away, so they planned to come to Barcelona for the first time to stay there with their granddaughter!

Just a few days before her due date, Marcela went into labor. It wasn't as bad as she thought it was going to be, but it still was extremely difficult. She was only in labor for about seven hours. She had heard the horror stories of women having two days of labor, the intense pain, etc. But Paris was ready to meet her parents and made it easier on Marcela.

She was beautiful, and Anastasio thought that she looked exactly like her mother. He had seen photos of Marcela as a baby, and the likeness was incredible. Anastasio hoped that Paris would grow up looking like her mother! No matter who or what she looked like, they were so happy and knew they would be proud of her. She was conceived in love and born in that same love!

His parents made their first trip to Barcelona to see their newborn granddaughter. They were so happy, and instantly Paris took to them. His mom was especially good at knowing what each cry meant and what to do in any situation. Marcela was so happy that they were able to come. She hoped that Paris would get to spend a lot of time with them as she grew up. Since her own parents weren't around, they were the only grandparents that she would get to meet.

His parents stayed for just over a month after Pairs was born. When they left, it was nice to have some privacy again. She loved every minute of them being there, but it was nice to be able to sit with her husband and not have anyone else around. She missed curling up with him and just watching a movie or listening to music as they talked. Before she was pregnant, they drank wine on a daily basis. But since she found out, she couldn't have it anymore. Anastasio wouldn't drink without her. She told him it was okay, but he cared too much about her to do something she couldn't.

Antonio and Lee proved to be the best godparents that Paris could have. Even though they weren't her real uncles, that's what they would be called. They were just as close as any family could have. They came over to her house every few days and spent time holding her and getting her familiar with them so when they would babysit, Paris wouldn't be afraid of them. The plan was working well as when Marcela and Anastasio went on a date night, Paris was in good hands.

Marcela started to only work half days after she went back to work. She stayed home for the first month. It was getting closer to their wedding date, and they couldn't wait to officially be married and a family in the eyes of God! It was getting so close. Everything was going according to their plan. Marcela fitted for her dress, and they finished up everything they needed to get done for the wedding.

They left for Italy a week before the wedding. Antonio and Lee came with them. They wanted to spend time with them before the wedding. And since they could stay at Anastasio's parents' place, all they really had to pay for were the flights. Jacqueline met them there was well. It was so much fun to have them all there together. His parents were great host for everyone. Marcela swore if she ate any more, she wouldn't be able to fit into her dress. But everyone else didn't seem to mind. His mom was constantly cooking, and the dad was showing everyone around the vineyard as everyone was curious how making wine worked. He was getting a lot of free help for the week. Jacqueline got to meet little Paris as well. She was really good with her also. Paris was going to have an amazing family around her!

Three days before the wedding, they had makeshift bachelor and bachelorette parties. They had different plans during the earlier part of the evening but planned to all meet up in the later part of the evening. It wasn't the standard way to do it, but they were all such good friends now that they all wanted to hang out together. Even though Antonio and Lee lived close to them, Jacqueline and his parents weren't. Marcela was surprised that Anastasio's dad wanted to be a part of it and was going to stay out late. He usually didn't go to bed early, but he never went out. His mom wanted to stay at home with Paris.

The morning of the wedding, Anastasio's mom, Jacqueline, and Marcela went to a spa, where they relaxed in the morning, then had pedicures, manicures, and their hair and makeup done. When they returned to the house, they helped Marcela into her dress and got her ready to walk down the aisle. Anastasio and the guys got ready as well. Since Marcela's dad wasn't in the picture, she asked Antonio to walk her down the aisle. She had asked Antonio to technically to be her maid of honor. He would stand as the best man for Anastasio. Jacqueline stood as her maid of honor.

The weather was perfect. It wasn't too hot or too cold. The early evening was amazing. That time of the year could be questionable with rain, but they lucked out. The planner also proved to be worth it. Everything—from the invitations, flowers, candles, to everything else set up outside—was perfect. They had a tent brought in, and under it housed the wedding table, cake, gift table, and dance floor. His parents insisted on paying for a band and DJ. Tiki torches lined the outside of the seating for the wedding and also led a path to the tent. They also lined a small area that one could go a little bit farther into the vineyard.

Anastasio was standing on the stage that was set up. He hadn't seen Marcela since last night. He hadn't seen the dress either. The procession started, and Jacqueline started down the aisle escorted by Lee since Antonio was walking Marcela down the aisle. She was smiling and seemed overjoyed. Lee was smiling broadly as well. Once Jacqueline was in place, Lee took a seat next to Anastasio's parents. Then like a beauty in the night, Marcela came out and started to walk down the aisle. Marcela looked stunning! Antonio was escorting her, and he looked like how a proud father would look. Anastasio knew he had to be beaming from head to toe.

They made their way slowly down the aisle. All the guests were standing, taking photos as they walked by. It seemed like she was walking in slow motion, like you see in movies. He wanted her beside him right now! He wanted to say "I do" and be married to the most amazing woman on the planet. When they made it to the stage, Antonio gave her away and kissed her cheek lightly. Then he went and straightened out her train and stood next to Anastasio. He was incredibly happy that Marcela had him as her best friend. He was irreplaceable!

The priest started the ceremony. They had decided against making their own vows because neither of them thought they could do it without getting too emotional. They planned to say something at the reception instead. The ceremony went off without a hitch. When they said "I do" and exchanged rings, there was nothing that could have made them happier. He kissed her, not as passionately as he would've liked, but he would be doing that later in the evening for sure.

Before the reception, they took photos by themselves, with the wedding party, and with his parents. After that they went to the tent and saw everyone that was there. Everyone was so happy for them, and they came up and gave them hugs and kisses. Anastasio's parents had become so close with Marcela. She never imagined that she would be close with his mom, but she was being like her own mother to her. She now understood why Anastasio was so loving to her. He saw that between his parents, and that's how he saw a relationship. They were his role models! She did see that his mom, at times, was somewhat controlling, but she was always good with Marcela.

They made their way to the wedding table that was set up at the head of the tent, so they were facing everyone. They didn't have a lot of people but enough to make it fun for the reception. It was mostly people in his family. They were an incredibly fun group. They were served dinner, and the music started. It was the DJ until dinner was over and then the live band when they would do the first dance and begin the rest of the evening. Marcela was actually looking forward to dancing with him. That was also part of the start for them.

Now that dinner was done, Anastasio and Marcela went to the dance floor. All eyes were on them, and Marcela got a little nervous. They had picked a song that both of them liked to have their first dance to. When the band came on, they weren't playing what they had chosen. It sounded vaguely familiar, and given Anastasio's response, he knew that this was going to happen. He came up to her and took her hand. "I know this isn't the song we picked, but I thought you would like this even more!"

"It sounds vaguely familiar. What is it?"

"Think back. Where have we danced to this before?"

It took her a moment longer, and she couldn't believe first that she remembered, second that he remembered, and third that he was able to find it. "How did you...?"

"You don't think that night was only memorable for you, do you?" He turned her to where she could see the band. It wasn't the band that they hired that was playing the song. It was the men she saw the first night she met him. She couldn't believe her eyes and ears!

"I just can't believe it! How did I get so lucky to find you?"

"I know I'm the lucky one. I love you so much! I haven't forgotten any moment that we have spent together."

They danced just how they danced the first night they met. She had subtle tears coming down her face from the sweet gesture that Anastasio had surprised her with. This day couldn't get better! Everything was turning out better than she had expected. "I love you, husband!"

He hadn't even thought about being called husband. He laughed a little. "I love you, wife!"

They danced close, and she closed her eyes. The memory of the first night came rushing to her senses. She could feel him, smell the air, hear the band playing, and taste the wine. She was back in Paris with him! She didn't want this feeling to ever go away. But she also knew that she would never forget that night or this night for the rest of her life. She knew that she would have many memories that she never would forget with him, and she looked forward to experiencing each one of them.

The song ended, and they announced that it was the father-and-daughter dance. They knew her father wasn't there, and his dad came and took her hand and started to dance. He was beaming with pride as they danced. She had learned a lot of Italian over the last several of months. They also were learning Spanish as well. She really had grown to love his family and was now happy to call him dad. Jacqueline brought Paris over, and Anastasio held her and danced around the dance floor with her.

The next few dances were with Antonio and Lee. She was so happy that they were a part of her life. They also loved Anastasio, and they all spent a lot of time together doing everything. Even if she was busy, they would call one another and hang out. It was like all of them were the family that she missed having. Her mom would've been so proud of her right now!

Anastasio and Marcela danced a few more times, and it was time to do the different toasts from everyone. They also had things they wanted to say since they didn't write their own vows. It was probably still going to be very emotional, but it was better now than during the ceremony. It was such a beautiful reception! Anastasio's parents were the main reason that it was so beautiful. They did so much to help.

Antonio stood and clinked his champagne glass. "First, I want to thank everyone for coming to celebrate the union of Anastasio and Marcela. I've known Marcela now for nine years now. I have known Anastasio for just about a year now. I couldn't be happier for either of them. There is no doubt in my mind that this is a love that will last forever. They were meant to be right from the start. I have never seen her as happy as she is now. I love you guys!"

Anastasio's father was next. "Thank you, Antonio, for a beautiful toast. You are family now! As many of you know, recently my son had cancer, and it was a tough time for him. But there was something inside of him that got him through it. Although he had amazing doctors, it was what he had in his heart that got him through it. It was the love he and Marcela had! I am proud to be here tonight with our new daughter, Marcela. As Antonio said, there is no doubt that this is a love for a lifetime. My wife and I couldn't be happier than we are now. To my son and my daughter. We love you both!"

His dad came and hugged and kissed them. Anastasio stood, raised his glass, and looked at Marcela. "To my wife! I hadn't thought of titles such as husband and wife until tonight. My wife, my love, my everything! We met in Paris by chance. It was such a day to remember. I remember the first time I looked into your eyes. It was like I was looking straight into your soul. At that moment, I knew my life was going to change forever. As luck would have it, it did! I can't imagine a life without you. You are my sun. Even when it's cloudy out, I know the sun is right there waiting for me. My sun is there to help me grow and be everything I want to be! Without my sun, I couldn't live very long. I can be anywhere in the world, and as long as my sun is with me, I will be fine. My sun is bright and makes me and others happy. I love my sun! I love this woman!" He shouted the last statement.

Marcela stood and hugged and kissed Anastasio, getting applause from the guests. During the hug, she said, "I love this man!" She turned toward the guests. "My husband is making me blush. The thing he didn't know, the sun isn't any good unless it has a world to shine upon. And the sun is a big, fiery ball that could explode at any moment." She laughed. "As all of you could probably tell, I was surprised by our first dance song. We had another picked out, and I didn't even think about or know that he would find that song. It was when I and he became an us! Right away I knew he was perfect for me! Well, I think he is perfect for anyone, and I'm glad it was me that gets that for the rest of my life. Just like this evening, his thoughtfulness is something that is almost impossible to find. But after meeting his parents, I know where that came from. Thank you, Mom and Dad, for everything you have done for us! I am proud to be your daughter now. Thank you, everyone, for being a part of our celebration!"

Everyone stood and raised their glasses and drank. The whole wedding party was overcome with emotion. The music started again, and people made their way to the dance floor. It was such a beautiful night, and everyone seemed to be enjoying themselves. Anastasio and Marcela made their way out to the dance floor and danced with most of the people that were attending the wedding. Many people that were attending were part of his family that she had just met this evening. They all were so kind and made her feel a part of the whole family, not just his mom and dad.

After some time, they cut the cake and did the traditional feeding of the cake to each other. Everything seemed to be going so fast. The food was amazing, the band and DJ were spectacular, and as always with being in Italy, the wine flowed like it was water. Everyone was having a great time! Anastasio's parents were even dancing to almost every song. She was surprised how much energy they had. She was glad that everyone was having such a good time. Everyone took turns holding Paris, and Jacqueline left early to put her to bed.

Anastasio's parents asked if they could talk to them for a few minutes toward the end of the night. They went to a table, and all sat down. His dad handed them a large envelope and told them to open it. They did, and inside it were documents. The first was the deed to Marcela's house. It was now paid for! Next was the deed to their home there in Italy. And next was the deed to Marcela's shop. Everything was free and clear of loans. They sat there and didn't even know what to say. They were more than shocked. His parents were smiling broadly.

"Dad, how is this possible?"

"Your mom and I have been talking about what was important for the future. And you two are the future! You have worked extremely hard to keep the vineyard alive. We have never taken that for granted! We have sold the vineyard. We only sold that land that the vineyard is on, and our house is free and clear of anything. We wanted to give you a good start to start the new chapter of your life. Once your mom and I are gone, you can decide what you want to do with this old place."

They didn't even have words to say. Anastasio took a few moments and finally spoke. "How? And why? The vineyard has been in our family for years!"

"Son, you know we've been fighting a losing battle for years now. Your mom and I want are ready to retire. You have your life in Spain and don't need to worry about this. You have your daughter to raise. We want to be able to spend time with Paris and not be married to this vineyard anymore. But don't worry, if you want to keep seeing clients, the people that bought the vineyard have some other ones and said they could use a salesman like you."

Anastasio and Marcela looked at each other. Her eyes were big, and her mouth was wide open. It was too much to try to take in at once. She wasn't even sure if she was awake and not dreaming at this point. With the house and the shop mortgages paid off, things were going to be so much easier for them. She had never told Anastasio about the money that she spent for his medical. She wasn't sure, but something told her that his parents had figured it out.

Neither of them still had any words to express themselves. Anastasio got up and hugged and kissed them. Marcela followed. Both had tears in their eyes. It was the most amazing gift they could have gotten! It was far from expected. They had already taken care of so many expenses for the wedding. Marcela couldn't feel closer to them as she did right at this moment.

The guests started thinning out, and the reception was winding down. Anastasio and Marcela were busy saying their goodbyes to everyone. They were still on the high of everything that was going on. It was almost like being in your own dream that you wondered if you were going to wake up and realize that it was just a dream! They danced a last song together and also with the parents.

They said goodbye to Antonio, Lee, and his parents. They would spend the night in a hotel suite that they had booked. And in the morning, they would catch their flight to Paris. There, they were going to stay in the same hotel that they originally met at. Jacqueline was going to be on their flight, and she was going to drive them to their hotel. They would have dinner with her and then spend the rest of the evening in the hotel. There was no real plan after that. They knew they wanted to do some of the same things that they did before and spend some time with Jacqueline there. Outside of the past week, Anastasio hadn't known Jacqueline before and wanted to get to know her more. She was such a good friend to Marcela! Therefore, she was a good friend to him.

They got to the hotel, and everything was already in place. Their room was the honeymoon suite, and there was a chilled bottle of champagne and strawberries waiting for them. It was a beautiful suite! They didn't drink much more as they had plenty at the reception. But it was nice to have some with the strawberries. They spent their time in bed for the first time as husband and wife. It was another first time for them both. They needed to be up early for their flight, but they still took their time sharing each moment together.

They woke the next morning, showered, and got ready to go to the airport. His dad was going to pick them up with Jacqueline and take them to the airport. They hadn't really been apart from Paris yet and wanted to see her before they left. He was hoping that since his parents were retiring that they would be able to come visit often and be with their granddaughter. They had only come once to Spain when Paris was born. Now especially since they paid off all the debt they had, he hoped they would come see everything.

The flight to Paris went well. They sat next to Jacqueline on the flight. It made for an eventful flight as Jacqueline loved to be silly, making everyone around them laugh. One thing was certain about her. She knew how to really enjoy life no matter what the situation was! Anastasio was really happy that Marcela had met her when she was in Paris. He was also glad that Jacqueline was able to come visit her when Marcela was going through rough times.

They arrived at the hotel a few hours before dinnertime, so Jacqueline dropped them off, and they agreed to meet later for dinner. Rocco was extremely happy to see them. It had been over a year since he had seen Anastasio. He never went that long without being there, but since he had been sick, he didn't travel there anymore. He showed them to their room and left them alone. They did plan to spend some time talking with him during their trip. But for now, they wanted to unpack and rest before dinner. It was nice to be back to where it all began! It brought tears to their eyes.

Over the next week, they were able to go to the places they had been before and experience some new things as well. They got to spend a good amount of time with Rocco and Jacqueline. It was the perfect start to their life being married to each other. They vowed that they would spend every anniversary there too. It was hard to leave there again, but they were really looking forward to spending time traveling through Greece.

The next week went by way too fast, but they got to see so many historical places. The islands were beautiful, and the people were very friendly to them. They wanted to see as much as they could. As much as they would've liked to go back, there were so many places they wanted to see together. Maybe if they won the lottery, they could spend their lives on vacations. But they both knew that even if they did win, they would still want to work. They enjoyed what they did in life.

The next year went by without a hitch. They both worked and spent a lot of time together and also made lots of time for their friends. Pairs was growing up faster than they thought was possible. It seemed like every day she was learning something new. They took lots of photos of Paris doing everything, from sleeping to laughing to bathing. Every picture she looked more and more like her mom. When they compared the photos from when Marcela was a baby to Paris, they looked like twins. Antonio and Lee spent a lot of time with her too. Anastasio and Marcela had one date night a week, and the uncles were more than happy to watch Paris. They treated her like she was their own child!

His parents also were traveling really for the first time in their life. It seemed like they were more in love than he had ever seen them. The mom that he had grown up with, who convinced him to not contact Marcela, was gone and replaced with someone that was always happy! Happy for Anastasio and Marcela, happy to have Paris in her life, and not worried about what could happen in life. They loved spending time with Paris!

Anastasio had rearranged his schedule the best he could to be home with them as much as possible. Almost all his clients understood and were happy to accommodate his schedule when they could. He was starting to think about other careers he could get into that would allow him not to travel or at least not as much as he did now. But all his work experience was in wine production and sales. There were vineyards in Spain that he would start talking with in the near future.

Marcela was hoping to be able to go back to working normal hours in the next six months. They had hired someone to take care of running the shop for at least the time being. If business was good, then she would keep them on after she returned. The hope was that it would be the case, and she could return only part-time. She didn't want to spend too much time away from Paris either.

Things were going better than expected over the next year. Anastasio got a job with a local vineyard as a quality control expert. Business at the store was doing very well, and she was able to keep her employee, and she got to work lots of less hours at the shop. They sold the house they were in and got one a little bigger to have room for a shop to design new pieces and be home with Paris. Anastasio's parents came every few months and a week or so to spend time with all of them. It was obvious that they loved being parents and grandparents. Nothing was more important to them than family!

Marcela missed her mom very much. But her new family made her feel like she was really a child of their own. Of course, they never treated her like a child though. They were always respectful of boundaries. They were also incredibly good at making sure Anastasio and Marcela got some time alone. The house that they bought had a room and living area that was on a different floor of the house. Even when they were there, it was like they weren't at times.

The next couple of years was much of the same. They still made it to Paris on their anniversary every year. They took Paris each time so Aunt Jacqueline could spend time with her, and it also allowed Anastasio and Marcela to have some alone time together. Even though they now stayed with Jacqueline on the trips, they always made sure they had a day or two in their favorite hotel. Rocco was still there and looked the exact same as the day she had met him.

The following year, Anastasio's dad got sick, and his illness was swift and quick. From the time he got sick to when he passed away, it took just over three months. His mom felt lost without him and spent most of her time with them in Spain. They offered to have her there permanently and to sell the house in Italy, but she wouldn't do it. She wanted the house to stay in the family. Anastasio and Marcela hadn't really thought about moving to Italy, but maybe they would like to when Paris was older. They didn't know where their careers and where life would take them.

His mom wasn't the same without his dad being with her. He was her life, and she was his. She was happy to have her son, daughter, and granddaughter to keep her mind somewhat occupied. Anastasio also missed his dad. They had a bond that was unbreakable! They would talk for hours on end when they were alone together. He wished Paris would've got to have really known him. She was too young to remember him later in her life. They hoped that his mom would be around for many years to come.

Paris was finding her own way. They hadn't started to try to have another child yet. They wanted her to have a brother or sister in the near future. She was so smart, and she picked up learning anything you put in front of her. They made sure to speak to her in Spanish and in Italian. Marcela was now mostly fluent in both languages as well. They wanted her to learn as much as possible while she was young. They soak it all up when they are at that age.

Aunt Jacqueline came to visit a few times a year. Paris loved seeing her! Jacqueline would play anything that Paris wanted and seemed to have endless energy, just like Paris. She always had a way with people, and seeing how she was with Paris, they guessed there wasn't anyone on the planet that wouldn't like her. Paris would even ask her to read a story to her each night and if she would sleep in her room with her. Marcela always told her that she didn't have to sleep with her, but she always said she wanted to anyways.

Uncle Lee and Uncle Antonio were great with her also. They made sure to stop by at least once a week to say hello, play with her, bring her little gifts, and to spoil her. They treated Paris like she was their own family. They would also babysit so Anastasio and Marcela could go to dinner or drinks or movies and have their private time together. There was never a shortage of people who wanted to be with Paris. And Paris loved all the attention she was getting!

As luck would have it, his mother passed when Paris was just over five years old. Paris would be starting school the following fall. Marcela's jewelry shop was doing really well. She was designing pieces now that bigger chain stores were paying her to mass-produce. They now had two stores and several employees at both of them. She still spent most of her time at home with Paris and worked from home most days of the week. Anastasio stayed pretty busy during the week but was always home in time for dinner and spent most every weekend at home with them.

They were now actively trying to have another child. A year went by and still no luck. They weren't to the point of seeking the advice of doctors, but it was getting close to that point. They were still incredibly happy with the family they already had. The love between Anastasio and Marcela never faded in the smallest amount. It was the exact opposite! They loved each other more every year they were together.

Paris had started school and was making many friends. She loved going to school, and she continued to thrive and soaked up anything that someone was teaching her. She had many playdates with her friends, and that also gave Anastasio and Marcela more time alone together again. Since both his parents had passed, they didn't have the normal free time that they had with his parents around. They liked being able to have a date night once a week again. The passion they had between each other wasn't something that many couple could say they had in their lives.

They picked up the hobby of sailing. Neither of them had done it before, but some of the parents of Paris's friends liked it. They learned to love it. They bought a small sailboat of their own. Every few weeks, they would sail either by themselves or in groups. They would take turns on whose boat they would take. They had a smaller boat than most, so they usually either went alone or on others' boats. Paris loved being on the water no matter if she was just with her parents or with her friends too. They were sure when she got older, she would take up sailing on her own. She was always curious and asking if she could help with what they were doing.

It was summer break for Paris now, and the weather was usually very nice. They found themselves sailing every weekend. They planned to go by themselves the weekend after next. They already had plans to go with another family that weekend. The family they were going with were Paris's favorite of all her friends. They were going just before sunset, and they would have dinner while out, and then they would come back in the early evening. This was something they all really enjoyed.

The sailing was perfect, and Paris stayed over at her friend's house afterward. It gave them a chance to go have some drinks and have the evening alone in the house. The main reason they liked these times was because they had made a habit of turning on some music, having some wine, and dancing in the living room, just like the first night that they met. Each time, it still meant the same to them. It was something they regarded as sacred!

The next week wasn't anything out of the ordinary. They both did their work during the day and, in the evenings, had dinner as a family and spent time playing with and teaching Paris. This is how they liked to spend the evenings. After Paris went to bed, they would watch a movie, sit, and talk or listen to music before they went to bed.

When Saturday rolled around, Marcela needed to go into one of the stores for a little while before they were going sailing for the day. She didn't have a long day there, but she would meet Anastasio and Paris where they kept the boat, and they would go from there. She didn't want them to have to wait for her to go there. Getting the boat prepared took some time, and she didn't want to waste time that wasn't needed.

Anastasio and Paris got to the boat slip about an hour before Marcela was supposed to be there. It usually didn't take that long to get everything ready, but he liked to have the extra time so Paris could help him. She loved being involved in everything. Each time, he tried to teach her something new. It obviously wasn't complex things but simple things that she could do and enjoy.

Marcela called and said she was running a little later than expected but would be there in the next half hour or hour depending on how traffic was. Paris usually napped around this time, so he laid her down, and she laid her head on his lap. He couldn't get over how much she looked like her mother. Her smile, her hair, and especially her eyes were like a clone of her mom. She was constantly changing, and sometimes she looked like him in some ways, but then as quick as she changed, she would change again. It was going to be interesting what she was going to look like when she got older. He guessed she would be a spitting imagine of her mother!

He stroked her hair as she was falling asleep. She would always smile when he or Marcela would do that as she was going to sleep. He remembered the first time he watched Marcela fall asleep as he stroked her hair and face. It only took a few minutes before Paris was sleeping. When she went to sleep, it was near impossible to wake her up before she was ready. If she wasn't awake by the time Marcela got there, they would start leaving the harbor, and Marcela would start to try to wake her. She was always excited to look at all the other boats, to wave to anyone passing by, and to help steer their way out.

Just over an hour passed by before Paris's eyes shot open and looked straight into her dad's eyes. She had never done this before, and he didn't know how to explain it but could see Marcela clearly in her eyes. Something was wrong. Not with Paris but with Marcela! There was not a question in his mind. He tried not to show any panic as he asked if she was okay. She looked close to tears. She said she had a bad dream about her mommy! Now Anastasio was really worried. For both of them to get the same vibe wasn't a good sign. He assured her it was just a bad dream.

He tried to call Marcela several times with no luck. Her phone would ring and then go to voice mail. He called the store she was at to see if and when she left. They told him that she had left over an hour ago. He didn't know exactly what to do. Never in their many years together had something like this happen. He didn't want to upset Paris either, so they stayed on the boat for about another thirty minutes before he got a call from her or so he thought. He answered the phone in a hurry, and after about thirty seconds of listening, he dropped the phone and started to cry and shake uncontrollably.

Paris felt pain but didn't know what it was. As her dad was on the floor of the boat, Paris put her hand on his shoulder and was drawn into looking out over the water. At that exact moment, she saw one of the most beautiful sunsets she had ever seen. Somehow it comforted her! She knew that that sunset would never be forgotten!

~

Marcela's day was going better than expected. Both of her stores were having a sale, and there were more people than anyone expected. Her employees and herself stayed terribly busy throughout the day. When it finally slowed down enough for her to breathe, she looked at the time and realized she was going to be later than expected to meet Anastasio and Paris at the boat. She called Anastasio and told him she was going to be on her way and that she would be there within an hour.

She got in her car and decided that she wanted to get some champagne for them to celebrate how well the news that she had received the day before and some flowers for Paris. She always loved flowers, whether they were for her or when Anastasio brought them for Marcela. She was in such a good mood and looked forward to being on the water with her family for the evening. Also, the weather was proving to be better than they had expected as well.

The day before, she had gotten a call from her doctor while Anastasio was at work. It had taken some time, but they were finally going to give Paris a brother or sister. She knew he was going to be extremely excited when she told him! She wanted to make it a special day for the family, and she thought sailing at sunset would be the perfect backdrop to the news she would tell them. Paris was going to be so happy too! She had asked over and over if she was going to have a brother or sister.

The store that she liked to get flowers from was a little out of the way, but their flowers were the best she had ever found. There was also a liquor store right next to it. She got the champagne first and then went in and found flowers she knew Paris would love. They were stargazers. It was her favorite! She paid and left the store and was on her way to her car. She heard someone scream and turned to look at what was going on. As soon as she saw who was screaming, she saw them pointing in her direction, and she didn't get her head turned all the way around before she felt intense pain in her hip and then her head.

When the police arrived on the scene extremely quick, there was a crowd of people standing over a woman. They knew immediately that they needed to act fast. There was a car that was just past her body, and the windshield was smashed, and there was blood over it and on the top of the car. Within minutes, an ambulance arrived, and they didn't waste any seconds getting her into the ambulance and on the way to the hospital.

The police found her phone in her purse as they tried to secure the scene. They found her phone and saw several missed calls. They dialed the number, and a man answered. They asked if he called that number and who he was in relation to her. He informed him that he was her husband, and they told him what had happened and that she was being taken to the closest hospital. Before they could say anything else, they heard the phone drop and the cries of a man in pain.

After a few minutes, he asked which hospital it was, and the police gave him the information. He felt Paris's hand on his shoulder, and when he started to get up, he saw her looking over the water at the sunset. He wouldn't realize until later how beautiful the sunset really was. His focus now was on getting to the hospital because it didn't sound good at all from what the police told him.

Marcela opened her eyes but couldn't see anything right away. There was something in her eyes that made it almost impossible to open. Within seconds, her body was screaming in pain. She couldn't seem to say anything, but she could hear her own voice as a scream. Someone told her to try to relax, and she felt someone wiping her eyes. A few seconds later, she could see that she was in some room and noticed the uniforms of doctors and nurses.

All of a sudden, she remembered the lady screaming at her and turning her head and the intense pain she felt just as she was feeling now. There was a doctor now speaking to her, asking if she could feel different things. She was in so much pain she couldn't feel anything he was touching. She was finally able to get some words out. "How is the baby? I'm pregnant! Tell me my baby is all right!"

The doctor looked at the nurse, and he didn't answer Marcela's question right away. "Just try to stay calm. We need to try to stabilize you!"

She knew what the lack of a response meant. She felt a wave of grief hit her, and she started to weep loudly. "No! No! No!" was all she kept saying.

Anastasio had a hard time focusing on driving. All he could think about was getting to the hospital as fast as he could. It only took him about fifteen minutes to get there. He got Paris out of the car and held her as he ran into the emergency part of the hospital. Once he got inside, he stopped the first nurse he saw. "I need to see my wife. She was in an accident!"

The nurse knew right away who he was referring to and immediately took her into a room that was lit with bright lights, and several doctors and nurses were leaving the room. There was just one doctor and a few nurses now around his wife. "Marcela! Marcela, I'm here!"

The doctor looked at him and moved to the side so that Anastasio could see her. Her whole head was swollen, and she was covered in blood. Without even realizing it, a nurse came and took Paris out of his hands to keep her from seeing her mom like this. Marcela looked up at him with tears in her eyes. "Anastasio, I lost the baby! I lost the baby!"

Anastasio thought his wife was not thinking clearly but wasn't going to tell her that now. "It's okay, baby! I'm here now. I'm here!"

The doctor looked at Anastasio and motioned for him to come a few feet away to talk with him. He didn't want to leave his wife's side but also needed to know what was going on. "I'll be right here, honey. I'm not leaving you!"

Once he was beside the doctor, he didn't waste any time telling him what was going on. "Your wife was struck by a car, and it broke her legs, her right arm, a few ribs, and broke her neck. She's lost a lot of blood, and although we have controlled it, with all her injuries and the loss of blood, she won't be able to make it more than a few minutes to possibly half an hour."

Anastasio felt like he left his own body and was in some kind of dreamland. "Was she pregnant?"

"Yes, she was! Go be with her. You will want to say goodbye fairly quickly!"

Anastasio felt a pain in his heart that he never knew. He went to her side and tried as hard as he could to mask his emotions. "Hi, baby! It's okay. I'm right here with you!"

She was able to look into his eyes, and they confirmed what she thought she already knew. She was dying! "I'm sorry, Anastasio!" She took a couple of deep breaths and was able to lift her hand to take his. "Where is Paris?"

"She's right behind me with the nurse."

"Please bring her here!"

Anastasio didn't think it was the best decision, but he wasn't going to deny her anything she wanted. He took Paris from the nurse, and he brought her over. Paris still hadn't cried yet, but she knew that this wasn't a happy moment. She was still too young to really understand.

"Hi, baby! I need you to do something for me. You know how you wake up and see me and daddy dancing in the living room?"

"You mean like you do every time we go to Paris?"

"Yes, baby. I need you to always remember to do that with Daddy. Can you promise me that?"

"Yes, Mommy."

Anastasio had to turn his head away to stifle the tears he had in his eyes. He couldn't believe all this was happening. Just a few hours ago, they were on their boat waiting for her to get there. Now they were standing in a hospital where she was about to die! How could this be?

Anastasio was able to look back at her and hold her hand. He wanted to break down in tears, but he knew there would be time for that later. He had to be here for his wife. He had to be strong for his wife. He didn't know what to say, so he just stood there where she could look into her eyes.

"Honey, do you remember the first time we danced? And how you surprised me with the song at our wedding and how we've never missed a year of it?" she asked as she was somehow able to give him a smile.

"Of course, I do! I could never forget that!"

"Well, I want one last dance with you!"

"Oh honey, I don't think you will be able to do that!" He had to fight as hard as he could not to start crying like he never had.

"I know that! But I can hear the music in my head. Let me see you dance with our daughter one last time as I will pretend it is us every year we have known each other!"

Anastasio wasn't sure he could do what she wanted, but he was going to do it anyways. He let go of her hand, kissed her lips, and looked into her eyes for the last time. He didn't want to leave her side, but he was going to do what she asked him to. He started to hum the song loud enough to be heard and danced with Paris around the room.

Toward the end of the dance, he could hear the sound of the heart monitor that told him what he knew was going to happen. Instead of going over to her right away, he kept humming even louder now to try to drown out the sound of the machine as he finished the dance with his daughter. As the dance ended, Paris heard him say, "I'll always have Paris!"

About the Author

Kevin Russell was born in 1974 in Louisville, Kentucky, where he only lived a short time before his family was relocated to North Carolina. At the age of six, his father died from lung cancer, and a few years later, the remainder of his family moved to Dallas, Texas. He received a full scholarship to play volleyball at Texas Tech University, where he studied international business, finance, and economics. After he received his master's of finance at DePaul University, he then set his sight on his volleyball and finance careers. He was successful as the vice president of an investment brokerage and then as the vice president and CFO of a movie studio. Kevin spent over fourteen years traveling all over the United States and most of the world for work. Since 1995, he has battled with cancer of the esophagus, which led him to retire from both careers in 2013. During his retirement, he found the passion to write this book, which was published by Fulton Books.

Printed in the USA
CPSIA information can be obtained
at www.ICGtesting.com
LVHW050443160224
771975LV00036B/385